LAKE SILENCE

THE WORLD OF THE OTHERS

ANNE BISHOP

ACE
New York

ACE
Published by Berkley
An imprint of Penguin Random House LLC
1745 Broadway, New York, NY 10019

ISBN: 9780399587269

Ace hardcover edition / March 2018
Ace mass-market edition / January 2019

Printed in the United States of America
1 3 5 7 9 10 8 6 4 2

Cover art by © Stephen Carroll/Trevillion Images
Cover design by Adam Auerbach
Book design by Laura K. Corless

BOOKS BY ANNE BISHOP

The Others Series

Written in Red
Murder of Crows
Vision in Silver
Marked in Flesh
Etched in Bone

The World of the Others

Lake Silence
Wild Country

The Black Jewels Series

Daughter of the Blood
Heir to the Shadows
Queen of the Darkness
The Invisible Ring
Dreams Made Flesh
Tangled Webs
The Shadow Queen
Shalador's Lady
Twilight's Dawn

The Ephemera Series

Sebastian
Belladonna
Bridge of Dreams

The Tir Alainn Trilogy

The Pillars of the World
Shadows and Light
The House of Gaian

In memory of
Mike Briggs
and
Emma Lee
You are missed.
January 2017

ACKNOWLEDGMENTS

My thanks to Blair Boone for continuing to be my first reader and for all the information he supplies that I transform to suit the Others' world; to Debra Dixon for being second reader; to Doranna Durgin for maintaining the Web site; to Adrienne Roehrich for running the official fan page on Facebook; to Nadine Fallacaro for information about things medical; to Jennifer Crow for pep talks when needed; to Ineke Prochazka for introducing me to Jubly-Umph and the quokka; to Paige and Dominique, the excellent Herders of Authors at Supanova 2016, who always knew when to lose us for a few minutes as we passed a booth full of shinies; to Anne Sowards and Jennifer Jackson for the feedback that helps me write a better story; and to Pat Feidner for always being supportive and encouraging.

THE FINGER/FEATHER LAKES

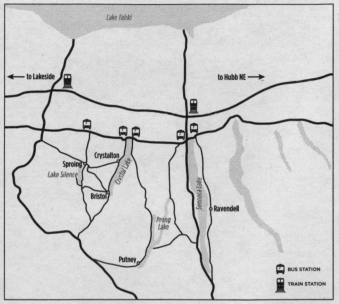

© 2017 Anne Bishop

Note: The geographically challenged author created this map and did her best to match the main roads to the story but makes no promises about accuracy.

CHAPTER 1

Vicki

Moonsday, Juin 12

I wouldn't have known about the dead man if I hadn't walked into the kitchen at the exact moment my one and only lodger was about to warm up an eyeball in the wave-cooker.

Until that moment, I hadn't known I had a scream that could crack glass; I hadn't wondered if an eyeball would puff up and explode in a wave-cooker like those animal-shaped marshmallows; and I hadn't realized my lodger—Agatha "call me Aggie" Crowe—was *that* kind of Crow.

She seemed so normal, if you overlooked her timely payment of the rent each week and the fact that she had taken up residence in The Jumble three weeks ago and seemed to be enjoying herself.

"You can't eat that!" I tried to sound firm, like a responsible human and business owner should. In truth, I sounded a wee bit hysterical, and I wished with all sincerity that I had walked into the kitchen five minutes later.

Then again, since the kitchen was one of the common rooms in the main building, I could have walked in when Aggie was halfway through her lunch, which I'm sure would have been more distressing for at least one of us.

"Why can't I eat it?" She looked at the eyeball rolling

around in the small bowl that was now sitting on the counter. "Nobody else wants it. It's starting to get squooshy. And the dead man doesn't need it."

The words got me past the physical evidence. "What dead man?"

"The one who doesn't need the eyeball." Little black feathers suddenly sprouted at her hairline, confirming the nature of my lodger. I was going to have to rework the rental agreement so that there was a space for unimportant bits of information like . . . oh, say . . . species.

"Where did you find the dead man?"

"On the farm track that runs alongside Crabby Man's place."

I should have pointed out that Mr. Milford wasn't usually crabby, but he did get exercised when someone took one bite out of all the ripe strawberries or pinched fruit from his trees, since he and his wife needed the income they made from selling fresh fruit and homemade preserves. But there were other priorities.

"Show me." I held up a hand. "Wait. And don't nibble."

"But . . ."

"You can't eat it. It could be evidence."

Her dark eyes filled with reproach. "If I hadn't wanted to warm it up because it was squooshy, you wouldn't have known about the dead man and I could have had eyeball for lunch."

I couldn't refute that statement, so I backed up until I reached the wall phone in the kitchen, and then I dialed the emergency number for the Bristol Police Station. Bristol was a human town located at the southern end of Crystal Lake. Sproing, the only human village near Lake Silence, was currently without its own police force, so Bristol had drawn the short straw and had to respond to any of our calls for help.

"Bristol Police Station. What is your emergency?"

"This is Victoria DeVine at The Jumble in Sproing. One of my lodgers found a dead man." Okay, Aggie was my only lodger, but there was no reason to advertise *that*. Right?

I started counting and reached seven before the dispatcher said, "Did you see the body?"

"No, but my lodger did."

"How do you know the body is dead?"

"I'm looking at an eyeball that used to be attached to the body."

This time I counted to eight.

"We'll send someone." The words were slow in coming, but at least they were said and would be officially noted somewhere.

I didn't blame the dispatcher for hesitating to send someone to Sproing—after all, the police officer we'd had before last year's Great Predation had been eaten, and a couple of officers who had answered calls since then had provoked something in the wild country and never made it back to their station—but I resented that I could feel her blaming me for whatever the police were going to find. On the other hand, I did withhold one tiny bit of information.

Just wait until the responding officer realized he had to interview one of the *terra indigene*.

A bit of useful information. My name is Victoria "call me Vicki" DeVine. I used to be Mrs. Yorick Dane, but giving up my married name was one of the conditions of my receiving valuable property—aka The Jumble—as part of the divorce settlement. Apparently the second official Mrs. Dane didn't like the idea that someone else had had the name first. Fortunately, she didn't seem as possessive about Yorick's Vigorous Appendage. I could have told her that a couple dozen other women had had it before she took possession. But it wasn't likely that she would keep solo possession of the appendage for long, so let her figure things out the hard way like I did. Of course, if she had been one of those indulgences, then she already knew the signs and might be able to nip them in the bud. Maybe that's why, before I had moved away from Hubb NE, I had seen her in the garden center buying long-handled loppers—the kind used to prune branches—when I'd heard her loudly proclaiming the previous week that gardening was a hobby for women who couldn't do anything else and so not of interest to *her*.

Anyway, I was married to Yorick Dane, an entrepreneur—aka wheeler-dealer—although I never understood what sort of deals were wheeled. He said I didn't have a head for business. I finally said I didn't have a head for cheating of any kind. Suddenly, after a decade of marriage, he said I wasn't living up to the promises that were implied by my name, meaning I wasn't hot or in any way sexy. The fact that it took him a decade to realize I was five foot four and plump instead of a five-foot-ten pole dancer with big tits was confusing. But once he made that discovery, he decided that he needed someone who would stand by him, and that would not be me.

So that's how I came to be the owner of The Jumble. According to the story that was muttered by Yorick's family once they'd had a little too much to drink, The Jumble was conceived and built by Yorick's great-great-aunt, Honoria Dane, a woman who was equal parts visionary and eccentric. She and her brothers were given equal shares in their father's fortune, the shares being dispersed upon the child's twenty-fifth birthday. Great-great (I never heard anyone refer to her by her given name) had sunk her part of the fortune into building The Jumble. It was supposed to be a self-sufficient and self-supporting community. It began its genteel decline almost from the moment Great-great finished building it.

The Jumble consisted of the sprawling two-story main house, which had a small but fully equipped apartment for the owner as well as two suites with private bathrooms for guests. It also had a big communal kitchen, a dining room, a library, a social room, an office for the owner, several empty rooms whose use I couldn't identify, and a large shower area off the kitchen that could accommodate up to four people at a time as long as they weren't shy. Besides the main house, there were four sets of cabins—three connected cabins to a set—within easy walking distance from the main building.

Each cabin was similar to an efficiency apartment with an open floor plan—no walls or doors for anything but the bathroom. Well, the three lakeside cabins that were closest to the main building had en suite bathrooms. The other nine cabins were a bit more primitive and an ongoing project.

There were acres of land that could be used by the . . . beings . . . in residence—plenty of room for growing food or raising a goat or two for whatever reason one keeps goats. There was even a chicken coop, sans chickens. It was probably sans a few other things, but if the chickens couldn't pay rent, I couldn't afford to update their lodgings. But The Jumble had one thing the village of Sproing did not—it included easy access to Lake Silence, which was an afterthought body of water compared to the other Finger Lakes. There *was* a public beach at the southern end of the lake, but I thought The Jumble's private beach and dock were a lot nicer.

Whoever negotiated the original lease agreement for the use of the land knew every devious loophole a person might try to use to rezone/repurpose/re-something the land. But the terms were brutally simple: it was The Jumble, with its set number of buildings of a particular size and so many acres of cultivated land (being a modest percentage of the overall acreage), or nothing. The Dane inheritance was actually the buildings and their contents. The land could be used only within the terms of the lease.

Last bit of information. Sproing is a human village with a population of less than three hundred. Like most, if not all, of the villages in the Finger Lakes area, it is not human controlled. Sure, we have an elected mayor and village council, and we pay taxes for garbage pickup and road maintenance and things like that. The main difference is this: on the continent of Thaisia, a human-controlled town is a defined piece of land with boundaries, and humans can do anything they want within those boundaries. But villages like Sproing don't have boundaries, don't have that distance from the *terra indigene*. The earth natives. The Others. The dominant predators that control most of the land throughout the world and all of the water.

When a place has no boundaries, you never really know what's out there watching you.

The surprising thing is there hadn't been a reported interaction with one of the Others in decades. At least around Sproing. Maybe the Others have been coming in and buying COME SPROING WITH ME or I ♥ SPROINGERS T-shirts without anyone realizing it, but even though the village lost about a quarter of its residents because of last summer's Great Predation, everyone still wanted to believe that the Others were Out There and didn't find us interesting enough—or bothersome enough—to hunt down and have as snacks.

Which made me wonder if the Others came into town seasonally, like tourists. And that made me wonder if everyone had missed the obvious when stores ran out of condiments like ketchup and hot sauce some weekends—and whether a run on ketchup and hot sauce coincided with people disappearing.

Something to ask Aggie once we got past the whole eyeball thing.

CHAPTER 2

Grimshaw

Moonsday, Juin 12

Officer Wayne Grimshaw drove toward the village of Sproing, the cruiser's flashing lights a warning to anyone else on the road that he was responding to a call and was all business. But the siren remained silent because that sound would have drawn the attention of everything for miles around—and when a man was in the wild country, even on a paved road that was a vaguely acknowledged right-of-way, it was better not to alert the earth natives to his presence.

Dead body reported at The Jumble near Sproing.

Sproing. By all the laughing gods, what kind of name was that for a village? It sounded like some kind of initiation or razzing—have the new guy respond to a call and then have to keep asking for directions to Sproing. Plenty of off-color jokes could be made about that.

Except he knew the name wasn't a joke. He had seen it on the map at the Bristol station and had been told calls from citizens living around Lake Silence were part of Bristol's jurisdiction. Added to that, the emergency dispatcher, who was a no-nonsense woman, had sounded reluctant to send him—and he'd been advised a couple of times by other officers at the station that if he had to answer a call around Lake Silence, he should get in and out as quickly as possible because things around that particular lake were a wee bit . . . hinky.

The village had a small police station but no longer had its own police force—not a single cop patrolling its streets. The people there were dependent on the highway patrol that worked out of the Bristol station, and even then . . .

Over the past few months, two officers who had answered calls around Sproing hadn't returned. One officer was found in his patrol car, which had been crushed by something powerful enough to flatten a car with its fists or paws or some freaking appendage. The other man . . . Most of that officer had been found, but no one knew what had set off the attack or why it had been so vicious. Both deaths were harsh reminders that the highway patrol traveled through the wild country as part of the job, and a man never knew what was watching him when he stepped out of his vehicle.

Grimshaw had been patrolling the secondary roads south of Bristol—a loop that would have taken him close to Lake Silence anyway—so when he spotted a sign for the lake, he turned onto the dirt road, hoping it would take him to The Jumble, which he'd been told was some kind of resort right on the lake. Instead he found himself in the parking area for the lake's public beach.

From what he had gathered from his captain's orientation speech, the land on the western side of Lake Silence was privately owned—or at least privately controlled—as was most of the eastern side. There was no vehicle access to the northern end of the lake, which left only the southern end for anyone who wanted to take a cool dip on a hot day or take a boat out for fishing or recreation.

Grimshaw frowned at the two signs attached to the low stone wall that separated the parking area from the beach.

The first sign read:

PACK OUT YOUR TRASH OR ELSE

The second sign read:

> YOU MAY SWIM, FISH, SAIL, ROW, CANOE, OR
> FLOAT ON RAFTS AT YOUR OWN RISK.
> IF YOU PUT A MOTOR IN THE WATER,
> YOU WILL DIE.

Nothing ambiguous about either message.

Grimshaw turned the cruiser around and got back on the main road, heading north. The next turnoff had a weathered sign for The Jumble. He made the turn and followed the gravel access road up to the main building. As he shut off the car, he pressed two fingers against his chest and felt the round gold medal for Mikhos, the guardian spirit of police officers, firemen, and medical personnel—a talisman he had worn under his uniform every day since he graduated from the police academy a decade ago.

"Mikhos, keep me safe." It was the prayer he whispered every time he answered a call.

A woman stepped into view, looking agitated. Curly brown hair, a pleasant enough face, and a build he would describe as stocky if she had been a man. He couldn't tell more than that from this distance, so Officer Wayne Grimshaw got out of the cruiser and went to see Ms. Victoria DeVine about a body.

CHAPTER 3

Vicki

Moonsday, Juin 12

"But I can't!" Aggie wailed, sprouting more feathers when I told her she would have to talk to the police.

The additional black feathers in her hair were less distressing than the ones that suddenly appeared on her face and forearms.

"You have to," I replied, striving to remain calm. I placed a saucer over the bowl with the eyeball. "You're the only one who knows where to find the body. You'll need to show the police when they get here."

"But I'll get in *trouble!*"

My breath caught and my heart thudded. Aggie was petite and had a small-boned physique—and my purse probably weighed more than she did. But being one of *those* Crows, she could be a lot stronger than she looked.

"Aggie, you didn't . . . ?" What would I do if she admitted that she had killed a man in order to eat his eyeball? I imagined myself being strong and brave and performing some kick-ass self-defense moves despite not actually knowing how to do them. Then I imagined myself smiling weakly right before I ran away.

I liked the idea of running away. Much more sensible.

"I didn't kill him!" Aggie sounded insulted. "He was already dead when I found him and only had the one eyeball."

"What happened to the other one?"

"Dunno. Probably got eaten."

Since I liked Aggie, I really didn't want to ask more questions. I grabbed the bowl with the eyeball and went outside to wait for the police. Aggie followed me out the front door but started edging toward the trees.

"Aggie . . ." Hearing tires on gravel, I turned to watch the police car as it drove up within sight of the house and stopped at a spot that blocked the access road. When I turned back, a pile of clothes lay under a tree and Aggie was gone. So I stood there, alone, holding the bowl while I waited for the police officer to get out of the car.

You know those cartoon heroes with the strong lower jaws, sparkly teeth, *broad* shoulders, and tiny waists? The man who stepped out of the police car could have been the model for the caricature, but he was correctly proportioned and looked really official with all the doodads on his belt. He was wearing sunglasses, so I couldn't see his eyes, couldn't tell if the expression in them was a warm "Can I help you, ma'am?" or a cold "You're being a pain in my ass, so talk fast."

If he had stopped to help when I was stranded on a dark, lonely road, I would have been happy to see him. But that presence was less reassuring when I wasn't sure I wouldn't be labeled the villain.

"Are you the lady who called about a suspicious death?" he asked, approaching warily.

He was a big man and had a big voice. Not that he was yelling at me or anything, but it was the kind of voice that could hammer a person—the kind of voice that, when used with a threatening tone, could trigger a panic attack.

He stopped and studied the claw marks on a tree—marks that were high enough that I hadn't noticed them because they weren't in my usual line of sight.

Something to think about on a hot summer night when I'm trying to convince myself that it's safe to leave the windows open to get some air. Safe from thieves maybe, since I have nothing to steal. Safe from the mysterious Clawman?

I'd read somewhere that an ordinary bear could hook its claws in a car door and rip the door off the hinges in order to get to the snacks someone foolishly left inside. Odds were good that whatever prowled around in The Jumble's woods didn't qualify as ordinary, although, to be fair, Aggie was the only *terra indigene* I had seen—"seen" being the qualifying word. If one of the crows hanging around The Jumble was Crowgard, how many others were more than they seemed?

"My lodger found a body near the farm track that is the boundary between my property and the Milfords' orchards," I replied, trying for matter-of-fact helpful. I held out the bowl. "Here. This is evidence."

He took the bowl, lifted the saucer, and stared at the eyeball. At least, I assumed he stared at the eyeball. Since he was wearing those mirrored sunglasses, he could have been staring at me—and it suddenly occurred to me that if he asked to look in my refrigerator, I had no idea what he might find.

"Wait there." He walked back to his car and opened the trunk. He returned in a minute without the eyeball. It didn't look like he was going to return my bowl and saucer either. "I'll need to speak to your lodger."

"She's a little shy about talking to the police."

He removed the sunglasses. The look in his blue-gray eyes said my lodger better get un-shy in a hurry. Or maybe I was projecting from past experience with men. Man. The one who used to leave me feeling that something was my fault even when I couldn't have controlled someone else's actions or thoughts or opinions.

"Did she tell you the location? Can you show me the alleged body?"

I had just given him an eyeball. How alleged could the body be? "I—"

"Caw."

I looked at the crow—or Crow—perched in a tree a couple of yards down one of the bridle paths, of which The Jumble has many.

"Yes, I can." I set off down the path and hoped really hard that I was following Aggie and not someone else.

The second time I tripped and would have landed face-first in the dirt if the officer hadn't grabbed my arm and kept me upright, he grumbled, "You might do better watching where you're walking than looking at the trees."

Sound advice. I wished I could take it, but I didn't want to explain that our guide was in the trees, because that would require explaining the nature of our guide.

"Stop," he said after we had been walking awhile. It felt like forever, and since I hadn't gone back inside the house to get my wristwatch before we headed out, time was measured by how it felt. "Do you have any idea where you're going?"

"Of course I do, Officer . . ." I realized he hadn't told me his name. Maybe that wasn't required?

"Grimshaw."

"Really?" So not the correct response, especially from someone named Vicki DeVine. "The Milfords' place is the land between The Jumble and the road that leads to Sproing. The body was found near the farm track between the Milfords' land and mine."

"So we should be heading east?"

I was about to agree but the affirmative words stuck in my throat. *Were* we supposed to be heading east? Was this a trick question? Couldn't be heading west. The lake was to the west of the main house—could, in fact, be seen from the back of the main house. But that left two other directions unaccounted for.

"Ms. DeVine?" Officer Grimshaw was not a happy camper.

"Um . . ."

"Caw."

I breathed a sigh of relief. "This way."

Suddenly there were three crows on the same branch, making me think of the shell game where you have to figure out which shell is hiding the pea.

Three black birds were sitting in a tree. Which one was *A-G-G-I-E*?

"Caw."

Only one took off, so I followed, hoping it was a Crow, and Officer Grimshaw followed me. Big mistake. I probably should have admitted to being geographically challenged *before* I led him into the woods.

"Caw!"

Open ground. Daylight. The dirt road, aka the farm track. And the body.

"Ew." That wasn't a professional response, but I wasn't a professional and I sincerely hoped I never met this man again. Either man.

"Stay there," Grimshaw said as he moved closer to the body.

Like I was going to get closer when my knees already felt rubbery and my stomach felt swoopy.

"This body has been disturbed."

"I'd be disturbed too if I was suddenly dead," I replied.

He twisted around enough to look at me and must have decided I wasn't trying to be a smart-ass; I just wasn't quite in control of what I was saying anymore. Since I had dealt with the eyeball pretty well, the only explanation was that my brain had decided that, with someone else here to handle the problem, it no longer had to be fully functional during this stage of the crisis and could enjoy a mini anxiety attack.

"Not a lot of predation," Grimshaw said, studying the body. "I don't think he's been here long."

"Aggie said his eyeball was squooshy. That's why she wanted to warm it up in the wave-cooker. Wouldn't it take a while for the eyeball to get squooshy?"

I watched him put his sunglasses back on before he turned to face me.

"Aggie is your lodger?" Arctic Voice.

I nodded, glad I couldn't see his eyes because my insides were quivering as I braced for Arctic Voice to become Hammer Voice.

"I really need to talk to her."

My quivering insides translated his Officially Polite Voice

as more encouraging than scary, so I pointed at the branch above me. "Go ahead."

His head moved, so I assumed he was looking up. Then, as he turned away, I heard him say, "Crap." It wasn't so much spoken as a breath shaped into sound.

Aggie lifted her wings in what might have been an apologetic shrug and let out a timid *caw*.

Grimshaw pulled out his mobile phone and made a call. The next couple of minutes sounded like a TV show with all the "officer needs assistance" and requests for the medical examiner and transport of the remains.

He hadn't gotten very far into explaining the situation when seven birds winged toward the body. They landed close and moved closer, despite Grimshaw waving an arm to keep them away.

"Friends of yours?" I asked, looking up at Aggie.

"Caw."

"Officer . . ."

"I heard."

Yeah. Regular crows would have been enough of a problem if you wanted to avoid having more body bits and pieces being taken away for someone's dinner. But dealing with the Crowgard? That made this a potential PR fiasco for the police department—and every other human service that could be affected by the *terra indigene*'s taking exception to someone keeping them away from the buffet.

Or *was* it the body that was so intriguing? I saw a glint of gold. A wristwatch. It looked like someone had been trying to pull it off and had been interrupted. By our arrival?

"I have to stay with the body until the Crime Investigation Unit gets here," Grimshaw said. "Can you find your way back to the house?"

"Sure."

"Can you find your way back?"

Could we call that a no-confidence vote for the geographically challenged?

"Caw." At least Aggie was confident of getting us back to the main house.

So there, Officer Smarty-Pants.

I headed back up the path, fairly sure that I could get out of sight before getting lost.

"Ms. DeVine?"

Grimshaw's voice stopped me but I didn't turn around. "Yes, Officer?"

"I'll still need to talk to you and your lodger. Don't go anywhere."

Like I could with his big official vehicle blocking the access road that led up to the main house. Somehow I couldn't see myself taking off on my bicycle in order to escape the law. Besides, all I did was report finding a body. How much trouble could I get into for doing that?

CHAPTER 4

Them

Moonsday, Juin 12

He studied the three men he had summoned for this late-night meeting. Two of them were top-tier members of the club, men who knew how to put together a deal and hold it together until it paid off. They were friends of long standing, and he had worked with them on several highly successful and lucrative projects. The third man came from money and a solid family name, but he was a third-rate schemer who thought he was a big shot—and could talk a good enough game to make other people believe he was as good as he believed himself to be, at least until a person started looking at the actual deals he'd made. Then it became clear that his success depended on his being the big fish in a very small pond.

Normally a man like that wouldn't be included in a deal this size, but the fool was the one who held the papers for the asset they wanted—an asset the man's family hadn't bothered to utilize for decades. Except the damn fool *didn't* hold the papers anymore, a detail he had "forgotten" to mention until the other men had shaken on the deal and couldn't exclude him without staining their reputations with the rest of the members of the club.

But that forgotten detail was the reason they were looking at trouble now.

"Franklin Cartwright is dead," he said, his voice full of harsh anger.

"Murdered?" the fool asked, sounding hopeful.

"Killed. My sources have confirmed nothing human could have done it."

"Did Cartwright get the papers we need before getting killed?" the oldest man asked. He had gray hair and a hefty build and was a decade older than the rest of the men involved in this deal.

"No, but another source is going to make sure those papers aren't available to anyone who might need them."

The oldest man nodded. "If the bitch can't prove she owns the asset . . ."

"It will give us time." He studied the fool. "Why did you ask if Cartwright was murdered? Do you think your lump of an ex-wife could do that?"

"Nah." The fool waved a hand as if erasing the words. "She's a dishrag. Just raise your voice and she'll do whatever she's told."

He looked at the two men he considered friends. "A murder charge won't stick, but I'll call one of our associates who is on the scene. Let's see if he can push the dishrag's buttons and convince her that she'll be held responsible for Cartwright's death."

Everyone thought that was a splendid idea. Since he knew the fool would go home and bleat the details of this secret meeting to the new wife, he didn't say anything more about their plans, even though the new wife happened to be his cousin. And he waited until he was sure the other men had left the building before calling the associates currently located in Sproing.

CHAPTER 5

Grimshaw

Sunday, Juin 13

The following morning, Grimshaw parked the cruiser in front of Sproing's police station and studied the building. The exterior looked more like a store that hadn't quite gone out of business but wasn't being cared for properly because the owner had given up on turning a profit.

Considering this was his new assignment, that did not bode well for him because it could be a visual opinion of the last police officer who had manned the station.

"It's a temporary reassignment," Captain Hargreaves had said.

"I don't work and play well with others. That's why I work highway patrol," Grimshaw had growled. "Why can't the town boys from the CIU team talk to the villagers? It's their investigation now. Let one of their own park behind a desk in Sproing."

Silence. He'd been working at the Bristol station under Hargreaves for only a couple of weeks, but he'd already learned to be wary of that weighty silence.

"There's something damn strange about the CIU team from Putney jumping on this case when it should be outside their jurisdiction," Hargreaves finally said. "So I want

someone in the village who reports to me and can handle the day-to-day business during this investigation, and I've decided that someone is going to be you." After a moment, he added, "We need to be careful. Can't afford to step on any toes. Town boys don't always appreciate that when they come into a small place like Sproing."

In other words, despite all the evidence over the past year of how the *terra indigene* respond to things they don't like, the CIU team might want to treat this investigation as if they were dealing strictly with other humans.

So there he was, the temporary officer in charge of the police station in Sproing while the Putney CIU team looked into the suspicious death of Franklin Cartwright—*if* the business cards he'd found near the body actually belonged to the victim.

Captain Hargreaves had told him the station would be unlocked, and if it wasn't, he should check with the mayor or with the tenants who had offices on the second floor. The door was unlocked, so Grimshaw went inside to look around, glad he didn't have to talk to anyone yet. Finding a set of keys in the middle drawer of one of the desks, he pocketed them, assuming they had been left for him. He also assumed the landlord—or the holding company that owned the building—had a set for the station as well as the two offices on the second floor. One office was rented by the village's lone attorney. The other? Hargreaves didn't have information on the other tenant.

Two desks, one on either side of the room. Two chairs to go with the desks and a visitors' chair in front of each. Gun cabinet empty of firearms. A cell in the back part of the building—more accurately, a room with a single bed and a rickety bedside table, bars on the window, and a barred cell door. Storage room for supplies and a wall of filing cabinets that actually had files, although nothing current. A bathroom that included a shower cubicle. A small kitchen area that contained an old refrigerator that still worked and a new coffeemaker.

If push came to shove, he could bunk at the station until he found temporary lodgings.

Grimshaw ran a finger over the desks and was surprised that he didn't swipe away more than a thin layer of dust—nothing more than what you'd expect just before the weekly cleaning. So the grungy feel was more from age and dingy walls, not a current lack of upkeep.

He wasn't sure if that was better or worse.

Having seen his new headquarters, he stepped outside. The village hall, which housed the courtroom as well as the offices for all the municipal services, was on one side of the station. The lone bank was on the other side.

Directly across the street from the police station was a store called Lettuce Reed.

"By all the laughing gods," Grimshaw muttered as he crossed the street. Was it some kind of produce market? Or something more esoteric and borderline legal?

As his foot hit the sidewalk and he saw the sign in the window announcing a sale on used books, it hit him. Lettuce Reed. Let Us Read.

"Cute." He hated cute and was already predisposed to dislike the froufrou owner of the place.

The wooden door stood wide open. Grimshaw opened the screen door and went in. As his eyes adjusted to the darker interior, he had the unsettling experience of recognizing the man standing behind the information island in the front part of the store.

"Hello, Julian," Grimshaw said.

"Hello, Wayne. If you got pulled into this business with the dead body, then I'm sorry for you."

A decade ago, they had been cadets together at one of the Northeast Region's police academies and had remained friends until Julian disappeared a few years after graduation. But it had only been because of the events of the past year—events that had rocked the whole continent of Thaisia—that Grimshaw had pieced together enough information to make some educated guesses about Julian Farrow.

Julian had been a brilliant cadet. While he didn't excel to the point of ruining the curve for the rest of them when it came to some of the tests, he had an uncanny ability to sense his surroundings and know when something was off, even when there was no indication of trouble.

During the academy drills, he knew when police needed to go down an alley with weapons drawn and when their mere presence would break up—or calm down—whatever trouble was stirring. Once he was on the force, that ability had saved his fellow officers too many times to count. Which was why the Incident was more damning than it might have been.

Julian had uncovered some bit of naughtiness—probably some kind of corruption within official or police circles. The kind of naughtiness that destroyed careers and came with prison sentences. But no one was really sure, because one night when he was on the late shift and his partner had called in sick, Julian responded to a call for assistance. When he arrived, he didn't find the frightened woman who had called the emergency number; he'd found five men wearing balaclavas waiting for him. Wielding clubs and knives, they jumped him before he could draw his weapon and fire.

Or tried to jump him. He hadn't walked far enough into that alley for them to make a thorough job of it. Two of them managed to stab him and a couple more landed damaging blows with clubs before Julian shook free and ran for his life.

Maybe he'd been disoriented. Or maybe his uncanny sense of place, which seemed to have let him down in that alley, started working for him again. How else to explain why he turned down another alley, one that ended at a solid wall. He'd scrambled up on the big garbage containers and managed to get over the wall before he blacked out, having lost a lot of blood.

That was the testimony he gave: he blacked out and couldn't provide any information about what walked into that alley behind the five men who were chasing him. But something did. Something large enough and powerful enough to eviscerate five men before ripping off their arms, their legs, and their heads. The savagery had shocked the entire police force in the Northeast Region, to say nothing of causing a panic among the citizens in human towns who had thought they were safe from the *terra indigene* as long as they stayed within town limits.

No one could prove Julian hadn't blacked out, that he hadn't heard everything that happened to those men. No one could prove he'd chosen that alley with the intention of trapping those men. No one could prove he was anything but the victim of attempted murder—or assault at the very least if the men were only supposed to "discourage" him from further investigations into the naughtiness.

No one could prove anything. But everyone on the force who had gone to the academy with him or had worked with him knew about his ability and were certain he hadn't chosen that alley at random, that he'd known in some way that it was his only chance of escape.

And no one could prove that he'd sensed what would happen to the men who followed him into that alley. But two of those men were fellow officers, which caused a stink and all kinds of investigations. In the end, Julian was awarded a settlement for his wounds, which were declared grievous enough to end his career as a police officer, and he disappeared.

Until now.

Grimshaw looked around. Didn't seem to be a thriving business, but that could just be the time of day. "A bookstore?"

"Have to make a living," Julian replied. "I like books, like to read."

And I know an evasive answer when I hear one. "Why here?"

"Why not?"

Grimshaw rested both forearms on the island, a relaxed "Let's shoot the bull" stance. After a moment, Julian mirrored his posture so that, at first glance anyway, they looked like two friends just catching up with the "How's your life been?" news.

"Why are you really here?" Grimshaw asked. "Before you try to bullshit me, let me remind you that I'm not stupid and we do go back a ways. And there was always something a little hinky about the way you left the force."

"You think there was anyone on the force who would want to work with me after the Incident?" Julian countered.

"I would have." Simple truth. He studied the man who had been his friend. "Why didn't you tell anyone you're an Intuit, that your ability wasn't exclusive to you?" He made it sound like he'd known for a while instead of waiting now for the answer that would confirm his educated guesses.

"And risk exposing my people to discrimination or persecution?" Julian's gray eyes looked as hard as stone. "We'd already been down that road, already had the experience of how other humans responded to our ability to sense things. That's why our communities are in the wild country—and why we don't admit what we are when there is a need to spend time away from our own."

"Now that some Intuits have come out of the closet, so to speak, it's been estimated that one out of three human communities in the Finger Lakes area is an Intuit community or a mix of Intuit and Simple Life folk," Grimshaw said.

"Something that still isn't commonly known outside of government and police circles, and *which* communities are Intuit hasn't been confirmed. And the Finger Lakes, or Feather Lakes as the Others call them, *are* the wild country. There isn't a single human-controlled village on any of these lakes. Being part of the highway patrol, that is a fact you know well."

Yes, he did. "If you had to keep what you are a secret, why not attend an Intuit police academy in one of your own communities?"

"There wasn't one. Not then. There are a couple of them now in the Northeast Region for the men who feel the need to serve and protect."

Grimshaw continued to study the man who had been his friend. Julian's dark hair was long enough to pull back in a tiny tail, but he wore it down so it looked shaggy—or maybe just disheveled in a way that might appeal to some women. A lean build and finely sculpted face with a thin scar across one cheekbone, a souvenir of that attack—or maybe just the scar that people could see. Grimshaw suspected Julian Farrow had a few other scars from that night that weren't on the skin or visible to the eye.

But he'd also been a good cop. Even more than that, he'd been a good investigator.

Which left the question: what *had* Julian Farrow really been doing all these years?

"You sure that's all you're doing here in Sproing? Selling books?"

Julian looked toward the screen door. Grimshaw thought he heard a quiet scratching on the screen, but when he looked over his shoulder he didn't see anything.

"I have just the thing for an evening read," Julian said. "Something I doubt you would have read before." He walked into the back area of the store and returned a minute later. He placed two books and what looked like a narrow trencher on the counter. Opening a container, he put ten pieces of carrot on the trencher and walked over to the screen door. He propped open the door with a gallon jug that must have been filled with sand or water—Grimshaw couldn't tell which from where he was standing—and set the trencher on the floor just inside the threshold.

As he walked back to the island, he held up two fingers and said, "Two pieces for each of you."

Grimshaw stared at the critters who gathered at the door. Five of them. For a moment, he wondered if Julian had gone completely out of his mind to be feeding giant rats. But the faces didn't belong to rats. What could look that happy about a piece of carrot?

"Alan Wolfgard writes thrillers," Julian said when he resumed his place on the other side of the island's counter. "And the other is a mystery written by an Intuit writer."

"What the fuck . . . ?" Grimshaw whispered. Then he caught the warning in Julian's eyes and picked up one of the books. "Never heard of Alan Wolfgard." But he knew the

name meant the author was a *terra indigene* Wolf. "You like
his stuff?"

"I do. And his perspective on the genre is . . . different."
I'll bet.

"And something you may find useful," Julian whispered.

Hearing a scraping at the door, Grimshaw looked back to
see the five whatever-they-were push the wooden tray to one
side of the door. Then they made that happy face and *hopped*
away. Not like a rabbit or anything else he'd ever seen.

"Those are Sproingers, from which this village takes its
name," Julian said.

"But what *are* they?"

"That's a question. I've collected books about places all
my life, especially books that have photographs of wildlife
and plants from other parts of this continent as well as other
parts of the world. My best guess is the template for the critters we know as Sproingers came from the continent of Australis."

"That's so far away it might as well be another world,"
Grimshaw protested. How many weeks on a ship would it
take to reach such a place? "How could a critter from . . ."
Then what Julian had said hit him. "The template?"

"Among the odd things about Sproingers, besides the fact
that they're here at all, is that there are always about a hundred of them, and on this continent they can only be found
around Lake Silence," Julian said. "They have no natural
enemies—they're big enough to take on any domestic cat,
and dogs back away from them—but there are never more
than a hundred. There are bobcats who live in the woods, as
well as coyotes—both ordinary animals and *terra indigene*.
Nothing touches the Sproingers. So they're a bit of a tourist
attraction with their happy little faces and the way they hop
around and stop at various stores for treats. And while they
stuff their faces, they listen to everything that's going on
around them."

"But they're not predators," Grimshaw said. "There has
never been a known form of *terra indigene* that wasn't a
predator." The *terra indigene*, the earth natives, the Others,

were, as a group, *the* dominant predators throughout the world, and they could be a terrifyingly efficient killing force, as humans had learned last summer.

"That's true," Julian agreed. "Sproingers aren't predators. I doubt the same can be said about their other form."

"Do you know what that is?"

"Something dangerous." Julian hesitated. "Did you wonder about the name of the store?"

"I thought some froufrou idiot owned the place."

Julian laughed softly. "I opened the store last fall. After the *terra indigene* swept through Thaisia last summer and killed so many humans during the Great Predation, a lot of stores in Sproing were suddenly without owners, either because the owners died or the people packed up and ran. The bookstore, such as it was at the time, was one of those places. The owner's heirs wanted to sell fast and get to anyplace that was human controlled. I bought it.

"It was around dusk one day before I officially opened, and someone stepped into the store. She looked small enough to be a child, but she never came all the way into the store and the light was such that I couldn't see her clearly. She asked if I was going to open the story place, and I said I was. She asked what the name would be, and I told her I hadn't decided yet and maybe she could help me pick a name.

"I didn't think anything of it; just a curious child. But two days later, she walked into the store at dusk and placed a scrap of paper on the counter with two words carefully printed out: Lettuce Reed."

"Let Us Read. She chose words that sounded correct."

Julian nodded. "Either she didn't know better, or she was testing me. Either way, that's how the store got its name. Now five of her kind come to the store once a week, at dusk. In fading light, you could mistake them for human. They have the right shape, mostly. But they're not human. I'm not sure what kind of *terra indigene* they are, but I am sure they're predators of the highest order, and they live somewhere around this lake. They come in and each of them buys one book. Sometimes they return a book for a used-book credit and tell me why they didn't like it. Other books they like a lot, so I suggest other stories that might appeal to them."

Grimshaw thought about that. "Five Sproingers come for carrots every day?"

"Most every day. They don't show up on Earthday, when the store is closed. But I don't think my book buyers and the Sproingers are the same beings—although it's possible that one kind of *terra indigene* has chosen to take two very different forms in order to keep an eye on things around this part of the Northeast." Julian looked at Grimshaw for a long moment. "Wayne, something is going on in Sproing. You should be careful about who you choose as allies."

A shiver went down Grimshaw's spine. No idle warning. Not when it came from Julian Farrow.

"What do you know about Victoria DeVine?"

Julian thought for a moment. Too long a moment?

"She's a nice woman," Julian finally said. "Smart with a sassy sense of humor; she doesn't hurt other people's feelings in order to be funny. The Jumble was part of her divorce settlement, along with a cash payment. She sunk the cash into the property, which needed repairs as well as new windows, new wiring, plumbing, septic tank. You name it, the place needed it. She managed to fix up the main house and three of the guest cabins. Now it's a game of wait and see if she can get enough guests on a regular basis to be able to keep the place going. I haven't witnessed one, but I gather she's experienced mild anxiety attacks since her separation and divorce, but for the most part has handled the challenges of living in an isolated spot like The Jumble. As far as having paying guests, she has a prime beach, which is available only to her guests—something some of the villagers resent because it's bigger than the public beach area at the southern end of the lake. I guess people got used to using The Jumble's beach as if it was public land and don't like it being off-limits."

"You like her."

Julian gave Grimshaw a sharp look. "I usually like people I call friends. That's why they're friends."

"Have you asked her out?" She wasn't his type—too nervy for one thing—but Julian had always had his own rules when it came to relationships.

"What are you, the dating police?" Julian demanded.

He grinned. "Just asking."

Julian looked away, making Grimshaw wonder about scars you couldn't see—and wonder if he'd just scraped across one of those scars.

"Julian?"

"My impression is that Vicki DeVine had a train wreck of a marriage and a car wreck of a divorce, and there are some deep wounds that haven't healed yet."

Grimshaw thought about her reaction to him, the way she had flinched a couple of times as if expecting a blow of some kind. "She has trouble being around men?" Owning a resort was a bad choice of profession if that was the case.

"Friends are fine. I didn't hear of her having problems with any of the contractors who did work at The Jumble. But when it gets too personal? The anxiety attack that follows can't be described as mild." Julian hesitated. "Vicki boarded with Ineke Xavier while The Jumble was being restored. One night one of the other guests tried some moves. I don't know any details except Ineke kicked the man to the curb and called the doctor to deal with Vicki's reaction."

"Crap," Grimshaw said softly. Nervy didn't begin to describe someone like that.

"We meet up for lunch sometimes or go to a movie with other friends. As long as no one calls it a date, with whatever physical demands that word conjures up for her, she's fine."

"And you're okay with that?"

"She's my friend. I'm okay with that." Julian blew out a breath. "There is a rumor that the dead man was connected to a developer who is going to build a significant lakeside resort."

An abrupt change of subject. Grimshaw took the hint. "You figure someone is looking at The Jumble for that?"

"That's the only land available, and it isn't really available."

"Unless a dead body shows up on the property and the investigation scares off the current owner." He thought for a moment. "What about the other side of the lake? Could someone be looking at that?"

Julian huffed out a laugh. "Silence Lodge is the home of the local group of Sanguinati. No one with brains, or any desire to live, would approach the vampires about developing land around the lake."

"What if I needed to talk to one of them?"

"Call your landlords. I believe they have the other office above the police station."

"Crap," Grimshaw said. "How many buildings do the Sanguinati own in this village?"

"More than the mayor or anyone else realizes. But that's just a guess."

Too much to think about, and he needed some time and quiet to think. "Anyplace around here to stay? Didn't see an inn or motel."

"Ineke Xavier's boardinghouse, if you're looking for short term. It's clean and the food is good. She can be a bit . . . difficult . . . at times, but it's your best choice. For longer term, there are some cabins along Mill Creek, which has a water mill that generates the electricity for the cabins. Come to think of it, I think it's the source of electricity for The Jumble too. The cabins are basic one-bedroom, but furniture can be included. I'm renting one of them and can't complain."

"Who owns the cabins?" But Grimshaw had a feeling he already knew.

"The residents of Silence Lodge. Don't let paved streets and storefronts fool you, Wayne. This is the wild country, and all of us are prey."

A *lot* to think about. "I guess I'd better go over to the boardinghouse and see if Ms. Xavier has a room to rent. How much do I owe you for the books?"

"Bring them back in decent shape and I can sell them to Vicki as good used books." Julian smiled. "She's building up a library for herself and for her potential guests, but she's on a budget."

It was tempting to ask if Julian knew that Victoria DeVine's lodger was one of the Crowgard, but that could wait for another day.

"See you around, Julian."

"Your business is just across the street from mine, so that's likely."

Following Julian's directions, Grimshaw got in his car and drove to the boardinghouse.

Yeah. He had a lot to think about, regardless of what the Crime Investigation Unit uncovered.

Like, what was Julian Farrow really doing in a place like Sproing?

CHAPTER 6

Vicki

Sunday, Juin 13

Ineke Xavier ran the boardinghouse in Sproing. She was a tall woman—at least compared to me—and wore black-framed glasses. What made her stand out was her hair. It was a dark brown that was almost black, streaked with bright burgundy and teal.

There had been a lot of rumors flying around Hubb NE last year about the *terra indigene* and some of their deadliest forms. One rumor was that there was a form of *terra indigene* that could kill with just a look and it could be recognized by its multicolored hair. So it was understandable that guests, when first seeing Ineke, might wonder what they were walking into. And, in truth, there were some who looked at Ineke and walked back out, preferring to stay in the camper park at the edge of town, renting a camper that didn't have its own toilet instead of staying in a clean room at the boardinghouse—an en suite room if you were willing to pay extra for one of the boardinghouse's deluxe suites.

Ineke was a good cook, but she wasn't much interested in baking. She left that to Dominique, one of the two young women who were somehow related to her and also worked for her. So when she showed up at The Jumble as soon as she finished serving breakfast at the boardinghouse, set a large bag on my kitchen table, and pulled out tins of chocolate chip cookies, cinnamon muffins, double-fudge brownies, and pecan-caramel rolls, I didn't need to be a blood prophet to know she wanted something.

"Is this a bribe?" I asked.

"Of course it's a bribe." She sounded insulted that I had to ask. "Do you think I would bring this many treats for anything less?"

Not when sugar and flour were still limited items that weren't always available.

I selected a chocolate chip cookie from the tin and took a bite. Delicious. Wonderful. And I flashed to the memory of Yorick giving me *that* smile and a little finger shake whenever I wanted to enjoy a sweet. Not gorge, mind you, just have an end-of-the-meal sweet—a family tradition he insisted on, claiming that none of the members of *his* family had ever gotten fat by having a small sweet after dinner. But I still got that smile and finger shake at the end of every meal—or a mild scold about being wasteful when I turned down the sweet.

I pushed aside memories that still soured my enjoyment of food most of the time while triggering a need to stuff my face. Feeling rebellious, I took another bite of the cookie. "Why the bribe?"

"People need time to get away from routine and relax. Now more than ever. And the Finger Lakes region has always been a popular destination. But the businesses in Sproing need something more than the Sproingers to give people a reason to stay here for a long weekend instead of spending time at one of the other lakes. I've been thinking about ways to hook the tourists, and I have a proposal for you." Ineke helped herself to a brownie. "I have an arrangement with the stable that adjoins the boardinghouse land."

Horses for hire and boarding for privately owned animals. I used to love to ride when I was younger, but I hadn't gone over to see about hiring a horse for an hour or two. Too much to do and not enough money for indulgences.

"Okay," I said, just to show I was listening, because Ineke wasn't someone you wanted to annoy. I had boarded with her while the repairs and upgrades were being done on The Jumble's main house. She usually gave her boarders a couple of prunes in the morning "to keep the plumbing clear," and you didn't get the rest of your breakfast until you ate them.

Feeding them to Ineke's dog, Maxwell, who was a border collie with a touch of OCD when it came to locating and herding his people-sheep, was a no-no. Maxwell loved prunes but did not need to have his plumbing cleared, and the result of feeding him prunes was a messy eviction. Ineke was a lovely woman most of the time, but cross her and she wouldn't hesitate to open a window and chuck your suitcase—and everything else you owned—onto the front lawn. And her aim was so good that at least half of what you owned landed in the dog's diarrhea.

While I stayed with her, I ate my prunes and never, ever fed Maxwell table scraps of any kind.

"I thought the stable closed," I said.

"Well, the previous owner was eaten, and the hands ran off to wherever people were running last year, but it was taken over shortly afterward by Horace and Hector Adams. They're Simple Life folk. Cousins, I think." She shrugged to indicate their actual relationship was none of her business. "They aren't as strict about following Simple Life customs as some of their people, so they were willing to take over a business in a village that's a mix of people and customs."

"What does that mean? They use electricity for their appliances and lights but don't own a television?"

"Pretty much. They have a radio, but only listen to the news in the morning and an hour of music at night. They have a telephone because they're running a business but don't have mobile phones. And they wear the traditional Simple Life style of clothes."

Ineke knew more about who was doing what and where than anyone else in the village, including Jane Argyle, the postmistress, which was saying something. But while Jane might pass on gossip or a rumor indiscriminately, Ineke passed on information only if she thought it was something someone needed to know.

"Last fall, we offered guided trail rides around Sproing, visiting a couple of the boutique wineries in the area and giving visitors a chance to see some wildlife that wasn't looking for lunch. Even after the Great Predation, there were people who wanted to get away from home for a day or two but didn't want to travel very far."

"People went to these wineries and sampled wines and then rode horses? Tall horses?"

"Dominique or Paige looked after the riders. Well, the horses mostly looked after the riders and knew enough to ignore the people on their backs and follow the girls. Anyway, I was thinking that, now that we're into the summer months and the heat is coming on, maybe we could arrange a guided trail ride through The Jumble. There are plenty of bridle paths. We could start out at my place, ride for an hour or so, and end up at your place, where guests could enjoy a swim in the lake or just enjoy the quiet of your private beach. You've got that big screened porch across the back of the main house, so we would offer lunch there before my guests were guided back to the boardinghouse, passing the Milfords' fruit stand on the way. I would supply the lunch—bringing enough for you and your lodgers—and would pay you twenty percent of the fee for the outing."

"You're charging for this?"

"Of course I'm charging. Hiring the horses and making the meal isn't free. And access to your beach is part of the package, not something that can be had separately. Unless you decide to open the beach on your own, but if you do, you'd better charge enough for the privilege and have someone around who can enforce who gets in and who doesn't or you'll be overrun."

"I'm not planning to make the beach available to anyone but my lodgers." I'd had enough trouble convincing people that The Jumble, and its beach, was private property. I wasn't going to encourage people to think otherwise. On the other hand, this sort of setup would bring in a little money. It might even bring a guest or two if someone wanted to spend time on the lake and had to rent one of my little cabins to do it.

"I'm willing to give it a try," I said.

"I'll be sure to put a disclaimer on the sign-up sheet, warning everyone that we aren't responsible for any injuries or accidents that are a result of anyone upsetting the Lady of the Lake." Ineke finished her brownie and licked the frosting off her fingers.

"The Lady of the Lake?"

Silence.

"No one told you about her?" Ineke finally asked.

I shook my head. "She's *terra indigene*?"

Ineke nodded. "It's one of the smaller Finger Lakes, being barely five miles long and less than a mile across, but Silence is one of the deepest. No one knows what the Lady is—people who might have seen her don't live to tell about it."

"Are you sure it's not just a story? I've been swimming out there—well, taking a quick dip since the water isn't warm enough yet to do more—and haven't seen anything. Not even a ripple."

"She's out there."

"Golly."

"Let's pick a couple of dates. Then I'll talk to Horace and Hector to make sure we can rent the horses," Ineke said.

I fetched my scheduling calendar and we chose a couple of days.

"I'm limiting it to six guests," she said. "We may not get that many the first time out since my current boarders are police officers of one sort or another, but they shouldn't be around much longer. If I don't fill all the slots, I'll open it up to Sproing residents, like the new owners of some of the stores. Julian Farrow is kind of dishy, don't you think?" She looked at me and waggled her eyebrows.

He certainly was dishy, and I liked him a lot, liked talking to him about books. Except for Ineke, he was the only close friend I had in Sproing, but I didn't want more than friendship from anyone who had a vigorous appendage, no matter how dishy he might be.

Shortly after coming to Sproing, I had read an article in an old magazine about "What Men Expect When They're Dating." It said men expected to have sex by the third date, which I found thoroughly intimidating because how could you know someone well enough in such a short amount of time to do something that intimate?

Anyway, I was staying at Ineke's when another guest, who was there for only a night, suggested we walk outside and take a look at the moon. Julian had loaned me a book about astronomy and I had planned to go out to the back of the property that evening and see if I could identify a few constellations, so going out to look at the moon didn't seem odd. And when the man hinted that a kiss or two would be a lovely way to end the evening . . . Well, that did seem a little pushy, but he'd been kind during dinner and had sounded interested in my opinions about a book we'd both read, and somehow the way he'd phrased the hint made it sound like everyone would think I was being mean and selfish if I said no after he'd been so kind to me during dinner. I didn't want Ineke, or anyone else, thinking I was mean and selfish, so I thought, *He's only here for the night and only asking for a kiss. We'll never reach third-date expectations. Why not see how it feels to kiss a man who isn't Yorick?* But I found out too late that he thought my agreeing to a kiss meant I had agreed to do a lot more, and when I pushed him away because he started to do more, he said I should be grateful anyone wanted to give me a fuck, and suddenly he sounded so much like Yorick that . . .

I don't remember much after that except Maxwell barking and snapping at the man and Ineke yelling. Then I was back in my room, hugging Maxwell, and Dr. Wallace was talking to Ineke—and the man was gone.

Before that night, I had daydreamed, just a little, about Julian maybe someday becoming more than a friend. After that night . . . I wasn't going to risk ruining the friendship I had in order to find out that wanting sex turned every man into a Yorick.

When I didn't respond, Ineke patted my hand and pushed

away from the kitchen table. I walked her to her car. She looked around, scanning the trees.

No sign of Aggie or any other Crow.

"The crime investigators are at the boardinghouse, and not just as guests," Ineke said. "The man who was killed was staying in one of my rooms. The investigators searched the room yesterday and they're doing it again this morning. It seems they can't find something they expected to find."

"So they know who he is." I breathed a sigh of relief. "That's good."

"I'm not so sure it's good." She sounded grim. "Listen, Vicki. I heard something that makes me think that *they* think the man knew you, was coming to see you."

"I didn't know him." Okay, I hadn't taken a good look at him since he had the missing eyeballs and I felt a bit squeamish. "I didn't have an appointment with anyone, wasn't expecting anyone."

She studied me. "All the same, if the investigators want to have a chat with you, I'd be real careful about what I said— and I would think hard about having a lawyer present before saying *anything* to them."

Ineke drove away, and I was left wondering where I would find a lawyer if I needed one.

As I went back to the house, I noticed the Crow on the ground near a tree. "Aggie?"

"Caw."

A soft sound. A troubled sound.

Just how much had she heard?

Around noon, two unmarked cars drove up to the house and I wondered if I should have paid more attention to Ineke's quiet warning and spent some time looking for a lawyer who would represent me if I needed one.

"Ms. DeVine?"

Two men got out of the first car. The older man had an insincere, oil-slick smile that reminded me too much of Yorick when he was talking "a chump" into some kind of deal. The younger one, who introduced himself as Officer Osgood, seemed uncomfortable with his partner or superior or whatever Mr. Oil Slick was in the CIU hierarchy.

Or was that Detective Oil Slick? Since he hadn't introduced himself, that name would do.

"We'd like you to come down to the station and answer a few questions," Oil Slick said.

"Why?" I stayed where I was, within reach of my front door. My heart pounded and I was getting that feeling in my arms and legs, like I was suddenly wrapped in another skin that was two sizes too small—a warning sign of excessive stress. "I already told Officer Grimshaw everything I knew. My lodger found the body yesterday, and I called the police."

"It appears the victim was here to discuss your squatting on land that belongs to your ex-husband's family."

"I beg your pardon?" That anxiety skin wrap tightened a little more. "I am not *squatting.* The Jumble was part of my divorce settlement. Whether it used to be family land or not, my ex-husband was happy to unload it on me." Then it clicked. "Oh. Did he send that man to see if I'd sunk enough money into the place and made enough improvements to make it worth his while to try to get it back?"

Typical Yorick. And typical me that it took me ten years to see his true nature. Of course, he'd been very good at making me believe that what I knew was true was really me making things up and getting confused.

Four other men stepped out of the second vehicle.

"You don't mind if my men look around, do you?" Oil Slick asked.

In another minute I was going to break down into uncontrollable weeping and Oil Slick would be able to push me into agreeing with whatever he wanted to do. But until that moment . . . "You think you can come into my house and look around? Maybe paw through cupboards and drawers and 'find' things to substantiate your allegations?"

"You've become overexcited, Ms. DeVine," Oil Slick

warned. "Pretending to have hysterics isn't going to change anything. You are coming to the station with us to answer some questions."

"Exactly where is this station?" Okay, I like reading thrillers, so I had this sudden image of me being driven away to some unknown destination and questioned until I confessed to whatever they wanted to hang on me.

"In Sproing." Oil Slick looked past me. "In the meantime . . ."

A hand latched onto my wrist, and Aggie pressed against my back and whispered, "Tell them what they are not allowed to do at your house. Say it really loud."

I didn't see how saying something really loud was any better than speaking in a normal volume, but I did what she suggested—if for no other reason than it seemed like a way to relieve a bit of stress. "No one is allowed to enter my house until I return. No one can open my car and look for alleged evidence. No one can enter the cabins and look around. No one is allowed to leave *anything* on my property. You can all stand outside and look at the trees, but that is all you are allowed to do."

Oil Slick lost even the veneer of courtesy as I listed, loudly, the things he and his men could not do.

"We can get a warrant to search your place," he said. "If we have to get a warrant, it will look like you have something to hide."

"Until you have that warrant, you don't set a toe inside any of these buildings." I felt very brave—or very lightheaded. It was hard to tell. "Now. I'll get my purse and lock up. Then I'll follow you to the station."

"You'll be riding with us, and you're not entering the house to destroy evidence while you're 'looking' for your purse."

"I could stand just outside the door," Officer Osgood said. "If Ms. DeVine leaves the door open . . ."

Then things got strange.

"Caw!"

"Caw!" "Caw!" "Caw!"

"My friends are here," Aggie whispered.

One Crow. Then three more. Then a dozen flew into the trees around the house. A dozen more took up position on the roof. The biggest hawk, or Hawk, I had ever seen landed on the roof of Oil Slick's car—and I'm sure it deliberately scraped its talons over the surface in a bird version of keying a car to put gouges in the paint. As I looked at the Hawk, it occurred to me that, until the car was repainted, those gouges would be so easy to spot from a bird's view of the roads.

A gust of air blew through the trees, making the leaves sound like sinister tambourines.

And something nearby and unseen *growled*.

"Miss Vicki told you the rules," Aggie said. She sounded a lot less like a teenager who was on her own than she usually did. "*Everyone* will make sure you humans follow the rules."

You humans. Battle line drawn.

"Get your purse," Oil Slick said.

I expected Aggie to keep holding on to my wrist, but she turned and ran to the back of the house. I got a glimpse of her clothing and would need to talk to her about wearing something more than a sheer cotton nightie when there were visitors. Especially when there were male visitors.

I fetched my purse, made sure the back porch's screen door was properly latched and the kitchen door was locked. When I was far enough into the house not to be heard, I pulled out my mobile phone and called Ineke, leaving a message on her answering machine, telling her the CIU investigators were taking me to the Sproing Police Station. Or so they claimed. I finished the message with the time, so she would know exactly when I had left. If Oil Slick was taking me somewhere else, maybe the time of departure would be useful. Assuming anyone tried to find me.

I made sure Officer Osgood saw me lock the front door, both regular lock and dead bolt. I made sure Oil Slick saw me tuck the keys into the big purse I used when I figured I would need everything.

"I have copies of the divorce papers, the settlement, and

the deed to The Jumble in my safe-deposit box at the bank. And, no, I won't give you my safe-deposit key so that you can fetch the papers." It was finally sinking in that something was far from right about all of this, including the presence of the man who had died on my land.

"Then we'll stop there first," Oil Slick said.

He made it sound like he was going to have to go miles out of his way when the bank was right next door to the police station. If he parked anywhere on Main Street, he wouldn't have to move his car in order to get from one place to the other.

"Caw!"

"Caw!" "Caw!" "Caw!"

Whether the Crows were acknowledging the destination or issuing a warning didn't matter. There were close to two dozen feathered witnesses who knew where I was *supposed* to be a few minutes from now.

As I was escorted to the first unmarked car by Oil Slick and one of the unnamed detectives who had been in the second car, I looked around. But I couldn't tell if Aggie was among the Crows watching us. If she hadn't rented one of the cabins, I wouldn't have had even this much support—and no one around to see what might happen.

CHAPTER 7

Aggie

Sunday, Juin 13

Aggie flew across Lake Silence as fast as she could. This was bad. This was so very, very bad. If she'd just eaten the squooshy eyeball instead of bringing it back to the house to warm up in the wave-cooker, the police humans wouldn't be causing trouble for Miss Vicki because they wouldn't have known about the dead man. But Miss Vicki had seen the eyeball and done what she felt was right by human rules, and now she was in trouble.

The Crowgard would keep watch around The Jumble, would even attack the humans if they disobeyed Miss Vicki's rules. But police humans had guns, and that made them an especially dangerous breed, so the Crowgard weren't enough protection. Not alone. And they didn't know enough about human rules. But she knew someone who did know about human rules and might be willing to help.

She flew across the lake until she reached Silence Lodge. Landing on the top level of the multilevel deck that stretched across the back of the lodge, she shifted to a feathered but mostly human form, gathered her courage, and knocked on the door.

CHAPTER 8

Grimshaw

Sunday, Juin 13

Grimshaw debated with himself if he wanted lunch enough to brave the inquisitive stares and prying questions he was bound to get the moment he walked into Come and Get It, the local diner. He'd already been grilled by Ineke Xavier when he asked about renting a room for a few days. She hadn't been keen to rent her last room to him—one of her rooms being a crime scene and the rest being appropriated by Detective Marmaduke Swinn and his CIU team—but when she understood that he *wasn't* part of the CIU team, she'd been willing to rent him the room with the en suite bathroom that she'd refused to give up for the CIU team.

He didn't know what Swinn had done to tick her off that she'd held back her best room, and he didn't care. He was just glad to have the room, and equally glad the CIU boys had been out and about when he arrived. Swinn had made it clear yesterday that he wasn't needed or welcome in their investigation, so showing up today as the new, if temporary, official police force in Sproing wasn't going to make for cordial dinners at the boardinghouse.

As he wondered how he was supposed to send Hargreaves

reports about an investigation he couldn't get near, Grimshaw watched Julian Farrow cross the street and make his way through the mob of Sproingers that had gathered in front of the bank and police station.

He waited until Julian entered the station and closed the door. "Has this ever happened before?"

"No." Julian sounded grim. "Listen, Wayne. I just got a call from Ineke Xavier. Apparently Vicki DeVine is being brought in for questioning."

"Not surprising. A dead body was found on her land, and the CIU boys will want an official statement." Grimshaw frowned. "If Ineke was concerned, why did she call you instead of me? I gave her my mobile phone number as well as the number for the station."

"You're still an unknown commodity. Highway patrol officer temporarily reassigned here, bringing with you a carryall that couldn't hold more than a couple of changes of clothes and a suit bag that probably has your other uniform and maybe a couple of dress shirts."

"Did she count my underwear the moment I was out of the room?"

"My point is, no one knows where you stand." Julian stood next to him at the window. Both of them watched the Sproingers. People going into or out of the bank could get around them. The critters did move out of the way, but they didn't move far—and if they suddenly felt inclined to attack someone's ankles or lower legs, a person had no room to maneuver.

"You need to be the good cop in this, Wayne."

"I don't think Ms. DeVine thinks of me as a good cop."

"Then you'd better do something to change her mind," Julian snapped.

Grimshaw studied the man who had been his friend. Maybe still was his friend. A man who had an uncanny sense of what was happening in a place.

"Okay. I'll be the good cop."

Julian nodded. "I told you that you'll need to be careful

about choosing your allies. Make sure everyone knows you're the good cop." He looked pointedly at the Sproingers. "And I do mean everyone."

"Crap."

An unmarked car pulled into one of the parking spaces in front of the bank. The Sproingers snapped to attention.

Grimshaw settled his duty belt and put on his hat. "Looks like that's my cue."

He walked outside just as one of the CIU boys opened the car's back door.

"Excuse me, fellas," Grimshaw said, looking at the Sproingers crowded around his legs. "I need to give the lady a hand."

They moved out of his way, giving him a clear path to the CIU car but closing ranks behind him.

He reached the car at the same time Vicki DeVine stepped out of the vehicle, swaying a little. The CIU man stared at her, so Grimshaw took a long step forward and extended his hand. She grabbed it. He wasn't sure she even knew whose hand she held.

Damn it, the woman was shaking, and if he was any judge of body language, she was a couple of breaths away from a complete meltdown.

"Anything I can do for you, Ms. DeVine?" he asked.

"We've got it covered," the CIU man said.

She looked at him and seemed to focus—and he wondered exactly what had happened during that car ride from The Jumble.

"The detective claims I'm squatting at The Jumble. He wants to see the paperwork that proves the land is mine. We're going into the bank to open my safe-deposit box."

"Do you want someone to go in with you?"

She focused on him a little more, as if who he was and what he was saying was finally getting through. "Thank you, Officer Grimshaw. That would be appreciated."

"Not necessary, *Officer*." Marmaduke Swinn came around the car to the sidewalk. He looked like he wanted to drop-kick a Sproinger or two to the other side of the street. The

Sproingers who stared back at him were not wearing their happy faces.

"Serve and protect." Grimshaw smiled and wondered what would happen if he pointed at Swinn and said, "That is a very bad man." How would the Sproingers react to such a statement? Would they shift to a *terra indigene* form that had a predator's teeth and claws? He estimated there were thirty of them filling the sidewalk in front of the bank and police station. If they had a lethal form, those were not good odds.

"Let's take a look at those papers and get this sorted out," he said. He released Vicki's hand, cupping her elbow instead to provide her with some support as they walked into the bank, trailed by Swinn and his man.

The bank manager stood near the teller windows and looked startled when Grimshaw walked in. Then he exchanged a quick look with Swinn.

Crap. What was going on between those two? The bank manager had expected Swinn to come in with Vicki DeVine, but Grimshaw's presence made the man nervous enough to sweat. Which meant a cop who wasn't part of Swinn's team was a problem for them.

"Surely we don't need so many people," he said as he fetched his keys and had Ms. DeVine sign the log.

Grimshaw gave the bank manager the look that made any wrongdoer squirm. And the man was squirming.

The safe-deposit box was removed from the vault and brought to the small room where people could add or remove things in private. Since the room wasn't bigger than a typical elevator and had a counter and chair taking up part of the space, the second CIU man stayed outside. The room was still crowded with four people. Grimshaw knew why he and Swinn were in the room, but why had the bank manager been allowed to stay? Was he supposed to be the witness to whatever was found in the box?

"They're gone," Vicki DeVine said, staring at the empty box. "The papers are gone. And the money! I had six thousand dollars in the box."

"This is a bank," Swinn said while the bank manager insisted that nothing could have been taken. "Why didn't you deposit the money? It doesn't earn interest sitting in the box."

She stared at him. "It also isn't lost if the bank goes under. This is a small institution, not a regional bank. Plenty of small banks went under in the past year. I wasn't taking that chance."

"Have a few trust issues?" Grimshaw murmured.

"Yes!"

She had color in her face again. He figured if she was pissed off, she was less likely to faint. That worked for him.

"Takes two keys to open the box," Swinn said. "I think you weren't being honest with us, Ms. DeVine."

"I know what was in the box," she protested.

"But you can't prove it." Swinn looked triumphant, like he'd made the winning point.

"That's right." The bank manager nodded vigorously. "You can't prove it."

"Of course I can," she snapped. "I made a list of everything I put in the box. And I took photos of all the items to corroborate the list."

More than a few trust issues—and a bit obsessive to boot. But Grimshaw was more interested in the way the bank manager started sweating again. Yes, opening the box required two keys. That didn't mean someone couldn't have made a duplicate before handing over the customer's key.

"The papers are missing, so you have no proof to your claim," Swinn said.

"I told you. Those were copies," Vicki DeVine replied. "The originals are in a lockbox in my bedroom at The Jumble."

Grimshaw focused his attention on Swinn before asking Vicki DeVine, "Is there anyone at your place to keep an eye on things?"

"I have a couple of men there," Swinn said, as if the question had been aimed at him.

"I think so," Vicki said. "Maybe."

Grimshaw nodded. "All right, then. We can drive back to The Jumble and—"

"She still has to answer some questions about the man who was killed on her property," Swinn snapped.

"A moment ago, you were certain it wasn't her property."

"Don't screw with me, Grimshaw. I've read your file, *Officer*."

Yep. He did not work or play well with others. Especially assholes like Swinn. Which was one of the reasons he was still just an officer while other men were promoted over him. But Swinn's reaction made him think the dead man was just the tip of the iceberg and Julian Farrow was right—there was something wrong in Sproing.

"Ms. DeVine?" Grimshaw waited until he had her attention. "Let's get your safe-deposit box locked up again, and then we'll go over to the station."

"What's the point of locking up an empty box?" she asked.

No point at all, he thought. But he wondered how many of Sproing's citizens were going to empty out their boxes once word got out that their valuables weren't any safer in the bank than they would be under the bed.

CHAPTER 9

Vicki

Sunday, Juin 13

We hadn't gone more than a couple of steps past the bank when a black luxury sedan with tinted windows glided into a parking space in front of the police station. It was so shiny, like road dust didn't dare touch its surface. Maybe they used a special wax that repelled dirt. If I asked the driver, would he tell me? My little green car was more a mottled brown these days, what with driving up the gravel access road to The Jumble's main house.

Then a man got out of the back seat.

He was . . . yummy. I mean, he was a double-scoop sundae with hot fudge and caramel sauce and a mountain of real whipped cream yummy. His hair was darker than Ineke's double-fudge brownies, and he had the most luscious melted-chocolate eyes.

He smiled at me, and I tried to move toward him, but Officer Grimshaw gripped my arm and wouldn't move at all. Didn't he know that gorgeous men never smiled that way at dumpy women with unruly hair? Stupid man.

"I'm Ms. DeVine's attorney," Yummy said. "I would like to speak to my client in private. We can use my office." He pointed toward the second floor of the police station. Then he handed Grimshaw a business card.

He was who? I was what?

"Crap." It was one of Grimshaw's breathed rather than spoken words.

"You're not a public defender," Swinn said, pushing forward. "And *she* can't afford anything more."

Too true, especially since someone stole the emergency fund I'd kept in the safe-deposit box.

"I will speak with my client in private," Yummy Attorney said. His eyes didn't look like melted chocolate anymore.

"Then you can talk to her in the station. We have a little room in the back just for that," Swinn said.

Sure, go ahead and smirk.

"Mr. Sanguinati and Ms. DeVine can talk in the front room, if that's acceptable," Grimshaw said.

Sanguin . . . Oh. It figured he wouldn't be a regular guy. Then again . . .

Grimshaw released my arm and I sort of teetered into the police station, followed by the yummy vampire attorney.

I took one of the visitors' seats. He brought the other visitors' chair over and sat facing me, our knees almost touching. Then he leaned forward and took my hands.

"You're trembling, Ms. DeVine." He rubbed a thumb over my knuckles. Was that supposed to calm me down, especially when he was looking at me as if I might be a plain vanilla cone but that was just what he was in the mood for? "Did those men hurt you in any way?"

"What men?"

"Are you unwell?"

Something was upsetting him, and when he glanced toward the door of the police station, I began to put it together. I wasn't the sharpest crayon in the box at that moment—stress does that to me—but like I said, I read a lot of thrillers, so I finally put the questions together. On the TV shows, the good guys refer to it as nonphysical interference or psychological intimidation.

That's what he wanted to know. Was his client shaking because of something that had been done? Trouble was, I'd developed a technique throughout my childhood and my marriage to Yorick where I would go to a safe and secret place in my mind, a closet that had a blankie and bunny slippers—a place no one else could find. I'd still hear whatever was being said to me or about me, still hear the list of my failings, but it was muffled by a thick door. So I heard and didn't hear.

Within a minute of driving away from The Jumble, I'd slammed that secret closet door shut. So I had absorbed but hadn't processed what Detective Oil Slick Swinn had said to me. I didn't come out of the closet until Grimshaw took my hand and I understood it was safe to be completely present again.

Not willing to pull away, I twisted my wrist to look at my watch. "Huh. It's past lunchtime. I get a little shaky when I'm stressed and forget to eat." And I hadn't eaten anything that day except the cookie, which was not smart.

"Wait here." He gave my hands a squeeze and stood up. Then he paused. "I didn't properly introduce myself. I'm Ilya Sanguinati."

"My attorney."

"Yes."

I sighed. "I appreciate the offer. I really do. But frankly, Mr. Sanguinati, I couldn't afford to pay for a sleeve of that very nice suit you're wearing, let alone your hourly rates."

"We can work out a payment plan."

I stared at him. A payment plan? I could guess what the interest might be while a person was paying off the principal on the bill. But . . . he was soooo yummy. And, really, what's a pint or two of blood between a girl and her attorney when she gets to have her neck nibbled by *that* mouth? And since neck nibbling wasn't the same as having sex, I was pretty sure I could handle it as well as the girls in the romances I'd read last week. I'd sure be willing to give it a try.

He opened the door partway and spoke to someone. I

heard Oil Slick Swinn squawk when Ilya Sanguinati closed the door and returned to the other seat.

"Now," he said. "Tell me how you came to be the caretaker of The Jumble and what you know about the human who had the poor taste to die on your land."

"Being dead is more inconvenient to him than it is to me," I pointed out.

His shoulders moved in what might have been a shrug. The movement was almost too subtle to see, but for all I knew, it could have been a wild, unrestrained gesture for someone like him.

I skipped the part about Yorick's Vigorous Appendage and explained about receiving The Jumble and some cash as my settlement in the divorce. I was happy to leave Hubb NE (aka Hubbney) since I wanted a fresh start and had hoped to turn The Jumble into a viable business that would provide me with a living. The fact that the property was on the western end of the Finger Lakes area was perfect since it was a happy distance from Hubbney and my former hubby.

I blamed low blood sugar for not being able to sound as upbeat and sassy as I wanted to sound. But Ilya Sanguinati didn't roll his eyes or sneer or make cute-but-cutting remarks. He just listened. I finished telling him about Aggie and the eyeball, which had led to me reporting the inconveniently dead man, moments before someone knocked on the station door.

Julian walked in. "I wasn't sure what you needed in the way of food, so I guessed. Grilled cheese sandwich and a chocolate milkshake. And there's a small bowl of sliced strawberries because Helen at the diner said you should have a little fruit with your meal."

"This is great. Thank you."

Julian set out the food on the desk blotter and pulled out the rolling desk chair.

"Now," Ilya Sanguinati said once I was seated behind the desk. "Let's get this settled."

My stomach rolled.

He raised a hand. "You eat and listen. *I'll* get this settled. And then we'll go back to The Jumble and take a look at the paperwork."

I noticed Julian took up a position behind me and a little to one side when the other men walked into the station. Officer Grimshaw took up a position at the far corner of the desk. And Ilya Sanguinati stood in front of the desk. It was like having a force field made out of male bodies, so I felt safe enough to stay out of the mental closet and listen while I ate my lunch.

Really good grilled cheese sandwich. Helen wouldn't say what she did to make them so good—a blend of cheeses, I think—but they were one of my favorite comfort foods when I ate at the diner.

Detective Swinn came in, attempting to swagger. He had a swagger attitude but not the build to pull it off. Rather like Yorick that way. The bank manager was the last one in. I guess the other CIU man wasn't invited to the party.

"Now," Ilya Sanguinati said. "Let's come to some small understanding."

"Ms. DeVine has to answer some questions," Swinn said.

My attorney ignored the CIU investigator and focused on the bank manager. "As we speak, two of my kin who deal with banks and banking issues are at the bank examining the contents of all the safe-deposit boxes held by the residents of Silence Lodge. Like Ms. DeVine, we keep a detailed list of everything we allow the bank to hold."

I looked at the bank manager, then at the dill pickle spear that had come with my sandwich. They were the same shade of green.

I nudged the pickle to one side and concentrated on the sandwich.

"More of my kin, the ones who are most interested in commerce and real estate, are also at the bank, withdrawing the funds we have on deposit."

"B-but you can't," the bank manager said. "If you withdraw that much . . ."

"The bank will no longer be a healthy, viable institution."

Ilya Sanguinati smiled. "I must also inform you that the lease for the building, which is owned by Silence Lodge, will not be renewed unless two conditions are met."

"But there isn't another building in Sproing that's suitable to be a bank, not without extensive renovations," the bank manager protested.

"I know." That smile again.

I blinked. Had I seen a hint of fang?

"What are your conditions?" Officer Grimshaw asked.

"Ms. DeVine will return tomorrow morning and open her safe-deposit box. If the missing papers and the missing seven thousand dollars have reappeared—"

"It was six thousand dollars," the bank manager said.

"Now it's seven."

Wow. This was better than the crime drama I'd watched on TV last week.

A light finger tap on the back of the chair reminded me that I was supposed to be eating. But, really, talk about bloodless bloodletting.

"The second condition is that you resign your position as bank manager before tomorrow morning. You will not retain any position with this bank. If those conditions are met and we have not discovered any discrepancies in our safe-deposit boxes, then we will restore enough of our funds to assist the bank in remaining solvent."

Now my attorney turned to the CIU investigator. But a movement at the window caught my attention.

"Is that a Sproinger?" I pointed at the face in the window. "Do they get that big?"

Ilya Sanguinati looked toward the window, then at me. "No. They are doing . . . Athletic human girls do this trick during sporting events."

"A pyramid? They've made a Sproinger pyramid?" I looked at the Sproinger. He—or she—made the happy face. "Can I get a picture?"

If I got out of this in one piece, I was going to buy an I ♥ SPROINGERS T-shirt.

Silence.

"Sorry," I muttered. "Brain-to-mouth disconnect."

"There are several people standing in the street taking pictures, including Dominique Xavier," Julian said. "I'm sure she'll give you one."

"This banking business is beside the point," Swinn said. "There are questions about why the dead man was lured to The Jumble."

"I agree," Ilya Sanguinati replied. "But you've already received the medical examiner's preliminary report, so you know there is no possible way that Ms. DeVine could have killed that man."

More silence.

"What did kill him?" Grimshaw asked. "I secured the scene but was relieved when the CIU team began their investigation."

"Spinal injury."

"That's not public knowledge," Swinn said, sounding unsure of himself.

"It is to us." Ilya Sanguinati looked at me. "Finished your lunch? You can bring the milkshake with you."

Even Oil Slick Swinn stepped out of the way when my attorney escorted me and the milkshake to his fancy black car. The driver, another Sanguinati judging by his looks, opened the back door for me, and Ilya Sanguinati blocked any attempt by Swinn to get close before we drove away.

"Thanks." I didn't know what else to say. Okay, I did know something else to say. "Why are you doing this?"

"You have been kind to Aggie. You are the first person since Honoria Dane to show some understanding about the nature of The Jumble."

"Which is?"

His eyes were back to looking like melted chocolate. "That it was built within a *terra indigene* settlement, with the understanding that the human caretaker would help those interested in learning to correctly mimic human ways."

Oh. Wow. That explained a few things about Aggie. She was the test volunteer to see if I was suitable. Now I wished I had talked to her about the nightie.

"There is no objection to your having human lodgers as well, as long as they are tolerant of their neighbors."

I sipped the milkshake to give myself time to think. "Does everyone know that about The Jumble? That it's really a *terra indigene* settlement?"

"During Honoria's time? I would think many of the residents in Sproing knew. Whether anyone outside the village understood . . ." He did that subtle shoulder movement.

That explained why Yorick's family always said Great-great's business venture was a failure. They hadn't known what she'd really built—or why.

Yes, visionary and eccentric. Maybe I could be like her when I grew up.

I looked out the window just as we passed the sign for Mill Creek Lane, which meant we'd missed the turn for my road. When we finally turned down an unmarked gravel road that I was pretty sure was on the other side of the lake, I started feeling nervous. "I thought we were going back to The Jumble to look at my papers."

"Not just yet," Ilya Sanguinati replied. "I am confident those papers are in order—or as much as they need to be. We're going to Silence Lodge so that you can assist me in reviewing some other papers."

"What other papers?"

He smiled, but there was a little bit of an edge to it. "The ones the dead man was carrying."

CHAPTER 10

Grimshaw

Sunday, Juin 13

Detective Swinn gave Grimshaw a look that would have scorched paint. Then he turned that look on Julian before he walked out of the police station.

"He doesn't like us," Julian said.

Grimshaw blew out a breath. "He's going to run a background check on you."

"Someone usually does, sooner or later."

And then that someone suggests that you move on?

"Why would the Sanguinati be interested in Vicki De-Vine?" he asked.

"Might be as simple as she's the person who has control of The Jumble," Julian replied. "She arrived in Sproing last fall and started renovating the main house and some of the cabins with an eye to having things ready for the summer, when you'd expect people to want to rent a place for a weekend getaway or a lakeside vacation. As far as I know, this is the first time the Sanguinati have made contact with her."

"If the vampires own as many buildings in this village as Ilya Sanguinati implied, then how did everyone pretend the Others kept their distance from the people who live here?"

Julian hesitated. "In another place where I lived for a

while, I took a job as the land agent—the person who collected the rent and arranged for repairs and listened to complaints. It was a small community like this one, and the humans swore there had never been a sighting of any kind of *terra indigene* in their village, despite the fact that they lived around the Addirondak Mountains and, occasionally, when the ground was soft after a rain, they would find huge prints under a window—evidence that *something* stood on its hind legs to look into the second-story window. There was a man in that town who had a side business making plaster casts of those prints. People would hang them on the walls of their family rooms and show them to guests—and they still swore the Others didn't prowl the streets at night, that some of the particularly gruesome deaths that occurred weren't caused by a large, angry predator. Wayne, a lot of people stay sane by pretending the *terra indigene* are Out There and not the individual sitting next to you at the counter in the diner."

"The only lodger currently at The Jumble is one of the Crowgard," Grimshaw said.

"Vicki knows?"

"If she didn't know before, she does now."

"But the Crow is still there?"

"Still there."

A hesitation. "The Crow she knows about may not be the only *terra indigene* living in one of the cabins or, at the very least, living on the land connected to The Jumble."

The phone rang. As Grimshaw reached for the receiver, he said, "That did occur to me." Then: "Sproing Police Station."

"O-officer down. O-officer needs a-assistance."

Gods. There weren't any other cops in the area, except . . .
"Where are you?"

"Th-The Jumble."

"Can you hold your position?"

"Yes."

"We're on our way." Grimshaw hung up and called the Bristol Police Station's number. "This is Officer Grimshaw in Sproing. Tell Captain Hargreaves I've got a situation at

The Jumble. Officer down and another officer requesting assistance. I'm heading there now. I need whoever you can send me."

"Isn't there a CIU team in the area? Can't they supply backup?" the dispatcher asked.

"I think it's the CIU team that got hit."

A heartbeat of silence. "I'll put out the call."

Grimshaw hung up and looked at Julian. "You're coming with me."

"No." Julian took a step back. "I'm not a cop anymore. I don't have a gun."

Grimshaw headed for the door. "You still have a gun. After what you went through, you wouldn't leave yourself without a weapon. I need someone to back me up, Julian. Someone I can trust."

He went out the door. He wasn't an Intuit like Julian, but he had a feeling that the man he remembered—the man who *had* been a damn good cop—wouldn't let him go into trouble alone.

"You can take the shotgun," he said when Julian got into the passenger seat.

"Which one of them called?" Julian asked.

Grimshaw pulled out of the parking space and made a U-turn to head for The Jumble, lights flashing and siren screaming. "My guess? The baby cop. Before Swinn sent me on my way, I saw a kid with the team who didn't look old enough to be in CIU. Barely looked old enough to have graduated from the academy."

"Swinn is his commanding officer. Why didn't the kid call him?"

"Maybe because Swinn *is* his commanding officer." Grimshaw concentrated on driving for a minute. Then he pulled a business card out of his shirt pocket. "Call Ilya Sanguinati and warn him not to take Vicki DeVine home until we know what's going on."

Julian took the card and pulled out his mobile phone.

"Mr. Sanguinati?" Julian said when the vampire answered the call. "There's some trouble at The Jumble. Officer Grimshaw is on his way there now. Could you . . . I see." Pause. "Yes, I understand. I appreciate the information." He ended the call. The hand holding the mobile phone flopped into his lap.

Grimshaw spared a glance at his friend, who looked unnaturally pale. "What?"

"Mr. Sanguinati is taking Vicki to Silence Lodge. He said the Elders aren't happy with humans at the moment, but the police will be safe enough to retrieve the survivor as long as no weapons are drawn."

He barely checked the reflex to slam on the brakes. "Elders? Gods, Julian."

When people spoke of the Others, they thought of the vampires or the ones who could shift to animal forms like Wolves and Bears and, yes, Crows. But as threats to humans went, those kinds of *terra indigene* paled in comparison to the *terra indigene* that were known as the Elders and the Elementals. *They* had been the killing force that had swept across the continent of Thaisia last summer—across the whole damn *world*. Unlike the shifters and vampires, who *might* let a human live if the encounter was peaceful, the Elders weren't that tolerant—a fact every police officer who did highway patrol recognized. Those men traveled the roads through the wild country every single day, and every day there was the chance that something watching from the verge would decide not to let the human driving the noisy metal box with the flashing lights live to reach his destination.

"He say anything else?"

"He said you should request an ambulance or whatever vehicle carries the dead when police answer a call. And you should bring some body bags."

Grimshaw slowed as he made the turn onto the gravel road that led to The Jumble's main house. He cut the siren but could hear other sirens in the distance, coming closer. Backup. Help. He hoped.

They saw the unmarked car where it had landed just off the gravel road. What was left of a car. Something had smashed the trunk and roof, punched in the doors, broken all the windows, and ripped off the front tires. Made sure the vehicle—and the people—couldn't escape.

"Let me out here," Julian said. "I'll see what I can do for anyone inside the car."

"You'll be in the open. Exposed," Grimshaw protested.

"I won't be carrying a weapon, so I should be safe enough."

The baby cop was still up ahead, so they had to split up in case anyone in the car was still alive.

"Watch your back," he said.

Julian opened the door but hesitated. "I have the feeling we'll be all right as long as everyone remains calm and professional."

And if fear makes someone twitchy? Didn't need, or want, an answer to that question.

Julian got out and Grimshaw continued up to the house. When he saw the young officer standing with his back to the house's front door, he put the car in PARK, touched the medal under his shirt, and whispered his prayer to Mikhos. Then he stepped out of the car, using the door as a shield while he looked around.

Man on the ground within sight of the house, not moving. The baby cop didn't look injured—at least he wasn't bleeding anywhere—but could be in shock.

Grimshaw stepped away from the car, closed the door, and approached the survivor. "Officer?"

"O-Osgood, sir. David Osgood."

"You hurt?"

"No, sir. I was . . . I was just . . ."

Grimshaw held up a hand. "We'll get to that. Anyone else around?"

An abrupt, hysterical laugh, quickly cut off.

"Caw."

"Caw." "Caw." "Caw."

One question answered but not in the way he wanted.

"Stay there." Not that he expected the kid to move while he approached the man on the ground.

He didn't know when he stopped moving. He just gradually realized his feet had frozen in place once his brain understood what he was seeing.

The CIU officer lay facedown. Grimshaw clearly saw the back of the man's sports jacket and the back of his head. He also saw the shoes that were pointing up.

Spinal injury. Gods above and below.

After that moment of shock, he approached the man to check for a pulse—and hoped he wouldn't find one.

Satisfied that he wasn't leaving an injured man, he returned to Osgood and led the young officer to his vehicle. Once inside the car with the doors locked—as if a locked door would provide any kind of safety—he called Captain Hargreaves to let him know backup wasn't required but another CIU team would be needed to investigate the reason for the attack—or at least to take possession of the damaged vehicle.

He finished the call to Hargreaves and turned in his seat to look at Osgood. "Can you tell me what happened?" They would need to take a formal statement, and maybe he shouldn't be the one asking questions now, but Swinn wasn't here and he didn't want anyone trying to convince Osgood to change his story.

"Detective Swinn and Detective Reynolds took Ms. DeVine to Sproing to answer some questions," Osgood said. "But not before Ms. DeVine made it real clear that we weren't allowed to snoop around inside her house or car or the cabins. And some of *them* heard her say it."

Snoop. An interesting word for a cop to use. What it said to him was the baby cop had felt uneasy about Swinn's orders.

"There was a girl with Ms. DeVine, a girl with black hair," Osgood continued. "I think she was one of *them*."

"She's one of the Crowgard." He studied Osgood. "They're called *terra indigene* or earth natives or Others. Talking about *us* and *them* is part of what caused the trouble and got a lot of people killed in the past year."

"Yes, sir." Osgood said nothing for a minute. "Once Detective Swinn left, Detective Calhoun told me to stay out front while he and Detective Chesnik took a look around back. I was checking out the wooden chair near the front door. Nice chair. I was thinking my grandma would like one like that when there was a . . . well, a scream from around back. Baker told me to stay put and ran around to the back of the house. The three of them returned in a minute. Calhoun and Baker had Chesnik between them. There was a necktie tied around Chesnik's leg, and his pants leg was soaked with blood. They yelled something about him being attacked and needing to get him to a hospital. So they put Chesnik in the back seat and Calhoun started driving down the gravel road."

"What was Chesnik doing when he was attacked?"

"I didn't see anything. I was out front."

Good guess that the next CIU team to come calling would find someone had tampered with a lock but didn't manage to get in.

"I heard the car crash into something," Osgood said. "I thought maybe Calhoun had been driving too fast on the gravel and hit a tree or something, and I started down the road to see if I could help. But Baker must have heard something in the trees over there because he headed away from the house and drew his service weapon, and I wasn't sure if I should stay and help him or go and help Calhoun. And then . . . then . . ."

"What did you see?" Grimshaw asked when Osgood stopped talking. "Officer! What did you see?"

"I didn't *see* anything!" A note of hysteria. "One moment Baker was running away from the house and had his weapon drawn and the next . . ." Osgood swallowed convulsively. "Something grabbed him and twisted him like it was squeezing water out of a wet rag."

Osgood scrabbled at the door. Grimshaw released the locks in time for the young man to bolt out of the car and stagger a few steps before he bent over and puked.

Grimshaw's mobile phone rang. Keeping an eye on Osgood, he answered. "Grimshaw."

"The driver is still alive but has severe head and neck injuries," Julian said. "I don't think he'll make it, but the EMTs are here. So is the Sproing volunteer fire department. They said someone called them and the EMTs and told them to get over to The Jumble. My guess is it was one of the Sanguinati who were at the bank. The volunteers and EMTs are working to get the driver out of the car so the ambulance can take him to Bristol Hospital."

The driver. That would be Calhoun. "Long drive for a seriously injured man."

"Nothing closer. One of Sproing's doctors is also here. He'll do what he can to help the EMTs stabilize the patient, but he says the man needs more help than he and his office can provide."

"And the other detective?" When Julian didn't answer, Grimshaw's voice sharpened. "Julian?"

"Something shredded his legs."

"Elders?"

"Not for me to say."

Yeah. Especially out in the open where you didn't know who, or what, was listening.

"What about you?" Julian asked. "You find the baby cop?"

"He's puking his guts out at the moment, but doesn't appear to be physically injured. The other man, Detective Baker . . ."

"What about him?"

"He's dead. Spinal injury."

He heard Julian suck in a breath.

"I'll walk up and meet you."

He wanted to tell Julian to stay put, but he realized if Julian Farrow felt all right about coming farther into The Jumble's land, they weren't at risk—until someone did something stupid.

CHAPTER 11

Vicki

Sunday, Juin 13

I went to the sliding screen door that opened out on a multi-level deck that overlooked the lake. There was a variety of very nice—and very expensive since it was handcrafted—outdoor furniture that I wished I could afford for my screened-in porch. Then again, Aggie thought my second-hand stuff was pretty fancy, so I guess it was a case of "eye of the beholder."

"Are you sure I shouldn't be there?" I asked, looking over my shoulder at Ilya Sanguinati. "Those sirens sounded like they were at The Jumble."

The Jumble was my responsibility—at least until I lost control of it—so I should be aware of what was happening. On the other hand, if I wasn't there, I couldn't be blamed for whatever had happened. Right?

"I'm sure you shouldn't be there," he replied. "The police caused a problem, and they'll have it fixed before I escort you home."

He seemed real certain of that. I was almost as certain about something else.

"Someone died," I said.

He looked up from the papers he had spread over a square coffee table that was bigger than my kitchen table. "Yes."

"It wasn't the young officer, was it?" In the thrillers I read, the young, less experienced officer was always the first one killed so the rest of the men would realize there was danger lurking nearby.

"No, it wasn't the young one."

"And Officer Grimshaw is all right?"

He studied me. "Is that important to you?"

There was nothing in Ilya Sanguinati's voice to indicate anything but mild curiosity, but I had a feeling Grimshaw's future depended on my answer.

"He was kind," I replied. "And he's a police officer you can depend on when you need help." *Unlike Detective Oil Slick,* I added silently.

I had revised my opinion of Officer Grimshaw during our second encounter, when his presence had helped me deal with Detective Swinn and the discovery of the theft of the items in my safe-deposit box. When he came to The Jumble, I was plenty nervous about leading him to a dead body, but he might have been nervous too and sounded a bit testy because of it. After all, cops really didn't like coming to Sproing because at least two of them had ended up inconveniently dead after responding to calls around here. At least, that's what I remember from the carefully edited news reports that were on TV a while ago. And now, if I understood what Ilya meant about a problem the police had to fix before I went home, they had at least one more reason to avoid the village whenever possible.

I returned to one of the chairs around the coffee table, determined to understand the papers the dead man had carried with him, but I kept looking at the items neatly lined up near the table. A knapsack and a thermos; a silver pen and pencil set; a silver business card holder; and a money clip, sans money.

I didn't know which kind of *terra indigene* would be interested in the knapsack and thermos, but I could guess who had taken possession of all the shiny items—and how much having to give them to Ilya had ruffled the Crowgard's feathers.

"Shouldn't those go to the police?" I asked.

"Why?" Ilya Sanguinati looked amused. "I believe the human phrase is 'finders keepers.'" After a moment, he added, "The Sanguinati didn't take those items, but I did require that they be brought here in case there was anything of import inside them."

"Like the papers." I almost pointed out that the police would like to have all this stuff for evidence, but being an attorney, Ilya already knew that—and he didn't care because, right now, helping the police investigate the first dead man meant helping Detective Swinn, and my yummy vampire attorney wasn't going to do that.

"Like the papers," Ilya agreed.

I looked through the papers again. After a few minutes, I shook my head. "This is wrong. This is all wrong."

"What, exactly, is wrong?"

I heard no condescension in the question, so I pulled out the first papers, which were an artist's rendering of cottages and the social center for a luxury resort. "All of these papers are plans for a luxury resort, very exclusive since there would be twenty-four row cottages as well as the social center, which would provide fine dining and an activities room, library, card room, et cetera. Within the grounds, the rendering shows tennis courts, as well as *two* docks. And look!" I jabbed at the rendering. "Motor boats. Who was the bozo who put this proposal together without looking at any of the conditions and restrictions? Because this . . ." And the last piece of paper was the one that tipped me over into pissed off and fighting mad. Which was quite an invigorating feeling—as long as I didn't have to fight with anyone who was bigger, stronger, or meaner than me. Which was just about everyone.

Unfortunately, the only person to fight with was a vampire. Who was my attorney. Whom I couldn't afford in the first place, so I probably didn't want to alienate him to the point of not helping me.

"This is The Jumble," I said with more control. Okay, I was gritting my teeth and kind of scratching at the paper, but I wasn't going all wild woman. Except for my hair. But that was its usual state. "When I took possession of the property, I studied the map that came with all the original documents that dictated what the person who owned the buildings could and couldn't do. So I know this is a map of The Jumble showing where all these luxury cottages would be located, where the tennis courts would go. And a parking lot, for crying out loud. None of which are permissible under the land-use terms of the original agreement."

I'd fretted over where to put cars if I actually had more than six lodgers. There *were* places near the cabins where you could park, but you reached those areas by driving on what amounted to an open track in the woods—single lane, unpaved. The grass between the tire tracks looked mown, more or less. Grazed might be a better description. Maybe that's why the old records that I'd been given had mentioned goats—nature's lawn mowers.

"What were the terms of the original agreement?" Ilya Sanguinati asked.

"If I could just get my papers, I could show you how this resort goes against the agreement."

"We don't need your documents. I already have the second set of originals."

I blinked. "You do?" I imagined giving myself a head slap. "You wrote up the original agreement."

"Not me personally. That was a bit before my time."

He looked to be in his mid- to late thirties. So either the Sanguinati aged differently than humans, which was likely with them being Others and all that, or he was lacing the words with dry humor when he said a few human generations was a bit before his time.

"A couple of residents from Silence Lodge did create the original contract, and we've enforced the terms of that agreement ever since."

"But I never saw you until now. No one came to check on the work to make sure it complied with the agreement."

He smiled, and I realized how naïve I sounded. Of course they'd checked on the work.

"We thought knowing about our presence might distress you, so we kept our distance. Now?" He did one of those subtle shrug movements with his shoulders. "Someone was interfering with you, so it was time to step in. Please tell me your understanding of the original documents."

I took a breath. The anger had burned off, leaving me a little shaky. "Well, the gist was that the person who owned The Jumble couldn't add more buildings and couldn't add on to existing structures to increase the overall square footage of any of the buildings, but could 'renovate and update the buildings to be in keeping with the times and local customs.' Only so many acres could be cleared for crops that would be used as a food source for the residents or to trade for other items. Trees could be cut for firewood or if they became a hazard to a structure due to death or disease. Any other changes could be made only with the consent of the land managers. Since there wasn't any contact information for these land managers, I was very careful about updating only what I needed to in order for the buildings to be sound and have the amenities paying guests would want, like en suite bathrooms, electricity, a roof that didn't leak, and plumbing that did what plumbing is supposed to do."

I finally took the next step. "Whoever that man worked for wanted to turn The Jumble into a posh lakeside resort. Which would mean buying me out—or forcing me out." I looked at Ilya Sanguinati. "Would someone really kill a man and try to implicate me in his death in order to get access to The Jumble? There has to be other land where someone could build a resort."

He took his time before answering. "There isn't any human-controlled land in the Feather Lakes area, so there isn't any-place where a *new* resort could be built. Investors would have to buy the buildings and the land lease for an existing place—and there are a few places similar to The Jumble throughout the Northeast Region where humans can take a lakeside va-cation or fish in the streams without having to totally 'rough it,' as I think you call it. But those places would have the same kinds of restrictions as The Jumble, and none of that land is 'owned' in the same way as The Jumble, making it even more dangerous for someone to come in and try to interfere with what already exists. And that doesn't take into account the difficulty of acquiring building materials—something the human who drew up those plans clearly hadn't considered."

Huh. Hadn't thought about that. After I arrived in Sproing and made a list of what I knew would have to be updated in the main house and the three lakeside cabins, I'd contacted companies in Bristol and Crystalton, the two towns of any size that were within range of Sproing. I'd ended up going with the companies in Crystalton—companies both Ineke and Julian Farrow had recommended. Well, Julian had recommended companies in Crystalton in general. It was Ineke who gave me specific names of contractors in Crystalton who could do the big renovations, as well as the names of reliable people in Sproing who could fix a leaky faucet or paint the rooms for a fair price. The Crystalton contractors said there was a waiting list for building supplies because there were further limits on raw materials after the war humans had foolishly waged against the *terra indigene* last summer.

Then the men had winked and said they would put in a good word for me. I don't know who they talked to or what they said, but the supplies came in and the work was done.

"Are the Sanguinati the land managers for The Jumble?" I asked, wondering how much financial interest the residents of Silence Lodge had in the land on the other side of the lake.

"No," Ilya replied.

"Then who is?"

A hesitation. "The rest of the *terra indigene* call them the Elders."

"You mentioned the Elders when Officer Grimshaw called about the new trouble. Who are they?"

"They are Namid's teeth and claws."

Oh crap. "So they're what, the *world's hit men*?"

He blinked. Then he laughed, a rich, deep sound.

Personally, I didn't think the question was that funny, especially when I started wondering how the dead man ended up dead.

"That is one way of putting it," Ilya finally said as he wiped his eyes.

Since he found that amusing, I really didn't want to know what other ways you could put it.

"If the Elders are the land managers, I'm guessing they aren't going to rub their paws together in greedy glee over the prospect of having the woodland overrun with humans."

I suddenly remembered a couple of bad jokes that were going around last summer just before Yorick started divorce proceedings and told me to find an apartment because he was keeping the upscale home in Hubbney that, apparently, the second official Mrs. Yorick Dane coveted.

Joke one. Why did the Bear chase the track team? He wanted some fast food.

Joke two. What do you call a flock of chickens caught in a fire tornado? Shake and bake.

On second thought, maybe the Elders would be happy about easy meals on their land—like campers who talk about tossing a line in the water and catching a couple of fish for dinner.

"Twelve cabins updated to match the times and social customs," Ilya said, sounding serious now. "No more and nothing more."

I pushed my fingers through my hair and wondered just how badly I'd been played. "What was that man doing here? *I* certainly wasn't going to try to build a resort on this land."

"Clearly someone thought it could be . . . finagled."

"Who? I could see my ex-husband showing up now that I've had a few months to realize how hard I'm going to have to work for so little return."

"Little return in human terms, perhaps, but there are other ways to measure a rich life," Ilya countered.

I tipped my head to indicate agreement. "But going with the reasoning in human terms, I could see him offering the cash equivalent of The Jumble as it had been valued at the time of the divorce settlement, completely ignoring all the money I'd put in for capital improvements. I could see him doing that, but he wasn't the person who emptied out my safe-deposit box."

"No, he wasn't."

"As long as I have the original documents that show Yorick ceded The Jumble to me, I can block whoever is trying to push in and change things."

"Yes, you can, and I will help you do that."

I nodded. I wasn't in the mood for self-examination, so I didn't want to wonder why I trusted a vampire more than I trusted most humans. Since I didn't want to wonder about that, I looked at the screen door and wondered about something else. "Do the Sanguinati have trouble with mosquitoes?"

"You mean, do the big bloodsuckers get pestered by the little bloodsuckers?"

Judging by my attorney's laughter, if I failed to turn The Jumble into a viable business, I could always get a job as a stand-up comedian in a vampire bar.

CHAPTER 12

Aggie

Sunday, Juin 13

Aggie moved back and forth on the tree branch, studying the dead man lying within sight of Miss Vicki's house.

The newest dead man? The last dead man? The dead detective man? How should the Crowgard identify this one? There had been an abundance of dead humans in The Jumble lately but a decided lack of easily acquired meat since they had died where alive humans had found them too quickly.

If the newest dead man couldn't be meat, maybe he had something else that was desirable? There had to be bits of treasure in the man's pockets, but she didn't want to get Miss Vicki into trouble by poking around, and the rest of the Crowgard who were watching the body—and the police—reluctantly agreed.

This body has been disturbed.

How had the human called Officer Grimshaw known that about the first dead man? He hadn't been there when the smaller *terra indigene* found the body and removed the useful items like the knapsack and thermos and the shiny that had rectangles of paper and the other things. Well, the eyeballs were gone, so that might have been a clue—police were always looking for clues in the TV shows Miss Vicki liked to watch—but had he known about the other things?

Ilya Sanguinati had known, or at least suspected, and had demanded that all the possessions be brought to Silence Lodge as his condition for helping Miss Vicki. And they *had* brought everything to the lodge. Except the eyeballs. Officer Grimshaw had taken the one she would have had for lunch yesterday, and Aggie suspected that one of the Weaselgard had made off with the other eyeball before the Crows had gathered to check out the first dead man. And the Weasels didn't even *like* eating eyeballs, so that was just them flipping their tails at the Crows.

On the other wing, Ilya Sanguinati had said he wanted to *see* what the first dead man had brought with him in order to figure out why the man had been trespassing at The Jumble. He hadn't said he would *keep* the useful things.

Still, she'd given up the shiny case that held the rectangles of paper in order to help Miss Vicki, and now there was this dead detective man who was bound to have *some* treasure.

Except Officer Grimshaw had already *seen* this body, so he would definitely know if it was disturbed by even tiny hands reaching into pockets to see what might be out of sight. He'd looked hard at the body, had even touched the neck like they did on TV in order to know if a human was dead, like they couldn't just tell by looking or smelling. Dead did *not* smell the same as alive. Even young Crows knew *that*. But apparently humans didn't and needed to touch.

Then she noticed a piece of cloth poking out from beneath the body. Humans called it a tie. One of her kin had seen a shiny clipped to the cloth, had seen it glint in a beam of sunlight as the detective man pulled out his weapon and challenged one of the Elders, who was already angry about the other two humans trying to enter Miss Vicki's house. Jozi had flown off to look for food, leaving Aggie to study the dead man.

She moved back and forth on the tree branch as she thought and thought about the shiny Jozi had seen. She could get that shiny without disturbing the body too much. All she needed to do was pull the tie out from under the body just enough to reach the clip.

Officer Grimshaw led Young Osgood to the car. She couldn't see them—which meant they couldn't see her.

She flew down to the dead man and looked again. Still couldn't see the car or the live humans.

She grabbed the end of the tie and pulled and pulled, tugging it out from under the body inch by inch. When she couldn't pull anymore out, she shifted her wings to tiny arms and hands that could squeeze between the ground and the body, following the tie until . . .

There!

She pulled out her prize, dropping it on the ground as she shifted arms and hands back to wings. Picking up the clip with her beak, she flew to the tree near the cabin she was renting from Miss Vicki—the tree that had a carefully built nest that hid a shallow hollow in the trunk. The hollow was just as carefully stuffed with sheets of paper that formed layers of hiding places for her little treasures.

Aggie studied the layers of paper for several minutes before finding just the right spot for her new shiny.

CHAPTER 13

Grimshaw

Sunday, Juin 13

Grimshaw drove slowly toward the main road, listening to the tires crunch on gravel—listening for the odd and terrible silence that usually meant the presence of Elders. He stopped when Julian approached the car.

"Is there anyone here who could give Officer Osgood a ride to the police station?" Grimshaw asked. He had left a crime scene unsecured, left a body unattended when he knew there were predators in the area. But this wasn't a human town or even a human place, and right now the need for caution—and the desire *not* to become the next dead body—overruled the basic protocol of investigation.

Besides, he wanted to get the baby cop out of there before someone told Swinn about the casualties to his team.

Julian rested an arm on the cruiser's door, leaning in to speak quietly. "The firemen got the driver out of the car. The EMTs have him and are on their way to the hospital in Bristol. I'm fairly certain he'll be DOA." He waved to a man dressed in a white shirt and sports coat, holding a medical bag. "Talk to the doc about that ride."

Julian stepped back to give Grimshaw room to open the door and get out of the cruiser.

"Doc?" Grimshaw said. The man looked too young to have his own practice, even in a small town. At least, that would have been true a year ago. Now, any doctor who was willing to practice in a small community like Sproing would be welcomed with open arms—and only a cursory check of his credentials.

"Steven Wallace. Junior partner at the medical office in Sproing."

They shook hands. Then Grimshaw crooked a finger at Osgood, who reluctantly got out of the cruiser, and said to Wallace, "If you're headed back to the village, could you give Officer Osgood a checkup, make sure he's all right?"

"I'm fine," Osgood protested, still looking sickly pale.

"Then you'll be in and out and can wait for me at the police station. Man the phones until I get there. Will you do that?"

"Yes, sir."

Wallace pointed at a vehicle parked behind the hearse. "That's my car over there."

Grimshaw waited until Osgood reached the car. "Doc? Are you the medical examiner?"

"More or less. I do determine cause of death among the residents of Sproing, as well as among the families who run the farms and vineyards all around this area, but if there's a criminal investigation or if it looks to be a suspicious death, the body is taken to Bristol for the autopsy."

That's what he figured, but he hoped for a little wiggle room. "There's another body near the main house. Is there anyplace in the village where you could take a look at it and give me an idea of the cause of death?"

Wallace took his time answering. "We can take the body to the funeral home, which also serves as our morgue, and examine it there." His lips curved in a grim smile. "Small town, small budget. The hearse is used to transport bodies. They already have the man who was killed in the car."

Grimshaw looked at the two men sitting in the front of the hearse, waiting for instructions. Then he heard a jangling and turned at the same time Julian said, "We've got company."

Two men walked down the road from the direction of the main house. The dark-haired one was a big man wearing jeans and a muscle shirt—and had way too much body hair to wear a shirt like that. The other one wasn't as heavily muscled and had golden-brown hair and eyes, but Grimshaw had the impression of speed and power that would easily match the other man's brawn.

Where had they come from? Grimshaw wondered, taking a step toward them. "Something I can do for you gentlemen?"

They ignored him and looked at the trees on either side of the road. Finding two that suited them, the leaner man padlocked two coils of chain around the trees. Then they uncoiled the chain the big man had carried over one shoulder. Simple hooks on each end were slipped through links in the padlocked chains. Attached to the middle of the long chain now blocking the access road was a wooden board with the words PRIVIT PROPERTEE, NO TRESPAZZING.

"You do know this is Ms. DeVine's property?" he asked. They stood on either side of the road, next to the trees.

"We're the groundskeepers and security," the muscled one said.

Had Vicki DeVine had groundskeepers and security before today? Or would she learn about her new employees when she returned from Silence Lodge?

"Your name, sir?" Too many civilians and not enough weapons, even if he dared draw a weapon.

"Conan Beargard."

Oh gods. That explained the build—and the hair. Grimshaw looked at the other male.

"Robert Panthera."

Grimshaw would bet a month's pay that the name was an alias. "Do people call you Robert?"

"Call me Cougar." A hand slapped the tree trunk. But in those seconds of movement, the hand changed, so what slapped the tree was a large, golden-furred paw with serious claws.

That explained who had used a tree near the main house as a scratching post. Did it also explain Detective Chesnik's shredded legs? Or had something even bigger done that damage?

"There's a body up near the main house. We need to retrieve it. I promised Ilya Sanguinati it would be gone before Ms. DeVine returns home."

"We know," Cougar said. "You can take the meat."

"You should tell that Swinn human that he and his packmates aren't welcome here," Conan Beargard growled.

"I'll tell him." Swinn would go ballistic when *that* message was delivered. "We'll go up to the main house, do our police things, and remove the body. Then we'll be on our way."

Turning his back on the two *terra indigene*, he looked at Julian. "Consider yourself deputized."

"No."

"I've got one shot at collecting evidence and looking around. I need another pair of eyes—and someone with better investigative skills than I have."

"I left the force, remember?"

"Get in the damn car, Julian." He waved to the men in the hearse. "You follow me up to the house." He looked at Wallace, who was still staring at Cougar's furry paw. "Doc? We'll meet you at the funeral home after you give Officer Osgood a checkup."

Wallace jerked. Then he regained his composure. "Of course." He walked to his car.

Cougar unhooked his side of the chain and walked across the road to stand beside Conan Beargard.

Grimshaw drove slowly, not giving any of the predators watching him a reason to attack. He parked at the main house, opened the cruiser's trunk, then addressed the men in the hearse.

"Give us a few minutes. I'll let you know when you can take the body."

"Make it fast, okay, Chief?" the driver said.

"I'm not the chief."

"That's not what I heard."

He'd deal with that later.

Relief breathed through him when he saw Julian taking the camera out of the trunk, along with the crime scene kit.

"You know what you're doing?" Julian asked softly.

"Doing what I can to supply my commanding officer with the evidence he may need." Of course, the evidence pointed to Swinn's men breaking into a house when they had been told they couldn't enter without a warrant. But that would be Captain Hargreaves's headache.

"I mean about having me involved. Swinn will chew bricks if he discovers I collected any evidence."

Another thing he'd deal with later. "Well, he'll never have a chance to look for himself, will he? Let's do this and get out of here."

The first thing he noticed when he approached the twisted body was the tie that was now partially visible. Which meant *someone* had fiddled with the corpse in the past few minutes.

"Gods above and below," Julian breathed. He didn't say another word, just started taking pictures of the body in situ.

Grimshaw looked around, moving out in an ever-widening circle. He found it unnerving that anything big enough to do *that* to a full-grown man also managed to leave no tracks—no sign of any kind of its presence. He bagged the service revolver that Baker had dropped.

"Done," Julian said.

Grimshaw waved to the men in the hearse. The older man, who had been driving, paled when he saw the body and realized what "facedown, feet up" meant. The younger one stumbled away and was sick.

"We're going to take a look around back," Grimshaw said. "Wait for us to escort you out."

"Caw!"

"Caw!" "Caw!" "Caw!"

The Crowgard didn't follow them to the back of the house,

but they weren't unsupervised, not with a big-ass Hawk perched in one of the trees that gave it a clear view of the screened-in porch that ran across the back of the house.

Blood in the grass. A lot of blood.

"Whatever attacked must have hit an artery," Julian said as he took pictures.

Grimshaw noticed something glinting in the grass. He pointed. "Take some shots of those before I bag them."

Julian huffed as he photographed the set of lock picks. "Damned fools, trying to break into this place."

Damned was right. Even the baby cop who wasn't physically hurt would be damaged by the experience. At the very least, he'd ride through a lot of nightmare-filled nights.

After bagging the lock picks, Grimshaw turned the handle on the screen door.

"Wayne!" Julian breathed the word.

The door opened, proving Chesnik had gotten the door unlatched before he was attacked—proving he had broken the rules of staying out of Ms. DeVine's house.

"Someone used lock picks to open this door," he said in a loud voice. "From what I can see from here, the intruder didn't actually enter Ms. DeVine's house or disturb any of her possessions, but we will inform her attorney about the attempted break-in." He started to shut the door.

"Wayne!"

Out of the corner of his eye, Grimshaw saw Julian drop to the ground. He hunched his shoulders and lowered his head a moment before he felt the tip of a wing brush across his back.

An aborted attack or a warning?

Shaken, and not daring to reach for the door again to shut it, he and Julian gathered the evidence and their equipment and headed for the front of the house.

Grimshaw glanced back. The Hawk they had seen was still in the tree, watching them. The attack, or warning, had come from a different direction.

Something to remember since he was certain he'd be coming back to The Jumble before this was over.

CHAPTER 14

Vicki

Sunday, Juin 13

After receiving a call from Officer Grimshaw, Ilya San-guinati gave me a ride to the Pizza Shack so that I could pick up dinner. He wouldn't explain why he had ordered a large Meat Eater's pizza with double meat as well as the mushroom and black olives pizza I had ordered for myself. Well, I'd be sharing it with Aggie if she decided to join me for cop and crime night on TV.

Then I met my new employee-lodgers, Conan Beargard and Robert "call me Cougar" Panthera, and I understood why I was bringing home what you could call the Carni-vore's Special pizza, which had so much meat you couldn't tell there was sauce, cheese, or a crust underneath.

I looked at Conan and Cougar and hoped it was meaty enough that they wouldn't be looking to nibble anything else. I rather liked having ten toes, not to mention a full set of fingers.

Aggie arrived before I could set out plates at the round kitchen table that seated four but could squeeze in five or six. She was a little wary of "the boys," but that wore off in a hurry. My wariness didn't wear off as fast, but I think I was entitled to a few moments of anxiety. After all, I, the dumpy

human, was sitting with a Bear, a Cougar, and a vampire—
because Ilya Sanguinati stayed and had a piece of pizza with
the rest of us. I wasn't sure if he liked it or just didn't want to
make it obvious that he had other dining preferences. Or
maybe he understood that having a known predator sitting at
the table would help me get acquainted with "the boys," who
were chowing down on the Carnivore's Special.

While we bonded over pizza, I learned that Conan had
settled into one of The Jumble's cabins near Mill Creek because the creek provided good fishing, and he liked eating
fish. Except for making patchwork repairs on the roofs and
replacing a couple of broken windows in order to prevent any
further weather damage to those cabins, I hadn't done any
renovating. By human standards, those cabins were still
"primitive," since anyone staying in them had to go to a separate building for toilets and showers. But Conan seemed to
think the cabin was very "human," although the bed puzzled
him and he couldn't figure out how to sleep on it, so he'd
been sleeping on the floor in his furry form.

I explained that the mattresses had rotted and been removed, and that I would purchase a new box spring and mattress, as well as linens and blankets. Cougar was also in one
of the primitive cabins, but he'd chosen one from the second
set of cabins that were close to the lake. He, too, had been
puzzled by the bed frame but hadn't given it much thought.

As we talked, I had the impression that Aggie had more
of what they called a human-centric education than the boys,
who made me think of young men in earlier times of human
history who would give up formal education before finishing
grade school in order to go to work. I didn't get the impression that Conan and Cougar wanted to get too humanized,
but they wanted *something* enough to settle into two of the
cabins and do some work in lieu of rent.

I put away what was left of the vegetable pizza. After
confirming what time Ilya would return in the morning to
take me to the bank, I said good night to my attorney and
settled in to watch cop and crime shows with my new friends.

The boys had never seen television, so I had to explain

that commercials weren't some weird schism in the story, that they were like their own little stories about something humans were selling and wanted other humans to buy. When Aggie said it was all right to talk during commercials because no one wanted to listen to them anyway, that started a whole round of questions about why the TV police did or didn't do the same things the police who had been sniffing around The Jumble had done. Which made me wonder if I should warn Officer Grimshaw about how carefully he was watched when he came around to investigate.

There were growls when the cops missed a clue and snarls when the bad humans did something sneaky—and more than a few eye rolls over human behavior in general. At one point, Aggie shouted at a woman who approached a villain who was pretending to be hurt. "It's a trick! There's no blood! Can't you smell that there's no blood?"

During commercials I tried to explain about human senses without sounding too apologetic for the inadequacies of my species. I ended up feeling that all I'd managed to do was convince my new friends that fish were smarter than humans even if humans did have those nifty opposable thumbs.

The other thing I realized by the end of the evening was that humans and the Others did have one thing in common—we both had a love for, and fascination with, stories. I learned that every form of *terra indigene* had its own teaching stories as well as stories that were the repository of their history and connection to the world. And they all had stories that were told for the fun of it.

After the last show of the evening, the boys and Aggie went to their own cabins, and I triple-checked the porch door to make sure it was locked. Ilya had said one of the detectives had opened the door but hadn't gone inside. As I did my walk around the rest of the house, I stopped in the library and looked at the books I'd been buying from Lettuce Reed. I hadn't purchased anything I didn't want to read. With only one lodger, what was the point, especially since Aggie seemed as enthusiastic about reading thrillers as I was? But now I looked at the books I had purchased and considered them with an eye to reading level. I was pretty sure Conan and Cougar would like the story lines in the thrillers. I was equally sure their reading skills weren't yet a match for those books, and making a trip to the story place had sounded like one of the big reasons those two had decided to interact with humans at all.

If Ilya Sanguinati was willing to stick around the village for a bit before taking me home tomorrow, I needed to talk to Julian Farrow about some appropriate books before I talked to the boys about a trip into town.

CHAPTER 15

Ilya

Sunday, Juin 13

Ilya Sanguinati walked to the lowest level of the lodge's deck and stared out over the lake. Had he made a mistake allowing Victoria DeVine to restore some of the buildings in The Jumble? If the *terra indigene* had prevented any human from taking up the agreed-upon caretaker duties for one more human generation, the agreement the Sanguinati had made with Honoria Dane and her designated heirs all those years ago would have been considered null and void, and the buildings could have been claimed as part of the *terra indigene* settlement. Humans could have been denied all access to Lake Silence except the southern tip, which, per the agreement with the first humans who had wanted to settle near the lake, was accessible to humans only as long as Sproing remained a viable human village.

But losing Sproing as a viable village would mean losing easy access to the Sanguinati's preferred prey. They had successfully hunted from the shadows since the village's founding, becoming more of a folktale that produced a delicious shiver than a real threat. Humans living and visiting Sproing believed themselves safe from those predators—even when the predators sat among their prey and became the seducers who were woven into a different kind of tale.

"This Victoria worries you."

Ilya waited until Natasha, his potential mate, stood beside him before answering. "She is not what I expected." Through the informants the Sanguinati maintained in the village, he had followed every step of Victoria's progress with the renovations so that he could reassure the *terra indigene* the rest of them feared that this human was behaving honorably. He'd also been careful to keep his distance—until the Crow had come winging across the lake looking for help because humans had come to The Jumble and had taken Miss Vicki away.

Perhaps keeping his distance had been another mistake. The informants had been less forthcoming than usual, leaving him unprepared to deal with a human who was emotionally outside of his experience.

"You could have fed from her today," Natasha said. "The rest of us could see it, feel it. She reads stories about a vampire's kiss and would have given her blood willingly."

He nodded. No point denying what even Officer Grimshaw had recognized when the police officer had tried to stop Victoria from moving toward him. "I could have fed from her, but only once. Then fledgling trust would have broken with whatever fantasy she has about our kind, and she would have run from any offer of help from us. No more flowing around the edges. With Victoria as caretaker, breaking the connection the Dane family had with the land, The Jumble can become a functional *terra indigene* settlement again, but we need direct access to her in order to deal with this potential threat." He hesitated, then added, "Something inside of her is wounded."

"I didn't notice any damage. She doesn't move as if she were injured."

"Not the body. This wound wasn't apparent—at least not to us. But the detective who was in the bank with her knew the wound was there and knew how to open it again."

"So she is vulnerable to attack."

"Yes. And like any other animal, she will hide the wound whenever possible to escape being targeted by a predator." But hiding a wound wasn't the same as healing it. Was there anything they could do to help Victoria heal? Their plan to reseed Sproing with humans of the Sanguinati's choosing hinged on The Jumble being restored and providing another source of transient prey. And The Jumble's restoration hinged on the Elders tolerating the designated caretaker. So far they were showing more than tolerance toward Victoria, and the warning should be clear enough for even humans to understand.

"Perhaps we should watch some of those cop and crime dramas to find out how humans think attorneys should act," Natasha said as they returned to the lodge.

"Perhaps." He had never been inside a courtroom to defend someone or argue a case. He specialized in leases for land and buildings, and his client had always been the *terra indigene*. Until now.

Victoria DeVine hadn't been wounded during all these months when she'd been restoring The Jumble, but she was wounded now. What was he supposed to do about that? His informants had failed to provide any information or give any warning. Perhaps that was as simple as loyalty to a friend, but that meant he wouldn't depend on them where Victoria was concerned. He needed another source of information.

"I'll join you soon," he told Natasha. Then he went into the room that served as an office for all of them, picked up the phone, and dialed the number for a Sanguinati who had access to other resources. "Vlad? It's Ilya. I need to understand wounds that affect the human mind and emotions. Could the Lakeside Courtyard's female pack help with that?"

CHAPTER 16

Grimshaw

Windsday, Juin 14

Grimshaw left the boardinghouse at first light and drove to a truck stop between Bristol and Crystalton. While he was on highway patrol, it was a regular stop for coffee or a meal—a place to sit and be quickly available without burning gasoline all day.

When he pulled into the lot, he noticed the new addition behind the diner. There had been toilets—a convenience for truckers who pulled in to a designated "safe" place after dark, especially after the diner closed for the night. Now there were also pay-by-the-minute showers, like the ones provided in a campground for those brave enough—or foolish enough—to stay that close to what watched them from the shadows of the woods. No sign advertising the new facilities, but the men and women who made a living on the road would know about the amenity.

Captain Walter Hargreaves was already in a booth, a cup of black coffee in front of him.

Grimshaw slid into the opposite seat, nodded to the waitress who lifted the coffeepot and raised an eyebrow in question, then studied his boss.

"Swinn and his CIU team work out of Putney on Prong Lake," Grimshaw said. "When I called the Bristol station to confirm a suspicious death, why didn't the CIU team from Bristol come to Sproing to investigate?"

"That's a good question," Hargreaves replied. Then he smiled at the waitress and ordered breakfast. He waited until Grimshaw placed his order and the waitress was out of ear-shot before continuing. "All I know is that Swinn called the Bristol station minutes after your call and said he and his team had been assigned to the case and Bristol was to stand down. He said he was already heading up to Sproing for a separate investigation and the suspicious death could be connected, so it made sense for him to take a look at the alleged body." He swallowed some coffee, his eyes never leaving Grimshaw's face. "His call came in so fast after yours, I started thinking he'd been tipped off, maybe even anticipated some trouble at The Jumble."

"I didn't call him," Grimshaw growled.

"I didn't think you did. But he was expecting a call and already had his team ready to roll."

"Including a baby cop who had no business doing more than directing traffic."

Hargreaves looked grim. "Tell me all of it. Tell me everything you didn't put in your report and wouldn't say over the telephone."

Grimshaw told him about the Sproingers gathering—and Julian Farrow's theory that they were a form the *terra indigene* had absorbed to be able to wander all around Sproing without humans thinking twice about their presence. He told Hargreaves about Vicki DeVine's state of mind when she got out of the car after Swinn and Reynolds brought her in for questioning, and the empty safe-deposit box, and the sudden appearance of one of the Sanguinati, who claimed to be her attorney. He recounted the terrified call from Osgood asking for backup, for help—and what he and Julian had found when they reached The Jumble.

Their breakfasts arrived. Grimshaw shoveled food into

his mouth for a couple of minutes, then put his fork down and sat back. "Osgood shouldn't have been there. He's too young to be on a CIU team."

Hargreaves kept eating for another minute. Then he, too, put his fork down—but he leaned forward. "Julian Farrow. You went into a bad situation with Julian Farrow as your backup? You're either crazy or suicidal."

"I trust him." Before Hargreaves could respond to that beyond swearing under his breath, Grimshaw asked the question that had been bothering him since he and Julian returned from The Jumble yesterday. "All those years ago, did the brass know Julian was an Intuit? Did they know *why* he had that uncanny ability to sense things?"

He saw genuine surprise on Hargreaves's face.

"Intuit? Are you sure?"

Grimshaw smiled when the waitress came over to refill their cups and ask if they wanted anything else. The smile faded as soon as she walked away. "I'm sure. Julian confirmed it."

Hargreaves was thinking hard. "Crystalton. The reputation it has of being a woo-woo place with people reading cards and talking about the properties of crystals and all that . . . bunk."

"Bunk? Or a smoke screen so that people coming into their community don't realize they're different?" Grimshaw countered.

"What's he doing in Sproing?"

"He owns the bookstore, which, as far as I can tell, is really a combination of a bookstore and the village's lending library since the front half of the store is more of a used-book swap than anything else. I didn't see it, but I'm guessing the back half has the new books that he sells for some kind of profit—enough to keep the doors open."

"Maybe," Hargreaves said softly. "Governor Hannigan created that Investigative Task Force last year—investigators who work with local police but answer to the governor."

"I know of it. Haven't met the ITF agent who has the Fin-

ger Lakes area." When he'd heard about the task force, he'd
considered applying for it, but a man had to have some skill
with working with a variety of police forces in the communities within his territory as well as being able to work on his
own, and the truth was he really didn't work well with others.

"There were some rumors that there are a few 'shadow'
agents as well as the ones who are visibly working with the
police."

"Undercover?"

Hargreaves nodded and drank some coffee. "What do you
think?"

"About what?" Grimshaw blinked. He almost laughed
until he thought about it. "Julian Farrow?"

"He was a damn good investigator, even when he was a
rookie. Of course, his being Intuit explains some of it, but he
had a real feel for it. He opened his store . . . when?"

"Last fall."

"Around the time we were all scrambling to figure out
what was left after the Humans First and Last movement set
the war against the *terra indigene* in motion. Silence is the
westernmost of the Finger Lakes, a gateway, you could say.
Sproing is a small community with lots of farms and vineyards around it, a lake to draw people to the area in the summer. If you needed a spy to alert you to possible trouble, it
might be a good place to position one."

Julian, an undercover agent for the governor? It sounded
like something out of a thriller. On the other hand, what *had*
Julian Farrow been doing since he left the police force? If
he'd ever really left.

"I trust Julian Farrow more than I trust Swinn," Grimshaw said.

Hargreaves finished his breakfast and pushed the plate to
one side. Then he nodded as if coming to a decision. "They
called him Swine at the academy. Don't know why. It was
one of those stupid things young men do, picking one or two
and giving them a hard time for no reason."

"Could be they saw him with a date."

Silence. "You think Detective Swinn acted inappropriately with Ms. DeVine, while one of his men was also in the car?"

"Something happened on the way in to the Sproing station. She was . . . scared—like, get her to the doctor's office before she collapses scared." But she had rallied when she took the hand he offered. He'd seen her come back from whatever had upset her.

"She did lead you to the body."

"No, the Crow who is her lodger led us to the body. Vicki DeVine couldn't find her way out of her own handbag." Seeing Hargreaves's stony look and knowing he'd dumped a potential scandal on the table, he added, "Of course, having seen her handbag, I don't think most people would be able to find their own way out."

Hargreaves leaned forward again. His voice was quiet and rough. "You remember that backup isn't down the street. You're out there in the wild country, Wayne, on your own, no matter who answers a call for help and how fast they respond."

"Business as usual, then."

They stared at each other.

"What do you want while you're manning the Sproing station?"

"I want Officer Osgood reassigned to the station. I want him away from Swinn."

"You think he'll back you up?"

Grimshaw hesitated. "I don't know. If nothing else, he can answer phones and type up reports. Walk down Main Street in uniform and look official. Keep his eyes and ears open."

"There is no safety in the dark, not even on the main street of a village," Hargreaves said quietly. "Humans screwed up last summer, and we're all paying for it. What happened to Chesnik and Baker . . ." He sighed. "I have an old friend, a patrol captain in Lakeside, who has a line to the governor. I'll wangle it so that Osgood ends up working under your temporary command."

"I'll have to find him a place to stay." Grimshaw smiled.

"The CIU team was staying at the boardinghouse. So am I. I can handle being in the same building as Swinn. I'm not sure it would be healthy for Osgood, especially once he's reassigned."

"Your call."

That was it? No, it wasn't. Hargreaves had something on his mind.

"Swinn is a good investigator. He finds the evidence, and prosecutors are glad to see his name on the reports. Nineteen cases out of twenty he is good."

"Then a few mistakes get made on number twenty?" Grimshaw guessed.

Hargreaves shook his head. "On number twenty, he's even better. All the i's are dotted and the t's are crossed. And somebody goes to jail, maybe even prison. But it never feels quite right. Swinn jumping on this case? It doesn't feel right, so you watch your back, you hear?"

"And Julian?"

The waitress brought over the bill. Hargreaves put enough money on the table to cover both meals and the tip. He slid out of the booth and gave Grimshaw a long look. "The less said about Julian Farrow, the better. But I won't comment about him giving you a hand as long as evidence isn't compromised."

"Not my job to look for evidence. That's what CIU is for."

"Maybe."

The word was said so quietly, Grimshaw wasn't sure he heard it. He looked at his watch and swore. He had to get moving if he was going to get back to Sproing in time to accompany Vicki DeVine and her attorney when they reopened her safe-deposit box.

CHAPTER 17

Vicki

Windsday, Juin 14

Opening the safe-deposit box the next morning was better than watching a magician pull a rabbit out of a hat. You got the happy surprise of something empty being filled without the brown presents at the bottom of the hat.

Everything had been returned—all the paperwork, which Ilya Sanguinati checked off the list he'd made from my record of the documents I'd put into the box. And there was even seven thousand dollars, nicely bundled.

Besides me and my attorney, there were three other people crowded into the privacy room to witness the Return of the Paperwork: Officer Grimshaw, Detective Swinn, and Valerie, who had been the head teller and was now the reluctant, and temporary, bank manager. When Ineke called me at the crack of dawn, telling me she'd pulled out all of her money as soon as she'd heard about yesterday's naughtiness with the safe-deposit box, I didn't ask how she'd found out—and I didn't need to talk to anyone else to know the bank was going to crash. The whole village was holding its breath, especially the folks who hadn't gotten to the bank yesterday and were now hoping that something would save them.

Frankly, I think everyone was hoping that the bloodsuckers who sucked blood would take over the bank. The penalties for a late payment might be steep, but at least there would be a brutal kind of honesty when they sucked you dry.

I placed each piece of paper in an old leather tote bag as Ilya Sanguinati checked it off. But when it came to the money, I hesitated. I had tucked six thousand into the box. Who had made up the other thousand? Had the bank manager taken it from his personal savings or had he used the bank's money, which would be another bit of naughtiness?

I hesitated. Then I looked at Valerie, said, "Sorry," and stuffed all the money in the tote bag.

"Don't be," Valerie replied. "I opened my box yesterday and removed the antique jewelry that belonged to my grandmother. It has more sentimental than monetary value, but I didn't want to discover it missing one day."

I hesitated a moment longer, wondering if I should put back the thousand dollars that didn't actually belong to me. Then I glanced at Detective Swinn and swiftly closed the box, which was empty once again.

Swinn wasn't old, but he looked a bit freeze-dried and his ash brown hair was cut short and stuck up across the top of his head, like it was iron filings being pulled by a magnet. He wore glasses with heavy black frames that dominated his face and didn't suit him at all. But the glasses didn't disguise the undiluted venom in the way he looked at me, and there was nothing I wanted more than to get away from him. Unfortunately, he was the person in the doorway and was, therefore, the person I had to squeeze past.

Valerie smiled at Swinn and moved her arm in an unspoken request for him to step aside so that we could all leave the privacy room and she and I could follow procedure and return the safe-deposit box to the vault.

As I eased past Swinn, he spoke one sentence so quietly no one else would have heard it. It was cutting and cruel and painfully familiar.

Valerie and I returned the box to the vault. Maybe, if it had just been Officer Grimshaw and Ilya Sanguinati waiting for me, I could have remained polite, could have clamped down on the hurt and anger churning inside me until I got home and could break down in private. But Swinn was still there, and he looked at me as if he knew what would hurt me most—and I couldn't breathe. Just couldn't draw in enough air for my heart to beat and my brain to work.

I bolted out of the bank, ignoring the "Ms. DeVine? Ms. DeVine!" behind me. A few Sproingers were out on the sidewalk. They were sitting up the way they do when they're given chunks of carrots for treats, but they weren't wearing their happy faces. Neither was I. I still wanted to talk to Julian Farrow about books, but I couldn't do that until I could breathe.

I marched next door and stomped into the police station. Officer Osgood, looking even younger in his official uniform, jumped to his feet. I might have jumped down his throat because he looked like a relatively safe target for the feelings building in my chest, but Officer Grimshaw and Ilya Sanguinati burst into the station, Grimshaw slamming the door in Swinn's face and pausing to turn the simple lock.

And Mount Victoria erupted.

"I know I'm not pretty, and I know I'm not smart, but I don't deserve to be treated like trash, to be pushed and pushed until I'm too tired and worn down and I agree to something that I don't believe." I pointed at the door, aiming my finger between Grimshaw's and Ilya's shoulders. "Why is Detective Swinn here? I didn't know the man who died. I didn't have an appointment to see him or talk to him. *And I didn't kill him.* So why is Swinn pushing and pushing, saying it's my fault and I'd better come clean about what I did, and how selling The Jumble will be the only way to pay for any kind of attorney who might be able to get me a reduced sentence? Why is he saying that?"

That's the trouble with hiding in your safe place and hearing but not hearing a verbal hammering. You do hear the words, and with the right trigger, all your feelings come out as word vomit or lava—a hot projectile that can't be controlled at all.

"And why would that bank manager help someone take

the things out of my safe-deposit box? I'll tell you why! Because no one thought I would make a fuss, and even if I did, who would listen to *me*? And I was just expected to swallow it. Well, I'm not going to swallow it. I was given The Jumble as the main part of the divorce settlement because everyone thought it wasn't worth much of anything but the assessed value looked good on paper. See how generous he was to give her some of the land that had been in his family for generations. But now someone thinks it is worth something and wants to take it away after I worked so hard to build a new home, a-and . . . a-and . . ."

I was done, drained, didn't even have a piddle of lava left to finish the sentence.

Three men stared at me. Osgood looked ready to crash through the window and run. Grimshaw looked grim. And my vampire attorney? I couldn't begin to figure out what he was thinking about my hysterics.

I took a couple of deep breaths to steady myself. "I still have some business with Julian Farrow that I would like to take care of before I go home."

"I'll walk you over," Officer Grimshaw said.

"Could Officer Osgood do that?" Ilya asked. "I can hold the bag with Ms. DeVine's valuables while she runs her errand."

Grimshaw hesitated, then looked at Osgood. "Officer?"

Osgood swallowed hard. He wasn't dill pickle green like the bank manager had been yesterday, but his brown skin did have a green tinge. "Yes, sir."

I wondered whom he feared more, me or Swinn? But I didn't ask, didn't make some lame joke designed to hurt feelings. I didn't want to be caught alone by Swinn either, and I was grateful for any escort, even if I should have been adult enough not to need one.

It turned out Officer Osgood and I both had an escort. The Sproingers formed two lines, a hopping honor guard for us to walk between as we crossed the street to Lettuce Reed.

Julian Farrow opened the screen door as we approached. The Sproingers sproinged into the shop, then clustered around the door. I hurried over to the island in the center of the front room.

"I handed out carrots this morning," Julian told the Sproingers.

They all gave him the happy face, but none of them crowded him as if they expected food.

Julian nodded to Officer Osgood, who took a position between me and the Sproingers, as if he couldn't decide what was more dangerous. I guess he hadn't seen them before. Otherwise he would have known he would be safe unless he wore orange socks. Apparently orange is the color of carrots and pumpkins, another Sproinger favorite food, and their little brains couldn't quite understand that not everything that was orange was tasty or food.

Or else they just liked biting things that were orange, and woe to the ankle under the orange sock.

"You look a bit flushed, Vicki," Julian said. "Would you like some water?"

"Yes. Thanks." I felt a little sick and desperately needed to regain control.

"Officer?"

"Thank you," Osgood said.

While we waited for Julian, I eyed the stacks of books on the island—books that had been returned for used-book credit but hadn't been processed yet to be put on the shelves.

Julian returned with a large wooden tray that held three glasses of water and a small dog bowl of water. He set the bowl near the door. I'm not sure any of the Sproingers drank any of the water, but they seemed to have a good time giving each other a bit of a splash before grooming.

Despite the splashing, at least half of them watched whatever was going on outside, standing on each other in order to look out the screen door.

Maybe their brains weren't so little. And maybe those ankle-biting incidents weren't mistakes caused by orange socks. At least, not all of them.

"Are you browsing, or are you looking for specific titles?" Julian asked.

Recalled to my task, I leaned forward. "I have some friends who really liked the cop and crime shows on TV last night and probably would enjoy reading thrillers, but I don't think they have the reading skills for the books I already have at The Jumble." I didn't want to buy something inappropriate that could sour their anticipated pleasure in visiting the story place—or sour their opinion of me.

"Would those friends be your new employees?" Julian had a knack for figuring things out. Oddly enough, he was rubbish at playing Murder, a board game where you tried to figure out who was murdered and how they died.

"Have you met Conan and Cougar?"

"Yeesss."

I went up on my tiptoes so I could lean a little farther before whispering, "I don't want to insult them by offering kiddie books. They are adults after all. But I don't want them frustrated either." And I didn't want them to blame me for being frustrated.

Julian stared at the counter. Then he looked at me. "Wait here."

Officer Osgood relaxed enough to look at the bookshelves closest to him, and I watched the Sproingers. The ones who noticed me watching made the happy face; the rest of them blocked the doorway and stared at something in the street.

Julian returned with a large stack of books. He set them on the counter, then held one up so that I could read the title and see the cover.

"The Wolf Team?"

He nodded. "They're stories about a group of adolescents with special skills who help . . . beings . . . in trouble."

Did they have a phone number? I could be a being who needed help.

"They're written for *terra indigene* youngsters." Julian opened the book to a random page and held it out. "Take a look."

I didn't know the characters or their mission because Julian had opened the book a few chapters into the story, but I started reading midway down the page just to get a feel for

the language and decide if I should add a couple of the books
to my guest library.

Oh.

Ew.

Goodness! Could *terra indigene* Wolves really do that?

A hand came down on the book, and I . . . squeaked . . .
and jumped back as far as my arms allowed without giving
up the book and losing my place. After all, I did have priorities.

My heart pounded. My lungs strained against muscles that
were corset tight. I heard chattering behind me, followed by
the thumps of several things hitting the floor. I stared at Julian
and realized he looked as startled by my reaction as I felt.

And then there was the weird way my slacks were twitch-
ing at knee height.

Maybe I should reorder my priorities until we sorted out
the whole thing about the dead man.

Julian lifted his hand off the book and offered a wary
smile. "Maybe you'd like to take the book with you and start
reading from the beginning?"

Why would Julian be wary of me? I turned my head just
enough to see the handful of books at Officer Osgood's
feet—probably the thumps I'd heard when I squeaked in
alarm.

Something patted my knee. I looked down at the Sproinger
standing next to me. The Sproinger looked up at me and patted my knee again, a silent query.

"I'm fine," I said. "Really. I'm fine." I smiled at the critter.

The Sproinger made the happy face and returned to his
buddies. They all looked at me and made the happy face
before resuming sentry duty.

I went back to staring at Julian. "He understood what I
said." Actually, I didn't know if that particular Sproinger had
a vigorous appendage. That wasn't important. The fact that
Sproingers *understood human speech* was important. Gods,
they hopped around the village every morning, cadging treats
from most of the businesses or browsing in people's yards.

"Uh-huh." Julian sounded like it wasn't the least bit important, and I took the hint. Sproingers probably knew every secret in the village, and if the people realized the critters not only heard but understood those secrets, there would be a lot fewer people handing out carrots.

But that sidestepped the real question. If the Sproingers understood everything, or almost everything, that was being said around them, whom did they tell? And how would they interpret the past few minutes and my squeak of alarm—and who might get blamed for alarming me?

I suddenly understood why Julian felt wary. "I zoned out."

"You got caught up in the story. That's a good sign. Do you want the series?" He held up a hand as if I had already protested that I couldn't afford them. "The human females in the early books are wimps. I fully acknowledge the lack of understanding about your gender, so don't come back and snarl at me about it. However, I'd heard that some of the writers of the Wolf Team books spent a few weeks in Lakeside last winter while planning some new stories, and the human female pack attached to the Courtyard helped them adjust their thinking, to say nothing of their attitude. The human girls in the latest story still can't take on the bad guys by themselves—it is a Wolf Team story, after all—but they're more kick-ass. Or as kick-ass as human females with no special powers beyond intelligence and good hearts can be."

"I can't burn through my whole book budget." I eyed the books, willing to be persuaded because, darn it, I wanted to find out what happened!

"I told you before I would open a line of credit for you."

I loved books, and given a line of credit, I could imagine having to sell my car to feed my book addiction and pay off my bookstore debt.

"Two-hundred-dollar limit," Julian said.

I needed some kind of solace, and it was either books or ice cream. If I bought the books, I'd have more than an evening's pleasure, and I could justify it because other beings would read them too.

But I'd ask Aggie if she liked ice cream, just for future reference.

I left the store with a stuffed Lettuce Reed carry bag, and Officer Osgood left with three of the five books he'd originally selected.

We scanned the street, noticed Officer Grimshaw's cruiser was gone, and scurried back to the police station, relieved that there was no sign of Detectives Swinn and Reynolds. Of course, that didn't mean anything. They could be waiting for me inside the station. The bad guys in stories always managed to slither out of hiding places just before the hapless protagonist thought she had reached safety.

But it was my yummy vampire attorney who opened the station door and stepped aside. As we walked in, I wondered— briefly—if I should switch to reading romances again. At least those stories wouldn't keep me up at night.

CHAPTER 18

Grimshaw

Windsday, Juin 14

Grimshaw studied Swinn's face as the man stepped out between two parked cars and then realized how much attention he would draw to himself if he tried to get through the line of Sproingers in order to reach Vicki DeVine.

Fury.

"I assume you wanted me to stay in order to discuss something in particular," Grimshaw said, glancing at Ilya Sanguinati, who was also watching Detective Swinn.

"How is your hearing, Officer Grimshaw?" the Sanguinati asked.

The words were polite, courteous even. But Grimshaw heard the frosty anger underneath. He understood the anger, felt it himself.

"My hearing is just fine," he replied. He'd seen the stunned hurt on Vicki DeVine's face when she walked past Swinn to leave the safe-deposit privacy room. And having heard the words, he understood why she'd erupted once she reached the police station.

"You humans have a saying about sticks and stones breaking bones but words not hurting."

"A dumb-ass piece of wisdom that has been proven wrong

too many times to count. Words can cause as much damage as a fist. They can leave deep scars that never fully heal. And they can kill."

Was that what had happened at The Jumble? Despite insisting otherwise, *had* Vicki DeVine met Franklin Cartwright on the farm track? Had he told her why he was there? Or had he made an excuse—surveying the property line or something like that—and didn't reveal he was there to evict her? Did he know enough about her to realize she could, and probably would, get lost on her own land? Had he counted on her wandering around while he hurried to The Jumble's main house to search for whatever he'd gone there to find?

Or had Cartwright said something, like Swinn had at the bank, thinking he had pushed the right button to make her cave in to his demands and, instead, had triggered a more physical and violent reaction?

The biggest problem with that theory was that nothing human could have killed Franklin Cartwright.

Ilya Sanguinati turned away from the window to look at him. "'You really do look like a fireplug with feet.' Would you say that to a stranger or a female you had met recently?"

"I wouldn't say it at all, even if it were true," Grimshaw snapped. Vicki DeVine was short and plump and shaped more like a box than an hourglass, but only a crass idiot would say something that mean to a woman he'd met in passing.

He stiffened when he realized what the vampire was driving at. "No, I wouldn't say it to a stranger or an acquaintance. Saying that to a woman . . . That's personal." Sexual. Intimate. Something an abusive lover might say, in jest of course, to undermine a woman's self-confidence.

Ilya Sanguinati nodded. "Yes, it's personal. And Detective Swinn's phrasing, to me, sounded like he was agreeing with something someone else had said."

Crap. There were a couple of questions he needed to ask Captain Hargreaves, but not here. He didn't want to bring anyone to the Sanguinati's attention.

"There are some things I need to do for the investigation,"

he said. "You're welcome to wait here until Ms. DeVine and Officer Osgood return. It shouldn't be much longer." He couldn't be certain of that, and if it had been anyone else, he might have insisted on locking up. But everyone on the police force knew the Sanguinati's other form was smoke, and they could flow through a keyhole if they wanted to enter a building—not to mention that Silence Lodge owned the building and Ilya most likely had keys to the station. He would show a little trust in the hope of having it reciprocated—especially if he discovered anything that was going to enrage the *terra indigene*.

"Thank you. I will wait."

Grimshaw scanned the street before getting into his vehicle. Swinn and Reynolds were nowhere in sight. Maybe they had gone back to the boardinghouse. He knew they weren't in the bookstore. He was pretty sure that would have caused a Sproinger riot.

Chesnik's body had been taken to Bristol for the autopsy, but the other two bodies might still be at the funeral home, and hopefully, the mortician and Dr. Wallace could supply a few answers.

Sheridan Ames, the public face of Ames Funeral Home, was a stringy woman in her late forties. Her hard features were accented by a severe black pantsuit. The only soft thing about her was her luxuriously thick hair, which was a rich brown with red highlights.

Yesterday she had been professionally pleasant when he'd stopped in to confirm that the two bodies had arrived at the funeral home. Today she was cold.

"If you've come to look at the bodies again, they've been taken to Bristol for autopsy to determine cause of death," she said.

Grimshaw studied her. Not just cold; she was seriously pissed off at police in general. Since that hadn't been her attitude yesterday, he took a guess at the reason she had changed. "Detective Swinn was already here."

"I don't appreciate being accused of tampering with evidence. I don't appreciate being accused of *taking* evidence. Dr. Wallace did go through the pockets of those two men, did confirm their ID. I was with him the whole time, and I made a list of every single item as it was removed and identified. And despite what *Detective* Swinn wants to put on the report, nothing human killed those three men."

"Three?" Calhoun had died of the head and neck injuries before the ambulance had reached the hospital in Bristol, but there was no reason Sheridan Ames would have known that.

"The first dead man. The one Vicki DeVine found at The Jumble."

"Any thoughts about what did kill them?" he asked.

"You should talk to Dr. Wallace."

"I will. But I'd like your opinion too."

She had been standing behind her desk, making it clear that she didn't want to give him time or answers. Now she sat down and invited him to do the same.

"Let's start with Detective Chesnik," Grimshaw said.

"The one who died of blood loss?"

He nodded. "His legs were ripped up. Clawed. Could a bear or a big cat have done that?" He remembered seeing a picture of a grizzly bear's paw next to a human head. The paw was bigger.

"Gods," Sheridan said. "It should have occurred to me, but I didn't think about the significance of big forms of *terra indigene* hunting in The Jumble. Has anyone warned Vicki DeVine?"

"The big shifters aren't hunting, exactly. Her employees now include one of the Beargard and one of the Panthergard." And the gods only knew what lived in the wooded land around the northern end of the lake.

She sat back. Grimshaw said nothing, just gave her time to think it through. Finally she shook her head.

"Whatever clawed that man's legs was bigger than a Bear or a Panther. A lot bigger," she said. "And I'm pretty sure it wasn't the same thing that killed the other two men. At least, it didn't take the same form. Clawed hand versus clawed paw."

"Big hands," he said softly. "Both Franklin Cartwright and Detective Baker had been killed by something strong enough to pick up grown men and twist them."

"Yes." Sheridan sat forward and folded her hands on her desk. "Concerning Detective Baker. Detective Swinn was particularly angry about a missing tie clip when he came by yesterday evening. He insisted that Baker had been wearing one that morning and wanted me to admit that Dr. Wallace or I had taken it. I gather he went back to the boardinghouse and searched Baker's room for the missing item and didn't find it, because he was back here this morning, demanding to look at the items that had been with the bodies. Of course, Dr. Wallace had made the arrangements and the bodies had been driven to Bristol at first light, along with everything that had been found with them. I asked him for a description of the tie clip; I know Ineke Xavier asked as well since he was so obsessed with finding it. But he wouldn't tell us what it looked like beyond being a tie clip."

"What about Chesnik? Did he have a tie clip?"

"He did. Swinn wasn't interested in that one."

Grimshaw thanked her and left the funeral home. But after returning to his car, he sat in the parking lot, thinking.

All the men on Swinn's team had worn ties and had used tie clips. What was significant about Baker's? A man wouldn't wear something expensive on the job, not when he was out investigating. There was always the possibility of losing it somewhere. But maybe it *was* expensive and Swinn wanted to return it to Baker's family. Or maybe it had some other significance. Was that why Swinn didn't want to describe it? Because he didn't want a description of a particular tie clip going into an official report?

If it had been logged in with the other personal effects, would it have disappeared after Swinn visited the funeral home? And would Swinn, despite being warned off, return to The Jumble to search for the missing item?

Grimshaw started the cruiser and returned to the station.

The black luxury sedan was gone from its parking spot. So were Ilya Sanguinati and Vicki DeVine. Officer Osgood looked desperate to find something official to do.

"Problem?" Grimshaw asked.

"Detective Swinn is upset that I've been transferred to this station and am under your command."

"You have any idea why Swinn pulled you into this assignment in the first place?"

"No, sir."

Grimshaw sighed. "Well, I'll talk to a couple of people and see if I can find you a place to stay while you're working here."

"I—I'm staying at the boardinghouse." Osgood's brown eyes looked huge. "Ms. Xavier threw Detectives Swinn and Reynolds out of her place. Somebody told them she was pitching their stuff onto the front lawn and when they got to the boardinghouse, she told them if they so much as set a toe inside her house again, she would report them."

To whom? Grimshaw wondered. "Did something happen to upset her?"

Osgood winced. "They fed their prunes to the dog this morning. I guess he got sick enough that the vet from Crystalton came to the house."

So Swinn would have to find accommodations at a nearby town or withdraw from the investigation. Swinn wasn't going to withdraw; he shouldn't have been there in the first place, so he'd be back for the same reason he got involved.

Osgood held out a pink message slip. "Ms. Xavier said to tell you that she's boxing up the other detectives' belongings and if you don't pick them up by tomorrow morning, she'll donate everything to the volunteer fire department to sell."

"Did you tell her she couldn't do that?"

"I've heard Ms. Xavier has a smoking gun tattoo on one thigh as a kind of warning."

Crap. Well, there was one good thing: Osgood seemed to be a gossip magnet, which was bound to be helpful as long as he just listened to gossip and didn't spread any information.

"I have an assignment for you," Grimshaw said. "Find out if anyplace around here is having a block sale, yard sale, moving sale, swap and shop. I need trinkets, shiny things that a teenage girl"—*or a Crow*—"would be drawn to. I need them as soon as you can get them." He pulled out his wallet and handed Osgood fifty dollars. "That's your budget. Nothing has to be expensive; it just has to shine."

"Yes, sir." One beat of silence. "Why?"

Grimshaw sighed. "Because I need to bribe someone to return a piece of evidence."

CHAPTER 19

Ilya

Windsday, Juin 14

As soon as he delivered Victoria DeVine back to The Jumble, Ilya asked Boris, his driver, to return to Sproing. He could have reached his quarry faster if he'd shifted to his smoke form and traveled cross-country, but the days of the Sanguinati being subtle about their control of the village were over.

"I won't be long," he said when Boris pulled into a parking space in front of the bookstore.

Going inside Lettuce Reed, Ilya walked up to the island counter, his dark eyes locked on Julian Farrow's gray ones. He set a piece of paper on the counter. "I'd like any of these books that you have in stock. New copies are preferable, but I'll take used copies."

Julian looked at the titles, froze for a moment, then met Ilya's eyes.

"You haven't lived up to your side of the bargain, Mr. Farrow," Ilya said softly.

"From what I can tell, Vicki's anxiety has its roots in damaged self-confidence and intimacy issues." Julian almost growled the words. "Those issues are personal, but she's dealing with them and they haven't interfered with the restoration of The Jumble or posed any threat to this village. Therefore, they were none of your business."

"Now they are." At least Farrow wasn't pretending he didn't understand the significance of Ilya wanting these particular books about human anxiety attacks and different forms of abuse. "You should have informed me that Victoria DeVine had a weakness."

"It's not a weakness," Farrow snapped.

"A wound, then. A vulnerability that leaves her open to attack."

"Show me a human living on this continent who isn't wounded in some way!"

Defensive. Cornered. A human dangerous enough not to be taken lightly. But that was the reason the Sanguinati had made a bargain with Julian Farrow in the first place.

As he noted how white the scar on Farrow's cheek looked on a face made harsh by anger, it occurred to Ilya that Julian hadn't pointed out that the other informant in the village also had failed to mention these anxiety attacks, hadn't tried to lessen his own failing. And Ilya suddenly understood, and appreciated, that the anger and defensiveness were . . . protective. Not Victoria's mate. Not yet. Maybe never. But the desire to protect was there nonetheless. Understanding that, he used the tone of voice that he used when discussing a problem with one of his own kind. With an equal.

"Detective Swinn used words to open that wound yesterday when he and his man drove Victoria to the village," Ilya said. "And this morning at the bank, what he said to her was not only wounding but very personal."

Farrow stared at Ilya, then looked past him, as if he was piecing together something that wasn't visible to anyone else. "Then he knows someone who knew her before she came to Sproing."

"Agreed."

Farrow continued to look toward the street. "The first body stirred up people and had them talking, worrying that the trouble might come into Sproing itself. But it didn't change the core feel of the village. Grimshaw being assigned here . . . A blanket feeling of relief—and budding hope in the villagers that they could take up the business of living without being afraid all the time."

"And the arrival of Swinn and his men?" Ilya asked.

All the color drained out of Farrow's face as he whispered, "The stench of overripe garbage spreading beyond the alley into the streets, into the shops, into the homes."

Interesting. Julian Farrow always said that he felt places, not people, but this was the first time the Intuit had revealed anything that descriptive about what he sensed. It sounded more like a memory than an observation about the here and now.

"Whatever really brought Swinn here will sour this village," he said.

Farrow nodded.

"The restoration of The Jumble is the key to Sproing's survival."

Farrow nodded again.

"Then perhaps we can work together to ensure that Victoria retains control over the human part of the *terra indigene* settlement."

Farrow gave him a tight smile. "We can do that. But it can be a fine line between helping someone and giving that person the impression that you don't think she's capable of helping herself."

Ilya repressed a sigh. That fine line in a wounded female like Victoria was probably smudged, and all he could hope for was not to stumble too far over that line and make matters worse.

"Do you still want these books?" Farrow asked.

"Yes." As Farrow turned away, Ilya added, "I didn't feed on her. In case you wondered."

Farrow didn't reply, but Ilya had the impression that the human male was relieved.

CHAPTER 20

Vicki

Windsday, Juin 14

I thought some rude things about Julian Farrow when I un-packed the bag of books and discovered he'd sold me the first five Wolf Team books instead of the whole set, filling the bottom of the bag with books by someone named Alan Wolfgard as well as other authors I hadn't heard of. Then I saw the boys' response to the Wolf Team books and could, grudgingly, appreciate Julian's strategy.

Conan and Cougar weren't swift readers—or accurate spellers, if the sign on the chain across my access road was anything to go by—so five books would be plenty for the four readers currently using my library. And when they had finished with those books, there would be more that could be purchased, either by me or by them, if I was very brave or incredibly stupid and took them into Sproing to visit Lettuce Reed and purchase books for themselves.

For a community that maintained that the Others were Out There, Conan and Cougar would be an eye-opener—and probably fill the doctors' office with a slew of people experiencing heart palpitations or dizzy spells, especially if someone forgot about looking human and slapped a paw on a counter to lay claim to something of interest.

Then again, if people signing up for the trail rides that Ineke had proposed weren't interested in seeing the *terra indigene*, they wouldn't be getting on horses and riding around in the Others' backyard, so to speak. But I could appreciate that there was a difference between seeing one of the Beargard in the woods and having one sit on the stool next to yours at the diner. There would always be the possibility that you would look tastier than the food on his plate.

I'd been more focused on Conan's and Cougar's reactions to the books because of the whole tooth and claw thing they had going for them, but eventually I realized Aggie was spending a lot of time looking at the covers and not saying anything.

"Nothing of interest?" I asked.

She traced the title on one of the books with a finger. "If there was a Reader at The Jumble, more of the *terra indigene* could enjoy the stories. Every *terra indigene* settlement has a Reader. Sometimes more than one."

Aggie looked at me. Conan and Cougar looked at me.

"You want me to be the designated Reader?" I could hear the capital *R* when Aggie said the word.

They all smiled at me. Conan and Cougar hadn't seen enough smiling humans to get all the teeth sorted out. The result was unsettling. It also made me wonder how they enunciated as well as they did.

"I guess we could start with the first Wolf Team book," I said. "Maybe I could read for an hour before dinner tonight?" It had been a while since I'd done any reading aloud, but I thought I could do a decent job reading to the three of them.

Aggie bounced up and down and clapped her hands. As she dashed out of the room, she said, "I'll tell my kin. They'll pass the word."

Kin? Word?

Conan took the second Wolf Team book and Cougar took the third before wandering off and leaving me to sort through the rest of the books Julian had tucked into the bag. I remembered seeing some of the titles in the stacks of books he'd had on the island counter. I didn't recognize the authors or the publishers. Of course, I didn't know Alan Wolfgard's work either, but the name offered a clue about *what* he was.

Using half a piece of heavyweight writing paper, I made a tent sign, put it on one shelf in the library, and shelved the new books I'd purchased that day. As I worked, I let my thoughts wander through the events of the past forty-eight hours. A lot had happened since I called the Bristol Police Station to report a dead body.

Detectives Swinn and Reynolds were forbidden to return to The Jumble, and Ilya Sanguinati had stressed on the ride home that if Swinn or anyone working for him contacted me, I was to hang up immediately and call *him*. Officers Grimshaw and Osgood were exempt from that gag order, but no one else.

It seemed excessive to insist on no contact at all since I wouldn't mind answering a question or two if it helped solve the puzzle of why the first dead man had ended up dead, but Ilya seemed to be holding back a fair amount of anger and I didn't want it spilling over on me, so I agreed to do what he asked.

Then it struck me. He had heard what Swinn had said. I doubt he understood why it had hurt so much or why I'd gotten so churned up instead of calling Swinn an asshat and moving on, but he'd witnessed the eruption of Mount Victoria and had decided to shut down the problem by denying Swinn any access to me without him being present.

So, yay, Team Vicki.

The shelf with the new books looked so nice, I made a few more tent signs and rearranged the books I'd previously acquired. I spent a happy hour putting the books into categories so that other residents, and potential guests, of The Jumble could find specific kinds of books.

I slipped the last book into place when Aggie's comment about having a Reader truly sank in.

Every *terra indigene* settlement has a Reader. I wasn't really the proprietor of a human business. Like Honoria

Dane, I was the token human who provided a valuable service by bridging the cultural gap between the Others and the residents of Sproing.

Given that the survival of humans on the continent of Thaisia depended on the Others' feeling some tolerance toward us, bridging the cultural gap should be a good thing. Which made me wonder if the attempt to force me out was part of a plan to have a particular person replace me in order to influence the *terra indigene* who lived around Lake Silence—or if it was part of a plan to break any chance of peace between our species.

When in doubt, call your attorney.

I didn't think I'd sounded urgent, but I'd barely had time to pick up my basket of gardening tools and start weeding the flower beds that bordered the screened porch when Ilya Sanguinati walked up behind me, startling me enough that I squeaked and would have fallen on my butt if he hadn't grabbed one of my arms and hauled me to my feet.

"I didn't hear the car." I had to stop squeaking and develop the full-bodied scream that actors in scary movies managed to achieve. Then again, they weren't really scared breathless, which I'm sure helped with scream volume.

"I came across the lake," Ilya said.

"You have a boat?" I couldn't imagine him rowing a boat or paddling a canoe, so maybe it was a little sailboat?

He laughed. "The Sanguinati's smoke form can travel over water as easily as land, and the direct route across the lake was faster than using the car." He waited a beat. "You had a question."

"Every *terra indigene* settlement has a Reader."

"That is a statement, not a question."

"Aggie and the boys are excited about me being the Reader here, but I'd like to know exactly what that means."

"Because of the sacrifice usually required to achieve it, being the Reader is a position of respect in a settlement."

Sacrifice? What kind of sacrifice?

"Would you like to work while we talk?" he asked. "I don't want to disrupt your schedule of chores."

I noticed he didn't offer to help. Then again, when the Sanguinati turned into smoke, their clothes also turned into smoke, which just added to their mystique. I had heard that the whole turning-into-smoke thing was the reason the Sanguinati always dressed in black or shades of gray. That might be something someone made up. Or it could be cultural, like Simple Life men wearing dark trousers, white shirts, and suspenders. But seeing Ilya crouch beside me as I weeded the flower bed, I really wanted to ask if it was as hard to get grass stains out of Sanguinati clothing as it was regular old human clothes.

"Every form of *terra indigene* has its own teaching stories, the lessons one generation passes on to the next," Ilya said. "And there are stories that are told as entertainment that appeal to many different forms. It's only in the past few decades that some of our stories have been written down and put into books that many can enjoy."

"Like the Wolf Team stories and the books by Alan Wolfgard?"

He smiled. "Exactly. But reading printed words is a human skill, and to most forms of *terra indigene*, acquiring human skills is considered a necessary contamination—a sacrifice a small percentage of us make in order to keep watch over the two-legged predators who are also prey."

Well, hearing that sure made me feel special. It also made me realize how The Jumble was different from other *terra indigene* settlements. "The Readers aren't usually human, are they? They're *terra indigene* who have learned to read well in order to share the stories with the rest of the . . . residents."

"Yes. Here, with you, the reading hour can be a point of interaction as well as entertainment."

And a lot of responsibility. "Every day?"

"Oh no. Perhaps one evening a week—and not on your cop and crime TV night—you could read a chapter from a book like the Wolf Team. On another evening, a folktale or one of your human teaching stories. On the third evening, you could read an article or two from a magazine like *Nature!*—something nonfiction."

I stopped weeding and looked at him. "I would think you would know more about the natural world than the humans writing about it."

"But knowing how humans view the world is valuable," Ilya countered.

Three evenings a week didn't sound too demanding. And most human social life finished up soon after sundown since everyone who didn't want to be eaten stayed home after dark, so I would still have plenty of time for my own reading and personal chores.

"Julian Farrow might have books of human folktales or short stories that The Jumble's residents would find appealing, and he could stand in as a second Reader," Ilya said casually.

Too casually? No. Uh-uh. I could not have heard what I thought I'd heard.

"Is there anything else?" Ilya asked.

"No, I just wanted to be clear about the duties of the Reader before tonight's story time."

"Then I'll wish you a good evening, Victoria."

I watched him walk away, kind of hoping I would see him do the smoke thing. But he still looked human when he walked down the grassy slope that led to the beach, and my thoughts circled back to what he'd said.

I sat back on my heels and stared at the flower bed. If Ineke had suggested that Julian could help me be the designated Reader, I would have said she was playing matchmaker. But Ilya Sanguinati?

Nah.

Conan fetched a chair from the kitchen and Cougar fetched a floor lamp from the social room along with a small table where I could set a glass of water. After they conferred with Aggie about potential locations for story time, the three of them had decided that I would stay in the screened porch so that biting insects wouldn't distract me from reading the story, and by using an extension cord to plug in the lamp, I could be positioned as close to the porch door as possible so that my voice would carry across at least part of the back lawn.

By the time I opened the kitchen door, ready for my first attempt at being The Jumble's Reader, I'd convinced myself that just because Aggie had spread the word, that didn't mean anyone would show up.

I'd had no idea that many Crows lived in The Jumble. I'd had no idea that many Crows could fit on my porch. I didn't know what to say about the large Hawk that was perched on the back of the chair I was supposed to use. I was pretty sure asking him—her?—to move was not a good idea. I was pretty sure having that beak a few inches above my head wasn't going to help my reading skills. I didn't know this story. What if there was a Hawk who worked with the villains instead of the good guys? And if this was the same Hawk who had gouged the paint on the roof of Detective Swinn's car, I didn't want to think about what those talons could do to me.

Breathe, Vicki. Breathe. And believe that no harm comes to the Reader.

Aggie, in human form, sat on the porch floor beside my chair. Conan and Cougar also sat on the porch floor.

"We're almost ready," Aggie said. "The Owlgard . . . Oh, there they are."

I watched two Owls glide in from somewhere and perch on a branch of the nearest tree. And I felt a gentle tug on my hair, as if someone was trying to figure out how to comb it. But the only being . . .

Oh gods. The Hawk was trying to preen my hair. I didn't want to imagine what would happen if one of his feet got tangled up in it, so I leaned forward a little, grabbed the book, and said with manic brightness, "Why don't we start?"

I couldn't see what was out there just beyond the porch. I caught a glimpse of tufted ears before something settled on the porch steps.

Breathe, Vicki, and make a note to schedule anxiety attacks after reading time.

"Today we'll start the first book about the Wolf Team," I said, raising my voice, although I wasn't sure that was necessary considering my listeners. "It's called *Sharp Justice*." I took a sip of water, then set the glass on the table. "Chapter One."

CHAPTER 21

Grimshaw

Thaisday, Juin 15

Grimshaw locked the door of his room and headed downstairs for breakfast. He'd been in charge of the Sproing Police Station for two full days and had three dead bodies. Four if he counted Franklin Cartwright, who was the reason he'd ended up in Sproing in the first place.

Last summer, most of the Northeast Region hadn't received the brunt of the *terra indigene*'s rage against humans, but he'd seen plenty of bad things during the Great Predation, enough that he considered a full night of dreamless sleep a blessing. Since Detectives Chesnik and Baker had wandered through his dreams last night, he really hoped today would be a corpse-free day.

He paused at the door to the dining room when he noticed Paige Xavier sitting next to David Osgood, a shoebox between them on the table.

"Come on," Paige coaxed. "You can tell me. What is it for?"

"I told you," Osgood replied, sounded cornered. "It's for a police investigation."

Paige gave the baby cop a smile that was two parts siren and one part terrifying. In other words, Female with a capital *F*. "What are you investigating? The loot you can buy at block sales and estate sales?" She tapped the shoe box. "Don't forget who showed you the Yard Sale and helped you pick out most of this stuff."

Grimshaw tipped his head back and looked at the ceiling, but the ceiling chose not to divulge any answers or even offer a paint flake or two of wisdom.

Maxwell, the border collie, dashed over to Grimshaw and gave him a sniff to confirm that his current flock of people-sheep was all accounted for.

The movement drew Osgood's and Paige's attention.

Grimshaw entered the room and took a seat. "Good morning."

"Coffee?" Paige asked, jumping up to pour him a cup.

"Thanks." He studied Osgood, who was squirming as if his breakfast prunes were working enthusiastically. "You found something?"

"I took David to a place in Crystalton called the Yard Sale," Paige replied as she filled Grimshaw's cup. "Most block sales and yard sales are done on the weekends, but the Yard Sale is a shop that buys from estate sales and such and is open during the week. I could have been more help in selecting things if I had known the reason behind this shopping spree."

"You helped?" He knew that, having just heard her say it. And there was no reason why she couldn't have helped Osgood select the items. She wasn't handling evidence or anything like that, but he was interested in *why* she had helped.

"I did." Paige set the coffeepot on a hot pad. "Since the two of you are our only guests at the moment, Ineke is doing omelets for breakfast instead of putting out a buffet. Would you like anything in particular in your omelet?"

"Nothing exotic," Grimshaw replied. "Otherwise, whatever Ms. Xavier has available." When Paige didn't show any sign of heading to the kitchen, he looked at Osgood and held out his hand for the box. "We need something to trade in order to recover a piece of evidence."

"Citizens are supposed to surrender evidence," Paige pointed out.

"True, but this citizen is one of the Crowgard—a juvenile female. I don't think she's much interested in surrendering anything that has caught her fancy."

"Ah." Paige flipped the lid off the box and barely avoided dunking a corner of the lid into Grimshaw's coffee. As she rummaged, Grimshaw saw a couple of cuff bracelets that might shine with some polish, an engraved lighter, and a few gewgaws he would have to inspect more closely to figure out what they were. "Here." She set a jingling object on the plate in front of him.

Grimshaw held it up to get a better look. The silver charms on the bracelet were all musical instruments—harp, piano, violin, trumpet, guitar, drum, saxophone. They jingled when he moved his hand, and they shone when they caught the light. "Perfect."

Paige gave Osgood a mischievous smile. "See? I told you it was a good choice." She took the plate and left the dining room, presumably to tell Ineke that the guests were ready for breakfast.

Grimshaw tucked the charm bracelet into his shirt pocket, put the lid back on the box, picked up his coffee . . . and waited.

"When I was picked for the initial assignment, Detective Swinn said to pack an overnight bag," Osgood said. "His team drove up in the two cars, so I didn't have a vehicle to drive over to the communities around Crystal Lake to look for the things you wanted. Miss Paige said she was going to the Yard Sale—I guess one of the Xaviers does that once a week to look for things that might be useful in the boarding-house or to sell on to someone else—and said I could go with her. She even made the extra trip to Putney so that I could pick up more clothes and my own car, in case you needed me to run another errand. But I didn't talk about the case."

Grimshaw was certain the baby cop believed that. He was equally certain Paige Xavier, like the other women in her family, was an expert at extracting information without seeming to do anything at all.

Paige returned and set the plates in front of them. Omelets and toast, and a small bowl of sliced seasonal fruit. She topped off Grimshaw's coffee, then left the room.

"No prunes?" Not that he minded; he was just curious and wanted to verify the potential of Osgood as a gossip magnet.

"Maxwell has a tender tummy after the episode yesterday, so Ms. Ineke didn't want to tempt him." Osgood bit into a strawberry. "I'd rather have the fresh stuff." He focused on eating for a minute. "Detective Swinn and Detective Reynolds are gone, but I think they're coming back."

Not a surprise. "I'm going to The Jumble to retrieve that piece of evidence. I want you to patrol Main Street and then man the phones at the office. Pay attention to anything being said about the bank—if it's going to close for good or will reopen under a new owner."

"Like the Sanguinati?" Osgood asked.

Grimshaw nodded. "Don't push for information; just pay attention to what the people around you are saying." He finished his breakfast and pushed away from the table. "I shouldn't be long, but I'll call in if I have to stop anywhere else."

"Yes, sir."

Grimshaw tapped the top of the shoe box. "Take that to the station and tuck it in an empty drawer. You never know when we'll need another shiny bribe."

Getting out of the cruiser, Grimshaw touched the medal of Mikhos under his shirt before he unhooked the chain across The Jumble's access road and lowered it to the ground. He didn't see anything, not even a sparrow or chipmunk, but he could feel the *terra indigene* watching him as he drove his car past the boundary and stopped to hook up the chain, cutting off his chance of a fast escape. He hoped the Others would understand the action to mean he had nothing to fear from them because he offered no threat to Vicki DeVine or any other resident of The Jumble. Whether they understood or not, nothing prevented him from reaching the main house—but *something* had warned Vicki that she was about to have a visitor because she opened the front door and stepped outside before he had time to get out of the car.

"Ms. DeVine."

"Officer Grimshaw."

Aggie rushed up wearing a mesh beach cover-up and nothing else. She latched onto one of Vicki's hands. Grimshaw wasn't sure who was supposed to be protecting whom.

"Why is he here? What does he want?" Aggie asked. "Should I call Cougar?"

"If you think he could help with this problem," Grimshaw replied. He'd skimmed a couple of cop and crime stories last evening, as well as reading a piece of the novel by Alan Wolfgard. He considered himself a good cop, a man who believed in the code of "serve and protect." But he'd realized last night that it would take more than being a good cop if he wanted to deal with some of the Others. He had to present himself as the kind of cop *they* would recognize as good. Trouble was, if he started representing himself as a persona rather than the person he was, at some point he would slip up, and he didn't think the Others ever forgave or forgot deceit.

But that didn't mean he couldn't adapt a few things from the books and TV shows Vicki and Aggie might use as reference for dealing with the police during this investigation.

"You *want* to talk to Cougar?" Vicki asked.

Of course not. No one in his right mind wanted to talk to one of the Panthergard—or the Beargard, for that matter. Or the Sanguinati.

"If you think he could help." Grimshaw pushed his hat back, a look that conveyed country friendliness. Sometimes people in the wild country needed help, and looking as official as possible made them feel uneasy. Sometimes looking a little more friendly made it easier for them to trust the man as well as the uniform.

"I guess it depends on the problem," Vicki said.

"A piece of evidence wasn't collected the other day when

Detective Swinn's team caused a fuss here while you were helping the police with their inquiries."

Vicki DeVine raised her eyebrows but said nothing.

"A tie clip wasn't bagged with the rest of Detective Baker's personal effects, which means it fell off when the body was collected." Grimshaw pointed to the area where Baker's body had been twisted. "Right around there." He focused on the two females. "It's possible that someone picked it up, thinking it wasn't significant—a pretty bauble that no one would miss. But it is an important piece of evidence, and we really need it returned."

Grimshaw took the charm bracelet out of his pocket and held it up, spreading it open over his fingers so they could see the charms.

"Oh!" Her dark eyes bright with excitement, Aggie released Vicki's hand and reached for the bracelet.

Grimshaw pulled his hand back just enough so that she couldn't grab the bracelet and run away.

Aggie gave him a look that held a touch of menace. She might be young, and she wasn't one of the forms of *terra indigene* that would be lethal as individuals—not like a Panther or Bear or Wolf—but he didn't think calling a gathering of crows a murder was a designation someone made up just for the fun of it. And a gathering of the Crowgard certainly could be a danger to a single human.

"I'm willing to trade this bracelet, which a young woman could wear as well as admire, for the tie clip Detective Baker was wearing when he came to The Jumble the other day."

"A lot of people could bring you tie clips in order to get the shiny," Aggie said, her eyes still focused on the charm bracelet. "How would you know which one belonged to *that* man?"

"I'm a cop. I'll know."

Aggie looked at Vicki in mute appeal.

"An experienced police officer would know, just like the investigator in the story we watched the other night," Vicki said.

Aggie sighed. Then she pulled the beach cover-up over

her head, giving Grimshaw a look at physical quirks that he didn't want, or need, to know about. Moments later, she shifted into her Crow form and flew away.

"You think Aggie took the tie clip," Vicki said.

"Someone here pulled the tie out from under the body and took the clip," Grimshaw replied. "If it wasn't Aggie, then I'd bet a month's wages that it was one of her kin."

"You really need it for the investigation? Why?"

"Because Detective Swinn was very upset about its disappearance, and I want to know what's so special about that particular tie clip."

They fell into an awkward silence. She seemed reluctant to be around him, and not because he was a cop. She was acting like someone had painted an insulting remark about her on a public wall, making her the focus of unhappy attention—and he was one of the people who had read it.

Before he could decide if he should say anything about the fireplug remark Swinn had made, Aggie returned. She landed on the wide arm of the chair near the front door and dropped the tie clip she carried in her beak. She nudged it this way and that until the tie clip was resting on the front edge of the arm, right in a narrow beam of sunlight that showed the clip to best advantage.

Grimshaw set the charm bracelet on the arm and scooped up the tie clip. Aggie grabbed the bracelet and flew off. Bargain set and sealed.

He looked at the tie clip and frowned, unable to see why Swinn had gone into conniptions about its loss. Okay, everything from a crime scene should be bagged, but he didn't think that was the reason Swinn had reacted the way he did.

Then he caught the look on Vicki DeVine's face. "What is it?"

"Yorick has a tie clip like that."

He held it up to give her a better look. "Your ex-husband has a tie clip like this or just similar to this?"

She looked at him, her eyes full of confusion. "Exactly like that."

CHAPTER 22

Vicki

Thaisday, Juin 15

Sitting in The Jumble's library with Ilya Sanguinati and Officer Grimshaw, I looked at the books I had shelved yesterday and had an epiphany. While I enjoyed reading thrillers, I didn't want to be the girl tangled in the plot of one because I would have been the heroine's best friend or the girl who had fallen for the hero—the girl he felt some affection for because she gave him sex while he was getting over the loss of his one true love. Those were the girls who ended up getting tossed in the wood chipper or left at the bottom of a deep, dry well full of spiders and millipedes—said well suddenly refilling, quite inconveniently, so that the girl would be found but not in time, especially if she was the passing love interest of the hero of the story. Those were also the girls who would be tied up in a cave and left to become the frame for a bat guano sculpture.

But even the epiphany didn't stop me from snorting out a laugh when Officer Grimshaw floated his theory about the tie clips.

"You think Yorick belongs to a secret society? An organization with secret handshakes and code words? A society that, wanting to remain secret, identifies its members *by a tie clip*? Are you *serious*?"

Apparently he was. I looked at Ilya Sanguinati to see what he thought about Grimshaw's theory. I don't know if it was because he was a vampire or an attorney, but he had mastered the poker face.

"You think it's possible," I said to Ilya.

"It should be considered," he replied. "It indicates a connection between Detective Swinn and your ex-husband."

Grimshaw leaned toward me, his forearms resting on his thighs, his face full of concerned sincerity. "Think about it. You were married to the man for how many years? Did he belong to any clubs, go out to monthly meetings that were members only?" He picked up an evidence bag containing the tie clip and held it up. "Your ex-husband and at least one of the detectives in a CIU team had this exact tie clip. A Bristol CIU team should have taken the assignment when I reported the suspicious death of Franklin Cartwright on your property. But a team from Putney, led by Marmaduke Swinn, showed up instead."

"The police in Putney have not concerned themselves with the citizens of Sproing until now," Ilya Sanguinati said.

"Bristol has two CIU teams that are supposed to handle any suspicious deaths or other incidents in Bristol and the area within Bristol's jurisdiction, which includes Lake Silence. Highway patrol out of Bristol is supposed to handle anything on the roads between Crystal Lake and Lake Silence, and that includes answering calls from Sproing." Grimshaw's expression hardened. "It was possible that both Bristol teams already had cases and couldn't send anyone that day, but I checked with Captain Hargreaves and he told me a team had been available. Somehow Swinn heard about Cartwright and claimed jurisdiction, saying it was related to a crime he was already investigating. Since no one in Bristol wanted to fight with Swinn over going to Sproing, they let him have the case."

"Geez," I said, "what do you guys do? Play rock, paper,

scissors to decide who has to take a call here?" I knew the police didn't like coming to Sproing—and to be fair, they had good reason to feel that way—but being told you sometimes got protection from someone like Swinn because no one else wanted to come didn't make me feel all warm and fuzzy—or safe.

I don't think I have a good poker face, because Grimshaw looked uncomfortable. Ilya Sanguinati's poker face didn't change, but I had the feeling he might have a few things to say to someone about how humans protected other humans.

"Right now, it doesn't matter how Swinn got the case," Grimshaw said. "What matters is why he wanted it."

"That man, Franklin Cartwright," Ilya said. "Did he have one of those tie clips?"

"I don't know," Grimshaw replied. "He was dressed casually when he was found. Swinn's team collected his things from the boardinghouse."

So now we had a conspiracy? This was getting better and better. Or worse and worse.

I raked my fingers through my hair, dislodging some of the clips that kept it under control. Ilya Sanguinati looked at my sproinging hair. His poker face cracked. His lips twitched. I promised myself that I would cover all the mirrors until I ran a brush through my hair so that I wouldn't scare myself.

We won't talk about the time I got a brush so tangled in my hair I had to make an emergency appointment with my stylist and have her perform a brushectomy to avoid having brush-head for the rest of my life.

"How many secret societies can there be?" I lobbed the question, not expecting an answer.

"Since they're secret, it's anyone's guess," Grimshaw replied.

His eyes went blank. I watched him swallow. We had momentarily forgotten that one of us was not like the others.

Now neither of us looked at the vampire in the room. The Humans First and Last movement hadn't been a secret. It had been a political pro-human, anti-Others group that started with speeches and ended with the acts of violence that started the war that killed a lot of people in Thaisia and destroyed the Cel-Romano Alliance of Nations on the other side of the Atlantik Ocean. But secret societies with secret agendas that might pose a threat to the *terra indigene*?

I had a bad feeling Grimshaw and I had just painted targets on the backs of several people—including my ex-husband. Yorick used to say a successful businessman was bound to make a few enemies. I don't think he'd considered that the Sanguinati might be one of them when he said that.

"It may not be a secret society," I said. "It could be a private or exclusive group that doesn't want their name splashed in the newspapers for doing charitable work. Or it could be a club. Yorick was a member of a couple of clubs where he hobnobbed with people who had money or social clout. Those clubs were exclusive but they weren't secret."

Grimshaw nodded. "That would make more sense, although I doubt that Marmaduke Swinn or Franklin Cartwright had money or the social clout to belong to such a club."

"It doesn't matter if Detective Swinn and Franklin Cartwright are part of that group," Ilya said. "It doesn't change the fact that humans with an agenda are causing trouble at The Jumble. Until we know who belongs to this tie clip club, we cannot determine if they are merely a nuisance or a real threat."

I had a feeling that everyone who was included in the *we* Ilya Sanguinati referred to had fangs at the very least. Which meant *we* didn't include Grimshaw and me.

"It's a human investigation," Grimshaw said, turning in his seat to look directly at Ilya.

"It's a human investigation because Victoria called the police instead of calling us," Ilya replied.

Oh golly. Had I stepped on some *terra indigene* toes by reporting the body to humans instead of calling Silence Lodge? Of course, I hadn't known about The Jumble being a *terra indigene* settlement or even the species of my neighbors across the lake, so I hoped the Sanguinati took that into account.

"Franklin Cartwright was staying at the boardinghouse, and he allegedly worked for Yorick," I said, trying to smooth any ruffled feathers—or fangs. "Even if I hadn't called the police when Aggie tried to warm up the eyeball in the wavecooker, someone would have noticed that he disappeared." I liked saying *allegedly*. It was such a cop-and-crime word.

"Humans disappear in the wild country all the time."

Grimshaw looked grim. I didn't blame him. We were being reminded that survival not only depended on fellow humans playing nice and sharing the sandbox but also depended on not bringing yourself to the attention of all the large, intelligent predators that prowled just beyond the boundary of the sandbox—and sometimes went hunting inside the sandbox when they had a reason to focus on particular prey.

"You should ask the Xaviers," I said, breaking the tense silence that followed Ilya's words. "Detective Swinn, his team, and the dead man had stayed at the boardinghouse. If any of them had one of those tie clips, Ineke might have seen it." I pointed to the tie clip in the evidence bag. "You could show her that one or even take a photo of it to show around."

It was the way Grimshaw didn't look at me that told me someone—or several someones—had already asked Ineke about the tie clip.

"The Xaviers are not the only individuals who could assist in finding out who wears that symbol," Ilya said, focusing a predator stare on Grimshaw. "We can assist with locating other humans who belong to this group. You can supply a photo."

Vampire and cop locked eyes.

"Belonging to an organization isn't proof of guilt or collusion," Grimshaw said.

"But obtaining a sample of who might belong to a particular group may assist in determining the group's agenda," Ilya countered. After a weighty silence, he added, "Our interest is in understanding why Franklin Cartwright came to

The Jumble and what he was supposed to achieve. Victoria is the owner of the buildings and caretaker of the land that makes up The Jumble. Someone thinks otherwise and is causing trouble. We will pursue this until we know why. We are willing to work with the police in this matter, or we will work on our own."

In other words, someone can go to jail if he or she has been naughty or that person can be eaten. Given those choices, I'm pretty sure I would choose jail. Then again, Ilya Sanguinati did look yummy, and dying from orgasms and blood loss might not be a bad way to go.

"Cooperation is always appreciated." Grimshaw didn't sound like he appreciated being backed into a corner, but he said the words that should at least delay more people getting killed.

But I was going to pay close attention to the shelves in the general store in case there was a sudden run on the ketchup and hot sauce.

CHAPTER 23

Aggie

Thaisday, Juin 15

Following Ilya Sanguinati's orders, Aggie gathered her Crowgard kin and flew to the woodland side of Silence Lodge, where they wouldn't be seen by any humans fishing on the lake. Many of the Crows chose to perch on the branches of nearby trees, but most settled on the ground since it was easier to shift to a human form when you didn't have to balance on a branch that might not hold that shape.

A dozen Sanguinati followed Miss Vicki's attorney out of the lodge. Several Crows fluffed and fluttered. Other Crows preened their feathers to show they weren't concerned by the number of vampires who were also attending this meeting. Normally the Crowgard had no reason to fear the Sanguinati. Being another form of *terra indigene*, they were not prey. But powerful predators should never be taken lightly.

"We would like your assistance in solving a puzzle," Ilya Sanguinati said.

Aggie stopped preening. Puzzles were fun, especially the ones that required figuring out how to claim a shiny.

Ilya Sanguinati held out a photograph of the shiny clip thing she had traded for the pretty bracelet. "We need to find out how many humans have a tie clip exactly like this one.

Once we know who they are, we'll be able to find out why they are interested in The Jumble."

<Miss Vicki is taking care of The Jumble now,> Eddie Crowgard said. <She is the Reader. We don't need another human there.>

"We think the humans who wear this clip are trying to force Miss Vicki to leave."

<Peck them!>

<Tell Cougar to claw them!>

<Tell the Bear to swat them!>

"Not yet."

All the Crows settled down. "Not yet" wasn't quite a promise that soon there would be eyeballs for lunch, but it was close.

"You cannot take these shinies," Ilya Sanguinati said. "They have to stay with the humans who own them."

Aggie stared at Ilya. No shinies? What kind of puzzle game was that?

"Find something else to bring back that will tell me who the humans are and where they live," Ilya said. "Something they won't miss, like mail humans toss in the recycle box as soon as it arrives or an envelope that has been thrown out. We need something with the human's name and address."

<What happens then?> Aggie asked. She wasn't sure how many of the Crows would play this puzzle game if they couldn't bring back any shinies.

Ilya smiled, showing his fangs. "Then we'll be able to identify the human enemies hiding among the rest."

CHAPTER 24

Grimshaw

Thaisday, Juin 15

Ineke Xavier walked into the boardinghouse's parlor wearing a one-piece bathing suit and an open robe. "You wanted to see me?"

When Grimshaw didn't answer, she looked amused. He understood her amusement—and felt grateful that she *was* amused because he couldn't stop looking at her thighs. Or more precisely, the two tattoos on her thighs.

On her left thigh was a revolver. The smoke coming out of the barrel rose toward her nether region. On her right thigh was a big-eyed caricature of Ineke with her multicolored hair piled on top of her head and a miniature of the boardinghouse tucked in the hair like an ornament. Around the caricature's neck was a necklace made of tombstones, and beneath them were the words "I Bury Trouble."

Gods, Grimshaw thought. *I'm renting a room from this woman.*

Ineke closed the robe, releasing Grimshaw from his involuntary fixation with the tattoos.

"Will this take long?" Ineke asked. "I'm going to The Jumble to talk to Vicki about our arrangements to offer guests a guided trail ride to the lake. I think she needs some girl time, and I could use a swim while we review the details."

Grimshaw wanted to shake his head to clear it, or at least splash some cold water on his face, but that would tell her too much about his reaction. Was there something mesmerizing about those tattoos, something hypnotic? Or was it just that he'd been caught unprepared?

He needed to close this case and get out of Sproing.

He held out the photo of the tie clip. "Have you seen this?"

"Have I seen a tie clip? I imagine every man has one, so I've seen plenty of them over the years. I think I even have a couple of them in the secondary jewelry box."

He hoped she had bought them for herself and he didn't have to look for bodies in the compost bin. "I'm looking for tie clips exactly like this one."

"I've covered this ground before." But she took the photo and studied the image. "Unless someone's behavior gives me a reason to look, I don't rummage through my guests' possessions. That doesn't mean I don't pay attention to anything that's left out in plain sight. Being tidy men, I can't say if you or Officer Osgood have a tie clip like this. Franklin Cartwright had rented one of the en suite rooms, but he didn't leave out so much as a tube of toothpaste, and despite planning to be here for a few days, he didn't remove anything from his luggage but a couple of shirts and a second pair of trousers that he hung in the closet. And his luggage was always locked when he left his room."

"How could you tell?"

"The luggage was secured with leather straps and padlocks." Ineke handed back the photo. "I don't mind guests having secrets or wearing the perfume of mystery. We all have secrets, and everyone should have a little mystery in their lives. But those padlocks and his talk about Vicki squatting at The Jumble when we'd all watched her pump money and sweat into the place didn't sit right. If Cartwright hadn't been killed, I was going to tell him to find another place to stay."

"There isn't another place to stay in Sproing."

She gave him a predatory smile. "Exactly." She waved a hand at the photo. "Detectives Reynolds and Baker had a tie clip like that. So did Detective Swinn."

"What about the bank manager?"

Ineke narrowed her eyes. "I never had a reason to pay attention, so I can't say for sure."

"Thanks for your help." Grimshaw started to turn away, then stopped.

Ineke picked up a large straw basket that held a rolled beach towel, a bottle of water, and a small purse. "Something else?"

He hesitated, then decided to ask the question. "What do you think will happen if Vicki DeVine leaves The Jumble?"

"I think that will depend on why she leaves."

"Do I look like I wear a tie?"

Grimshaw looked up at Gershwin Jones, the owner of Grace Notes, Sproing's store for all things musical. Looking up at someone was a novel experience he didn't enjoy.

"No, you don't," Grimshaw replied. "But I'm asking business owners if they've seen a tie clip like this."

Gershwin Jones was a large, well-proportioned man. A first-generation Thaisian whose parents had emigrated from the Eastern Storm Islands, he had brown skin and dark eyes. He wore his dark hair in dreadlocks that fell below his shoulder blades, and the knee-length caftan he wore over sand-colored trousers looked like a rainbow that had overdosed on caffeine.

"All the business owners or a select few?"

Like Julian Farrow, Gershwin Jones was a newcomer, someone who had moved to Sproing last fall after so many people in small, isolated places like this one had died or bolted to towns that were human controlled—or at least provided more of an illusion that there was a boundary between them and the *terra indigene*.

Grimshaw might not sense things like Julian did, but a cop had his own kind of intuition. "A select few—the people who moved into the area within the past year. Lots of people have been looking for new opportunities, looking for a different place to settle down. You've got Simple Life folk running the livery, and I understand that a few Intuits have become residents of Sproing." *And I think you're one of them,* he added silently.

Jones went over to the bins of sheet music and began straightening the already tidy bins. "Julian says you're a friend of his, says you're open-minded about the gifts that come to a person at birth."

Which just confirmed his thought that Jones was an Intuit. "I try to be open-minded about things that don't hurt another person or break the law."

Jones just kept tidying the bins. Finally he stopped but didn't look at Grimshaw. "I have a feeling the men who wear that tie clip wouldn't be doing business with someone like me. They don't feel the rhythm of a place or the people who live there. They don't have a feel for anything but profit. You hear what I'm saying? Those detectives causing trouble for Miss Vicki. They didn't come in, but Officer Osgood has come in to look at the sheet music, look at the instruments I have for sale. He feels the rhythm."

Well, asking people about the tie clips had been a long shot.

A faraway look came into Jones's eyes. Then he focused on Grimshaw. "You got a connection to any of the special girls?"

For a moment, Grimshaw's body clenched. Special girls. Blood prophets. The *cassandra sangue*. Girls who could see the future when their skin was cut.

"No, I don't have a connection to any of those girls," he said. Not directly, anyway.

Some of the girls still lived in the compounds where they had been raised and trained. Others had left that "benevolent ownership" and tried to survive in the chaotic everyday world. Many hadn't survived, and the ones who had were hidden away.

If you wanted to hide vulnerable girls, you'd ask someone

who had an intuitive sense about a place to find communities where those girls would be safe. And Grimshaw didn't know anyone who was better at sensing a place than Julian Farrow.

"Thanks for your help," Grimshaw said. He hurried out of Grace Notes and went straight to Lettuce Reed.

"You alone?" he asked Julian as soon as he walked into the store.

"For the moment," Julian replied. "Had a run on romantic suspense novels an hour ago. Probably not the type of story that is of interest to you."

Grimshaw waved off the comment. "I need help answering a question. I need a special kind of help." Too cryptic? No. Julian knew exactly what, or who, he was talking about—and said nothing. Expecting that to be Julian's response, he added, "I know a man who knows a man who might know a blood prophet."

Julian looked away. "What are we playing? Six degrees of separation or connect the dots?"

"Maybe both. What do detectives working in Putney, a bank manager in Sproing, and a businessman living in Hubb NE have in common?"

"You tell me."

"They all have the same tie clip, which could be coincidence or could be a connection."

Julian said nothing.

Grimshaw decided to push. "You helped hide some of those girls, didn't you? Before you opened the store here."

"We're not talking about it. Ever," Julian said fiercely.

No, Julian wouldn't talk. Blood prophets were worth a fortune because of their ability to see the future, and a man who admitted that he knew where to find even one of them would be wearing a target on his back.

But there was one blood prophet who might be within reach.

"Captain Hargreaves knows a patrol captain in Lakeside. He might be able to reach out." He didn't want to ask Hargreaves to call in another favor on his behalf, but he also didn't want this trouble at The Jumble to be the incident that started the next Great Predation.

"Do you really need this?"

"Gershwin Jones seems to think I do. He's the one who asked if I knew any of the special girls."

A crackling silence. Finally Julian sighed. "Some Intuits have a private information exchange. There's been talk that some of the special girls are exploring ways to reveal prophecy without their skin being cut." He smiled grimly. "I know a man who knows a Wolf who knows a girl who might be able to answer a question by reading cards."

"If you could reach out," Grimshaw said. "I trust Captain Hargreaves, but Swinn's involvement raises the question of who else might be connected to this mess."

"Work out exactly what you want to ask, and I'll send the question. Might help if I can e-mail the photo of the tie clip too."

"Thanks. I'll be back."

Grimshaw crossed the street and went inside the police station. Osgood was there, reading one of the books he'd purchased at Lettuce Reed.

"Why don't you do a foot patrol?" Grimshaw said. He pulled out his wallet and handed Osgood a couple of bills. "Pick up some lunch for the two of us while you're out and about."

"Yes, sir." Osgood hesitated. "What are you going to do?"

"I'm going to take some alone time to consider a question."

CHAPTER 25

Vicki

Firesday, Juin 16

We were trapped in a building. Lots of pipes overhead and exposed steel support beams. Something was in there with us, hunting us. We'd found Dominique Xavier lying in a pool of her own blood, her blank eyes staring at us as we turned and ran, searching for a way out, desperate to escape the monster.

Ineke, Paige, and I fled in the same direction. As I swung around a corner, I heard Paige scream. I turned back, but Ineke shouted, "Run, Vicki, run! Get help!"

Then came a sound that didn't—couldn't—come from one of us.

I ran through a maze of rooms—gray metal walls, metal ceiling, wood floor. My heart pounded; my lungs struggled to breathe. Had to get out; had to find help.

The next room had baskets of bright-colored toys filling a row of metal tables—little bits of plastic no bigger than a thumb in the shape of animals. In a world reduced to metallic gray, the colors were startling, unnerving, life-affirming. I picked up a basket—and heard a sound behind me.

I don't know what it was. It was human-shaped but noth-

*ing human. The head rising from a soiled white shirt and
thin-striped brown suit looked like papier-mâché draped
with dirty strips of gauze that settled around its shoulders.
Instead of eyes, a pair of black goggles were somehow attached to the gauze—not tight, not like there were straps
holding them on to provide some shape to the white lump. It
was as if the goggles were its eyes. Several tie clips decorated the lapels of the suit.*

*I flung the plastic toys out of the basket, scattering them
over the floor like wash water. The gauze-headed thing
stumbled over the plastic bits, just a moment of unbalance.
I dropped the empty basket, grabbed another that was full
of the colored toys, and ran, pursued by the terrible thing
that was dressed like a businessman but was deadly and
monstrous.*

*I heard a ding, saw the freight elevator's doors open. If I
could get to the elevator, I could get to the ground floor, get
out, get help. Paige was hurt—no one screamed that way if
they weren't hurt—and I didn't know what had happened to
Ineke.*

*I looked back—and it was there, right there, coming
toward me. Did I have time to get in the elevator and press
the button? Would the elevator doors close before that thing
reached them—and me?*

*I threw the basket at it, but the basket turned into a pillow
that bounced off its chest. I leaped into the elevator, slapped
at the panel, and pushed the B button. Wrong button! There
were bad things in the basement. There were always bad
things in the basement. I pushed the button for the ground
floor. The gauze-headed thing reached in as the elevator
doors began to close. Reached in to grab me, to drag me
back into something unspeakable. I flung myself to the side
of the compartment, desperate to avoid that touch and . . .*

I woke up on the floor next to my bed, my heart pounding
and a sharp pain above my left eye, surrounded by a sense of
ow and a trickle of something wet.

It took a couple of tries to get to my feet. I wobbled my

way to the bathroom, turned on the light, and stared at the blood trickling from the area above the corner of my left eyebrow.

That was so not good, especially when I could see the swelling already starting. I rinsed a washcloth in cold water and applied it to the wound as I studied my face in the mirror. Did my eyes look weird? I didn't feel like I'd banged my head against anything, but I'd obviously hit *something* on my way to the floor.

I lowered the washcloth and leaned closer to the mirror. The bleeding had stopped for the moment, revealing a couple of scrapes and a shallow gouge surrounded by swelling and shades of purple.

Wow.

As I dabbed antibiotic ointment on the scrape and covered it with a small bandage, it occurred to me that I would never feel the same when the hero in a story got hit in the face during a fight because faces really object to getting hit or hurt in any way and didn't hold back when it came to letting you know about it.

Back in the bedroom, I turned on the light and wiped up the drops of blood that had fallen on the floor. The culprit—the square corner of the bedside table—didn't have any obvious forensic evidence, but I wiped it off anyway.

Having done whatever I could do, I shut off the light and lay diagonally on the bed, my head as far from the table as possible. I entertained my mini anxiety attack by wondering if I should stay awake in case I had a concussion, which seemed unlikely, and by wondering how *terra indigene* Bears and Panthers reacted to minor blood spillage. I fell asleep while trying out different versions of how to explain this to Aggie.

CHAPTER 26

Aggie

Firesday, Juin 16

At first light, the Crowgard who lived around Lake Silence flew to the houses in Sproing for the treasure hunt. It wasn't garbage day, so the trash cans weren't at the curb, but it was the day when the recycling truck traveled the streets for paper, plastic, and glass.

An hour later, when humans were stirring and beginning to notice the Crows, most of the Crowgard flew away, bored and disappointed. Better to perch near the businesses and watch the humans and see if any of them wore the shiny that the Sanguinati wanted to find.

Determined to find *something*, Aggie flew to the house that belonged to the human who used to work at the bank. The houses were bigger on this street, and sometimes the humans here discarded things that weren't even broken.

Just so she could say she'd been thorough, in case that was something the Sanguinati would reward, she poked through several recycling bins before she reached the bank human's house and perched on the first recycling bin. Glass jars, plastic jugs. Nothing interesting.

She hop-flapped to the paper recycling bin. The Crows

couldn't get inside the houses to look for shinies, and paper wasn't interesting unless it was a book that had a story.

Most of the humans in Sproing brought books to Lettuce Reed, but sometimes Julian Farrow put books into the recycling bin because pages were missing or the book was falling apart. Sometimes, if there were several stories in the book, most of them would be intact. The *terra indigene* rescued some of those books, willing to skip the stories that had missing pieces and read the ones that were complete.

Would the bank human throw away books? Probably. And not because they were old and broken. He would do it because he was *that* kind of human.

Movement around the house distracted her for a moment. Poised to fly away if there was danger, Aggie watched dozens of Sproingers take turns hopping up the steps to the bank human's front door and pooping on the stoop. Then they hopped away, letting everyone on the street know their opinion of the human who lived there.

Air ruffled the papers in the recycling bin and directed the breeze so that the scent of poop blew into the house's open windows.

The Elementals weren't usually playful or obvious about targeting a particular human, which made Aggie wonder if the Sanguinati had approached that form of *terra indigene* to look for the tie clips.

Discouraged, Aggie almost flew away when a bit of gold shiny caught her eye. She pushed and pecked a few pieces of paper, flinging them out of the bin until she found the envelope that had a logo on the left-hand corner made of metallic gold ink.

A small treasure. Maybe useful to the Sanguinati, maybe not. But if the vampires didn't want the envelope, she would keep it.

Hearing the front door open and the swearing that followed, Aggie grabbed her prize and flew back to The Jumble. Maybe Ilya Sanguinati would trade a different shiny for the envelope the way Officer Grimshaw had traded the pretty bracelet for the tie clip.

Shifting to human form when she reached her little cabin near the lake, Aggie went inside and dressed, choosing casual clothes similar to what she had seen Dominique Xavier wear last week. They both had dark hair, although Aggie's hair was Crow black and Dominique's hair was dark brown, but Aggie figured it was close enough that clothes and colors that Dominique chose would be appropriate, allowing Aggie to blend in with the humans. Blending in was important when approaching humans.

She brushed her long black hair and put on the charm bracelet. She couldn't ask the Sanguinati for a reward for finding the bit of shiny paper, but wearing the bracelet would be a hint that, maybe, a reward should be given. Hinting wasn't the same as asking and should be safe.

Aggie grabbed the envelope and ran out of the cabin. First she would show Miss Vicki and also make sure she hadn't missed any clothing she should be wearing. She had studied humans carefully before renting the cabin at The Jumble, but sometimes she didn't get the human things quite right.

Reaching the screened porch that ran across the back of the main house, Aggie turned the handle on the door and was a little surprised that it was unlocked. But Miss Vicki had planted flowers and did come out early to water them. That must be the reason.

Moving silently across the wooden floor, she reached the screen door that opened into the kitchen. She raised her hand to knock because that would be polite. Then Miss Vicki turned and Aggie saw the bandage, saw the purple shadows that were on one side of Miss Vicki's face.

Aggie backed away from the door. She'd read enough stories to know what bandages and *those* kinds of shadows meant.

She dropped the envelope as she bolted across the screened porch and out, letting the door bang behind her, forgetting that she'd intended to be quiet. No, she should *not* be quiet. This was bad. So very, very bad.

She didn't just send the warning to her Crowgard kin. She sent the warning to *all* the *terra indigene* around Lake Silence.

<Somebody attacked Miss Vicki!>

CHAPTER 27

Grimshaw

Firesday, Juin 16

Partially dressed, Grimshaw grabbed his mobile phone on the second ring, knowing no one called a cop early unless they needed something.

"Grimshaw."

"Wayne, get to The Jumble," Julian said. "Something is happening, and I don't think it's good for any of *us*. I'm heading there now to see if there's anything I can do."

"You have a feeling?"

"I saw . . . Gods, I'm not even sure what I just saw. A male and female on horses, galloping toward Vicki's place."

"A man and woman on horseback doesn't sound serious." But Julian sounded . . . odd. Scared. And *that* was not good.

"The riders weren't human, and despite what the animals looked like, I don't think they were actual horses."

Police officers who worked highway patrol studied every scrap of information they could about the kinds of *terra indigene* they might encounter, and what Julian had just described was among the most dangerous and feared. "Elementals."

"That would be my guess."

"I'll be there. Wait for me at the chain. Don't go up to the main house on your own."

Instead of answering, Julian hung up.

Swearing fiercely, Grimshaw finished dressing and rushed out of his room and down the stairs.

"Coffee's ready," Paige said with her usual cheer. "We have—"

"No time." He went past her as Osgood popped out of the dining room.

"Sir?"

"Man the phones." Grimshaw kept going. He yanked open the front door and almost knocked down the bank's former manager.

"I want to make a complaint!" The man was red-faced.

"Osgood!" Grimshaw shouted. "Deal with this."

He heard indignant whining about being fobbed off to the *junior* officer, but he ignored it as he ran to his car. He pulled out of the parking lot, spraying gravel. He hit the lights and the siren.

He should call for backup, shouldn't go into this thing blind. He didn't want to bring Osgood. The kid had already had a bad experience at The Jumble and he couldn't be sure Osgood wouldn't freeze if he encountered more *terra indigene*. If he called dispatch for backup, the closest cops around were Swinn and Reynolds, and *their* presence would aggravate the situation, whatever it might be. And, gods, if they were dealing with angry Elementals, the whole community could be kindling and corpses in the blink of an eye.

No, he'd count on Julian Farrow for backup and hope they both survived long enough to get the situation under control before the *terra indigene* took care of things in their own lethal way.

CHAPTER 28

Vicki

Firesday, Juin 16

I answered the phone at the same moment a column of smoke flowed through the kitchen's screen door and shifted into a very angry attorney. Okay, partially shifted, which raised all kinds of questions about anatomy that I was sure the Sanguinati would never answer.

"Vicki? Vicki!" Ineke's voice blasted out of the receiver and sounded stressed.

"Uh." I'm not at my best first thing in the morning, and under the circumstances that was the sum total of my vocabulary.

"Something is happening. Grimshaw just peeled out of here like a maniac."

I heard the siren. It was getting closer. Then I heard a jingle and looked past Ilya Sanguinati. Aggie stood on the other side of the screen door. I thought I'd seen her on the porch a few minutes ago, but she was gone by the time I walked across the kitchen.

A gust of wind rattled the house. I started adding things up and wished I had my little calculator handy because there was a lot to add.

The siren sounded so loud now, I pictured Grimshaw

driving right through the front of the house like one of the cops had done in a recent TV show.

A car door slammed. Then another door slammed. Then someone—or something—growled as it headed toward the kitchen.

"Vicki!"

"Ms. DeVine!"

Add one Crow, one angry attorney, one police officer, one bookstore-owning friend, a second gust of wind that might be an opinion, and one Panther that entered the kitchen just ahead of the two men.

"I'll call you back." I hung up on Ineke and considered the variety of upset males filling up my kitchen and staring at my face. Oh crap. Crappity crap crap.

"What happened?" Officer Grimshaw asked at the same time Julian said, "You need a doctor."

"I don't need a doctor, and nothing happened," I replied.

Ilya Sanguinati hissed. Cougar growled. Julian made a huffing sound that might have been an angry laugh.

Grimshaw said nothing. Somehow that made him the scariest one of all.

"Nothing happened?" Julian said. "What? You walked into a door? Do you know how many times police officers hear that excuse?"

Double crappity crap crap.

Aggie had eased into the kitchen and worked her way around all the male bodies until she stood next to me. She took my hand—gently. That told me who had blabbed to Ilya and Cougar, but who had said what to Julian and Grimshaw that had them tearing up here right on the Others' heels?

Suddenly feeling tired and achy, I pulled out a kitchen chair and sat. Then I sighed. "I had a very weird, very scary dream, and when I tried to get away from the gauze-headed monster, I fell out of bed and scraped my head on the bedside table. It's embarrassing, and it's nothing to fuss about."

"You have a blackberry toe!" Aggie said, pointing at my left foot.

We all looked at my big toe, most of which was a solid purple-black.

"Huh. I thought that was a shadow." I hadn't turned on the bathroom light when I'd taken a shower, figuring the dim morning light was sufficient—and a lot less upsetting when I could look at my face and pretend I was seeing shadows and not bruises.

"You need to see a doctor," Grimshaw insisted.

"I agree," Ilya Sanguinati said.

"No." I was firm about that, despite my ribs starting to clamp around my lungs in response to male voices that were too loud to be safe. But I was firm until . . . *whomp.*

I'd always thought my thighs were chunky, but I couldn't see me under Cougar's paw. It was a big paw. And when he wrinkled his lips and showed me his teeth, I noticed that they were a perfect set of cat teeth—not a misplaced human tooth among them.

I should have been intimidated. Gods, I should have been terrified. Maybe I would have been if Cougar had growled at me. But he was one of the boys here at The Jumble, and while it wouldn't be smart to trust him not to mistake me for lunch if I was actively bleeding, the paw on my thigh felt oddly comforting, like it was his way of telling me it was safe to stop and think.

"All right. I'll go to the doctor's—but I don't want to ride in the police car." I sounded like a whiny six-year-old, but I didn't care. I'd had enough of riding in cop cars, and I could feel the anxiety attack starting again, just waiting for the final push.

Focused on my breathing in an effort to avoid the meltdown, I almost missed the significant looks between Grimshaw and Ilya Sanguinati.

"Fine," Grimshaw said. "Julian can drive you."

"Happy to," Julian said.

Ilya shook his head. "My car is on the way. I will escort Victoria to the doctor." He focused on Aggie for a moment. "But perhaps we can all meet up after the doctor's visit?"

"At the boardinghouse?" Julian suggested. "I can call Ineke and see if she can provide lunch."

"Can I say something?" I raised my hand halfway, which was childish or snarky. Hard to tell at that point.

"Of course," Grimshaw said smoothly as he removed a small notebook and pen from his shirt pocket. "You can describe your dream. Anything that frightened you that much could have relevance to the investigation."

I stared at him. "How? I'm not an Intuit or a blood prophet." I was pretty sure asking me to describe the dream was his way of getting back at me for being snarky, but now that he'd tossed that idea out there, I could see that they *all* wanted details. More embarrassed than ever, I grumbled, "It was just a silly dream. Have you seen any papier-mâché creatures in business suits running around Sproing?"

"The creature could be symbolic, since paper seems to be at the center of your current difficulties," Julian said, frowning. "And this dream might be trying to tell you that you understand more about what is going on than you realize."

I wanted to punch Julian for validating the dream, but I would have needed to push Cougar's paw off my leg in order to stand up, and I didn't think I'd succeed. So I described in excruciating detail—because three of the four males in the kitchen kept interrupting to ask for more details—the dream that had caused my various bumps and bruises when my sleeping body obeyed my fuzzy brain and tried to run away without having any clue about its current location.

Stupid body. Stupider brain for not posting a sign that said DREAM THREAT—PLEASE IGNORE.

Of course, even surrounded by guns and fangs, the image of the gauze-headed monster made me want to run, so maybe my various parts, while misguided, weren't all that stupid. After all, running away was a valid choice.

Which meant Julian might be right about my subconscious trying to tell me something important.

"The car is here," Ilya said.

"You need your purse?" Julian asked.

Of course I needed my purse. "I can get it."

"You sit." Julian disappeared, moving as if he were familiar with the main house and knew how to find my suite of rooms.

I was trying to think of how to tell two men who were so obviously trying not to look like they were wondering if Julian and I were friends or *friends* that I wouldn't consider thinking of Julian like that. He was human and he was my friend, not a romantic fantasy. The only thing thinking about *that* in real terms did for me since the divorce was produce anxiety attacks.

Julian returned with my purse. Ilya and Grimshaw made sure the doors were all locked while Julian escorted me to the Sanguinati car.

"Vicki, go and get checked out," Julian whispered as he opened the car's back door. "Seeing the doctor has little to do with you right now."

I studied his face, parsing out what he was trying to tell me when neither of us knew who or what was listening. And that was the point. An alarm had gone out, and while Ilya Sanguinati, Aggie, and Cougar may have been the only *terra indigene* visible in the kitchen, they weren't the only ones who had responded and now needed to be appeased.

Ilya joined me a minute later and we drove to the doctor's office. Someone had called ahead, warning Dr. Wallace that I was being brought in for unspecified injuries. The people in the waiting room looked surprised when I walked in with my attorney—and a few looked put out when we were immediately led to an exam room. But no one so much as muttered about special treatment.

There was tut-tutting from Dr. Wallace about the bruised toe and comments about me being lucky I didn't hit my eye, which I had figured out for myself. Otherwise, he didn't have much to say. The wound above my eye was minor and already healing. The area would be sore for a while, and I should be prepared for soreness and secondary bruises that would show up in another day or two. Goody.

He sounded more like a doctor assuring an anxious parent

that the child hadn't seriously damaged herself. I resented the tone but understood the reasoning. After all, Dr. Wallace wasn't really talking to *me*.

A few minutes later, we were back in the car and heading for the Xavier boardinghouse.

"You'll tell everyone that this happened because I had a bad dream, all right?"

Ilya gave me a curious look. "Does it matter?"

When we left the office, the women looked at my face and then looked away, some with sympathy and a couple with recognition. If humans made a mistaken assumption because it was true more often than not . . . "I don't want anyone to be blamed for something that was no one's fault."

A weighted silence. Then Ilya said, "I'll pass along the message."

CHAPTER 29

Grimshaw

Firesday, Juin 16

Grimshaw had never wanted to be an investigator. He didn't want a desk job or to expend energy on being nice to a small pool of citizens who would comment on or criticize the fact that he was not, and never would be, a people person who knew how to glad-hand and grease the wheel. He wanted to serve and protect. He wanted to be a cop. He accepted that being on highway patrol wasn't the way to move up the promotion ladder, but he had made that choice because he liked highway patrol. He liked helping people who needed help or apprehending people who broke the law—and he liked that he rarely had to see them again. But like it or not, he was now in league with the Sanguinati and wouldn't extricate himself from this place or problem anytime soon.

He wanted Ineke at this meeting but had enough political savvy and survival instinct to ask Ilya Sanguinati if that was all right. Getting the vampire's agreement, he and Ilya settled in the boardinghouse's parlor with Ineke and Vicki, all of them waiting for Julian to finish a phone call and join them.

Julian entered the parlor, holding a worn box that contained some kind of kids' game. He closed the door, set the box to one side, and looked at Grimshaw. "I have an answer to your question. You owe someone a favor."

"I'm good for it."

"I know."

"Perhaps we should begin with the dream so that Ms. Xavier can appreciate why we asked her to participate in this meeting," Ilya Sanguinati suggested.

Vicki DeVine looked a little pale, but that could have been her normal skin tone in contrast to the dark bruises above her left eye. Either way, Grimshaw pulled out his notebook and recounted the dream to spare Vicki from having to repeat it.

"Well, gods," Ineke said, taking Vicki's hand. "If I'd had a dream like that, I would have done my best to run away too."

Vicki wrinkled her face, then winced, telling all of them that even that much movement hurt. "Bed to floor. Not much room to run."

"I find it interesting that Victoria's dream included three other women," Ilya said.

"That struck me too," Julian said.

Grimshaw looked at the other men and blew out a breath. So he wasn't the only one who thought that was significant.

Vicki shook her head. "It's not a big thing. In thrillers, a lot more women are running from the bad thing. The men in those stories are more inclined to look for a pipe or a big stick to whack the bad thing than run away—especially when the men are a group of friends."

"But one or two still get mauled or slashed or eviscerated before the rest run away," Ineke said.

"True."

"Regardless of what happens in thrillers, I think Vicki unconsciously recognized that Ineke could also be a target and was in equal danger," Julian said with strained patience.

"From Mr. Paperhead." Vicki's tone was a swipe at Julian—something Grimshaw didn't appreciate but was willing to overlook since it could be defensive rather than intentionally hurtful.

"*Victoria.*" Ilya imbued that single word with disapproval. Didn't sound like *he* was willing to overlook the tone. "The shape of the monster that frightened you may be symbolic, but I think the paper head and the business suit are significant. You are embarrassed and are, therefore, trying to diminish the experience by snapping at Mr. Farrow and dismissing his opinion. You should not. Instead you should ask what you and Ms. Xavier have in common."

"They run their own businesses," Grimshaw said.

"Other women run businesses in Sproing," Ineke said. "Sheridan Ames owns the funeral home, and Helen Hearse runs Come and Get It."

"Necessary businesses in a community, but you two have the only properties that provide accommodations for visitors or short-term residents," Julian said. "The campers that are available to rent at the far end of the village are old and seedy, without running water. There are toilets and pay showers on the grounds, and a couple of pipes where you can fill your own jugs with potable water. I know because I considered renting one of those campers when I first relocated to Sproing and was looking for a temporary place to live."

"But you stayed here at the boardinghouse," Ineke said.

"You bet I did. Given a choice between a clean room with its own bathroom and a musty camper with access to public toilets and showers, it was an easy decision."

"I have three cabins that have been updated and nine that are serviceable if primitive, with the same kind of sanitary facilities as the camper area," Vicki said.

"You have rustic cabins on the lake," Julian countered. "You have a large main house with all kinds of extras for your lodgers, including shower facilities, kitchen privileges, and several common rooms where people can read or watch television or socialize. And you have a private beach that is equal in size to the public beach on the southern end of the lake." He leaned forward. "When it comes to desirable accommodations in Sproing or around Lake Silence, you two are the only game in town."

There was a look in Ineke's eyes that helped Grimshaw

remember the tattoos he'd seen yesterday morning—and wonder if he should mention them to Julian. Instead he asked, "Do you have a mortgage on this place?"

"No." Ineke said the word fiercely, but a moment later she looked uncertain. "Not a mortgage, but there are a couple of liens on the house and other buildings—money I borrowed for repairs and improvements."

"The bank holds the liens?"

"Yes." She aborted a glance at Ilya when she said it, which told Grimshaw that she wasn't paying a loan back to the bank and knew it.

"No," Ilya Sanguinati said. "The bank had a few cash-flow problems a few years ago due to . . . I believe humans refer to it as having one's hand in the till. Or maybe this was the creative bookkeeping that is mentioned in some crime stories." He moved his shoulders enough that the movement could be translated as a shrug. "Since the bank was privately owned, and since we saw advantages to preventing its collapse, Silence Lodge bought all of the bank's paper, including liens like the ones on Ms. Xavier's boardinghouse. We did not want to upset Sproing's human residents, so the Lake Silence Mortgage and Loan Company came into being and worked through the bank, an invisible but vital part of the bank's health—and the Sanguinati interested in the banking and investment business became the bank's officers, allowing the president to keep his title as the human figurehead in exchange for a modest salary. And, technically, he still owned the bank. One of his last independent acts was to hire the recently removed bank manager to run the bank. Since the man had the education and credentials for such a position, we did not object."

"Does the bank's president live here?" Grimshaw asked.

Ilya shook his head. "He relocated to Putney. My kin who are interested in banking informed me last evening that the recently removed bank manager had lived in Putney before coming to Sproing. That had not been significant until now, when too many humans from Putney are showing too much interest in The Jumble."

Putney was the human town on Prong Lake—and the Putney Police Station was home base for Detective Marmaduke Swinn and his team. Like Ilya said, the connection to Putney was a little too strong to be coincidence.

"I wonder if your figurehead president has a particular tie clip," Julian said.

Ilya smiled, showing a hint of fang. "An interesting thing to wonder. I can tell you that, one way or another, we are acquiring his remaining shares in the bank."

"One way or another?" Grimshaw asked.

"The house he purchased in Putney was far beyond his means, and has continued to be more than he could afford."

Vicki pointed at Ilya. "The Sanguinati hold the mortgage on his house?"

Ilya's smiled widened. "The first *and* the second mortgages. The documents he signed when we provided the second mortgage—for terms that were far more forgiving than the human moneylenders he had considered when he ran into financial trouble again—gave us an option of demanding immediate payment in full of all that he owed us. The papers were served the morning after Detective Swinn brought Miss Vicki to the station for a chat. The difference between what he owed us and the current worth of his shares in the bank was petty cash."

"So he had to choose between giving up what was left of the bank or losing his home in a way that would tell the rest of his creditors that he's bankrupt," Julian said. "One is a silent transaction up here, and the other would be public humiliation—worse if you make it obvious who is evicting him and his family."

"The bank will close at its usual time today. It will reopen sometime next week as Lake Silence Bank." Ilya looked at Ineke and Vicki. "We will, of course, retain any of the human employees who want to continue working for the bank. The honest ones, anyway."

And the people in Sproing could do business with the Sanguinati knowingly or drive to Bristol or Crystalton, which were the closest human communities. That meant they would have to choose between holding their receipts until morning and then driving along those two-lane roads in the wild country to reach another human town to make their deposits, or keeping money in the store's safe and hoping they wouldn't be robbed.

Grimshaw almost felt sorry for his own people, but the Sanguinati would have learned cutthroat business practices by observing humans—or having been burned themselves because they had believed the humans would deal with them honestly.

"What's that got to do with Vicki's dream and my boardinghouse?" Ineke demanded.

"Someone who thinks he can force Ms. DeVine out of The Jumble might also think he can buy the liens from the bank and call them in, forcing you to sell or forfeit this place when you can't pay the debt," Grimshaw said.

"I don't think Yorick has the business savvy to plan this kind of hostile takeover," Vicki said.

Julian looked at Grimshaw. "Which brings us to the phone call and the answer to a question." He looked at each of them. "I contacted Steve Ferryman. He's the mayor of Ferryman's Landing, which is an Intuit village on Great Island. He knows some . . . people . . . in Lakeside."

"The Sanguinati at Silence Lodge know about the sweet blood who lives in the Lakeside Courtyard," Ilya said quietly.

"Do they?" Grimshaw asked just as quietly. What did "sweet blood" mean to a vampire?

"She has friends among the Sanguinati who live in that Courtyard—and we are all entertained by stories about Broomstick Girl." The vampire's smiled sharpened. "What did she say?"

"I e-mailed a picture of the tie clip to Steve and briefly explained what was happening in Sproing," Julian said. "The question that was sent to Lakeside was this: besides this tie clip, what do detectives working in Putney, a bank manager in Sproing, and a businessman living in Hubb NE have in common?"

"And the answer?" Grimshaw asked.

"Schools and . . ." Julian retrieved the box and set it on the table in front of the sofa. "Somehow this is part of the answer. Big wheels and little wheels."

Judging by the picture on the cover, the box held sticks and wheels that children could put together to form different shapes.

"Is this the literal answer or a symbolic one?" Vicki asked.

"Difficult to say," Julian replied. "I don't know exactly how blood prophets see the future."

"But you didn't ask about the future."

"No, but the girl who answered the question is working with a prototype deck of prophecy cards, which is making it possible to ask questions that aren't specifically about the future. However, I was warned that this is a new skill that is still being learned, and the answer depends as much on the person interpreting the information as on the person who is guided to selecting particular images."

"May I . . . ?" Vicki waved a hand at the box.

Julian shrugged. "Go ahead."

Vicki opened the box and smiled. "I had a set of these when I was a child. I loved playing with them, putting the sticks and wheels into all kinds of odd shapes or structures. My mother disapproved because I built shelters for my little stuffed animals instead of building a proper home for the dollies I didn't want to play with."

"Why didn't you want to play with them?" Ilya asked.

"Dollies are creepy," Vicki and Ineke said. They shuddered. Then they began taking pieces out of the box.

Grimshaw looked at Ilya Sanguinati, who was looking at the women as if he'd just discovered a hitherto-unknown predator and wasn't sure what to think about that. Well, Grimshaw knew what to think about it. He was certain he could subdue Vicki DeVine if he had to. After all, she was short and plump and didn't have the kind of muscle mass that indicated that she routinely worked out. Ineke, on the other hand, advertised that she buried trouble—and he still wasn't sure if that was figurative or literal.

It made him glad he was the only person in the room carrying a real gun.

Vicki cocked her head. She set three small wheels on the table, equally spaced, then waited for Ineke to connect the wheels with short colored sticks before she pointed to each one in turn. "The first dead man. Detective Swinn and his team. The bank manager." She placed a larger wheel below those three. "The bank president now living in Putney." She placed another large wheel up and away from the others. "Yorick up in Hubb NE."

"Big wheels and little wheels," Grimshaw said as Ineke attached long colored sticks to the wheel representing Vicki's ex-husband, connecting him to the three small wheels and the bank president's wheel.

"Social status," Ineke said before Vicki could respond. "Odds are better that the businessman and bank president would move in the same social circles—circles that would not include minions like detectives and employees." She smiled at him. "No offense."

"None taken," Grimshaw replied. "The blood prophet had said 'schools.' Ms. DeVine, where did your ex-husband go to school?"

"Yorick's family has lived in Hubb NE for generations," Vicki replied. "He went to Smythe and Blake, the private college in the city."

"It may be a private college where the future movers and shakers are sent to learn how to take over the family businesses, but land constriction made it necessary to share some things with the University of Hubb NE as well as the technical college and the police academy located in that city," Julian said.

"Like the athletic fields and some of the general-use buildings," Grimshaw said. "I remember how, at the dances, there would be four distinct groups holding their own piece of the room, and may the gods help anyone who dared to cross into another territory to ask a girl for a dance."

Julian tapped one of the connected wheels. "But there

were clubs and societies that crossed those lines. I never paid attention to them because I wasn't interested in joining."

No, Grimshaw thought, Julian wouldn't have joined a club. That would have been an additional risk of someone figuring out what he was. "So what are we saying? That a secret club has been working out of the schools around Hubbney, recruiting members?"

"Probably working out of the private college and spreading out from there," Julian said. "Think of the announcements on the bulletin board at the academy. Clubs like the chess club and drama club were obvious, but some groups had names that sounded so dumb you couldn't figure out why anyone would want to join."

Like a group that claimed to be interested in tie clips? Had they been operating when he and Julian had been at the academy? Must have been, but he hadn't noticed. "Hiding in plain sight."

Julian nodded. "And promising that all the members would benefit from a helping hand. So a man comes to The Jumble to pressure Vicki to give up the property. When he is killed, someone alerts Swinn so that he makes sure he takes the case and can try to apply a different kind of pressure, along with the bank manager removing any paperwork that would prove Vicki's claim that she was the rightful owner of the property."

"Even if there is a conspiracy to take The Jumble, the terms of the original agreement are clear," Vicki protested. "As far as having access to the land that makes up The Jumble, humans keep it as it is, which is some cultivated land and limited dwellings and outbuildings. If they don't, the deal is off and the whole thing is reclaimed by the *terra indigene*. That's the biggest reason Yorick pawned it off on me—he knew there wasn't any commercial use for the land. Why would he try to get it back?"

"Maybe someone else thinks there is a loophole that will allow a developer to come in and build a resort or private community on the lake," Ineke said.

Ilya brushed a few dog hairs off his trousers. "Being

aware that your ex-husband had claim to some potentially lucrative land, perhaps other members of his pack put together a plan that would make them money and didn't realize that Yorick no longer held the paper for The Jumble. If they didn't want to walk away from the deal, they might pressure him to reacquire The Jumble."

"How much information would this cabal have about The Jumble?" Grimshaw asked. "By now, they have to know that people were killed there. Why try a land grab and tangle with the *terra indigene*? I would have thought last summer would be a sufficient lesson in how well that works."

"It's been our observation that humans often willfully believe that they can repeat the actions of those who went before them and not suffer the same consequences," Ilya said.

"But none of this is aimed at the Others," Ineke protested. "It's all aimed at Vicki, as if this was strictly a human-against-human conflict and all they have to do is get her out of the way."

"Maybe this group has people in government who have promised to find a loophole in the agreement or have the original agreement contested in court and thrown out," Grimshaw said.

"There are no loopholes," Ilya said. "And contesting it in a human court would not change the *terra indigene*'s response to invaders."

Grimshaw had expected that answer. Didn't mean he liked it.

Julian crouched near the table and tapped one of the wheels as he looked at Vicki. "What it comes down to is your ex-husband could be just a cog in this deal, and whoever is behind it is a much bigger wheel and is going to come after you again."

CHAPTER 30

Ilya

Firesday, Juin 16

"I have something to show you," Natasha said the moment Ilya returned to the lodge. "Aggie Crowgard brought it over after you left to take Miss Vicki to the doctor."

Ilya took the envelope and studied the former bank manager's name. "We already suspected him of having one of the tie clips and being involved in the threats to Victoria."

"Aggie thought it was important because it had shiny gold ink." Natasha smiled, showing a hint of fang. "She mentioned a couple of times that the police might be interested in a shiny envelope and that *they* sometimes exchanged one shiny for another."

"Not a precedent I want to follow, and one Officer Grimshaw may come to regret," Ilya murmured as he considered the return address. "TCC, with a Hubb NE address. Tie Clip Club?" That would fit in with Grimshaw's and Farrow's thinking that the group had a name that would be overlooked by most of the humans attending the schools in Hubbney.

"Would an enemy be that bold to display the location of where they can be found?" Natasha asked.

"Organizations send information to members all the time.

Nothing unusual about that. Nothing suspicious. All out in the open. Except the part that is hidden."

"If these humans have dug in to three locations in the Northeast Region, they could have their claws in many more."

Ilya nodded. In human-controlled cities, there were Courtyards—a separate place within the city that was the territory of the *terra indigene* who kept watch over the humans and made sure they honored their agreements. Because Hubb NE was the seat of government for the Northeast Region, the Courtyard there had a strong gathering of Sanguinati. It was possible they already knew about these tie clip humans but had not interfered because the humans had interacted only with other humans. With this gambit against Victoria DeVine, the tie clip humans had crossed a line and were now dealing with the *terra indigene* whether they knew it or not.

"What are you going to do?" Natasha asked.

Ilya tapped the return address on the envelope and smiled. "I'm going to ask the Sanguinati in Hubbney for any information they might have about these humans."

He went into the office at the lodge, turned on the computer, and composed the e-mail he would send to the Sanguinati in Hubb NE. Then his hand hovered over the SEND button.

Human-controlled cities were watched by a collective of *terra indigene* living in a Courtyard. Here the humans had been watched by the residents of Silence Lodge. They had been a shadow that touched Sproing and Crystalton. But despite their fiercely human-centric educations, their training in how to speak and how to dress—even what vehicles to purchase— they had been isolated. And not just from the humans in Sproing who had thought they were mysterious, rich city dwellers slumming in the wild country. Their ability to be urban predators also had kept them apart from the rest of the *terra indigene* who lived around Lake Silence and the northern half of Crystal Lake. Even the ones who had some interest in human things were wary of the sleek beings who dressed in black and exuded a blended threat of human and Other.

Then things had changed in the Courtyard at Lakeside. Interesting things that had altered passive watching to interacting. And things changed even more because of the war between the Others and humans, followed by the Great Predation. New humans had arrived in Sproing—and a caretaker had arrived to restore The Jumble. Various forms of *terra indigene* wanted some knowledge of human things without too much human contact. More a Simple Life than city kind of knowledge.

It could happen now. *Was* happening now. And, he admitted to himself, he was no longer bored with his important assignment of being the leader of Silence Lodge.

Ilya sat back, the message still waiting to be sent. Last year he had envied Vladimir and the rest of the Sanguinati living in the Lakeside Courtyard. They had been at the center of events that had rippled through the whole of Thaisia. Did he want the Tie Clip Club to be a serious threat because he wanted to be at the center of a new event that might create another, if significantly smaller, ripple? Was he already thinking too much like a human, wanting a problem to solve in order to garner attention and praise from the most powerful among the Sanguinati?

Did it matter? Someone was trying to force Victoria to leave The Jumble. Until she was safe and her position was secure again, even an innocuous-sounding organization could be an enemy.

Ilya sent the e-mail to the Sanguinati in Hubb NE. Then he sent an e-mail to the leader of the Sanguinati in Lakeside— a progress report on the status of The Jumble and his interactions with the caretaker.

CHAPTER 31

Vicki

Moonsday, Juin 19

Julian Farrow looked at my face and winced. I thought having the deep purple bruising above my eyebrow looked bad enough, but when the secondary bruises showed up yesterday, coloring the whole eye area, I decided purple wasn't a bad look in comparison.

Two middle-aged women were browsing the shelves of used romances. In such a small community, you would think I would know everyone, at least by sight, but I didn't know these two women beyond type—they were Sproing's country club set, if Sproing was a place that could afford to build a country club for the handful of families that were too important to rub elbows with the rest of us. These were the women who wouldn't think of going into Come and Get It for lunch or to the local clothing store unless they wanted everyone to know they were slumming. They were the kind who made a seasonal trip to Hubbney or Toland for a clothes-buying spree, which impressed no one except themselves.

My ex-mother-in-law had been like them, smiling and keeping her voice devastatingly pleasant while she listed my inadequacies and all the reasons Yorick could have done better if he'd thought with his head instead of letting his loins respond to a moment's temptation, which was the only reason I had ensnared him into marriage. The fact that he didn't have access to any of the family money when we got married and needed someone to help support him while he "grew into his potential" meant none of the posh girls would have been of any use to him since they, too, needed someone to support them while they grew into *their* potential.

At a party for our fifth anniversary, one of his friends asked him why he was holding on to his starter wife now that he was established. When Yorick just laughed, that should have told me something, but by then I believed him when he told me that no one else would want to screw, let alone marry, someone who looked dumpy even in the most expensive dress, and I was lucky that he still wanted to stay with me.

"Should expect something like that to happen when you live around brutes."

I don't know which woman said it, but I felt the punch behind the words. Easier to blame the woman for the black eye until it's your eye. Then I saw the look on Julian's face as he turned toward the women, and I leaped to stop him from doing or saying something he would regret.

"What do you think?" I said loudly, moving into his line of sight. "I'm trying it out for a friend who does stage makeup. The color is called Bruise Yellow."

Julian studied me. Did he understand what I was trying to do? Would he play along?

"It looks real," he said after a moment. "But why only do one eye?"

"To make it look realistic."

He nodded as if that made sense.

A muttered remark from one of the women. I didn't catch it, but that look filled Julian's face again—a look that made me think he'd been other things in his life besides an amiable bookstore owner.

"You know what else my friend told me?" I asked Julian, once more pulling him away from a potential confrontation.

"What?"

"That there is a shade of red lipstick favored by women of mature years that has a special, very secret ingredient. Know what it is?"

"What?" he said again.

"Bull urine."

He blinked. The women, who had their backs to us, gasped.

"What?" Julian said for the third time, making me wonder if something was wrong with him. He usually wasn't so limited in his vocabulary.

"Bull urine. It's the ingredient that adds that hint of yellow under the red. So instead of asking someone if he would kiss his mother with that mouth after he uses really bad swearwords, you should be asking if he'd want to be kissed by someone wearing that shade of red lipstick." I looked at the two women and gave them a Sproinger happy face.

They stared at me as if I'd suddenly grown fangs. Which made me wonder if there were any of those costume shops left where you could buy things like fake teeth for Trickster Night. Might be fun to greet the Proud and the Huffy with a fanged happy face. But I wouldn't want to insult my attorney, whose fangs were anything but fake.

One of the women lifted the books she had selected to make sure we were watching. Then she dropped them on the floor and sniffed at Julian. "If you're going to let riffraff into your establishment, we'll take our business elsewhere."

"Do that," Julian snapped. "And just so there are no misunderstandings in the future, if you do decide to purchase books here, I won't accept any used books from you in exchange. The last time you brought books in, one had been dropped in dirty water and the other two smelled like cat piss. Any books you buy here from now on, you pay the going price."

"Well!" the first woman huffed.

"I'm going to report you!" the other snipped.

"To whom? I own the place," Julian said.

The second woman hesitated, then dropped her stack of

used books on the floor in a show of solidarity. The first woman kicked a book out of her way as she marched to the door and out, her friend trailing behind her.

Julian came out from behind the island counter and began to pick up the books the women had dropped. When I took a step to help him, he snapped, "Don't." Then, more softly, "Bitches."

Since I didn't think any business in Sproing could afford to lose customers, I felt badly for him—and felt guilty because my coming into the store had contributed to his trouble with some of his customers.

I watched the women cross the street. "They're going to the police station." I turned and looked at him. "They're going to report you to the police?"

Julian had been checking the books for damage. He glanced toward the police station and sighed. "Gods, I hope Wayne isn't in the station right now. This is the kind of bullshit that makes him crazy and is the reason he chose highway patrol in the first place."

I didn't feel all warm and fuzzy thinking about a large man with a gun going crazy. Then again, I woke up that morning with a Panther-shaped Cougar standing next to my bed, staring at me as if trying to decide if I was still alive and was going to get up and make breakfast or had died and could now *be* breakfast. Since it looked like this was going to be my new normal, I might not be using the straightest ruler when it came to measuring crazy.

I went into the back half of the store, where the new books were shelved. Julian had a small display next to the island counter that held the newest releases, but the rest of the new books were back here. It seemed like a less-than-stellar business plan, having the more profitable part of your stock where it wasn't easily visible, but the used books really were more like a lending library than a store.

Maybe Julian should make up a membership card and charge a modest annual fee that allowed people to do the buy and swap of used books like they did now, and people who didn't pay the fee could just buy the used books.

I'd float the idea past Ineke first and see what she thought. In the meantime, I gave in to the need for some kind of treat to take away the sting of the woman's words and my guilt over hurting Julian's business. I browsed the shelves, picking up another thriller by Alan Wolfgard as well as a mystery by an author I hadn't read before. According to her bio, she lived in the Finger Lakes area in a village I'd never heard of.

Looking at the *terra indigene* names on the covers of some of the books, I realized why Julian kept the new stock in the back half of the store. Sure, he carried the books by human authors that could be found in any bookstore in human-controlled towns, but he also had books by authors who would be unknown in cities like Hubbney or Toland— authors he kept in stock for a clientele that wasn't human.

I selected a few thrillers and mysteries, then perused the romance shelves, finally choosing one about a ship's captain and a female stowaway who faced danger on the high seas— the biggest danger being the Sea itself. The capital *S* was the only hint that the captain and his stowaway might be squaring off with an Elemental, so of course I had to buy it.

I brought my selections to the counter. Julian looked at the stack and sighed.

"You don't have to buy more than you want in an effort to support the store," he said. "Those women did nothing for my bottom line."

"I like to read." It wasn't a snappy or clever reply, but it was the truth.

Julian rang up my purchases and deducted the total from my revolving line of credit. Me buying books on credit didn't help his bottom line either, but I would pay him. Eventually.

He put the books in a cloth Lettuce Reed bag and held it out. I took the bag but hesitated to leave the store.

"Does the eye really look that bad?" I asked.

"Compared to what?"

Now I sighed. I'd planned to stop at the general store to pick up a few things since I wasn't feeling up to driving to a grocery store in Crystalton or Bristol for a full load of victuals. Besides, Pops Davies carried all the basics, and he bought the food fresh from local farmers, and that included the milk, cheese, and ice cream. What more did I need? Well, I needed big sunglasses that hid half my face so I wouldn't have to answer the "What happened to you?" question at every store I entered.

When I asked Ilya Sanguinati to spread the word about how I got hurt, he knew I wasn't thinking about the humans in Sproing, but maybe I should let certain people know. Problem was, I really didn't want to tell humans I had a black eye because I had a nightmare and fell out of bed.

While I considered if I really needed milk and fruit, Detective Swinn slammed into the store, looking triumphant. Officer Osgood trailed behind him, looking worried. Looking scared.

"You're coming with me, Farrow," Swinn said.

"Why?" Julian asked calmly.

"To answer the charges of abusive language and threats of bodily harm."

"Come again?"

"Are you resisting?" Swinn's expression made it clear he really wanted the smallest indication of resistance.

"I'm asking for clarification."

"Two women made a complaint about you," Osgood said.

"You mean the two women who marched over to the police station after insulting another customer and damaging some of my stock?" Julian asked so pleasantly I knew he was furious. "The two women who come in at least once a week to complain that I don't carry their preferred authors? I do carry those authors, by the way, but the women would have to buy new copies of the books because I don't have those titles as used books. Are we talking about the two women who come in and complain about what I charge for used books, saying they can get them cheaper in Bristol? The two women who bring in damaged books that I can't possibly use and expect to be given full credit toward their next selection? Are those the women who made the complaint?"

"Julian didn't say anything objectionable," I said.

"No one asked you, missy," Swinn snapped. Then he

studied my face and smiled. "That's a good look for you. Fireplug."

Julian almost leaped over the counter, but Osgood said loudly, "Something is going on at the bank."

Swinn had been pushing for it, hoping Julian would react. I silently thanked Osgood for the diversion. Then I looked out the bookstore's big front window and realized it wasn't a diversion. A mob of people crowded the sidewalk in front of the bank and no one was getting inside.

Of course. The Sanguinati had closed the bank after the end of business on Firesday. It looked like it was still closed, which was not a good way to start the workweek. I wondered if anyone had thought to put a sign on the door to let people know the bank *would* reopen.

"Looks like the bank is closed today." Julian took a step back from the counter as he regained control of himself. "You might want to go over and assist with crowd control."

"Not my job," Swinn said.

"Neither is following up on a ludicrous complaint, but you're here."

Marmaduke Swinn locked eyes with Julian Farrow.

"The bank's president sold out to save himself," Julian said quietly. "He and the bank manager are off the game board. So is Franklin Cartwright. So are Chesnik, Baker, and Calhoun. Are you and Reynolds also pawns in someone's scheme? What is the price of loyalty?"

The hatred that filled Swinn's eyes was totally out of proportion to Julian's words—unless Swinn really was a pawn in someone's scheme.

"Someone should have put a bullet in your brain years ago," Swinn snarled.

I froze, shocked. Osgood looked equally shocked. Maybe more so because Swinn had been his commanding officer a few days ago.

"Better men than you have tried, and I'm still here," Julian replied.

"Your luck won't hold forever."

"Maybe not. But I have allies too, and I'll let them know

that if something happens to me, you should be the first person they check out."

"That's enough," Grimshaw said.

I don't know how long he'd been standing just inside the door. I didn't see him come in, didn't know how much he'd heard.

"Officer Osgood, go over to the bank and start dispersing the crowd. I've been informed that the bank will reopen tomorrow under new management. People should bring in proof of their checking and savings accounts. Every account with confirmed paperwork will be honored. Pass the message."

"Yes, sir." Osgood fled.

"Detective Swinn," Grimshaw continued. "This isn't your territory. You came in to investigate a man's death. It has been determined that no human agent was involved in his death, so the case is closed."

"Just because a human didn't kill him doesn't mean a human wasn't involved." Swinn looked at me when he said it.

"The investigation is done."

"It's done when I say it's done."

Grimshaw took a step toward Swinn. "It's done when your captain says it's done. He called you this morning, telling you to return to Putney. You and Reynolds. I know because your captain called mine to request that any follow-up be handled through the Bristol station."

Swinn's face turned an unhealthy shade of red. "This isn't over." He laced the words with venom.

"Unfortunately, you're right about that." Grimshaw stepped aside, giving Swinn a clear path to the door. He watched Swinn until the other man pushed through the crowd still milling around the bank and got into the unmarked car. Then he looked at Julian. "We need to talk."

Julian hesitated. "You know where I live."

Now Grimshaw focused on me. "Do you feel all right?"

"My face is sore. Otherwise, I think I look worse than I feel."

"That's good."

I guess that was his way of telling me I really didn't want to visit any more stores until the bruises faded.

"Call Pops with an order and ask him to drop it off at the boardinghouse," Julian said.

"Why there?" I asked. Although getting a snack at the boardinghouse had a lot of appeal. And I could give Ineke the gossip firsthand. Between the showdown at the bookstore and the run on the bank there was a lot to talk about. "Scratch that question. Dropping off an order at Ineke's would save Pops some time and gasoline."

Julian's smile didn't reach his eyes. "Exactly."

Grimshaw walked me to my car. "They shouldn't bother you, but if Swinn or Reynolds shows up at The Jumble—or anywhere else—I want to know about it. Understood?"

"Did Swinn mean what he said about Julian?"

Grimshaw opened my car door and didn't reply.

CHAPTER 32

Grimshaw

Moonsday, Juin 19

Grimshaw found the Mill Creek Cabins easily enough. They were larger than he'd expected, with either a loft or an attic space above the ground floor. A covered porch ran across the front of each cabin, and low stone walls enclosed front yards that weren't any wider than their respective cabins.

Julian lived in the last of the six cabins, the one farthest away from the main road. Grimshaw parked next to his friend's car, picked up the insulated box, and came around to the wooden gate in the wall, studying the raised gardens that hugged the stone walls on three sides.

"You raising flowers and vegetables now?" Grimshaw asked.

"Thought I would give it a try." Julian held up a bottle of beer. "There are more cold ones in the fridge, unless you're out of uniform but still on duty."

Grimshaw wasn't sure he was ever off duty anymore, but he had changed to summer-weight trousers and a pullover shirt as a way to indicate this wasn't an official call. But he didn't think the conversation was going to be easy either. He held up the insulated box. "Dinner, compliments of Ineke."

"That's a fair trade."

Grimshaw went inside. An open floor plan for the most part. Pocket doors to provide privacy for the bedroom and bathroom. Stairs on one side of the main room, going up to the loft area that might be considered a guest room or home office. A fan on the ceiling. He wondered if the fireplace provided the sole source of heat. That would explain the open floor plan.

He put the food in the fridge, took out a beer. The bottle opener was on the counter, so there was no reason to look through drawers. Going back out, he settled in the other chair on the porch and decided to circle around what they needed to discuss.

"Did you know Ineke has tattoos?" he asked.

The beer bottle hovered near Julian's lips before he lowered his hand. "Ineke? Where?"

"Her thighs. She was wearing a bathing suit. The tats were hard to miss." He described the tattoos.

"Gods," Julian said. "I used to rent a room from her."

"I *am* renting a room from her." He studied Julian. "What?"

"It's nothing."

"With you it's never nothing. Spit it out."

"Just . . . the Xaviers are a bit possessive about their compost bins. Have you noticed that?"

"Can't say I have. Why did you?"

"I offered to turn over the compost while I was there and was politely told to keep my hands off."

"Maybe they have a system." Or a convenient place to dispose of inconvenient bodies?

Nah.

Then again, a lot of people disappeared during the troubles last year. One more might be noticed but the disappearance wouldn't draw a lot of attention.

Grimshaw stared at Julian, who looked way too innocent, and realized he'd been played. "Bastard."

"You started it. *I* never saw those tattoos."

They sat quietly, enjoying shade and a cold beer on a hot summer evening.

"I heard what Swinn said to you," Grimshaw said quietly.

"By tomorrow morning all of Sproing will have heard some version of it," Julian replied. "The community doesn't need a newspaper. If you want the latest news, go to the diner. Helen can tell you everything from how the Sproing bowling team did in the Bristol bowling tournament to who slept on the couch after an argument—and what the argument was about."

"Good to know, but I seem to have my own gossip magnet—at least until Osgood is reassigned."

"You heard what Swinn said to me," Julian said. "And I heard what you said to him. He's really off the case?"

Grimshaw nodded. "Investigation is done. One of the Others killed Franklin Cartwright. There's no question about that."

"But Swinn still has Vicki DeVine in the crosshairs."

"Yeah. And that only makes sense if someone besides his boss is encouraging him to pursue this and find some way to push her out of The Jumble."

"There's one surefire permanent way to do that."

Grimshaw stared at the flowers in the raised beds. "You're talking about a cop. You're talking about premeditated murder."

"Was Swinn promised enough of a payoff from this scheme to make that worth a serious thought?" Julian countered. "Not likely. He's part of the muscle, not the money."

"But he would get something from the deal. They would all get something." Grimshaw waited a beat. "Where have you been since that night in the alley?"

"I haven't been a spy for the police force or the government if that's what you're asking."

"I didn't have the impression the allies you mentioned belonged to either group."

Julian huffed out a breath. "I wasn't doing anything illegal or immoral. That's all you need to know."

No, that wasn't all. "Why are you here? Why Sproing? Why a bookstore?"

Julian shot out of the chair and went inside. He returned a minute later with two more bottles of beer. One he set beside Grimshaw's chair. The other he kept, drinking deep as he leaned against one of the porch's supports.

"I don't know why one of the *terra indigene* followed me that night or why it killed the men who wanted to hurt me—or let's be honest, kill me. But I've stayed away from human-controlled towns since I received that settlement and left the force. I've moved around. A lot. A place would feel all right when I first arrived and found work and a place to live. But something would sour in a few months, sometimes even in a few weeks. I didn't fit in, not long-term, not even in Intuit villages. I put my hand to a lot of work during those years; even taught at a *terra indigene* school for a while. Because of that, I would get a call every so often to help with a problem. Investigate something or someone. Check out a place and report what I sensed."

"What happened?" Grimshaw asked when Julian stopped talking.

"I got tired of wandering. I wanted to put down roots. I was on my way to Ravendell on Senneca Lake. I have family there. Sproing was supposed to be a stopover, but I saw the For Sale sign in the bookstore window, and it felt right. Like everywhere else, the community was experiencing an upheaval, with people leaving one way or another. And new people were coming in—Simple Life folk and Intuits. A fresh start. A little pocket of ordinary within the wild country."

"Not so ordinary since the place contains hoppy things that hit up store owners for carrots," Grimshaw said.

"I didn't know about the Sproingers until after I bought the store." Julian resumed his seat. "In a way, the bookstore is a kind of payoff for services rendered."

"How so?"

"The store changed hands during the time I was inquiring about its availability. The owner's heirs received their full asking price, and the deal went through fast, even for a cash transaction. I know that because I checked. But the business was still for sale, and I paid about a third of what it's worth when you take the building and the stock into account."

"Silence Lodge?"

Julian nodded. "Someone gave the orders to set the price within a range I could afford. Just like my rent for this cabin is almost too reasonable."

"The Sanguinati—or some kind of *terra indigene*—want you here. Any idea why?"

"No. Except . . . Gershwin Jones is another Intuit who settled here within the past few months. Grace Notes should have closed within a month of opening. A music store in a place this small? But the building, which includes the apartment above the store, was offered at a rent that he wouldn't have found anywhere else in the Northeast." Julian sipped his beer for a minute. "The Dane family wasn't liked around here. The families who live on High Street aren't much liked either."

"I drove around to get acquainted with the streets and noticed half the houses on that street are empty, and not all the unoccupied ones have For Sale signs on the lawn."

"According to the gossip at the diner, some families fled but are intending to return. Other homeowners died last summer when the *terra indigene* tore through human places."

Grimshaw nodded. "So those who are left are still trying to reestablish their superiority and are discovering they don't have enough social weight to carry it off." He waited a beat. "Do you think the Sanguinati are seeding the community to create a new dynamic?"

"They're the form of *terra indigene* that often acts as the front man for more . . . disturbing . . . forms, so my sense is that restoring The Jumble to its original purpose has been something they've wanted but didn't quite know how to manage because they didn't want the Dane family to come back to Sproing. Then Vicki DeVine showed up with the deed and a need to make a go of the place. Right person, right time."

"Openly running the bank is also a declaration: work with us or leave."

Julian pushed out of the chair. "Let's get something to eat."

Grimshaw stood and stretched, his eyes scanning the land around the cabin.

"After what Swinn said about a bullet in the brain, are you looking for a shooter's sweet spot?" Julian asked.

"Yeah. I am." Grimshaw looked at his friend. "But you've already thought of that."

"I have. I've also thought about why Swinn hates me when we've never met. I've wondered what he had hoped to gain by trying to bring me in for questioning over accusations made by women who had caused the trouble in the first place—especially when he didn't have any authority to bring me in for questioning since Sproing has an official, if temporary, police force."

"And I'm wondering about that night in the alley and what kind of tie clip the men who went after you wore."

CHAPTER 33

Vicki

Sunday, Juin 20

My hair was long, golden brown, and straight except for a slight curl at the ends. That should have been my first clue. The filmy nightgown that was slipping off my nicely defined shoulders and pushed up to my slender thighs should have been the second. But the man held my attention, making my heart pound as he approached the bed. He wore skin-tight black pants and an open-to-the-waist white shirt with big sleeves. His smile was assured, almost smug.

"There's nowhere to run, so you're going to do as you're told," he said. He sounded like Yorick—had Yorick's voice, anyway, although Yorick never sounded that sexy except when he was having an affair and wanted me to know what he *could* be like with someone else.

Oh yeah? I thought, feeling defiant and scared. *I got away before and I can do it again.*

"First lesson." He held up gold nipple clamps connected by a chain, but the clamps were the size of the thingies mechanics connected to batteries to jump-start cars.

His face morphed into someone who looked like Grimshaw's nastier brother. That only lasted for a moment. As he leaned over me, smiling because I couldn't seem to move enough to get out of reach, his hair darkened, and the face, now lean and sculpted, had a thin scar beneath the left cheekbone. Then the gray eyes changed to melted-chocolate brown as he settled the clamps over my big toes and said . . .

"Caw?"

I snapped awake. My left arm had gotten tangled in the top sheet, securing me to the bed, creating the sensation of not being able to move.

Jingle, jingle.

I lifted my head off the pillow and looked at the Crow perched on my big toes. The charm bracelet around its neck jingled as it wibble-wobbled on my toes, its nails digging in as it tried to maintain its balance.

"Aggie?"

"Caw."

Freeing myself from the sheet, I rubbed my hands over my face—and then whimpered because the area around my left eye was still living in the Land of Ow.

"Could you get off my toes? I need to use the bathroom."

Aggie hopped to the mattress. A jingle Crow is not a stealthy Crow. Then again, since she had access to purchased food and whatever was growing wild in the kitchen gardens that I hadn't had a chance to restore, maybe her meals didn't require any more stealth than mine did.

I wobbled my way to the bathroom. I had a low-grade headache and my stomach felt a little swoopy. Those might be symptoms of setting off the *ow* around my eye, but it was also my body's typical response when the weather turned so humid it felt like I was breathing water.

That thought froze my brain for a moment. I turned on the bathroom lights and studied my neck carefully to make sure I hadn't acquired gills overnight. Of course, I hadn't eaten the strange food that was the only sustenance given to the plucky woman who had been abducted by the mysterious pirate who was taking her to his secret island.

I carefully splashed cold water on my face and checked

my neck again. Still gill free. I made a note to myself that, for the next few days anyway, I should read a milder form of romance before bedtime.

I returned to my bedroom to find Aggie exploring my jewelry box. I didn't have much that wasn't costume jewelry, and even the nicer pendants hadn't been worn in a while because the chains had knotted sometime during my move to an apartment in Hubbney when Yorick and I first separated and then to The Jumble, and I couldn't seem to untangle them.

Apparently a Crow's beak could do what human fingers couldn't. Aggie had worked out the knots on four of the necklaces and had laid them out on the dresser.

"Thanks." Maybe Pops Davies would have a jewelry box that would allow me to hang up some of these pieces. Just because I hadn't noticed something like that at the general store didn't mean Pops didn't carry it.

Barely awake and I was already tired and crabby and achy. The to-do list never seemed to get shorter, and if I didn't get into a routine to handle the day-to-day I would never be able to handle having more than one lodger and provide them with amenities in the main house, to say nothing of providing some kind of cleaning service in the cabins.

But I didn't have any other lodgers besides Aggie. I didn't count Conan and Cougar because they weren't paying me anything to use the primitive cabins. Of course, I wasn't paying them for whatever they were doing around The Jumble as a trade for the lodgings.

Maybe I should ask what they were doing besides blocking the access road so that people couldn't just drive up to the main house. Cougar had been around every morning to watch me breathe and decide if I was still alive or now qualified as a snack, but I hadn't seen Conan except for the story-time evenings. The Bear showed up then in human form, but I had the impression that was the only time he wasn't seriously furry.

Tired of working, tired of worrying, tired of thinking about why someone who might or might not be Yorick wanted The Jumble enough to cause so much trouble, I grabbed my bathing suit and went into the bathroom to change. Sure, Aggie was a girl, and she was so engrossed in discovering what else might be tangled in my jewelry box it wasn't likely she would even notice if I changed out of my nightie, but I had a full load of body image issues, so being seen by someone else did matter to me.

I put on the bathing suit, a little surprised that it fit a wee bit better than it had a couple of weeks ago. Pulling on a beach cover-up, I returned to the bedroom and found my sandals next to the bed. I studied the golden-haired pirate on the cover of the romance novel I'd been reading last night. Yep. Could have been Grimshaw's less trustworthy brother.

So not something I was going to mention to the large police officer who had a gun and handcuffs and already thought I was a pain in his ass. Teasing Grimshaw would be like rolling up a newspaper and whacking Cougar over the head. I would expect the results to be pretty similar.

I packed two beach towels into my big woven bag, along with a bottle of water and a smaller bottle of juice. I also stuffed one of the Alan Wolfgard novels into the bag's pocket. Then Aggie and I left the house. She flew off and I went down to my private beach.

Some of the shoreline that was part of The Jumble was stony, but a long stretch nearest to the house was sand. I had been meaning to ask if that was typical of the Finger Lakes, but in the end I didn't care. It was a pleasant place to walk even when the water was too cold for swimming, and I had a feeling someone had done some work to make this beach as nice as it was.

I spread one towel, anchoring it with the woven bag. I put the cover-up in the bag and used the sandals as a second anchor. Then I walked down to the water, letting it wash over my ankles. It was still early enough in summer for the water to be cold, but you could go out a few yards before the gradual slope turned into a steep drop-off, and the shallow water felt more like a refreshingly cool shower. So I waded in up to my knees, then my thighs. Finally I lifted my legs and tipped back into the water, spreading my arms as the water covered everything but my face and my hair floated around my head.

The water felt delicious. Every so often, I kicked my feet and used my hands to steer. Every so often, I righted myself and touched bottom to confirm I hadn't slipped into deep water. Finally starting to let go of all the various worries, I closed my eyes and enjoyed the water.

Then a hand touched my shoulder, gently pushing it down.

My body turned with the push and I went under. I came up sputtering and scared because I hadn't heard anyone enter the lake. Planting my feet in the sand, I shoved my hair away from my face and got ready to blast the person who had no business being there. Then I got a good look at her.

From the hips up, she was water, shaped like a human female. I knew she was water because I watched minnows leaping out of her torso, creating little splashes as they returned to the lake. She had a delicate build, slender and sinuous. She had webbing between her fingers. She had dark eyes, but I couldn't tell if the eyes came from another *terra indigene* form she could assume or were formed from shadows. Even her hair was water, but it was the color of shale.

"Don't you like my lake?" If the sound of water murmuring over sand could be shaped into words, that was her voice.

"Yes, I do," I replied. "It's a lovely lake."

"But you remain anchored to the land." She didn't seem upset; more curious about my behavior.

"I know how to swim, but I'm not a strong swimmer. Not yet, anyway. So I feel more comfortable swimming the length of the beach and being able to touch bottom rather than swimming into deep water." I didn't mention the potential danger of being struck by a rowboat or canoe, or that the deeper water was still too cold for a human to be in for any length of time. She might understand the danger of being struck, but I didn't think water temperature would mean much to her.

"I'm Vicki."

"I know. You are the land's caretaker now."

I waited but she didn't offer a name. Maybe she didn't have one humans could pronounce. Maybe she assumed her identity was obvious.

"Ineke—do you know Ineke?—and I were talking about doing some trail ride beach parties for her boarders and my lodgers. Would it be okay with you if other humans came swimming at this beach?"

"Why do you ask?"

"Well . . ." I waved an arm toward the center of the lake, my fingertips trailing in the water. "This is your home. We're guests."

She smiled, clearly pleased that I understood. "Your guests will be my guests." Then she raised a hand and looked stern. "But no motor-things."

"No motor-things." Since we were chatting, it was my chance to ask. "Why no motors? Do they spoil the water?"

"Some Elders live in the northern end of the lake, but they hunt the length and breadth of my home. The sound of the motor-things is the sound of both prey and challenger—and the sound annoys them, so they will attack even if they are not hungry."

Oh golly. "What about the way humans splash around when they're swimming? Sharks are attracted to that sound because it sounds like a fish in distress. At least, that's what I've read."

She laughed. "There are no sharks, or Sharkgard, in the Feather Lakes." She thought for a moment before adding, "The Elders in the lake are smaller than many of the old forms of *terra indigene*, but they are fast and fierce. However, they do not attack humans who behave as guests—unless those humans enter their home water at the northern end of the lake."

The Elders in the lake might be smaller, but there was at least one form of *terra indigene* living in The Jumble that was big enough to pick up a grown man and twist him. How big was the biggest Elder living in the lake? And what were we talking about? Something that looked like an alligator but was big enough that it could ram a motorboat? And what about the smaller ones? Were they dog size? People size? And if they *did* get hungry, just how fast could a human be consumed?

My brain stuttered. Was that a minnow trying to nibble on my ankle or something else?

I focused on my companion. It was like watching water ebb and flow in a human-shaped container. She watched me as if I was the most entertaining thing she'd seen in quite a while. I wondered if that was true.

"Vicki? Vicki!"

I turned toward the shore. "That's my friend Ineke. Would you like to meet her?"

"Not today." She sank to the waist. Then the human shape rose on a column of water, like one of those leaping game fish. As she reached the apex of the leap and headed down, her shape dissolved until only a spray of sun-sparkled water met the rest of the lake.

I stumbled out of the water, stopping where the wet sand changed to dry—and hot—sand.

"Vicki?" Ineke's voice sounded worried.

"Here!"

She appeared a minute later. "I thought you might be cooling off. It's a good day for it, and . . . Gods! What happened?" She led me to the towel, dug in my bag, and opened the bottle of juice. "Drink some of this. You're white as a sheet."

"I just met the Lady of the Lake."

Ineke stared at me. "What's she like?"

"Watery. And quite nice." I drank some of the juice. "She has no objections to our beach days as long as we give her home the same care and respect as our own."

Ineke took the juice and drank some before giving the bottle back to me. "Sounds fair."

I leaned toward her. "She said Elders live in the lake. Their home is the northern end of Lake Silence, but they hunt in and along the whole of the lake, and they're the ones who don't like things with motors."

"Then we should be safe enough." She eyed me. "Right?"

"Right." But the next time I went to Lettuce Reed, I was going to see what books Julian had about alligators and ancient freshwater predators. Just in case.

CHAPTER 34

Grimshaw

Sunday, Juin 20

Pulling into the truck stop, Grimshaw parked next to the other police car and sat for a minute. He still worked for Captain Hargreaves, was still on the Bristol payroll as a highway patrol officer since his stint in Sproing was a temporary assignment. So he had to wonder why he wasn't being asked to report to the Bristol Police Station instead of his captain going off the clock to meet him here—because he was sure Hargreaves had taken personal time instead of officially meeting one of his officers.

Grimshaw slid into one side of the booth and set his hat and a manila envelope on the seat. "Captain."

"This . . ."

Hargreaves broke off and smiled at the waitress who hustled up to their table. He ordered the steak sandwich special and iced coffee. Grimshaw ordered the same to save time.

"This should have been an easy assignment," Hargreaves said. "A human killed by one of the *terra indigene*? It's unfortunate, but everything points to the man being seen as an intruder."

"Should have been easy, but that death turned over a rock and a lot of nastiness has crawled out." Grimshaw picked up the envelope and slid it across the table. "My report. Didn't want to send it by e-mail."

While Hargreaves read the report, Grimshaw stared out the window. Vicki DeVine should be safe in The Jumble. A sharpshooter might set up across the lake or on the water and try for her when she went for a swim, but it would be a suicide mission because he didn't think anyone could get away fast enough once the shot was fired. But Julian? Someone could walk into Lettuce Reed and open fire. If the attack was timed right, he and Osgood wouldn't be nearby, and no one else would take on an armed man.

No one human, anyway.

Hargreaves tucked the report back in the envelope and set the envelope under his own hat. "I heard that Swinn is taking personal time. So is Reynolds."

"What does that mean?"

"It means they can spend time in Sproing without having to explain themselves to their own captain."

"If they break the law, I'll toss their asses in a cell until you can arrange for them to be transferred to the Bristol lockup."

Hargreaves smiled again when the waitress brought their meals. The smile faded as soon as she walked away. "It was easy enough to request Swinn's and Reynolds's transcripts from the police academy. Both men attended the academy in Hubbney, but not at the same time; there is almost a decade between them in age. Finding out about the other men . . ." Shrugging, he picked up his sandwich and took a big bite.

"If this does have its roots in some kind of club or organization that these men joined while they were at school, there's no way to tell if you're asking for help from someone who might be part of the scheme," Grimshaw said. The steak sandwich looked good, but he didn't have much appetite.

"I made a roundabout inquiry into the other men—where they went to school, that sort of thing," Hargreaves said. "The request will reach an agent in the governor's Investigative Task Force."

"Who might have a special tie clip."

"Doubt it. The agent is Governor Hannigan's nephew and is trusted by the *terra indigene*. If anyone can make inquiries without sounding any alarms, it's him. In the meantime . . ."

"I'll maintain order in a town that is so small its main street doesn't have a single stoplight and yet has been as much trouble as a tavern brawl on a Watersday night." Grimshaw bit into his sandwich. Which would be worse: being responsible for a friend's survival and possibly failing or someday picking up a newspaper and reading about Julian Farrow's murder?

No contest. Being nearby was the only way to succeed.

Hargreaves drank half his iced coffee. "I'll apologize for sticking you with this assignment if that makes you feel better. But, Wayne? Consider what might be happening in Sproing right now if someone connected to Swinn and the rest of them had answered that call for assistance instead of you."

CHAPTER 35

Them

Sunday, Juin 20

Useless, incompetent dickheads. How could so many of them screw up something so *easy* and get *killed* on top of it?

"The bitch is still there, still in control of our asset," he told the other three men. He didn't look at the dick his cousin had married—the fool who had tossed the property away in the first place. Once they had control of the property, he would find a way to cut the asshole out of the deal. And wouldn't his cousin bust the fool's balls over *that*?

Served her right for not choosing someone who was top tier.

"What are we going to do?" the oldest man asked.

"What we should have done in the first place." He smiled. "Take care of it ourselves."

CHAPTER 36

Vicki

Watersday, Juin 24

It rained for two days. All the green things needed the rain, and even the rain barrels that collected water from the downspouts had been close to empty. So while I didn't complain—not out loud, anyway—the initial storm taught me how isolated I would have been at the main house if I'd been on my own. Which I wasn't, but I can't say with any honesty that wet Panther or wet Bear smells any better than wet dog.

When the storm rolled in across the lake on Thaisday evening, I'd been at the renovated cabins, giving the two unoccupied ones a quick dust and vacuum and helping Aggie change the sheets on her bed. We gathered up the sheets and towels and stuffed them into large carry sacks. Then I saw the flash of lightning and heard the *boom* of thunder.

We went out on Aggie's porch.

"The Elementals are playing," Aggie said. She stepped closer to me. "Or they're angry about something."

Flash. *Boom.*

"What makes you think the Elementals are doing this? It's just a storm."

"Thunder and Lightning are running together."

Flash. *Boom!*

Aggie looked toward Silence Lodge, which was hidden behind a wall of rain making its way across the mile-wide lake. "And Ilya Sanguinati says if you don't leave for your house now, you should plan to stay in the cabins here until the storm quiets."

"How long will that take?"

She shrugged.

There wasn't any food in the unoccupied cabins, and I wasn't sure if Aggie had anything stored—or if what she had was something I, being human, would want to eat for any reason short of desperation.

Flash. *Boom*. That spear of lightning struck the lake.

"I'm going to make a run for it." I looked at Aggie, who carefully didn't look at me. Where were her kin? Would they join her here to huddle on the porch, somewhat protected from the weather? Or did they already have their own shelters? "If you want to come with me, stuff a couple of changes of clothes in a bag, and do it fast. And remember to bring your toothbrush," I shouted when she dashed into the cabin.

The storm seemed to stall over the lake for a few minutes—long enough for Aggie to pack and make sure the cabin's windows were closed. She didn't lock the door, and I didn't comment. After all, if she wanted to let her kin have use of the cabin during the storm, I wasn't going to be mean about it.

I had left the door of the screened porch unlatched, and I was glad because someone had kept the storm on a tight rein just long enough for us to reach the porch. Then it came thundering over The Jumble.

I unlocked the kitchen door and dumped the carry sacks. "Close the windows," I said as I ran around the house doing exactly that. Not fast enough in some cases—the wind scattered papers in my office, knocked over a lamp in another room, and soaked the curtains in a couple of rooms.

Breathless, I ran back to the kitchen and pulled out the sheets and towels, handing the hand towel and facecloth to

Aggie. "These need to be washed anyway, so let's use them to wipe up any water on the windowsills and floor."

She didn't ask questions, didn't indicate if this was a familiar human behavior or a new experience.

Flash! *BOOM!*

The weatherman on the TV news had talked about a storm coming in from the west that could be fierce enough to cause some flooding and close roads. Viewers had been warned to have emergency lanterns and food for a couple of days in case they were cut off from nearby towns. I had assumed the warning was for the farmers and vintners, but I suddenly realized the warning was also meant for someone like me. And I was glad that Aggie had chosen to join me at the main house.

When I returned to the porch to see if I'd left anything that could be damaged by water, I found a wet Cougar and equally wet Conan waiting for me by the kitchen door. They were in their furry forms and each carried a sack that I assumed contained some human clothes.

I stepped aside in invitation. "Aggie is here too. Do you want to join us?"

They entered the kitchen and dropped their sacks next to the ones Aggie and I had carried from her cabin. They came back out with me while I did a quick check of the porch. Since the porch ran the length of the house, a quick check to rescue a couple of books and move a couple of plants from tables to the floor wasn't all that quick and I was clothes-clinging wet by the time I returned to the kitchen. Conan and Cougar had tipped over the lightweight chairs on the porch— an activity I appreciated when a blast of wind knocked me into Conan. I wasn't sure the Bear even noticed; I was pretty sure I would have some interesting bruises the next day. I couldn't wait to explain *those* to the doctor—or Ilya Sanguinati. Or Officer Grimshaw.

It wasn't my fault. The wind knocked me into a Bear.

I wasn't sure Dr. Wallace would want to believe me. After all, he was one of the Sproing residents who had lived in the safe little bubble of believing the Others were Out There before the events of the past few days had shown everyone that Out There really meant Right Here.

I went to my suite and changed into dry clothes. I looked at my hair and put enough clips in it to hold it away from my face, planning to take a hot shower later and use extra hair conditioner in the hope of combing out all the tangles.

When I returned to the common rooms, Cougar and Conan had shifted to human form and were dressed. They still smelled a bit like wet animal, but I decided not to comment about that since it occurred to me that I had no idea what a wet human might smell like to them.

On Firesday, the first full day of rain, I made hourly checks of the rooms, reassuring myself that I hadn't left a window open or had any leaks that I could ill afford to have fixed at the moment. One of my companions came with me during each inspection, watching everything I did but not asking why I needed to check something I'd already checked. They just rotated keeping me company. In between inspections we napped or read. I turned on the TV to watch the noon news. Serious faces advising viewers to stay indoors as much as possible. Some flooded roads; some blocked by downed trees.

"Why do humans need other humans to tell them things they should be able to know by themselves?" Conan asked.

"There is comfort in confirmation," I replied. "It's easier to believe something if someone else thinks the same thing."

They looked at the windows as the wind chose that moment to drive the rain against the house with enough force it sounded like pebbles hitting the glass. Then they looked at me.

"It is raining," Cougar said solemnly. "If you go outside, you will get wet."

I wasn't sure if he was trying to be snarky or helpful, but I decided to go with helpful. "That's what I think too."

He nodded, yawned, then closed his eyes as he stretched out on the floor. I studied him. Could he really fall asleep that fast? Conan was also dozing. Even Aggie was curled up at one end of a sofa, looking too young to be on her own. Then again, a lot of her kin might live in The Jumble, so her staying here probably wasn't much different from a human teenager going away to college.

"I'm going to take a shower."

Three pairs of eyes opened, fixed on me for a moment, then closed again.

Going upstairs to my suite, I stripped out of my clothes, turned on the shower to bring up the hot water—and hesitated as I listened to the storm. I hadn't heard a rumble of thunder or seen a flash of lightning in a while. I wasn't keen to become a morbid headline—"Woman Struck by Lightning While Taking a Shower"—but I thought I would be safe if I was quick.

Warmed by the shower, I combed through my hair and wondered if I should try the hairstylist in Sproing—an old barber who had a monopoly on the haircutting trade because he hadn't run away or been eaten last summer—or take Ineke's advice and go to the stylist in Crystalton who cut and colored her hair. Someone who, according to Ineke, had an extra sense about how to do the most with the hair a person had. Then I thought about the income that wasn't coming in and wondered if I wanted to throw away money on a lost cause. So not something I would say to Ineke, who would give me a lecture about letting someone else's opinion sour *my* opinion of myself.

Easy for her to say.

Feeling a bit defiant, or maybe just not caring for the moment, I pulled on clothes that were comfortable and warm and in no way flattering—things I wouldn't wear around anyone human. Then I thought about Aggie's questions about what to wear and when to wear it and changed into clothes that were a little less disreputable. Not being happy with the way I looked or any of the clothes in my closet didn't mean I had any right to spoil Aggie's fashion adventure.

As I returned to the social room, it occurred to me that Paige Xavier had the same light-boned build as Aggie, if not the same coloring, and might be better at suggesting outfits suitable for the Crow. If the weather cooperated, we would have our first trail ride beach party in a few days, and I could introduce Aggie to Paige and let them work things out for themselves.

The rest of Firesday passed quietly. We read our own books. I thawed out all the meatballs in the freezer and made spaghetti and meatballs for dinner, which was a new food for the boys and required teaching them how to twirl the spaghetti on a fork. Since that slowed down food consumption, I suspected that, on their own, they would have picked up the spaghetti by the handful and ignored the saucy mess. But they were sufficiently intrigued in learning how to eat this meal the human way that they persevered, and in the end everyone had plenty to eat.

By Watersday afternoon, the novelty of staying inside napping and reading had worn off, even for me. I opened the cupboard where I had stored board games and the shoe boxes filled with plastic figures I had purchased as toys for the children of my future guests. I dismissed the jigsaw puzzles as being too sedate, even if the four of us worked on one together. I dismissed the games that were too young for my companions. Finally I pulled out a box and held it up to show Aggie and the boys. "Let's play Murder."

I tried not to think too long or too hard about the way all their eyes brightened and the amount of enthusiasm they showed as we set up the game. They looked a little puzzled as I explained the game, but they recognized the fireplace poker, rope, revolver, knife, and hammer as weapons. I had to explain the garrote.

"Teeth would work better to choke your prey," Conan said, studying the game piece.

"Yours, maybe. Mine? Not so much." Could you garrote a Bear or Panther? Could someone get a wire around a neck and through all that fur fast enough not to get clawed to pieces? Another question to ponder when I couldn't fall asleep.

I let each of them fan a different set of cards while I selected victim, weapon, and location and tucked them in the little envelope. Then I shuffled all the cards and dealt them.

"Now we have to figure out who died and—"

Aggie, Conan, and Cougar immediately laid down the character cards they were holding, then looked at me.

"Do you have any humans?" Aggie asked.

I revealed my character card.

"Now we know which human is dead," Conan said.

"But we still need to figure out where that human died," I said.

They laid their location cards over the rooms on the game board and looked at me again. I put my location card over the kitchen, which left the dining room as the only location uncovered. I held up a hand before the three of them could put down the weapon cards. "To make it more interesting, let's say that a player has to fetch a weapon and bring it to the dining room, and if a person has the card to show that weapon *wasn't* used, he, or she, only shows it to that one player."

Needing to roll dice and move their pieces along the squares to reach a room suddenly added more interest to the game. Since even Aggie was more of a predator than me, I didn't point out that I had explained the rules before we had started, so the whole thing would have been more interesting if we were trying to figure out the who, what, and where instead of just the what.

Even then, the *terra indigene* didn't seem to understand that every player worked alone. Maybe that was something I should mention to Officer Grimshaw. They might not cooperate if one brought down a deer and wanted to keep his lunch for himself, but when it came to finding a human who did a bad thing, they scattered and regrouped. Each of them clumped over the board to reach the closest room with a weapon, and then they headed for the dining room, taking the weapon with them. Since I was considered part of this odd pack, I followed their example and fetched the knife that had been in the kitchen, leaving the garrote that had been discarded there. Maybe it would have been a weapon of opportunity in a crime show. Not a likely weapon since I didn't think most people knew how to kill someone with a garrote. You probably had to go to assassin school or something and take the garroting class to learn how to do it properly. Which didn't mean someone couldn't do it badly but still be effective in the end.

I think they all figured out the knife was the weapon, but they all guessed incorrectly, letting me reveal the final piece of evidence.

"That was pretty good," Cougar said, making me think he would offer a cub the same encouragement for almost catching a bunny or some other small edible.

"Yes," Conan agreed. "But our way of playing the game is better."

"You all play a different version of Murder?" I asked.

They nodded.

I considered making an excuse to stay in my suite for a few hours. Then I considered that this was good practice for entertaining lodgers on a rainy day. Not that I would be expected to play games with my lodgers. I would be expected to provide drinks and snacks and fight with the rabbit ears that provided sketchy TV reception in this kind of weather since there was bound to be someone who preferred television over board games.

"Why don't you set things up for your version of the game while I see what I can rustle up for snacks?" That suggestion went over well and gave me an excuse to retreat for a few minutes.

I was pondering what I had available that would feed two carnivores and two omnivores when the phone rang.

"The Jumble, Vicki speaking."

"It's Julian. How are you doing out there?"

"Since I'm not planning to leave until I run out of food or the rain stops, I'm doing pretty well. Aggie, the boys, and I are about to play the *terra indigene* version of Murder."

"Oh." A single word followed by the slightest pause. "Well, I'm glad you're not on your own there in the storm."

Something in his voice. It suddenly occurred to me that Julian might be lonely. He lived in one of the Mill Creek Cabins, but he was the only tenant. That meant he was as isolated there as I was at The Jumble. Of course, if the roads were passable and he could reach the village, he could rent one of Ineke's rooms for a night to avoid being alone.

"I don't know what the main roads are like or if my access road is passable, but if you'd like to join us . . ." I did have two guest suites on the second floor of the main building, so I could offer him a place to stay instead of going out on slick roads after dark. And since I'd already said Aggie and the boys were here, he wouldn't mistake the offer as more than an invitation for friendly company.

"I'd like that. Is there anything I can pick up since I can stop at Pops's store before I leave Sproing?"

"You're already in the village? Are you sure you want to come out in this weather?"

"I'm sure."

I wasn't sure I would brave the roads today for anything less than an emergency, but I took him at his word and considered what I was going to run out of by tomorrow morning. "Bread, milk, sandwich fixings?"

"Got it. I'll see you in a little while."

The larder was a little more bare than I'd thought, even for snacks. I cut up some carrots, cut some cheddar cheese into squares, and made peanut butter and jelly sandwiches. I eyed the jar of sweet pickles but put them back unopened.

There were good reasons why, unlike Ineke, I didn't include meals with the cabin rentals—or with the suites upstairs for that matter. Use of the kitchen? Yes. Me putting out more than snacks? Not a chance. Since Aggie and the boys were more of a mind to eat whatever was available and hadn't yet acquired any discernment about what foods were a good or bad combination, they were quite happy with what I brought out.

I hadn't been gone that long, but they had rummaged through all the supplies and toys I had purchased and had transformed the Murder game.

The original board was in the center of the table, but the rooms now had labels that matched the downstairs rooms in The Jumble, even if the layout couldn't match. They had taken sheets of colored construction paper and added green woodland on three sides of the board. On the fourth side, they had snugged three little houses together to represent the lakeside cabins, added a strip of tan paper to represent the beach and, finally, blue paper to represent the lake. Aggie was busy making strips of squares that matched the size of the squares on the board, while Conan carefully secured the strips to the construction paper to indicate paths in the woods and paths from the kitchen down to the cabins and the lake. Cougar had found the sets of little plastic toys and created a cluster of trees on each of the green sheets of paper. There were farm animals—cow, pig, chicken, horse—scattered on the papers, positioned next to squares. There were also foxes, hawks, owls, a family of deer, and a moose. And there was a wolf and a coyote.

The bear, cougar, and crow were set on three of the places where players started the game. As for the people . . .

"Look!" Aggie beamed at me as she paused in her square making to hold up a figure in a police uniform. "It's a teeny Grimshaw. And here is a teeny Vicki!"

They were plastic figures that had come out of molds. They had no relevance to the real world. It still gave me a thrill to see that teeny Vicki was just as tall as teeny Grimshaw.

Teeny Vicki was also placed on the game board in a starting position. Teeny Grimshaw was in the library. I had no idea why. Other teeny people included a dark-haired man dressed in casual business attire that made me think of Julian. There was a man in a white coat with a stethoscope around his neck and a woman in a nurse's uniform. There was a woman wearing an apron, like a short-order cook. There was a curvy, dark-haired woman in a business suit. And a man in a business suit. Except for teeny Grimshaw, the other people were placed on the edges of the board, as if they weren't part of the game yet. Except for the woman in the long blue dress who was placed in the center of the blue paper that represented the lake.

I didn't have to ask who *she* was.

But there was one other creature on the board. I put down the tray of snacks and picked up one of my fuzzy white socks. It had been stuffed with a partial roll of toilet paper. The sock now had frowny eyes drawn on with a permanent black marker, as well as a mouth full of a ghastly number of teeth, and arms that ended with paw-hands that had serious claws.

"What is this?" I asked.

"That's the Elder," Aggie said, taking it from me and replacing it on the board.

I would never be able to wear that sock without either stepping on an Elder or looking down and seeing that face looking up at me.

Besides the die that was rolled for movement, there was another pair of dice that, I was told, was used for a number of things. And there was a small stack of cards made from index cards that had been cut in half. Since those were turned over and placed in the center of the board where the envelope with the answers usually resided, they weren't part of the human version of the game. Then again, neither were the question marks that were randomly placed on some of the squares, both on the board and on the newly created paths.

We had our snacks while Aggie and the boys finished making the pieces for their version of the game. I took the dishes back to the kitchen and returned to the social room with a pitcher of cold water and several plastic glasses.

"We're ready to play," Aggie said.

Cougar wrinkled his lips, revealing his mismatched teeth, and said, "Heh-heh-heh-heh."

Oh golly. Did I really want to play a game that made Cougar that gleeful?

I gave them my brightest smile. "Alrighty! Let's—" I heard a car pull up and headed for the front door. "That must be Julian." I heard two car doors close, then two more, and hesitated. Maybe that wasn't Julian. Maybe it was someone else, someone who thought I would be alone here.

I was aware of Conan coming up behind me and Cougar moving past me toward the front door.

The doorbell rang.

CHAPTER 37

Grimshaw

Watersday, Juin 24

Grimshaw glanced in the rearview mirror at the two bags of groceries and the three large pizzas filling up the back seat of the cruiser before focusing on the wet road. "You expecting Vicki DeVine to live on pizza for the next few days?" Or few weeks?

"She said Aggie and the boys were staying with her during the storm," Julian replied. "I wanted to make sure she had enough food in the house."

He wasn't sure pizza would be the best choice of food for a Bear and Panther, but he didn't argue. Besides, he liked pizza.

"I could have taken my own car," Julian said.

"This one handles better on wet roads."

Julian said nothing for a minute. "Were you worried about her too?"

It was his turn to choose his words. "Not worried as such. But I've been patrolling the village since the storm hit to make note of any flooded streets or downed power lines." And giving quiet thanks last night that he wasn't one of the highway patrol officers driving those dark roads in the wild country in this weather. "The Jumble and its residents are also part of my territory, so it was time to check up on them."

"And to show the *terra indigene* that human authority isn't ignoring someone they've taken an interest in."

"That too."

He turned onto the access road to The Jumble. Someone had removed the chain across the road. Had one of the boys, as Vicki DeVine called them, come out to do it? Or had it been down a while, maybe indicating that someone else had gone up to the main house?

"Julian?"

"We're not walking into anything," Julian said after a long moment.

Then he would assess the situation and decide if he should mention the chain to Conan or Cougar. After all, they were the ones who had put it up in the first place.

They got out of the car. Julian grabbed the three pizzas and Grimshaw grabbed the two bags of groceries. They closed the car doors and ran for the overhang protecting the front door. Julian juggled the pizzas and managed to ring the doorbell.

When the door opened, it wasn't Vicki DeVine standing there to greet them. It was Cougar, and he didn't look like greeting them was what he had in mind.

"We brought pizza," Julian said.

"Hi, Julian," Vicki said brightly, peering around Cougar. "You're just in time!" She hesitated for a moment. "Officer Grimshaw."

"Hope it's all right for me to stop by," he said. He wasn't in uniform and had left Osgood on call for the evening.

"Oh, sure." Vicki tapped her fingers against the Panther's arm. "Cougar, let them come in out of the rain."

They followed her to the kitchen—and Conan and Cougar followed them. He listened to Vicki and Julian wrangling about the cost of the groceries and paying for the pizzas while he put the milk and orange juice into the refrigerator. He noticed the Others were also listening to the wrangling, but neither male was showing any further sign of hostility toward Julian.

Vicki paid for her groceries and accepted the pizzas

as Julian's contribution for a social evening. Grimshaw took note that Conan and Cougar knew enough about the main house to know where to find the dishes, glasses, and flatware.

They piled pizza onto the plates, took plenty of napkins, and went into the social room. Vicki and Julian went back for the glasses and a pitcher of water. Grimshaw would have preferred a beer, but he was driving, and it wasn't a night to have his reflexes even slightly dulled.

Then they all looked at the *terra indigene*'s version of Murder—and Grimshaw watched Julian Farrow pale.

"It's The Jumble," Julian said, sounding as if he were choking.

To give Julian time to recover before anyone started asking questions, Grimshaw pointed to what he hoped was a clean sock and said, "What's that?"

"Fuzzy Sock Elder," Vicki replied.

Crap.

He ate pizza and listened to the Others explain their version of the game. Land on a question mark and you pick a card that might allow you to take an extra move or allow you to escape a predator—or be attacked by one. The pair of dice were thrown to decide conflicts—an even number meant the player entering the room would not attack the player already in the room; an odd number equaled an attack and the number itself determined the severity of the attack. A low number indicated a small, nonlethal bite, while a high number equaled being eaten or at least desperately injured unless you had a "Doctor!" card and could get help or had a "Friend" card that meant the other player would now work with you instead of munching on you.

No way to get out of playing now, so he resigned himself to losing the game and reminded himself that he'd gotten pizza out of the deal.

And hoped he really wasn't seeing the signs that Julian was sensing something terribly wrong now.

* * *

They agreed on the rules: the initial victim was a character from the original game, the weapon would be one of the human ones that came with the game, and the location would be one of the rooms on the board. But the Others insisted that they had to play by Miss Vicki's rule that you had to bring the weapon to the room to make your guesses. Which would have been fine, except Grimshaw noticed almost all of the weapons had been scattered in the north, south, and east woods. The revolver was in the lake, placed on the last square located on the blue paper.

Six weapons, six players. They rolled the die and moved their pieces on the squares to reach one of the two doors that would get them outside to fetch the weapons.

"I could go out a window," Aggie said, after rolling a two for the third time. "I'm a Crow. I could do that."

"No squares under the windows," Vicki said. "You can't move your piece except on the squares, so you have to reach a door."

Julian moved teeny Julian out the kitchen door and headed for the lake—and the revolver. Teeny Vicki went out the front door and headed for the garrote in the north woods. Teeny Cougar headed for the rope but got distracted when he landed on a square and had the chance to eat a fawn. He didn't roll a number high enough for a serious injury so the fawn got away, and he growled softly about the missed kill until Vicki went into the kitchen and returned with the rest of the pizzas, much to Grimshaw's relief since he was sitting next to the Panther.

They were still wandering outside, retrieving the weapons, when Grimshaw felt the first ripple of unease. Julian had been heading for the lake during his turns and had rolled a six—enough to reach the last square on the blue paper and get the revolver. Except Julian moved his piece to the last square on "land" and stopped. He stared at the "lake" and the female in the blue dress for so long that Vicki started to reach out and touch his arm. Then Julian turned his playing piece around and marched teeny Julian back toward the house.

"But you didn't fetch the revolver," Vicki said.

"No," Julian replied, beads of sweat popping up on his forehead.

He's afraid, Grimshaw thought. *What is he sensing that would make him afraid? It's just a game.*

Could this game version of The Jumble be just close enough to represent the real thing? He'd never seen Julian react this way when they'd been in the academy.

Grimshaw landed on a question mark square and drew a "Friend" card, meaning when he finally entered a room or confronted a predator, he could use the card instead of rolling the dice to determine the outcome of a fight. Vicki also landed on a question mark square.

"Help from an Elder," she read. She looked at the fuzzy sock guarding the north woods and smiled. "That's a good card."

"Yes," Aggie said, not smiling. "It's a very good card. You should keep it with you."

Grimshaw fetched the revolver from the lake and Julian managed to bring the fireplace poker to the kitchen and seemed to be all right, had even regained his color.

Then Vicki landed on another question mark and drew a card that said, "A predator blocks your path. The next player chooses the predator."

Aggie was the next player and didn't hesitate. She grabbed the businessman with the briefcase and set him on the square right in front of teeny Vicki—the square that had the garrote next to it.

Julian leaped up and ran for the nearest bathroom.

Conan and Cougar looked at Julian's empty place at the table, then looked at the board.

Grimshaw counted the seconds. When a full minute had passed, he rose casually. "I'll go check on him. Make sure he's all right. Hope he's not coming down with a stomach bug."

Following Vicki's directions, he found the powder room and knocked on the door. "Julian?" He didn't hear vomiting.

Didn't hear anything. He turned the knob and was surprised it wasn't locked. He opened the door a couple of inches. "Julian?"

"I'm all right."

Grimshaw opened the door a bit more and leaned in. Seeing Julian bent over the sink, face dripping with water, he squeezed into the room and closed the door. "What happened?"

"Not now, Wayne. Not here." Julian straightened and wiped his face with the hand towel. "Let's finish the game and get out of here."

"Are you reacting to the game?"

Julian hesitated. "I hope so."

He studied his friend. "But you don't think so."

"No," Julian said grimly. "I don't think so."

They returned to the social room and the game. Julian made excuses for his hasty retreat. Grimshaw didn't know if Vicki believed him, but she pretended to and the Others followed her example. Figuring out the solution was a bit slapdash, but they finished the game and said their good-byes.

"Are you sure you're all right?" Vicki asked.

"I'm fine," Julian replied. "Thanks for the interesting evening." He ran to the car.

"I'll persuade him to stay at Ineke's," Grimshaw said. "In case he does have a touch of something." And if he couldn't persuade Julian to stay at Ineke's, he'd sleep on his friend's couch at the cabin. One way or another, Julian wasn't going to be alone tonight.

"I'll call tomorrow," Vicki said.

As they approached the intersection, Grimshaw said, "Which way? To your cabin or to Sproing?"

"Neither," Julian replied. "Pull over here. Put your lights on so we don't get rear-ended."

Not sure of the condition of the shoulder, Grimshaw eased the right-side tires off the road and turned on the cruiser's flashing lights.

Julian punched a number into his mobile phone. Grimshaw was surprised that it worked, but the storm was spent and would be cleared out by morning.

"This is Julian Farrow. Grimshaw and I were at The Jumble and we're heading back to Sproing. I need to see you. Now."

He waited until Julian finished the call. "Before you put that away, call Ineke and see if she's got a room."

Julian stared out the window for a minute, then called Ineke and arranged to stay at the boardinghouse overnight.

Grimshaw didn't see another car on the road, didn't see anything approach *his* car. But a few minutes after Julian made the first call, the back door opened and Ilya Sanguinati slipped inside.

"Is this a typical kind of meeting for humans?" Ilya asked.

"Sometimes," Julian replied. "When there is a need for secrecy."

"And what secrets are we sharing?"

Julian turned in his seat in order to look at Ilya. "What happened tonight has never happened to me before, so I can't give you any assurances that what I sensed is accurate."

"Understood."

No questions from the Sanguinati about how or why Julian sensing something would be significant. Which meant Ilya, at least, knew Julian was an Intuit.

"A predator in a business suit is going to come to The Jumble," Julian said. "Maybe more than one. When that happens, you need to get Vicki DeVine out of there. Not just have her stay with you or at Ineke's while she fights to hold on to that place. You have to go along with whatever scam the predators are going to play and make them believe they succeeded in taking The Jumble away from her."

Silence. His eyes fixed on the rearview mirror, Grimshaw saw the cold look on Ilya's face and wondered if Julian realized how close he was to being killed. How close they both were.

"And why should I do that?" the Sanguinati finally asked.

Julian looked Ilya in the eyes. "If you don't, Vicki DeVine is going to die."

CHAPTER 38

Vicki

Windsday, Juin 28

I sat in Ineke's kitchen and watched her cut up carrots for the Sproingers while I sorted out the order of the things I wanted to discuss. Should I start with the good news that had some concerns or the development that had me more than a little concerned?

Good news could wait. "Julian and Grimshaw are acting weird."

"They're men," Ineke replied. "That's normal."

Clearly she hadn't seen Julian in the past couple of days and didn't appreciate the depth of my concern. And she probably hadn't seen much of Grimshaw except for meals, and maybe not even then since Paige and Dominique usually served the guests in the dining room. "Weirder than normal."

"Oh." Ineke set the knife on the cutting board. "Well, that's disturbing."

"Ever since we played the *terra indigene* version of Murder—which, according to Aggie, changes from place to place—the men have been acting like Maxwell when he sees a duckling that has strayed too far from its mother."

She raised her eyebrows. "They want to snatch you and hide you under the porch?"

"Okay, not like Maxwell." The border collie was fine with the duck family that lived in the pond on Ineke's property as long as the ducklings stayed close to their mama. But if one got so much as a collie-length away from mama, Maxwell snatched it and took it to the nest he'd made for himself under the porch, sure that the duckling was now orphaned and wouldn't survive without his intervention. Of course, that resulted in skirmishes with mama duck on an almost daily basis.

I knew Maxwell could count at least up to ten; that's how he knew when one of his people-sheep needed to be rounded up. Turned out the ducklings' mama knew how to count too and didn't approve of a dog being a duck-sitter.

Since Ineke had found dog, duck, and ducklings under the porch after the storm, snuggled together on the old quilt Maxwell had appropriated from the clothesline a few months ago, it was felt that the mama's squawking was more for form's sake than because she thought Maxwell would harm her little ones. And any duckling he did borrow he would herd back to the pond the next morning.

It was understood that if Maxwell didn't come when called, Paige or Dominique would check under the porch.

"But they *are* acting weird," I said. "And the weirdest thing is that Julian is rubbish when it comes to playing Murder, and this time it was like he was tuned to a different channel." I thought about that and what I knew about Julian. "No. More like he was tuned *between* two channels; like he was seeing the picture of one show and hearing another, but the shows were close enough in story line that he reacted as if they were one and the same."

Ineke finished cutting the carrots, put them in a container and the knife in the sink. Then she sat down across from me.

"You know what Julian is," she said, not quite a question.

"An Intuit? Yes. And I wondered if he had sensed something about The Jumble and that's why he's been acting weird, calling a couple of times a day just to see how things are going, like something should be different. He's never done that before." Sometimes he had invited me to lunch when I'd been running errands in the village, and talking to him then had felt friendly and enjoyable. The phone calls didn't feel like a friend wanting to chat. The phone calls felt . . . smothering, as if Julian no longer trusted me to be competent and able to take care of myself. And that was too strong a reminder of living with Yorick, who would review my list of plans for the day and then correct *something* to reinforce the belief in my inability to function on my own, despite my being the person who had the job that supported both of us for most of our marriage.

Had Yorick given up The Jumble because he *expected* me to fail, to be too incompetent to restore the buildings enough to receive paying guests?

Ineke reached across the table and touched my hand, pulling my thoughts back to the here and now. "If Julian did sense something and told Grimshaw, maybe that's the reason our police chief is also acting weird."

Did Grimshaw know about his verbal promotion? Officially he might be a Bristol highway patrol officer on loan to the village of Sproing, but a whole lot of people now referred to him as the chief. Not to his face, of course. They didn't want to spook him with the idea that his position was permanent before he had a chance to get used to the possibility. And there was a contingent of residents who wanted to see the back of him, blaming him for the Sanguinati ousting the bank manager and taking over the bank. Which wasn't his doing.

"Then why won't they tell me?" I said, getting back to my concern. "The Jumble is my responsibility, and if something might happen there, Julian should be telling me, not Grimshaw. Well, not only Grimshaw."

"I don't think an Intuit can always tell you why he, or she, feels what he feels. Why does someone back out of a leisurely boat ride with a group of friends because she feels uneasy about the weather when there isn't a cloud in the sky or the slightest breeze—and ends up being the only survivor because a wild storm blew in out of nowhere and the friends on the boat couldn't get to safety?" Ineke shrugged. "Julian may not be able to tell you why the game spooked him, but I think using his behavior as a barometer for trouble would be smart."

Yes, that would be smart. Just like it would be smart to remember that Julian and Grimshaw weren't new friends; clearly they were old friends reunited. Because of that, there were things Julian might be willing to say to Grimshaw that he wouldn't say to anyone else. Even me, the person who was the reason they were acting weird.

So maybe Julian wasn't trying to make me feel incompetent. Maybe he *needed* to make those phone calls and check on me for his own peace of mind, even if he couldn't articulate *why*—at least not to me.

That made sense in an uncomfortable sort of way, so I went on to the other things that concerned me. "I have good news. I'm going to have more lodgers this weekend. A couple reserved one of the renovated lakeside cabins, and two couples have taken the suites in the main house. And they're all coming in for a long weekend, arriving Firesday afternoon and staying through Moonsday."

"That is good news." Ineke studied me. "Why aren't you happier?"

"I explained, twice, that The Jumble is a rustic getaway and that outside of me providing some fruit and pastries for breakfast, guests are responsible for their own meals, even if they rent the suites in the main house."

"Very smart."

Considering my cooking skills, it was more than smart. Although, since my cooking skills were pretty much in the range of making salads, heating up soup, and putting together a sandwich, I wasn't sure what I was supposed to do with the big kitchen garden that Aggie and the boys thought I should restore to provide food for The Jumble's residents. Then again, if I put in enough carrots, maybe I could trade with Ineke, becoming her carrot supplier in exchange for cooked food. What I knew for certain was that I had to arrange for some trees to be harvested for firewood, both for my own use and to sell. And the kitchen garden and the orchard had to be restored, whether or not I prepared any meals for anyone but myself. I'd been so focused on getting the house and the first three cabins renovated that I only had a vague idea of what I, as the caretaker of a *terra indigene* settlement, should be doing with the land. Of course, no one had told me the true nature of The Jumble, so I should be excused for thinking of leaky roofs before food.

"What are you thinking?" Ineke asked.

"Are we still doing the trail ride beach party tomorrow?"

"Yes. We need to try it out before offering it to guests. Besides, this might be the last quiet day I have for the rest of the season."

"Then I think I should go home and get ready for my guests. Or maybe I should sit on the porch and read for the rest of the day and let everything sort itself out."

"Clean sheets don't automatically appear on beds or clean towels in the bathrooms. So you're going to go home and get ready for your guests, just like I'll be doing."

"You have guests coming in?"

"A man and his wife who wanted time away from the city. Or so she said."

"Which city?"

"That she didn't say. But they're also coming for a full four days. My rooms fill up in the summer—and even after the things that happened last year, people who have stayed with me in previous years have been calling to make reservations for a little getaway—so I made sure the wife understood that she was lucky to get a reservation when she called so close to the date she wanted. Oh, just so you know, I have a three-day minimum for my rooms during the summer and fall. You might want to do something similar for your cabins and suites since most people stay for at least a weekend if they're going to drive or take a train here. Besides, you never intended to be an overnight billet like a motel."

"Good point. That's something I'll do for future guests."

"It's better for us to be a unified front in that regard." Ineke smiled. "So we'll have our trail ride beach party tomorrow, which will be fun and should keep you from fretting about the guests on Firesday. It will be our trial run since Julian and Grimshaw will be playing the part of our potential guests."

Julian and Grimshaw, who were already acting weird. Goody. "So it's the two of them plus you, me, and Paige . . ."

"And Hector, since he's coming along to tend the horses and get a free lunch."

I pushed away from the table. "I have to go."

"Going to tidy up?" Ineke asked.

"I am." And the first bit of tidying I was going to do was hide the Murder game.

CHAPTER 39

Grimshaw

Windsday, Juin 28

Grimshaw studied the OUT TO LUNCH, BACK IN ONE HOUR sign on Lettuce Reed's locked front door. Then he walked down the driveway to the small parking lot behind the building. Julian's car was there, so even if Julian *was* having lunch, he hadn't gone far. And it wasn't likely he'd gone anywhere since the windows were open and Grimshaw could hear at least one fan running to battle the heat and humidity. The storm hadn't brought cooler or drier air; if anything, it was even hotter and stickier. Oppressive.

Unnatural? Would that be an appropriate word if the *terra indigene* were manipulating the weather for their own purpose? If they did play with the weather, would they take a request for a blast of northern air to knock down the wet heat for a few days?

Natural or unnatural, this weather had meant more work for him, not only dealing with storm damage around Sproing but also dealing with the incidents that had happened to people who should have known better, even if they were youngsters. He appreciated that the public beach was crowded, and the portable potties were being overused to the point where the smell knocked a man back a couple of steps when he opened the door. So he understood the mutters and resentment about being kept away from Lake Silence's other beach now that it was, once again, unquestionably private property. He understood why some of the teenage boys tried to sneak into The Jumble and make use of the beach. And he had to admit—just not out loud—that while he wasn't looking forward to tomorrow's trail ride except as a way to get a better sense of the land around Sproing and within The Jumble itself, he was looking forward to spending some time on The Jumble's beach and in cool water that wasn't so crowded with other people that you felt like a sardine in a can.

While he wasn't going to turn a blind eye to trespassing, the incidents were ranging from the ridiculous to the serious. Moonsday night, Osgood had brought in a kid who had been running down the road buck naked and almost dove through the cruiser's open window in an effort to get away from the clawed monster that had ripped off his swim trunks while trying to catch him. Oh, the kid had scratches on his ass that proved *something* had tried to grab him after he'd gone swimming at The Jumble. The identity of the attacker came the following morning when Vicki DeVine brought in a pair of torn swim trunks and said that, according to Aggie Crowe, one of the Owlgard had grabbed the trunks while trying to get to the wiggly mouse inside. The boy made some noises about suing for injuries—apparently he'd been watching too many cop shows and not enough of the news reports about the *terra indigene*—but after Grimshaw impressed on the kid what could have happened if the Owl *had* managed to get its talons on the "wiggly mouse" while the kid was knowingly trespassing, the opinion of all concerned was that the scratches were sufficient punishment for a first-time trespasser but being caught a second time would mean a minimum of three nights in jail—if the kid got out of The Jumble alive.

When the father picked up his son, he, at least, understood that the three nights in jail would be more for the boy's protection than a punishment, because an Owl was one thing; the other hunters in The Jumble were something else.

First thing this morning, three teenagers came into the station, admitting that they had ignored the after-dark curfew and had gone for a swim at The Jumble the previous night. They swore they'd heard voices—angry female voices that were so close the females must have been in the water too, giving the boys a reason to scramble out and go home. The words? Something about a monkey, which was an animal that lived in Afrikah. So that made no sense. Either the boys hadn't heard what was said or they were too scared to repeat what they'd really heard.

It didn't matter to Grimshaw what was said. What mattered was the gut-level belief that warnings had been issued. From now on, anyone trespassing at The Jumble wouldn't be so lucky to get away with a few scratches on his ass or hearing weird voices. And he and Osgood would be filling out Deceased, Location Unknown forms instead of incident reports.

Which was something he wanted to discuss with Julian Farrow.

He raised a fist to whack the door, then thought about the OUT TO LUNCH sign and walked over to Come and Get It. He ordered two of the sandwich specials and returned to the bookstore a few minutes later. Then he whacked on the door.

Julian stared at him through the glass for what felt like minutes before unlocking the door and letting him in.

The man looked like he hadn't slept in a couple of days. Or shaved. Since the clothes were clean and he didn't smell, Grimshaw figured Julian had at least gone home long enough to shower and change.

"I brought lunch." He held up the carry bag from the diner.

Julian led him to the back room that served as an office and break room. Grimshaw unpacked the carry bag and wondered where to set the food since most of the table was covered with an enhanced version of the Murder game.

Leaving the food, Grimshaw studied the game and the little figures scattered throughout the rooms and outdoor areas. He knew from Pops Davies that Julian had bought the game and as many different sets of little figures as Pops had available. The people weren't quite the same as the figures in the set Vicki DeVine had. For one thing, the police officer had brown skin and black hair like Osgood and the figure that had been teeny Vicki was now a long-haired redhead. No, wait. There was a figure with shorter brown hair standing next to an upright athletic sock that had a face drawn on a square of paper that was attached with a safety pin.

"That's your Fuzzy Sock Elder?" Grimshaw asked.

Julian moved to the other side of the table. It wasn't casual enough to be anything but a man trying to put something between himself and a potential adversary, which Grimshaw found disturbing in too many ways.

"My great-grandfather's brother on my mother's side," Julian said. "He could sense a place. Worked construction, building houses mostly. The work took him beyond Intuit villages, but he was good and was hired on whenever he wanted the work. The company was scheduled to build a rich man's house, and when the uncle saw the land, he went to the foreman and told him it wasn't a good place, that the land was weak there and couldn't support the house. He pointed out a couple of other locations on the property where the house could be built safely, but the owner and the architect were firm about wanting the house to be built on the spot they'd chosen. He insisted that location would only bring darkness and sorrow to the family. He refused to work on the house, so he was assigned to the crew who built the barn and other outbuildings.

"The house was built. A month after it was completed, a sinkhole opened up and swallowed the house. The edges of the hole kept collapsing, so within hours, the house was buried under so much earth there was no way to save the man's family."

Grimshaw felt a bead of sweat trickle down his spine. "What happened?"

"People said the uncle had cursed the man and that was why the ground opened up and swallowed the house and family. One night a mob came to the uncle's house. They dragged him out of bed and hanged him, and when his pregnant wife ran out and pleaded with them to stop, they beat her so badly she and the baby died." Julian stared at Grimshaw. "A family story, told as a warning of what can happen to us when we tell people who aren't Intuits what we sense."

That explained a few things about Julian Farrow.

Not knowing what to say, Grimshaw pointed to the game. "Have you figured out anything from that?"

"I figured out that the reason I had so much trouble playing this game in the past is because the game board represented a place without *being* a place. So I was trying to sense something that didn't have enough markers—like trying to breathe in the scent of a rose by smelling a photograph of one. But this?" Julian waved a hand over the board with its additional woods and blue-paper lake. "That's close enough to act like a model for The Jumble."

"Do you think the same thing would happen with a model of a place you didn't know?" Could an Intuit look at a model of a village and sense a coming storm or a human-made problem like a bank robbery? Considering the story Julian had just told him, convincing Intuits to participate in such an experiment would take a lot of persuasion.

"I don't know," Julian replied. "We usually have a feel for the place where we live and the people around us. And unlike the blood prophets, who can see the future, what Intuits sense is immediate most of the time."

A thought for another day. "So what have you figured out about The Jumble?" He noticed a figure that could be teeny Julian standing two squares into the water and several other figures in the space between the "lake" and the house. "You're okay with your piece being in the water now?"

Julian paled, making the dark smudges under his eyes more pronounced, but he nodded. "If Vicki is around The Jumble, the water feels safe."

"And if she's not around?" Grimshaw picked up teeny Vicki and set her beyond the playing area.

Julian seemed to be fighting some impulse, but after a few

seconds, he grabbed teeny Julian and placed him in the kitchen on the game board. His breathing sounded labored.

Worried that Julian would need an emergency trip to the doctor's, Grimshaw set teeny Vicki in one of the wooded areas near a bear that was twice her size.

Julian's breathing returned to normal. "Sorry. I've been working through scenarios since yesterday. Guess I need a break."

"Sounds like a good idea." He looked at the little figures that were scattered around the board and the few that were out-of-bounds. "Last question." He picked up the business-man who had been out-of-bounds and set it right in front of teeny Vicki.

Julian's reaction was instantaneous. He jerked away from the table and shouted, "No!"

Grimshaw took the businessman off the board. "That's the trigger, isn't it? That's what set you off when we played the game the other night." Concerned about his friend, he moved around the table but stopped when Julian stumbled away from him, blind panic in the gray eyes.

"It's all right," Grimshaw said quietly. "Julian? It's Wayne. You're safe here. We're safe here." He pulled a chair away from the table. "Come on. Sit down before you fall down. You can't help them if you can't think clearly. Come on, Julian. Sit down."

Julian reached for the chair and fell into it. Grimshaw slipped the businessman figure into his pocket, poured glasses of water, and handed one to Julian.

"Yeah," Julian said after drinking the water. "That's the trigger."

"How many times did you test that while you were here alone?"

Julian hesitated. "I got used to working alone."

"Well, wrap your mind around the idea of working as part of a team," Grimshaw snapped. Coming from him, that was almost funny, but he didn't remember Julian being this spooked when he sensed something during their time at the academy or when they were working the streets together at the beginning of their careers. Then again, he didn't know how many times Julian had played out this scenario and had to work through his reaction on his own.

Wanting to think about something else, he focused on the sock and cocked a thumb in its direction. "The Crow did a better job."

Julian made a hand gesture that expressed his opinion quite clearly, then said, "Did you bring anything good for lunch?"

"I did." He fetched the covered plates and placed them on the two narrow strips of table that weren't covered by the game. He concentrated on eating for several minutes, glad to have the silence. As they finished the meal, he asked, "You still coming out for the trail ride and beach thing tomorrow?"

Julian nodded. "I did the trail ride wine tour when I first came to Sproing. It was . . . interesting."

"I'll bet."

Grimshaw collected the dishes and put them back in the carry bag. "I'll walk these over to the diner. See you tomorrow."

As he turned to go, Julian said, "Wayne? I think you still have a piece from the game."

"Yes, I do. I'm going to keep it for a while." He walked out, too aware of the teeny businessman in his pocket.

CHAPTER 40

Vicki

Thaisday, Juin 29

The morning of the trail ride beach party, I walked out of the laundry room and found a pony in the kitchen. To be precise, I found a pony with his head in the fridge, rummaging around. I wasn't sure if he was really looking for something or just enjoying the cold air that was wafting out of the fridge, but I realized the tried-and-true phrase "Were you born in a barn?" wasn't going to convey what I wanted it to convey.

I hurried around the table, giving myself plenty of distance from his back end, then skidded a little on some water. Gods, I hadn't been out of the kitchen long enough for the fridge to start defrosting from the heat, but where else could the water have come from?

Looking at the pony's tail, I chose not to contemplate the alternate answer to that question.

"Hey," I said sharply.

The pony pulled his head out of the fridge, a bunch of carrots dangling from his mouth.

He was a small white pony with a barrel-shaped body and chubby legs, and clompy hooves the size of dinner plates. Okay, they weren't that big, but I was wearing sandals and felt a little nervous about anyone who could stomp on my toes, intentionally or otherwise. Once I got over the surprise of finding a pony in the kitchen and stopped wondering if Hector or Horace had brought him over early for some reason, I started to wonder about the color of the pony's mane and tail. They were aquamarine, a lovely shade of greenish blue, with streaks of stormy gray. I wanted to believe there was some colored glass in the kitchen somewhere that was coloring those bits of him, but I knew there wasn't any colored glass. Maybe someone dyed the mane and tail? Not likely.

Which meant that whatever he was, he wasn't quite what he seemed. Which meant I should do the neighborly thing and let him have a carrot.

"I'll take those." I reached for the bunch of carrots. The open fridge door blocked him on one side and the kitchen table created a barrier behind him. Short of running me down to make his escape, there was nowhere for the carrot thief to go.

My hand closed on the carrots. His ears went straight out from his head, like little handlebars. I had a momentary crazy thought of grabbing the ears and saying *vroom-vroom*, but he still had clompy feet and I was still wearing sandals. After a brief tug-and-pull, I ended up with the carrots and he ended up with the green bits—which he dropped on the floor before following me to the counter beside the sink.

I washed one carrot and prepped it as if he were a human guest. As I cut up the carrot, I said casually, "I don't know if your person lets you have carrots."

Vigorous head bobbing, as if to say of course he was allowed to have carrots.

"You might be allergic to them."

Equally vigorous head shakes. Or maybe he was fluffing his mane as a prelude to flirting with me.

I fed him one of the carrot chunks and said, "Let's go outside."

I shut the fridge door, thinking hard as the pony and I walked out. I had a hand towel attached to the fridge's handle, so he could have pulled on that to open the door. And the screen door into the kitchen had a handle, so he could have pushed it down and then pulled on it to open that door. But the porch's screen door had a different kind of lock and latch, and there was no way a pony could get *that* one open.

"Caw!"

Unless he had an accomplice.

I studied the crow—or Crow—happily splashing in the birdbath. Could have been Aggie; I didn't see her in her Crow form often enough to be sure I could identify her in a lineup. Didn't matter. The pony had wanted to come in and someone had helped him. Why? No idea. Okay, I had an idea about why he had wanted to come in, but how would he have known about the carrots?

I also didn't know why a strip of the porch floor was wet, just like the floor from the kitchen door to the fridge was wet.

Every few yards I stopped and fed the pony another chunk of carrot. We continued that way until we arrived at the beach. Feeding him the last bit of carrot, I slipped off my sandals and dashed across the already hot sand to the water, intending to stand in the shallows for a few minutes before going back to wipe up the kitchen floor and get on with preparations for my part of this party.

The pony followed me into the water, and we both stood knee-deep in water that was refreshingly cool. Then the water began swirling around me, like a friendly animal circling my legs. There was no natural reason for it to do that all of a sudden, and the motion was causing the sand to shift under my feet.

Before I could become more than mildly alarmed, the Lady of the Lake rose out of the water to my left and said, "You shouldn't tease Miss Vicki after she gave you a carrot."

The swirling stopped. I looked to my right. The pony had disappeared.

"He's curious," she said, "but he won't hurt you."

I heard the slight emphasis on "you." "I'm glad you're here. I wanted to tell you that Ineke and I are hosting a beach party this afternoon, so there will be a few humans who will be swimming and using the beach. Maybe even taking a walk farther up the beach."

"These are friends?"

"Well, this group of people are friends. If this party is a success, Ineke and I will offer more trail ride beach parties to her paying guests and mine."

"Why offer parties to humans who are not friends?"

"They will be guests—humans who pay to stay in the cabins for a few days and spend time swimming in the lake."

"This is important, having humans who pay?"

"The money I earn from renting out the cabins will help me take care of The Jumble." And provide me with food and clothes and other essentials, but I figured The Jumble would be of more interest to her.

After a moment's consideration, she nodded. "I will tell the others. They may want to observe, but I will tell them to keep their distance from your guests."

Who wanted to observe?

"What happened to the pony?"

She laughed. "Whirlpool? He's around."

She sank into the water until only a vaguely human head and chest showed. Then she leaped high, her human-shaped torso becoming a column of water below the hips—becoming an arching prism of colors as she dove back into the lake.

I waited a minute, then headed back to the house.

Whirlpool. Really? I thought about the water swirling around my legs and decided it was better to think of something else before a party that had swimming as part of the activities. Like, who were the others who wanted to observe us? And why would the Lady tell them to keep their distance?

"Miss Vicki!"

I stopped and waited for Aggie, who came running up the path from the lakeside cabins to the main house.

"Did you let the pony into the house?" I asked when she reached me.

"Can I help you with your party? I've never been to a human party and—" Aggie stopped. Stared at me. "Pony?" She looked toward the lake, then focused on me again. *"Pony?"* She leaned toward me and whispered loudly, "One of *them*?"

Not knowing who *they* were, I couldn't answer that. "Maybe. His name is Whirlpool."

"Don't let him near your bathtubs."

Well, that sounded ominous—and made me deliriously happy that I preferred taking showers.

"Okay. But if you didn't let him into the house, please tell your pals not to help him get inside until we establish some ground rules for taking things out of the fridge."

"But you said the food in the kitchen was for all the guests," Aggie pointed out.

I could have pointed out in turn that, technically, Whirlpool wasn't a guest, but I had a feeling that broadening my definition of "guest" was right up there with "don't smack a Panther on the head" as a basic rule of how to live with all my neighbors.

"Even so, standing in front of an open refrigerator and staring at the food is a human boy behavior that females everywhere should discourage. So Whirlpool should wait for someone to help him if he wants a treat. And, really, a cold treat might not be good for his tummy."

Was a pony like Whirlpool in any way like a regular pony or horse? Would the same gastric rules apply? Something to ask Hector when he came over this afternoon.

"Can I help?" Aggie asked again.

As my lodger, she was entitled to join the party, and enlisting her help might encourage the rest of the Crowgard to prove they had good manners. Or not. It was worth a try. "Yes, you can help." I opened the porch's screen door. "The first thing we need to do is wipe up the water on these floors."

CHAPTER 41

Grimshaw

Thaisday, Juin 29

The horse called Buster studied Grimshaw. Grimshaw studied the horse. Horace said that a big rider needed a big horse. Grimshaw wasn't sure he needed anything *this* big, but there were a limited number of horses available for this trail ride, so he had to take what he was given.

As he moved to Buster's side to mount, he said quietly, "I may be off duty, but I'm still carrying."

Buster's response to that warning was to produce a copious amount of urine that Grimshaw swore had been aimed at his shoes before he skipped back a step.

When no one commented on this byplay, he gathered the reins and prepared to mount, grumbling, "Someday we'll have a vehicle that will be able to think for itself and get its passengers wherever they want to go."

"We already have such a thing," Hector replied, smiling as he gave Buster a pointed look. "Although, to be fair, our thinking vehicle doesn't always take you where *you* want to go."

"Great."

It wasn't feeling competitive—well, not much anyway—

that made him glad Julian's horse also looked like a plodder so he wasn't the only one riding a horse that might as well have a sign pinned to its tail that read, MY RIDER IS A STUPID BEGINNER. I'LL HANDLE THIS.

Or maybe it was just because Paige Xavier was riding this pretty mare named Blackie who pranced and flirted and tossed her head. A little like Paige herself, since she also enjoyed a little harmless flirtation, her blue eyes often filled with gentle mischief, especially when she talked to Officer Osgood. But Grimshaw felt better about her pretty mare when Horace mentioned that Blackie was Paige's horse and that she boarded the mare at the livery since it was just down the road from the boardinghouse.

Paige kept the horses to an active walk that allowed them to cover some distance but also allowed the riders to look around. Cultivated land, swaths of land full of grass and wildflowers, and woodland. He wasn't an expert, but the vineyard they rode past looked well tended. And well watched, he noted as he studied the hawks. Or were those Hawks? Even when one was perched on a fence post so that you could take a good look at it and judge the size, you couldn't really tell if it was one of the *terra indigene* watching you. He figured news about the trail ride beach party had spread and anything that was trailing them was one of the Others.

"Keep a firm hand on Buster," Hector called. "He's been to a few of the wine-tasting trail rides and we're coming up on . . ."

The familiar trail, Grimshaw concluded when Buster suddenly veered toward a wide track between rows of grapevines. Grimshaw reined in the horse and tried to turn him to follow the rest of the party, but Buster aimed himself toward the track and planted his feet. Clearly, if he wasn't allowed to go down *this* track, he wasn't going anywhere.

Then a Coyote dashed in front of him, startling the horse enough that, with Hector's help, Grimshaw finally turned the stubborn beast and continued on the trail toward The Jumble.

"Still want a vehicle that can think for itself?" Hector asked, laughing, before he dropped back to the end of the line.

Every time Buster thought about testing rider and rules, the Coyote showed up at the side of the trail. Grimshaw didn't think one Coyote was a real threat to a horse, but maybe Buster believed the one Coyote he could see meant there were many he couldn't see and cooperating with a human was his best chance of seeing his stall again.

They crossed the two-lane road that ran from the southern end of Lake Silence up to the crossroads leading to Sproing. As he guided Buster, Grimshaw noticed a small—and new—sign that read, JUMBLE TRAIL RIDE.

Woods. Trickles of water that might have been offshoots of Mill Creek or runoff from the rain. Grimshaw was beginning to enjoy the ride when the bridle path suddenly ran along plowed land that was being worked by a dozen . . . creatures.

He glanced at Paige when she reined in, looking startled and a little scared. Clearly this wasn't an expected part of the tour. But after a moment, Paige rallied, even if her tour guide voice was a little shaky. "This is The Jumble's kitchen garden. Many of the individuals who reside on this land are helping Miss Vicki to provide a variety of fresh food for her guests."

What Grimshaw saw were rough human forms—beings who, unlike Aggie Crowgard, would never be able to pass for human for an instant. Based on the shapes of their heads and the patches of fur covering their limbs and torsos, there were Coyotes and Foxes, as well as Crows and Hawks. And was that a Bobcat? He'd have to ask Vicki DeVine if any of the cabins were nearby. Were these *terra indigene* squatters? Did Vicki know about them? Did she know they were planting the garden? Maybe that was something to ask Ilya Sanguinati. After all, there was nothing a human police officer could do about the Others, but if they were taking over The Jumble, someone should be told.

The bridle path forked beyond the garden. Paige looked from one fork to the other and frowned.

Well, Grimshaw thought as he watched their guide, *we are the dry run for a paying trip.*

The Other that looked like a cross between human and Bobcat walked toward them, stopping when the horses tossed their heads and snorted. Getting them used to creatures that looked human—at least to a horse—but didn't smell human was probably another reason for this little party.

Paige gave the Bobcat a bright smile, as if seeing *terra indigene* working the garden wasn't the least bit surprising. "We're going to Miss Vicki's house. Do you know which one . . . ?" She gestured to the trails.

The Bobcat stared at her. Finally he pointed toward the right-hand trail. "House that way."

Rough voice. A Bobcat's throat shaping human words. Was this a first attempt to speak to an actual human? Grimshaw kept his focus on the Bobcat and wished he could study the rest of the *terra indigene* working in the garden. Were they all like that, having learned human speech from others of their kind but were now attempting to communicate with actual humans?

What had Vicki DeVine gotten herself into?

As they rode past, he and Julian raised a hand in a casual salute. After a moment, the Bobcat copied the movement.

Grimshaw made a note to talk to Ilya Sanguinati about that too. If the Others were going to observe and copy humans who came on these trail rides, they needed to understand that the tourists who came for one of these parties might not be the best role models. Some would be, certainly. Other guests would not.

The bridle path hugged a tumble of boulders that looked like they'd been tossed there casually and settled together. He saw Julian look up as they approached, which made him scan the boulders closely. If Julian hadn't sensed something, hadn't given him a reason to look with a cop's eyes, he

wouldn't have spotted Cougar crouched among the boulders,
watching them. The Cat didn't move, and the wind was in the
wrong direction for the horses to catch his scent. Good thing
too since one of the Panthergard *could* bring down a horse,
and the horses knew it.

He breathed a sigh of relief when they reached The Jumble's main house, rode around to the back, and dismounted.
Vicki and Ineke came out of the house to greet them. Ineke
looked confident, which was nothing new. Vicki looked nervy,
but not meltdown anxious about putting on this shindig.

"Would everyone like to go down to the lake for a bit to
cool off, or would you like some lunch first?" Vicki asked.

"Lake," Julian said, smiling.

"I vote for the lake," Paige said.

When Hector nodded, Grimshaw made it unanimous. He
wanted to see the beach here, to say nothing of spending a
little time in cool water.

Vicki led the men to the communal showers on one side
of the kitchen. Four showerheads, no dividers. Reminded
him of a locker room except it was decorated in blues and
greens and soft grays. Plants provided lush greenery, giving
the whole area an outdoor feel. But there were racks of folded
towels and a long wooden bench where people could sit.
There were pegs for clothes and little baskets for personal
items. A good place for guests to rinse off and dress after an
afternoon on the beach.

He didn't pay attention to Julian as he stripped off his own
clothes and pulled on swimming trunks, but he saw Hector's
face when the Simple Life man slipped into the room and
looked at Julian.

There were scars. More than he'd expected from what
he'd heard about the attack that had ended Julian's career as
a cop. He'd expected those scars to be deep and significant,
but there were others that looked like they had been acquired
in other life-threatening situations—and some that didn't
look old enough to have been acquired during Julian's years
on the force.

Julian met his eyes and shrugged into a white threadbare shirt to wear over the swim trunks, saying nothing. What was there to say? The scars spoke quite eloquently, and Grimshaw had a better understanding of why Julian Farrow had been looking for a quiet place to live.

Not wanting to make his friend self-conscious, Grimshaw looked away—and smiled when he saw Hector's swim attire. The trunks snugly covered the man from waist to knees, and the tank top was long enough to cover the crotch, probably for additional modesty.

"Is that traditional?" he asked.

"It is," Hector replied.

They took the provided beach towels and went outside to find the three women studying a small white pony who was grazing on the lawn.

"Where did he come from?" Grimshaw asked.

"I haven't seen him before," Hector replied.

Ineke moved closer to the pony, who stopped grazing to watch her. She pulled one of the sapphire streaks in her hair forward. She studied it, then studied the pony's greenish blue mane and tail before turning to Paige and Vicki. "What do you think about that color on me?"

"Gods," Julian muttered.

The women ignored him.

"I don't think aquamarine would work for you," Vicki said. "But on Paige . . . ?"

Paige pulled her braid over her shoulder and held it out for study. It was a soft red that had a glint of gold in sunlight.

"Yes," Ineke said. "That color would look better on Paige."

The men, and the pony, watched the women head for the water. Then Ineke turned and looked at them. "Are you guys coming?"

A man could get into all kinds of trouble answering a question that was phrased that way, but those tattoos on her thighs were intimidating enough to discourage any smart-ass remarks.

"On our way," Grimshaw said.

Julian blew out a breath. "I'm so glad I didn't know about those tattoos when I lived at the boardinghouse."

"Told you." Grimshaw headed for the water, looking forward to cooling off. Then he noticed the women had gone in up to their ankles and stopped—and seemed to be having an intense, whispered discussion. It was easier to figure out what the *terra indigene* were thinking than a human female, but he had the impression the discussion was about the knee-length cover-up Vicki was still wearing.

"You divorced him," Ineke said, sounding sharp, "which proves you have some sense. So forget what he said. What's a little cellulite among friends?"

Grimshaw saw Vicki's face flush, and he figured she was going to bolt and lock herself in the house, pretty much ending what might have been a pleasant afternoon.

Then Julian stepped forward and looked at Vicki. "We are among friends who don't judge us by how we look but by who we are, right?" He didn't wait for an answer. He shrugged out of the shirt, tossed it toward blankets spread out on the sand, and walked into the water—knees, thighs, waist. Then he dove under.

Ineke looked at Vicki. No question everyone had seen Julian's scars. Vicki hesitated a moment longer, then pulled off the cover-up and went into the water with Ineke and Paige.

Hector eased up next to him and whispered, "What's cellulite?"

Grimshaw shrugged. "A female obsession?" He eyed the other man. "But not among the Simple Life women?"

"If it is, it is not spoken of in the presence of men."

Lucky men.

Watching Julian swimming parallel to the beach, Grimshaw struck out in the same direction, angling to eventually meet up with his friend. They swam together for several minutes before Julian stopped to tread water.

Grimshaw looked around. Another beach but not sand. Stones and shale?

"This is a boundary," Julian said.

"For what?"

"Don't know. But I have the feeling we've crossed a line and are now in a part of the lake where we shouldn't be without permission."

Grimshaw scanned the shore. Was something hiding among the trees, unseen?

"Wayne," Julian breathed.

He turned and noticed Julian was looking at the water farther out from shore. Ripples, as if a large fish had broken the surface. "You see something?"

"I'm not sure, but I think we should join Vicki and the rest of her guests."

Something broke the surface. Maybe a large fish catching a meal, or was it something else coming up for air—or for a look at him and Julian? The arch of a back. A glimpse of a delicate, translucent dorsal fin. And at the last moment . . . "Was that a tail?" By all the gods, what had he just seen?

"We need to get back to the beach," Julian said.

He didn't argue. And if it felt more like they were racing on the way back, he thought they had good reason.

neke had brought a beach ball along with the blankets and towels. When Grimshaw and Julian reached them, Vicki and Paige were on one team and Ineke and Hector were on the other, playing water volleyball—except the idea seemed to be how long they could keep passing the ball between the teams before someone slipped and went under. Since Julian joined Vicki and Paige, Grimshaw went over to Ineke's team.

He wasn't sure how long they played—couldn't have been more than a few minutes—when Vicki and Ineke excused themselves and went up to the house to set out the lunch. A couple of minutes after that, Paige caught the ball and said, laughing, "We should go up now."

They got out of the water and dried off, but Grimshaw lingered, looking toward the lake. So did Julian. That was why they were the only ones who watched the white pony with the weird-colored mane and tail trot into the water and disappear. That was why they were the only ones who saw the water begin to swirl, a small circle at first but getting wider and wider—and deeper and deeper.

He didn't ask Julian, didn't really want confirmation that someone else could see a powerfully built yet insubstantial horse with that same coloring galloping round and round the edge of the whirlpool before the horse vanished and the lake rushed into the funnel shaped by the swirling water. A moment later, water lapped the sand and there wasn't any sign that anything had happened.

Grimshaw looked at Julian. Julian looked at him.

"This isn't new," he said quietly.

"No, this isn't new," Julian agreed. "But I think someone has decided to allow us to see it . . . and live."

CHAPTER 42

Vicki

Firesday, Juin 30

The guest suites in the main house were ready, and the renovated cabins were clean. I dithered about putting a vase of fresh flowers in each room along with a welcome basket, but I didn't have three vases. Well, I did, but they were old, chipped ones I'd found haphazardly packed away in the attic—all right for my use but not something you put out for guests.

The Milfords sold what they called weekend jars of jams and jellies—small containers that would be sufficient for one or two people for a couple of days without wasting the contents of larger jars since most people didn't want to eat from an opened container when they didn't know who had had their utensils—or fingers—in it. At breakfast, Ineke put out jams and jellies in small bowls to avoid waste, and I would need to figure out which way was the most practical for guests coming to The Jumble. The weekend jars could be something guests took with them, whether or not they had opened the jars during their stay. If I did that, it might provide more business for the Milfords, and that would be a good thing.

"Why do we need more humans here?" Aggie asked.

She had watched me go through my list of preparations since early that morning and had become more and more unhappy the closer we got to the arrival of the three couples who would be spending a long weekend with us.

"We need paying guests," I replied.

"I pay."

I stopped dithering and looked at her. She reminded me of a resentful teenager, but maybe she wasn't resentful of intruders, however temporary, as much as she wanted reassurance that she was equally valued.

"Yes, you do, and you're a great lodger." *If we overlook the whole squooshy eyeball thing.* "But I need more paying guests. In order to stay here and be the Reader and help all of you restore The Jumble as a *terra indigene* settlement, I need to make a living, need to make enough money to pay the bills. I can't do that with only one lodger. Do you understand?"

"Are you going to make the other *terra indigene* move out of the cabins?" she asked after a moment.

"Conan and Cougar? No, Aggie. They're helping me with the heavy work in exchange for using those cabins."

"I meant the *terra indigene* who are using the meadow cabins near the kitchen garden."

When Paige mentioned my having helpers to tend the kitchen garden, I thought she'd meant Conan and Cougar. "There are more *terra indigene* living in the cabins?"

Aggie nodded. "There's a Bobcat and a pair of Coyotes for sure. I think the Owlgard took the third cabin there." She moved this way and that, twitchy movements. "Maybe they should have told you?"

"Yes, they should have told me." When she seemed to shrink into herself, I added, "If I'd known, I would have gone over and introduced myself and made sure those cabins were habitable." Enough work had been done to stop further weather damage, but I hadn't expected anyone to stay there so the furniture I'd left in those cabins had been rickety at best. Then again, maybe the Others often took over aban-

doned human buildings and thought wobbly chairs and tables with peeling paint or stains in the wood were normal.

That made me sad, so I pushed the thought aside until I
could talk to Ilya Sanguinati. He would know if the Others
in those cabins were happy with the arrangement or felt
slighted in some way. And really, if anyone had felt slighted,
I wouldn't have been hearing about this from Aggie days
after my new residents had moved in. I'm sure the Bobcat or
the Coyotes—or even the Owls—would have expressed an
opinion in a way that was unmistakable.

Which suddenly made me wonder if they had been among
the *terra indigene* who had shown up for the story hours and
had moved into the cabins to be nearby. The sites for the four
guest buildings had been chosen to provide a sense of
privacy—or as much privacy as you could have when each
building was made up of three connected cabins—but none
of the buildings were more than a quarter mile from the main
house, and the renovated cabins were within sight of both the
lake and the main house—or would be if the bushes and
trees between the house and cabins didn't provide a natural
privacy screen.

"The humans are here," Aggie said.

"I didn't hear the cars." I touched my hair, hoping all the
effort I'd put in that morning to look professional hadn't gone
to waste. I could easily end up looking like Electric Shock
Lady when I greeted my guests.

"Eddie just told me that Cougar moved the chain across
the road to let them through. Eddie says the humans have
fancy cars, but not as nice as the ones the Sanguinati drive."

"Of course their cars aren't as nice."

She grinned and followed me to the front door to wait for
these visitors, now more curious than tense about what kind
of human would come to The Jumble.

I was curious about that too. But I can't say I wasn't tense.

CHAPTER 43

Aggie and Ilya

Firesday, Juin 30

Aggie flew across the lake as fast as she could. This was bad. This was very, very bad, and she was going to make sure the Sanguinati at Silence Lodge knew how very bad it was because those . . . *humans* . . . made her *so* angry.

When she reached the lodge, she perched on a railing for a moment before hopping down to the deck and shifting to her human form. Then she turned and stared at The Jumble's beach on the other side of the lake.

"Since Miss Vicki has human guests and you look human, you might want to put some clothes on so they don't see more than they're used to seeing," Ilya Sanguinati said as he stepped out of the lodge and joined her on the deck. "Not that they could see this far across the lake without binoculars, but humans often carry such things when they're in the wild country. Or so I've been told."

Aggie turned to face the vampire, whose lips were curved in a hint of a smile. "If the Crowgard peck out their eyes, they won't see anything."

The smile faded. "What happened?"

"They were mean to Miss Vicki. They made her *cry*!"

No amusement now. Ilya stared across the lake, then took a seat in one of the chairs. "Tell me."

Aggie and Miss Vicki watched three shiny cars drive up to the main house. At least, she thought they were cars. Miss Vicki had called them utility vehicles and said they were a good choice for camping and rougher roads. The humans got out and looked around, the females wrinkling their noses like they had smelled a wheelbarrow of poop—which they couldn't have because Cougar hadn't buried much poop in the flower beds at the front of the house since he had been careful not to dig up the flowers Miss Vicki had planted.

The humans were called Trina and Vaughn, and Darren and Pam-EL-la. They were staying in the main house with Miss Vicki. Hershel and Heidi were staying in the cabin next to Aggie's.

The humans didn't say much while Miss Vicki did the registering thing, took the payment, and told Hershel and Heidi that she would walk down to the cabin with them and help with the luggage because there wasn't a track to the cabins wide enough to accommodate anything bigger than a donkey cart, which she didn't have. Well, she had the cart, which was in pretty good shape—Conan had found it in the big shed with the tools—but not the donkey.

No, she hadn't told Miss Vicki about the herd of donkeys that lived in The Jumble. There had been no reason to say anything since the donkeys weren't *terra indigene* and Miss Vicki hadn't said she *wanted* a donkey; she just explained to the guest humans that their cars wouldn't fit on the track to the cabins.

They used the footpath between the main house and the cabins since that was shorter than using the track. The Heidi human carried her own carryall, but that Hershel gave the heaviest bag to Miss Vicki instead of carrying it himself. Once they reached the cabin and went inside, Miss Vicki returned to the house, intending to bring the guests a basket of fruit and treats, since Darren and Pam-EL-la had gone down to the cabin as soon as they dropped off their luggage in their suite. And Miss Vicki did bring the fruit and treats. But when she got back to the cabin, she heard the four humans talking and . . .

"And?" Ilya Sanguinati said. "What did they say?"

"They said Miss Vicki was as pathetic as they'd heard, and they were going to say so in their reviews, and The Jumble wasn't rustic or quaint; it was decrepit and wouldn't amount to anything—and *these* were the cabins she claimed were renovated when it was clear to anyone who bothered to look that she'd barely done anything at all. And then that Pam-EL-la said . . ."

Flight feathers sprouted from Aggie's arms and smaller feathers framed her face as she remembered the wounded look in Miss Vicki's eyes.

"She said Miss Vicki should hire someone presentable to deal with guests because no one with any social standing would want to deal with a person who looked like she'd been dragged through a bush backwards."

"This Pam-EL-la female is the one who said that?" Ilya asked mildly.

Aggie rounded on him, forgetting caution in her desire to remind him that Miss Vicki had been the first human to act as Reader in The Jumble for a long, long time, and she was *nice* and . . .

When she looked at him, she realized Ilya's mild voice hid the same burning fury that she felt.

"Yes, she said that."

Ilya thought for a moment. "Humans say unkind things about each other all the time when the person being . . . pecked . . . with words isn't around to hear."

"They knew she was there. Eddie Crowgard heard them talking before Miss Vicki came back to the cabins with the treats. They were *waiting* for her, *watching* so they would be sure she heard them."

"I see."

She was certain that he did see, and whatever happened to these humans would be a reflection of that seeing.

Aggie hesitated, but if the Sanguinati were going to take vengeful payment for the humans being mean, she should mention the one human who hadn't been mean. "The Heidi human . . . After Miss Vicki left the treats and went back to her nest to cry, Heidi said that maybe they shouldn't have let Miss Vicki believe they were reviewers from important travel magazines who were here in-cog-ni-to to tell other humans about The Jumble. But even her mate said she was being softhearted—or softheaded—and the sooner Miss Vicki was out of the way, the sooner their own deal could go through."

Ilya stared at her. "Out of the way. Is that the exact phrase they used?"

She nodded.

They said nothing for several minutes, just stared at the other side of the lake.

Finally Ilya stirred. "Who among the Crowgard here can take a human form well enough to pass for human?"

The answer was simple, but Aggie thought about it, trying to figure out why he would want to know. "Besides me? Clara. Eddie. Jozi."

"Eddie and Jozi are closer to your age, yes?"

"Yes. Why?"

"They're going to stay at the cabin with you. The three of you rented the cabin for the entire summer. The girls sleep in the bed and Eddie sleeps on the sofa."

"But Miss Vicki didn't rent it to three of us," Aggie protested. "We all decided that *I* would be the lodger." The Crowgard had discussed it and squabbled over it and finally voted on it, and she'd been so proud to be the one the rest of the Crows had selected for this important first contact with the human who had been working to repair The Jumble.

Ilya rose from his chair. Aggie tried not to flinch. In Crow form, she could fly fast, but the Sanguinati, in smoke form, could move even faster, could wrap around their prey and draw blood through the prey's skin. In human form, she didn't stand a chance against him.

Then again, neither did humans.

"You need to stay close to Miss Vicki and help her—and report to me everything the humans do and say around her. But these are dangerous humans, Aggie, and a lone Crow is vulnerable. I don't want you to be alone with those humans living so close."

"My kin live all around The Jumble."

"But not seen—or not understood for what they are. Three Crowgard in human form staying in a cabin? Better odds. Knowing there is a young male present, one who claims kinship to you, will discourage the males from being . . . inappropriate."

"Who is going to stop them from being inappropriate with Miss Vicki?" Aggie asked.

Ilya smiled, showing his fangs. "I will."

It wasn't until she was flying back to The Jumble that she remembered that, in the thriller books she liked to read, "out of the way" usually meant dead.

Ilya watched the Crow fly across the lake as he considered the information she had provided. Humans arriving at The Jumble under false pretenses, using words to open wounds. They knew one another, had come here as a pack. Had come incognito.

"Problem?"

Ilya glanced at Boris, who usually filled the role of chauffeur, insisting that a human who had a driver had more status than one who drove himself. Ilya wasn't sure that was true, but driving the car pleased Boris, so Ilya didn't argue about it. Besides, a chauffeur was considered to be in a different social class than an attorney, making it easier for Boris to talk to shopkeepers and flirt with—and feed on—the women who worked at the diner or the Pizza Shack.

Of course, feeding in Sproing might be more difficult now that the Sanguinati had taken over the bank, forcing the citizens to acknowledge their presence. All the more reason to protect the places that provided shelter for transient humans—like The Jumble and Ineke Xavier's boarding-house.

"Yes, there is a problem," Ilya replied. "The guests used words to harm Victoria, told lies to make her think they are something they are not."

"Easy enough to eliminate problems," Boris said blandly.

The thought of how to eliminate those problems made him hungry, so he pushed it aside—with regret. "Killing the first guests at The Jumble would not encourage other humans to visit."

"It might, if we started a rumor that one of the cabins was haunted. We could even assist with the props—a chair that rocked on its own; a radio that turned on by itself; a blank pad of paper that had the beginning of a note written on the first page the next time a human walked by. Easy enough for one of us to do."

Ilya huffed out a laugh. "We'll save that possibility." He sobered quickly, his anger returning full force. "For now, we need to know who these humans really are and where they're from. We need to know if they're the danger Julian Farrow sensed closing in on Victoria, or if these humans are like Detective Swinn and his men. Are they more hounds to chase and harry, or are they the hunters, the real threat to Victoria?"

"I could fetch the car," Boris said. "We could drive over and pay a call."

"No, I don't want to announce our connection to The Jumble. Not yet." His lips curved in a savage smile. "But that doesn't mean we can't cross the lake and wait for an oppor-tunity to find out more about Victoria's guests."

CHAPTER 44

Vicki

Moonsday, Sumor 3

"If these are the kind of people I'll have to deal with on a regular basis, I don't think I'm cut out for this business," I told Ineke as I sat in her kitchen instead of running the errands I had told my guests I needed to run. The truth? I hadn't *needed* to run errands first thing that morning. I had needed to run away from my guests.

"They're checking out tomorrow morning, so you're almost done with them. You can hang on for one more day." Ineke pushed a plate of double-fudge brownies closer to me. "Eat a few of these. You might end up in a chocolate coma and not wake up until it's time for them to check out."

"I agreed to pick up pastries and other appropriate breakfast foods since I can't be bothered with serving meals, which is what I *should* be doing if I want to keep up the pretense that The Jumble is a vacation spot."

"Is that a direct quote?"

"Close enough." I reached for a brownie. Then I thought about the "helpful pointers" that had been made for the past three days every time I saw one of my guests. Well, screw them. If I was already a ginormous, slovenly glutton with a permanent bad hair day, I might as well stuff my face with food because, with my lack of looks, style, or fashion sense, a man who wasn't desperate wouldn't give me the time of day let alone a screw. As if I wanted one! Yorick had cured me of *that* little fantasy, and now I knew the only good, romantic sex was found in romance books.

I bit into the brownie and chewed furiously, struggling against the tears stinging my eyes. Then I noticed the way Ineke stared at me.

I swallowed, forcing the bite of brownie down a tight throat.

"How much of that did I say out loud?"

I never found out how much I'd said because Dominique and Maxwell walked into the kitchen from outdoors at the same moment Paige slammed into the kitchen, a plate full of food held between her shaking hands.

"He said the eggs are cold and rubbery. He told me to take his plate away and he would make do with something else. Then he said—" She choked and would have dropped the plate if Dominique hadn't grabbed it and set it on the table. "He said he wouldn't mention the eggs or the inferior service he'd received so far if I was *nice* to him. And then he—"

"Sweetie, he's a terrible person," Dominique said, guiding Paige to a chair. "We agreed yesterday that you shouldn't go in by yourself if he was the only one in the dining room." She looked at me. "Grabby hands."

I didn't remember setting the brownie down, but I wasn't holding it when I pushed away from the table. "That's awful! Ineke . . ." I stopped and watched Ineke calmly remove a large pair of shears from one of the kitchen drawers.

"Would you like to come with me while I explain a few things to Mr. and Mrs. Daniel Yates?"

I didn't know what to do about my own guests—they weren't attacking anyone but me, after all, and words weren't a weapon you could report to the police—but I would stand with Ineke to put a stop to her girls being harassed by someone who probably would argue that grabbing a girl's ass was a form of flirtation and the girl was overreacting and just trying to stir up trouble.

Ineke and I walked into the dining room, followed by Maxwell, who whined because he knew something was very wrong with his family but didn't know what to do.

"Mr. Yates," Ineke said at the same time a thin, dark-haired woman who looked like she would kill for a candy bar pushed past us and entered the dining room.

I recognized her. I recognized him too, the blond-haired, blue-eyed man who had more of a paunch than he'd been carrying a few months ago. "Oh gods, you have got to be kidding." I turned to Ineke. "That isn't Daniel Yates. That's my ex-husband, Yorick Dane, the second Mrs. Dane, and the Vigorous Appendage."

"Shit," Ineke snarled.

Maxwell zipped around the room, then started talking to us in that growly, barky, yip-yip way he used when conversing with humans, clearly wanting some kind of answer.

"Can't you shut that thing up?" Mrs. Dane said, further endearing herself to the whole Xavier family.

"Vicki named three and he can only find two," Ineke said.

"Well, if *that's* what Maxwell is asking about . . ." I pointed at Yorick's crotch and said, very loudly, "That's where Mr. Grabby Hands is hiding the Vigorous Appendage!"

CHAPTER 45

Grimshaw

Moonsday, Sumor 3

Dressing for work and wondering what Ineke was serving for breakfast, Grimshaw suddenly cocked his head, his khaki short-sleeve shirt dangling from his fingers, and listened to voices loud enough to penetrate the door to his room on the second floor—male and female, punctuated by Maxwell barking.

When he heard the piercing scream, Grimshaw dropped his shirt, grabbed his service weapon, and rushed out of his room, colliding with Osgood. The baby cop wore nothing but a pair of cutoffs and still had beads of water on his chest from the shower, but he also had his weapon.

They ran down the stairs and followed the screams. Easy enough to see the action was in the dining room, but getting to it might be a problem. Vicki DeVine was trying to hold on to Maxwell, telling him it was all right, that Mr. Grabby Hands hadn't eaten the Vigorous Appendage; he'd just hidden it. The woman he couldn't see but could hear yelling for someone to call an ambulance had to be Mrs. Yates, one of the new guests. And Ineke . . .

"What were you planning to do with the shears, Ineke?" he asked.

She turned toward him, a murderous look in her dark eyes. She raised the shears and focused on them. Open, close. Open, close.

"Nothing," she said with a smile that made Grimshaw's balls shrink and sweat trickle down his spine. "Maxwell took care of it."

"Somebody call an ambulance!" Mrs. Yates screamed.

Grimshaw held out his left hand, reluctant to move too close to Ineke. She stared at him a moment too long before offering the shears. He quickly handed them off to Osgood and stepped into the dining room, putting the safety on before tucking his gun into the waistband of his trousers.

Mr. Yates was on the floor, holding his crotch and screaming. More like whimpering now. Then he saw Grimshaw and yelled, "That fucking dog attacked me! Shoot it!"

"Don't be so melodramatic, Yorick," Vicki snapped. "Maxwell didn't attack *you*. He was trying to rescue the Vigorous Appendage." She rubbed the border collie's head. "Weren't you, Maxwell? You just wanted to rescue the wiggly duckling from the grabby man."

Oh gods.

Then . . . Grabby man? Yorick? That wasn't the name he'd been given when they'd all had dinner here last night.

He thought about Vicki's words and the look in Ineke's eyes—and the way Paige had gone quiet at some point during the weekend. No flirting with Osgood. No teasing him. Not even a smile. As if she didn't want to be noticed.

"Ms. DeVine, would you take Maxwell into the kitchen and wait for me there?" he asked.

"I really should be going. I'm supposed to . . ."

He gave her the "Don't mess with me" stare.

Vicki stared back, her defiance lasting longer than he'd expected. Then she nodded. "We'll wait for you in the kitchen."

"You too, Ms. Xavier."

Ineke left the dining room without a word in protest, and that worried him. He took the shears from Osgood and said quietly, "Talk to Paige and Dominique. See if you can coax them into telling you what's going on."

Finally he turned to the Yateses. Or, more correctly, Mr. and Mrs. Dane. Yorick Dane had managed to get off the floor and collapse into a chair.

"You want to tell me what happened?" The wording sounded friendly, as if they had a choice.

"That beast attacked me!" Dane said. "It's a danger to people and should be shot."

"Well, Maxwell is protective of his people."

"It's the fault of Vicki DeVine," Mrs. Dane said. "She's the one who riled up the beast to attack my husband out of spite and jealousy. Just because we're going to—"

"*Constance.*"

The word came out breathy, but Grimshaw heard the warning in Dane's voice.

"What are you doing in Sproing?" he asked.

"We wanted to get away from the city," Mrs. Dane said.

"There are resorts on the lakes closer to Hubb NE. Why here?" He kept his voice friendly.

"I have property here," Dane said.

"You had property here," Grimshaw corrected. "Unless you've purchased something the residents haven't heard about yet—which is unlikely—the only property that had formerly belonged to the Dane family is The Jumble. And that now belongs to Vicki DeVine."

"It still belongs to the Dane family, since Vicki didn't fulfill the terms of the agreement," Dane corrected in turn. "But I had hoped to discuss this with her quietly, like adults. Avoid embarrassing her in front of her neighbors, since I'm sure she didn't make anyone privy to the arrangement."

"Except her attorney." Grimshaw smiled. "I'm sure he's reviewed all the documents that pertain to transfer of ownership."

Dane went pale. Or paler, since he hadn't regained any color yet.

Didn't know about the attorney, did you? Which means

you probably don't know who represents Ms. Victoria DeVine.

"I'll contact Dr. Wallace and ask him to make a house call."

"I want that woman charged with assault," Dane snapped.

Grimshaw nodded. "Assault with a border collie. Not something I put in a report every day."

"You think this is funny?" Mrs. Dane demanded.

"No, I never think assault is funny. Which is why I will write up the report against Ms. Xavier—just as soon as I determine if I'm also writing up a report against Mr. Dane for sexual assault."

He walked out of the dining room, leaving them sputtering.

CHAPTER 46

Vicki

Moonsday, Sumor 3

"It was a stupid and impulsive thing to do, and it's my fault, so you can't blame poor Maxwell for trying to rescue a small critter," I said as soon as Officer Grimshaw walked into the kitchen.

Even only wearing the khaki trousers and a white undershirt, he still looked intimidating and official—especially now that I was having trouble holding on to my mad—and intriguing because he also wore a round gold medal on a chain, a medal that looked like the ones sold at the Universal Temples as an acknowledgment of a person's guardian spirit. Somehow I hadn't thought of Grimshaw as a spiritual man.

Yorick and I had attended the neighborhood Universal Temple while we were married for the same reason we'd gone to parties or other social events that were attended by people he claimed to despise—to be seen so that another checkmark would be made in the proper column. He'd scoffed at having any material reminder of the gods and guardian spirits who were supposed to watch over humans.

I should ask Ineke if there was a guardian spirit who looked out for innkeepers of all sorts, including caretakers of *terra indigene* settlements.

Grimshaw didn't respond to my opening confession. He just stared out the kitchen door to where Osgood and Paige were slowly walking across the lawn to a bench under one of the big maple trees. Then he sat at the table and leaned toward Ineke.

"Does Paige need to see a doctor?" he asked. He looked at Dominique, who was standing at the counter. "Do you?"

Dominique shook her head, and Ineke said, "If either of them had needed a doctor because of him, he wouldn't have been curled up on my floor like a cooked shrimp."

She didn't say what *would* have happened, but I didn't think Grimshaw had forgotten about the "I Bury Trouble" tattoo on her thigh. I sure hadn't.

Maybe I didn't want to ask Ineke about the compost she used in her kitchen garden to make the vegetables grow so well.

"Do you want some breakfast, Officer Grimshaw?" Dominique asked.

He shook his head. "Just coffee, if it's convenient."

She poured him a cup, then went outside to join Paige and Osgood.

"What happened?" He held up a hand. "Not just now in the dining room. What has happened since the Danes arrived using an alias? And, damn it, Ineke, you have two cops in the house. Why didn't you say something about Dane's behavior?"

Ineke shrugged. "We've dealt with men like him before."

I thought about the vacations Yorick and I had taken. I thought about the look on the faces of the young women who had worked in the hotels or resorts. I thought about how I'd believed for so long that there was no connection between the poor service we received and the way those women looked at him—and the blend of pity and resentment aimed at me.

"If I'd known your guest was Yorick, I would have warned you," I said quietly.

"I know," Ineke replied. Then she smiled. "I don't think Mr. Dane was prepared to get head butted by Maxwell—or have him trying to dig through the pants to reach the wiggly."

"I think it was when Maxwell got his teeth around the zipper—and maybe a bit more—that . . ."

"Stop," Grimshaw said.

I'd forgotten about him. Which wasn't easy to do since he was sitting right there. Although he did look a wee bit green.

"If Dane presses charges, you'll press charges, and if he drops the assault charges, you'll do the same?"

Ineke studied him. "Are you asking or telling?"

"Asking."

"I won't file an official complaint against him as long as he does the same."

After living in Sproing these past few months, I knew what that meant. Ineke didn't have to file an official complaint because, by now, all the people who worked in service businesses had already heard about Yorick's wandering hands and his view that there was nothing wrong with "trying it on" to see if "no" really meant "yes." Once word spread that Mr. Yates was actually one of the Danes, there wouldn't be a girl in the village Yorick could even look at without a father or older brother blocking his view.

Ineke might be one of the odd Xaviers who ran a boardinghouse, but she had considerable influence within a certain segment of the village's population—and as Grimshaw had pointed out, she had the village's two cops rooming with her right now.

And while I would never, ever, *ever* say this when there was any possibility of Grimshaw hearing me, it occurred to me that if I quietly pointed out Yorick to the Sproingers as well as the Crows, he wouldn't be able to sneak off to meet anyone for any reason without someone—or something—paying attention.

CHAPTER 47

Grimshaw

Moonsday, Sumor 3

Grimshaw parked his cruiser in the space next to the black luxury sedan. He got out and nodded to the man standing in front of the sedan, wearing a chauffeur's hat. He knew Ilya Sanguinati usually had a driver, but this was the first time that individual was making a point of being seen.

Was it a coincidence that the point was being made today, or was it a deliberate message?

The Sanguinati had controlled this village from behind the scenes for who knew how many generations. Now they weren't being subtle about the businesses and property they owned. Some of that might be due to the upheaval last summer, when someone somewhere had made the decision to show the humans living on the continent of Thaisia that there were fewer human places than they had wanted to believe, and none of those places were safe. Here in Sproing, the trouble at The Jumble and the pressure on Vicki DeVine—and the Others' interest in her—had been the tipping point when it came to the Sanguinati's decision to come out of the shadows. When the *terra indigene* not only controlled all the natural resources but also openly controlled things like banks and commerce, arrogance was an indulgence humans could not afford.

Which made whatever was going on here even more dangerous.

"Is Mr. Sanguinati in his office?" Grimshaw asked the driver.

"He is." The vampire's voice was stiffly polite and offered nothing.

"Thanks." Grimshaw opened the glass door that led to the second floor and went halfway up the stairs before he stopped and pulled out his mobile phone to make a call.

"Lettuce Reed."

"Julian, it's Wayne. Can you close up for a few minutes?"

"I'm not officially open yet. You're at the station?"

"Going up to Ilya Sanguinati's office. I'd like your input." He waited for Julian's usual protest about not being on the police force anymore.

"Does this have something to do with what I sensed when we played the Murder game?"

"I think so."

"I'll be right over."

Grimshaw waited at the top of the stairs. When Julian joined him, he knocked on the door that didn't have a company name before turning the knob and going in.

The small receptionist's desk was bare of everything but a notepad, a pen, and a telephone. It looked old and ornate and in pristine condition, making Grimshaw wonder when the furnishings had been moved into this office—and how anyone had gotten the furniture up the narrow flight of stairs. Floor-to-ceiling bookcases created a partial wall that divided the reception area from what he assumed was a private office.

"Come in, gentlemen," Ilya Sanguinati said.

No surprise that Ilya had known who had entered his space. The *terra indigene* could communicate with one another over distances, and the driver would have told him who was climbing the stairs for a meeting.

Grimshaw walked to the opening that served as a doorway and stopped, surprised at the lush plants that filled the credenza beneath the windows overlooking Main Street. The desk in this room was twice the size of the other and was also an antique, but it had a monitor and keyboard on one side and a telephone and trays for paperwork on the other side.

Ilya Sanguinati looked up and blanked the screen on the monitor. "Officer Grimshaw. Mr. Farrow. Is there something I can do for you?"

Grimshaw settled in one of the visitors' chairs while Julian took the other. "Yorick Dane is in town, staying at Ineke's."

Julian snapped to attention and swore quietly.

"I'm surprised she let him through the door," Ilya said.

"He used an alias. Vicki DeVine identified him during a ruckus this morning. He and his wife aren't scheduled to check out until tomorrow, but I'm sure Ineke will want to toss him out as soon as Dr. Wallace examines him. I need your help to persuade her to let him stay for the rest of today."

"Why would I do that?" Ilya asked in a mild way that filled Grimshaw with dread.

"Yes, Wayne, why let that man stay another hour?" Julian asked with an edge in his voice.

"According to Dane, his family still controls The Jumble because Vicki didn't fulfill the terms of the agreement," Grimshaw replied, watching Ilya.

Something cold and ugly moved in Ilya's eyes, a reminder that a taste for antiques and expensive clothes didn't change the fact that the Sanguinati were lethal predators.

"I read through all the paperwork with regard to the divorce settlement and Victoria's claim to The Jumble," Ilya said. "There were no conditions to her receiving The Jumble, no terms that needed to be fulfilled."

Grimshaw nodded. "I figured as much. If everything was aboveboard, Dane wouldn't have come here using a false name." Well, it would have been hard for Dane to find a place to stay if he'd used his own name unless he wanted to rent one of the houses on High Street for a month—or stay in one of the run-down campers at the edge of town.

Ilya hesitated, then handed Grimshaw a sheet of paper from a legal pad. "He isn't the only one who has come here under false pretenses. The humans staying at The Jumble also gave aliases. And they're pretending to be reviewers for travel magazines. Also, they were overheard to say that Victoria had to be removed from The Jumble before their own deal could go through."

"How did you get these names?" Grimshaw looked up. "You didn't ask Aggie Crowgard to go poking around in their rooms, did you?"

"Of course not. For one thing, Crows can't get through the screens in the windows, something which is not an impediment to the Sanguinati in our smoke form. I entered the suites in the main house, found the humans' identity cards, and memorized the names and addresses. My driver uncovered the real identities of the two humans who are staying in one of the renovated cabins."

"What's the second reason you didn't ask the Crows?" Julian asked.

Ilya gave him an arch look. "I didn't want them to be tempted by the shinies scattered on the dressers—at least not while Victoria still has control of The Jumble. If ownership should change hands . . ." His shoulders moved in a minute shrug.

Grimshaw handed back the paper and pinched the bridge of his nose, as if that would relieve the headache building behind his eyes. "Any thoughts about what's really going on? Because I'm not buying Dane's claim that Vicki failed to meet part of the agreement and the Dane family can reclaim The Jumble by default."

Ilya sat back in his chair. "When I reviewed all the legal documents that dealt with Victoria's divorce and settlement, I found it interesting that the listed value of the house, automobile, and furnishings that Yorick Dane retained was considerably less than the value of The Jumble, despite the automobile being fairly new and the house needing nothing more than annual maintenance. The liquid assets were divided based on those assessments."

"The Jumble is a business venture made up of several buildings and acres of land, not to mention private access to the lake," Grimshaw said. "It stands to reason it would be worth more than the residence."

"No one had put any work into those buildings in decades," Julian countered. "That should have been taken into account by whoever had done the assessment."

Ilya smiled, showing a hint of fang. "A good point, Mr. Farrow, and one I believe was, in fact, taken into account. Among the papers Franklin Cartwright had been carrying on the day he was killed were notes indicating that he had been in Sproing prior to the date when Yorick Dane filed for divorce and had made a careful assessment of The Jumble's condition at that time and what it would cost to turn the place into a 'stage-one income stream.' The cash settlement to Victoria was sufficient for her to make all the major repairs to the main house and at least some of the cabins. Perhaps all of the cabins, but she was practical about holding back the money she needed to live on during the months of renovation and the time it would take to attract paying guests."

"I don't remember the CIU team finding any paperwork near Cartwright's body," Grimshaw said. He certainly hadn't seen any when he'd secured the scene and waited for the CIU boys to show up.

"They didn't," Ilya replied so pleasantly there was no question that the subject was closed.

Meaning, whatever information the Sanguinati had would be shared when *they* wanted to share, and there was nothing the human police could do about it.

Grimshaw frowned. "So Dane knew how much Vicki DeVine would have to sink into the buildings to turn The Jumble into a rustic resort because he had hired Franklin Cartwright to assess the property. And then he had Cartwright come back here to find out if she'd done enough work to make it worth his while to reclaim it?"

"To reclaim it as a stage-one income stream," Julian said. "Which means there is a stage two." He stared at Ilya. "Did you find anything else in those papers Franklin Cartwright was carrying when he died?"

A weighted silence. Then Ilya opened a drawer and removed a stack of papers. He unfolded one and turned it so that Grimshaw and Julian could see it.

A map of The Jumble. But not The Jumble as it was today. Not a rustic resort. This was a luxury resort. And that made no sense.

"Mr. Paperhead," Julian whispered. His hand clamped on Grimshaw's wrist. "Ineke, Vicki, Paige, Dominique. All in danger. That was Vicki's dream."

By itself, Vicki's dream had been nothing more than a weird dream—a concoction of images her subconscious had burped into her sleep. He'd taken down the details to appease the Others and, all right, to be a hard-ass about being called to The Jumble because of a dream. But, for him, it had been Julian's response to the dream that had given weight to the whole thing then—and now.

"Eight people arrive in Sproing at the same time, using false names," Ilya said. "Six of them know each other. It stands to reason they also know Yorick Dane since one of them referred to a deal involving The Jumble."

Grimshaw nodded. "Odds are building a luxury resort would require investors, and those people would want to take a look at their property. Dane couldn't have stayed with them at The Jumble even under an assumed name. Vicki recognized him as soon as she saw him."

But was that the only reason Dane had stayed at the boardinghouse? Or was he scouting? As Julian had pointed out when they'd sat in Ineke's parlor the other day discussing the dream, Ineke and Vicki owned the two properties around Sproing that accommodated travelers. Still, when he considered all the potential people involved in Dane's attempt to reclaim The Jumble, it just didn't add up.

"Is The Jumble as it is now really a lucrative enough business for a group of people to conspire to take it from Vicki DeVine?" Grimshaw asked.

"I've heard that fishermen lust for a chance to fish in Mill Creek, but the best runs aren't on easily accessible—or safe—land," Julian replied. "It may be seasonal, but I can see Vicki's creekside cabins providing a nice income, even in their primitive state, as long as permission to fish in the creek was part of the rental agreement. And the cabins near the lake would make some money too." Julian shrugged. "I think an individual could make a living from renting the cabins, but the only way I can see for a group of investors to make enough would be to develop the land."

"Which still belongs to the *terra indigene*," Ilya said. "The Dane family owned the buildings, and only as long as they abided by the terms of the original agreement. They never controlled any part of the land."

"Does Yorick Dane know that?" Julian asked.

Ilya looked surprised. "How could he not know? He supplied a copy of the original agreement with the rest of the papers Victoria received with regard to the divorce settlement." He waved a hand at the map. "This luxury resort will never be built."

Because the moment someone digs up a spade of earth for something other than a flower bed or garden, people are going to die, Grimshaw thought.

"If the people staying at The Jumble are investors in this scheme of Dane's, I wonder if he's told any of them about the original agreement and the building restrictions," Julian said. "After all, he finagled the divorce settlement so that it looked like he was being fair. Why be truthful with potential investors?"

"And if they all belong to the Tie Clip Club?" Grimshaw asked.

"Then someone believes, in the face of all reason, that they can build this thing without the *terra indigene* noticing. It's a kind of willful blindness that occurs most often in humans who live in human-controlled cities. Some people still believe they can make the Others disappear simply by insisting that everything that lives in the wild country doesn't exist."

"Enough," Ilya said. "We have stripped the meat from the bone and there is nothing left but gristle."

Grimshaw had to agree. Outside of giving false names, the people staying at The Jumble hadn't done anything wrong—at least, nothing that had been reported to the police. "I'll see what I can find out about Vicki's guests."

"Inquiries are already being made about them, but your

sources may have access to different information." Ilya tore a sheet of paper off a legal pad and copied the names and addresses he'd found. He handed the sheet to Grimshaw.

"If I find out anything useful, I'll let you know." Grimshaw stood and folded the paper until it fit into a pocket. "Are you going to ask Vicki DeVine to leave The Jumble?"

Instead of answering, Ilya looked at Julian, who stared out the window behind Ilya's desk.

"The village is all stirred up and doesn't feel . . . comfortable, but I'm not sensing physical danger within the village boundaries," Julian said slowly. "I don't think the real danger has arrived yet, so Vicki doesn't have to leave The Jumble today." He thought for a moment. "But soon. Soon."

"When that time comes, I'll get her away from The Jumble," Ilya said, standing up to indicate the discussion was finished.

Grimshaw didn't offer his hand. Neither did Julian. They left the office and walked down the stairs but stood just inside the glass door at street level.

"This was a setup from the start," Julian said, staring at the street.

"Yep." And so far, Yorick Dane's scheme had been indirectly responsible for the deaths of four men. He needed to apprise Captain Hargreaves that there was a serious situation brewing around Sproing.

As they stepped outside, Grimshaw heard the phone ringing in the police station. When it kept ringing, he hurried to unlock the door. It stopped ringing the moment he walked inside, but his mobile phone started.

"Grimshaw."

"Sir? Sir, are you there?" Osgood didn't sound steady.

He didn't point out to the baby cop that, since he answered his own phone, he was there. "Problem?"

"There's a situation at The Jumble."

"What kind of situation?"

"I guess you would call it vandalism. Or threatening behavior."

He looked at Julian, who gave him the "I'm not a cop

anymore" look in return. But he couldn't count on Osgood if he had to deal with any of the furred or feathered residents at The Jumble. Not yet, anyway.

"What, exactly?" he asked.

"Something opened a back window on one of the cars and peed—well, sprayed a lot of urine on the seats. And one of the cars was flipped over on its roof."

"That's the vandalism. What's the threatening behavior?"

"Unspecified."

"Are you still at the boardinghouse?"

"Yes, sir."

"Is Vicki DeVine?"

"Yes."

"Then let her know I'm going out to investigate. Tell her to stay in town until I give the all clear. You got that?"

"She'll be concerned about her guests."

"Then you take her car keys. And try to impress on Ineke that Vicki should stay with her."

"Yes, sir."

Julian didn't say a thing. He got in the cruiser on the passenger side before Grimshaw opened the driver's side door.

"You're not a cop anymore. I know." He looked at his friend. "But this is a bit of yahoo frontier law at this point." Not that highway patrol didn't always have a bit of yahoo frontier law. Not that highway patrol officers didn't walk into dangerous situations before backup could reach them. But screwing up in the wild country usually meant a single life at risk, not a chain reaction that could lead to an entire village disappearing if he lost control of the situation.

"I want to take a look at these guests," Julian said. "I want to know if the feel of The Jumble has changed because of them. For all our sakes."

Grimshaw pulled out of the parking space, turned on his lights, and headed for The Jumble.

CHAPTER 48

Vicki

Moonsday, Sumor 3

Poor Osgood. He never stood a chance. If he'd come in like Grimshaw would have done, all official and imposing, held out his hand, and told me to hand over my car keys, I would have been sufficiently intimidated to do exactly that. But despite being dressed in his uniform, Osgood had radiated nerves when he asked for my keys. Nerves made him a regular person instead of an official police person, so I, quite reasonably, asked him why he needed the keys, and Paige asked if there was something wrong with his car that he needed to borrow mine. By that time, Ineke had realized something was a trifle off and flanked him.

The three of us and Osgood in the middle. It made me think of a nature show I'd watched last year about a pride of lions in Afrikah. The little critter caught by the lionesses hadn't stood a chance either.

A pride of lions. A pride of Xaviers. Would Ineke find humor in the comparison? Maybe it was something Julian Farrow would appreciate.

Or not.

In short order, we knew why Osgood wanted the keys, where Grimshaw had gone, and that there was some kind of disagreement between the guests and The Jumble's residents. It took a few minutes more to fully appreciate that Osgood was so freshly out of the police academy that coming to Sproing with Detective Oil Slick Swinn and the rest of that team—and encountering the *terra indigene* who killed some of those men—was his first assignment. So while he had the academy training for what to do with lawbreakers and ordinary people things, he didn't have any on-the-job training yet that would help him cope with the Elders—or with women like the Xaviers.

All to my advantage.

Since we didn't want Osgood to get into trouble with Grimshaw, who was his boss, at least for the short term, I gave him my car keys, which were what he'd been told to acquire. Then Ineke and I packed up what food she could spare, ran out to *her* car—which did not fall under Osgood's orders—and drove to The Jumble, leaving Paige to handle Osgood, which wouldn't be hard if she fibbed a little and told him that Dominique and Maxwell were out and she felt uneasy about being at the boardinghouse alone while Yorick was still there and couldn't Osgood stay until Ineke got back?

"When do you think Osgood will realize Paige wouldn't have been alone?" I asked.

"She would have been," Ineke replied, making a sharp turn. "Dominique took Maxwell for a walk so he wouldn't spend the whole day standing in front of the Danes' bedroom door, growling."

"Do you think he'll forget about the Vigorous Appendage by the time he gets back from the walk?"

"He's a border collie. He doesn't forget anything he can possibly herd."

"Well, that should shorten Yorick's visit."

Ineke suddenly looked grim. "Don't count on it."

When we reached The Jumble, I didn't recognize the young man who unhooked the chain across the access road, but he had the look of one of the Crowgard.

"I'm Eddie," he said as we rolled slowly past him. "I'm helping Aggie and Jozi. And the Sanguinati."

Helping them with what?

Grimshaw's cruiser was parked in front of the main house, as far from the three utility vehicles as he could manage and still turn around without hitting a tree. The UV in the middle looked untouched. The one I approached after getting out of Ineke's car had an open back window and . . .

I clapped both hands over my nose and mouth, while Ineke said, "Gods above and below, that's a stink!"

Maybe human pee smelled just as bad to Cougar—or whatever had sprayed an opinion into the interior of the UV—but the vehicle smelled like a well-used litter box without the litter.

The third UV, which was a greenish brown, looked like a rubber-footed turtle that had been flipped on its back.

I decided right then and there that she who lives in The Jumble should never, ever, *ever* think too long or too hard about the large beings that also lived in The Jumble because thinking about them being out there would lead to anxiety attacks and an inability to go outside.

Even though we arrived bringing brunch and lunch, Grimshaw wasn't happy to see us, and Julian looked wary, although he tried to hide it. My guests weren't trying to hide anything. Four of them were expressing themselves at full volume about the lack of service, about their being threatened, about damage to property. Trina wasn't in the hall. Heidi was, and she was trying to say something, but I couldn't hear her.

"Enough!" Conan roared as he walked down the stairs.

"I agree."

I turned toward the front door. When had Ilya Sanguinati arrived and how much had he heard?

"Who are you?" Vaughn demanded.

"Ms. DeVine's attorney." Ilya walked in and stood beside me.

Vaughn gave me a cold look. "You're going to need one."

"I'll put the food in the fridge," Ineke murmured. She took the bags of food and headed for the kitchen.

Wondering what else she planned to do once she was out

of Grimshaw's sight—and wishing I could go with her—I resigned myself to enduring extreme unpleasantness. The rental agreement did have a separate clause guests had to sign that said I wasn't responsible for any damage to their property during their stay, but I was reluctant to point that out since I was pretty sure the men would start hollering again, and men hollering tended to trigger anxiety attacks.

"What provoked them?" Ilya asked, directing the question to Conan.

Grimshaw didn't growl about someone else asking questions, so either he hadn't gotten any answers that he believed from the humans or he wanted to hear the Others' version of events and hadn't had a chance to ask before Ineke and I arrived—or hadn't been successful in getting any of my lodger-employees to talk to him.

Conan pointed at Darren and Pamella. "Aggie and Jozi found these two humans in Miss Vicki's private den, going through her belongings. When Aggie told them to leave, they refused and said . . . insults . . . before I came up and helped the Crowgard drive them from the den."

The perverse part of me wanted to hear what they had said, even knowing I would be hurt by it. The tiny part of me that was an enthusiastic supporter of self-preservation understood that while Conan would tell Ilya at some point—and might even tell Grimshaw—exactly what was said, the Bear had already decided not to tell me.

"He manhandled me," Pamella said, her voice shrill as she showed everyone the torn pockets in her capris. "And he threatened Darren."

"Threatened to disembowel me," Darren said.

"Did they take anything?" Ilya asked Conan, ignoring the humans.

"They tried," Conan replied. "But they did not leave with anything that did not belong to them."

Hopefully they also didn't leave anything in my suite, like intestines. Not likely, since Darren was waving his arms and down here with the rest of his friends, but I really liked the carpet I had put in my bedroom and didn't want it stained by people innards.

"Hershel was at our cabin, resting, and I was in the library, looking for a book to read," Heidi volunteered, sounding anxious to establish the legitimacy of their activities. "You did say we could borrow a book while we were here."

I wasn't the only one who saw the disgusted looks Pamella, Vaughn, and Darren gave her, and I felt sorry for Heidi. She was older than the other two women and even rounder than me, so she probably endured a bushel of verbal cuts whenever she and her husband socialized with the other two couples. She actually seemed like a nice person, much nicer than her husband, which must have made her the odd man out even in her own home.

I could relate to that. I could also relate to her husband looking at her as if she had farted at the moment he introduced her to an important client.

"And the female who is missing?" Ilya asked. "Where was she?"

"Trina isn't well," Vaughn said. "She had some kind of dizzy spell. I was going to take her to the doctor. Then we discovered the vandalism . . ."

"Where was she when she had this dizzy spell?" Ilya was using his scary mild voice.

A woman walked into the hallway and said, "She had picked the lock on Ms. DeVine's office, but she couldn't go through the files or take anything because I was there." She smiled at me.

She wasn't beautiful—at least by current standards—but her face was arresting and she looked great in the sharply tailored black business suit. And with the long black hair, dark eyes, and olive-toned skin, she was definitely Sanguinati.

"What was *she* doing in there?" Vaughn demanded. "And how did my wife end up having a dizzy spell just by being in that room? Is this place contaminated with mold or something else perilous to human health?"

Definitely something else. Was Vaughn the only one who hadn't figured that out? Sanguinati plus intruder equals lunch.

"I'm the CPA," she said, managing to imply in those three words that she had been in my office because she was *my* CPA.

Since I hadn't seen her before, I hoped no one asked me to introduce her.

"Ms. DeVine," she said, "since you weren't involved in this incident, perhaps I could have a few minutes now to review the accounts?"

Grimshaw immediately focused on her. "I might have some questions, Ms. . . . ?"

"Natasha Sanguinati."

They all looked at Natasha. They all looked at Ilya. At least some of my guests were beginning to figure things out—or not. Or maybe they counted on nothing happening to them while Grimshaw was there upholding the law.

I wasn't sure how much law he could uphold, but his presence seemed like the assurance they all needed to continue to yap at the Sanguinati.

The lightest touch of Ilya's hand on my back. Clearly he wanted me away from the rest of the humans, so I followed Natasha to my office—and saw the sharp way Julian stared at her for a moment before relaxing just enough to be noticeable.

Natasha held the office door for me, then closed it behind me, isolating us from whatever was going on in the hall.

"I hadn't intended to be in your office without your consent," Natasha said. "But when the Crowgard reported that the humans were acting sneaky and scratching at the doors to places where they didn't belong, a couple of us came over to investigate. I was sitting at your desk, writing a note to you—I like the stationery you created for The Jumble— when that Trina female scratched at the door until it opened. She wanted me to leave, insisted that you had asked her to find a couple of legal papers. She was offended that I didn't believe her."

Natasha seemed quite amused by that.

"So you bit her?"

"Oh no. A bite can be so intimate, don't you think?"

Considering some of the fantasies I'd had about Ilya, apparently I did think biting and intimacy could go together.

"Besides, there are other ways to feed," Natasha added.

I was not going to think about that because thinking about it made me feel like a walking juice bar.

Raised voices, muffled by the closed door, were silenced by the sound of something large and metallic being dropped. I didn't know much about cars, even when they weren't being dropped, but I guessed it had sounded like that because the tires were now flat.

"How many Elders does it take to flip a car?" I asked.

She gave me a puzzled smile. "Is that a human joke?"

Not likely. "Maybe."

"While we're waiting for the police officer to ask his questions, why don't we review your accounts?"

I figured she already knew I couldn't afford what she usually charged any more than I could afford my attorney, so I told her that was a nifty idea and began counting the hours until I could shove my first guests out the door.

CHAPTER 49

Grimshaw

Moonsday, Sumor 3

As far as Grimshaw was concerned, situations like this were exactly the reason why cops hated coming to places like Sproing or The Jumble unless it was to help a stranded motorist or look for a missing child. The Others in the wild country usually left you alone if you were helping a motorist, and they sometimes assisted in the search if they understood you were looking for a lost child. But when humans ran afoul of the *terra indigene*? Nothing a cop could do except try to extract the humans without antagonizing the Others.

Well, he could shoot the humans. He was pretty sure the Others wouldn't object to that. Explaining that to Captain Hargreaves or a board of inquiry might be tricky—assuming the bodies didn't just disappear before he had time to file his report.

Which made him wonder why the body of Franklin Cartwright had been left in a place where it would be found and hadn't shown much sign of predation. Had the man been left as a warning about the penalties of trespassing in The Jumble, or was it a case of the smaller *terra indigene* not daring to grab anything from a kill made by an Elder?

Or most anything, he amended, remembering the call Vicki DeVine had made about the eyeball that had started the initial inquiry.

Hershel, a large gray-haired man who was older than the other two men, arrived at the main house and was as vocal as Vaughn and Darren about their treatment here and the damage to their vehicles. Grimshaw figured Hershel really had been in his cabin resting, or at least doing nothing that upset the Others, since his UV was the only one that hadn't been damaged or vandalized.

"Let's go into the library and see if we can work this out," he said. He didn't see the point of standing in the hall, and he wanted to get a look at Trina. She might need a doctor. Then again, she might need nothing more than a glass of juice and rest to make up for the blood donation she'd made as a penalty for picking a lock on a door that was clearly marked PRIVATE.

They just argued more loudly until the crash of something large and metallic.

"I'll go," Julian said. He hurried out, then hurried back in. "The overturned UV has been righted. The tires are flat, and there is some other damage—mostly dents and scratches."

Vaughn ran out to take a look. They heard a shocked sound, almost a scream, before he ran back in.

"Someone is going to pay for that," he shouted.

"You will," Ilya said. "And for the tow truck unless it is your intention to abandon the vehicle."

Vaughn's eyes were filled with fury and hatred, and Grimshaw wondered if the man had been a member of the Humans First and Last movement before most of the humans who had joined the HFL were killed by the Elders and Elementals. Anyone left had survived by hiding their affiliation. But if Vaughn was one of the investors in this luxury resort nonsense, that would be sufficient reason to hate the Sanguinati's interference.

Finally Grimshaw had enough. "Anyone who wants me to make an official report will come into the library. It's a one-time offer. You blow me off now and then want a report because your insurance company won't pay for repairs without one, then you'll have to pocket the expense."

"This is outrageous!" Hershel said. "Who is your superior? I'm going to file a complaint."

Oh, he didn't want to do what he was about to do because this was the first step in becoming entangled in the briars that were the village of Sproing. It was also the fastest way to make sure he wasn't hamstrung by orders that might come from someone other than Captain Hargreaves. "I'm currently the chief of police in Sproing, so if you want to file a complaint, you file it with me. I can tell you already where I'll put it."

Grimshaw walked into the library and waited. At first, the only individual to follow him was Ilya Sanguinati. Then the five humans entered the room, grumbling and complaining.

A minute later, Julian slipped into the library. "Definite signs that someone picked the lock on the office door. Not what I would call a professional job, but it was done by someone who has had some practice. You might want to take fingerprints and send them on to see if they match any unsolved burglaries at resorts around the Finger Lakes."

That started all of them yapping again, even Trina, who didn't look as wan as she had a minute ago. Which made sense since he was certain that her fingerprints would be on the door.

Grimshaw wanted to smack his friend, but all he said was, "Fox. Henhouse."

The guests didn't get the reference. Ilya Sanguinati laughed.

The laughter shut everyone up.

"We aren't staying here unless you deal with those . . . *creatures*," Darren said.

"You're guests," Ilya said. "The *terra indigene* live here. You can talk to Ms. DeVine about an early checkout. I believe I can convince her to forgive the rest of your bills as long as the checks you sent for the deposits on the cabin and suites didn't bounce."

"Ms. Xavier, who runs the boardinghouse in Sproing, is

in the kitchen," Grimshaw said, looking pointedly at Julian. "You could inquire if she has sufficient rooms available."

"I'll do that." Julian left the library.

"Boardinghouse?" Pamella sounded offended that he would suggest such a thing. "I don't think so. Where is the nearest hotel that isn't a dump?"

"Bristol," Grimshaw replied.

Pamella sniffed in a way that said there was *nothing* suitable in *Bristol*.

Julian returned. "As a favor to Ms. DeVine, Ineke will rent them rooms for the rest of today. But they need to be out by eleven a.m. tomorrow because, after that, all her rooms are booked through the rest of the month."

"That's unacceptable," Vaughn said. "We may need to stay longer to settle legal issues."

"Then you'll have to stay somewhere else," Julian replied.

"Where?" Vaughn snapped.

Grimshaw thought about the Mill Creek Cabins, but realized that not only were those rented on an annual lease; they were owned by the Sanguinati at Silence Lodge. Not the kind of landlords these humans would want.

Darren, Vaughn, and Hershel looked at one another. One by one, they nodded, as if casting a vote.

"Fine," Darren said. "We'll stay at the boardinghouse until we conclude our business."

"Until eleven a.m. tomorrow," Grimshaw corrected.

He was sure getting him reassigned to some remote human village in the Northeast was going to be a high priority for these men. He'd call Captain Hargreaves and give him a heads-up, but they would be out of the boardinghouse before they could put anything in motion.

He hoped that was true.

"Ms. Xavier will be going back to her place in about half an hour," Julian said. "She can fit two people and some luggage in her car. The rest of you will have to ride in the available UV."

"What are you going to do with the other two vehicles?" Grimshaw asked Vaughn and Darren.

"We'll leave them here. For now," Vaughn replied.

As the humans filed out of the room, Ilya plucked the book out of Heidi's hands and gave her a fang-tipped smile. "This is Ms. DeVine's property."

"Oh, but . . ." Heidi began.

"We wouldn't want anyone to think you were trying to leave with something that wasn't yours."

"Who would cut up stiff about a paperback?" Hershel snapped.

"Do you know where you are the moment you walk out the door of this building?" Ilya asked, his focus still on Heidi.

"The Jumble?" she replied hesitantly.

He shook his head slowly. "You're in the wild country, and there are a lot of beings between you and the nearest human place who would 'cut up stiff.'"

Heidi trembled. Tears filled her eyes.

Her husband didn't put an arm around her, didn't do so much as take her hand.

Dismissing the man, Grimshaw studied Ilya and realized the vampire hadn't been trying to frighten Heidi; he'd been trying to warn her.

Mikhos, watch over me.

Thirty minutes later, Vicki DeVine was still in her office with Natasha Sanguinati. Grimshaw figured that was Ilya's doing. Ineke was at the front door, tapping one foot as she waited for Heidi and Hershel to get their things packed. Or repacked, since Conan insisted on looking inside their luggage to make sure they hadn't taken anything from the cabin.

None of the Others took pity on the humans who had to haul their luggage back to the cars unassisted. Neither did Julian. And Grimshaw decided he needed to keep his distance from these people, just in case Darren or Vaughn upset something that had bigger claws than Conan Beargard.

It took more than thirty minutes, but the three couples finally headed for the boardinghouse, leaving him and Julian in the hall with Ilya Sanguinati until Vicki and Natasha came out of the office.

"They're gone?" Vicki asked.

"They're gone," Ilya replied.

"Thanks for your help."

Grimshaw wasn't sure who was being thanked, but since the Sanguinati seemed to be waiting for him and Julian to leave, they walked to the cruiser and drove back to Sproing.

He didn't say anything until they turned off the access road and were heading for the village. "You get any feeling about those people?"

"I don't get feelings about people, Wayne," Julian said. "I sense places."

"What's your sense of The Jumble?"

Julian looked out the passenger window. They were pulling into a space in front of the police station before he finally said, "It's no longer a safe place."

CHAPTER 50

Them

Moonsday, Sumor 3

The four men and their wives met in the Danes' room in the boardinghouse because Yorick couldn't even leave to go to the bathroom without that damn dog trying to dig a hole in his groin looking for who knew what.

Damn Vicki. He wasn't sure there was a way to pay her back for shooting off her mouth like that, but he'd sure like to try.

Vaughn poured the wine, looking pissed and pleased in equal measure. He hadn't expected to be thrown out of The Jumble; hadn't expected to be thwarted when he sent Trina to look through the papers in the office and pull out anything that could support Vicki's claim to The Jumble. But Vaughn said those things were a temporary setback in turning The Jumble into a high-end moneymaking resort.

Yorick wasn't so sure they would be able to turn The Jumble into anything. Not anymore. The other men had done these kinds of deals before, buying a run-down property and fiddling with the deed in order to add a few more acres of land from neighboring plots. Then they built what they pleased with none of those *creatures* being the wiser. But those deals, from start to finish, had been made with other humans, had been done *quietly*, and they had been done before the Humans First and Last movement made that colossal blunder last year that riled up the scary forms of Others that usually didn't even notice humans. But this? People dying and Vicki making such a fuss, bringing in cops who had no allegiance to Vaughn or the rest of them, to say nothing of those freaking vampires. Too many people, too many *things*, were watching them now.

When he'd first started flirting with Constance, he had bragged about owning a rustic resort right on the shores of one of the Finger Lakes. He'd known from family stories that there was no practical way to do anything with the place. But it had impressed Constance, who was Vaughn's cousin, and Vaughn was a top-tier member of the TCC and had barely noticed him before he started dating Constance and had sneered at his business deals, as if they were too insignificant to impress a *true* entrepreneur.

Then the dating became a hot affair, and Vaughn and other top members of the TCC began commenting on the affair drawing too much attention within their social circle, and Constance no longer found it amusing to be the Other Woman. She demanded that he divorce Vicki and marry her, but she had wanted to keep the house in Hubbney, and the car, and all his other assets, and he *had* to put up something that he could claim was of equal value and then browbeat Vicki into taking it as her half of the assets. He'd known the buildings in The Jumble were in poor condition, but signing over the place to her made him look generous, especially when he added the cash settlement that almost matched Franklin Cartwright's estimate of what it would cost to upgrade those buildings enough for people to use them.

Days after the divorce was pushed through, he and Constance were married—and Vaughn introduced him to Darren and Hershel and said they were all interested in investing in this resort he owned to help him bring it up to quality standards. Yes, Constance had told her cousin all about the resort, had talked it up because *he* had talked it up to impress her. But she hadn't known he'd signed it over to Vicki so that

Constance could keep the house and expensive car and all
the other things she had claimed they just *had* to keep.

Vaughn had been furious when he'd learned about the
division of the assets because *he* had talked up The Jumble
and had Darren and Hershel salivating over the chance at
running a posh lakeside resort. After seeing that side of
Vaughn's temper, which wasn't half as unnerving as Hershel's cold sympathy about troublesome divorces, Yorick had
been afraid to tell the men about the wording of the original
agreement and that it wasn't laziness or lack of vision that
had stopped any of his relatives from making money off The
Jumble.

"Here's to the Tie Clip Club's next successful business
venture," Vaughn said, raising his glass.

"*We* will make a success of it," Constance said.

"Where would the Clippers be without their women?"
Hershel said, giving Yorick a chilling smile.

The Tie Clip Club. People collected all kinds of rubbish,
and in school there had been all kinds of clubs. Who would
suspect that the movers and shakers in all kinds of businesses, and even in the police and government, formed their
alliances by belonging to a club that collected tie clips? Who
would suspect that the tie clip that had been specially designed for club members would have real significance when
those young men left school and began working in their
various fields? While they were in school, members who
weren't society boys endured being laughed at for belonging
to such a dorky club—and never forgot the names and faces
of the ones who had laughed when it came to awarding job
contracts or hamstringing someone's climb up the business
or social ladder.

Members helped members. Saying no was not an option.
And that was the catch. When a member asked for help, the
rest of the membership was expected to provide whatever
assistance they could. It was one reason why the founding
members hadn't stuck to their own social circle when they
began recruiting a couple of generations ago. Rubbing el-

bows with young men who were attending the public university, the tech college, and the police academy hadn't felt right, but when those men became the owners of their own construction companies, or owned the garages where you could get your expensive luxury car fixed, or became high-ranking members of the police force, putting up with them while you attended the private college along with your real peers made sense.

Just like marrying Vicki had made sense. She had been such a social nobody, it had been easy to dazzle her with the great future they would have together, and he had dangled that dream in front of her during the years when she'd worked to support them while he'd waited for his trust fund to kick in and dabbled with working whenever she balked at making a payment on his tailor's bill instead of paying the electric company to keep them from turning off the service. She wasn't the right wife for a man like him, but she'd been useful, and it had been so easy to convince her that his affairs were her fault because she wasn't enough for any man when it came to sex.

A lot like Heidi, in fact. After he'd gotten Vicki off his back, Yorick hadn't understood why Hershel hadn't dumped Heidi years ago. But that was before he realized that Hershel sometimes needed to tune up his partner a bit in order to really enjoy sex, and Heidi was enough of a doormat to take it.

If he hadn't needed to divorce Vicki and marry Constance in order to remain in good standing with Vaughn and the rest of the Tie Clippers, would he and Vicki have reached the point where foreplay included the back of his hand to make things good? Not something he could try on Constance, of course, with her being Vaughn's cousin.

"If Vicki showed that attorney all the paperwork, he'll wonder about me presenting this document now," Yorick said.

"We'll swear we saw it with the rest of the paperwork when you were working out the terms of the settlement,"

Darren said. "She destroyed her copy in order to retain her hold on property that was no longer hers. Her signature is on the document, same as yours. And it's notarized."

"First thing tomorrow morning, you'll go to the police station and insist that Officer Grimshaw, in his capacity as the chief of police, help you issue the eviction notice," Vaughn said with a nasty smile.

Yeah. He liked that idea.

They discussed going out to eat, not that there was anything remotely adequate in Sproing, but the rooms included breakfast and dinner in their price, and not eating at the boardinghouse didn't reduce the price of the rooms. Hershel had already checked.

Pamella claimed a severe allergy to dogs, so at least that beast wasn't tormenting him while they ate dinner.

"Ms. Xavier," Vaughn said when Ineke filled the coffee cups and set out plates of fruit, cheese, and chocolate at the end of the meal. "If we decide to stay a bit longer tomorrow . . ."

"Checkout is eleven o'clock," Ineke said. "Other guests are coming in and we need to turn over the rooms, so I'm not offering extensions."

"If we choose not to leave, what are you going to do?" Vaughn persisted. "Call the police?"

She stared at Vaughn for so long, Yorick began to squirm in his seat.

Then she smiled. "No, I wouldn't call the police. There's someone else I call when I need to eliminate vermin."

CHAPTER 51

Vicki

Sunday, Sumor 4

I had just finished washing the breakfast dishes when I heard a quick *whoop* of a police siren—a *bloop* of sound, there and gone so fast I wasn't even sure I had heard it until Aggie ran into the kitchen.

"Jozi says Officer Grimshaw is here with those other humans," Aggie said. "He flashed the lights and made the car howl, but just a little."

Since Aggie was naked and had more feathers than usual in her hair and framing her face, I deduced that she had been in her Crow form when Jozi gave the warning. Or maybe it was more accurate to say Jozi was passing along Grimshaw's warning.

Grimshaw didn't make idle warnings.

Trembling, I hurried to the kitchen phone and called Ilya Sanguinati.

"I'll be there," he said when I stumbled out the reason for the call. "Make sure the porch door and kitchen door are unlocked. Take your time answering the front door. Make some excuse."

Doing the dishes. Had soapy hands. Wasn't sure I'd heard the bell with the water running.

Since I'd seen Ilya flow through a screen door, I figured unlocking the doors was for the convenience of someone—or something—else who would deal with a lock by ripping the door off its hinges. Wanting to save myself the expense of repairs, I made sure the back doors were unlocked before heading toward the front of the house. The doorbell rang again, immediately followed by someone pounding on the door.

"Damn it, Vicki!" Yorick shouted. "Open this door!"

What was *he* doing here?

"Miss Vicki?"

Had I stopped moving toward the door because I had stopped to respond to Aggie? Or had I frozen the moment I heard the anger in Yorick's voice? But he couldn't shove me against the wall and tell me how angry I had made him, not with Grimshaw right there. Could he?

"Better if you're not here right now," I told Aggie. "Not undressed in human form."

She shifted to her Crow form and flew up to the railing at the top of the stairs—not in anyone's line of sight but able to see and hear everything.

In Crow form, there wasn't much she could do against a human—not much she could do against a grown man in her human form either—but I felt braver knowing Aggie was there as a witness.

I opened the door and saw Yorick's fist coming toward my face before Grimshaw grabbed his wrist and stopped the movement.

"Sorry," I said. "I was washing dishes and didn't hear the doorbell."

"Ms. DeVine, we need to come in," Grimshaw said.

His police-issue sunglasses made it impossible to see his eyes, but I had the impression he was either really ticked off about being here or had a vicious case of indigestion and needed some seltzer. Either way, he wasn't asking permission to come in; he was telling me I didn't have a choice.

I backed up and kept moving back as Yorick, Darren,

Vaughn, and Hershel strode in, followed by their wives and, finally, Grimshaw, who didn't fully shut the door.

"Ms. DeVine," Grimshaw said, coming to the front of the group, "it is my unpleasant task to serve you with this eviction notice, effective immediately."

"Eviction?" I wanted to wiggle a finger in my ear like they do in movies to show that the person couldn't possibly have heard what they had heard. "How can you evict me? I'm the legal owner of this property."

"No, you're not," Yorick said, looking insufferably smug.

Grimshaw held out the folded paper. "You have to take it."

Ilya Sanguinati strolled in from the back of the house, carrying a thin briefcase that must have been really expensive and top quality, judging by the envy in Yorick's and Darren's eyes when they spotted it. Even Vaughn looked uncomfortably impressed.

"I'll take it." Ilya held out his hand.

Grimshaw didn't hesitate to hand over the paper. I suppose giving it to my attorney was the same as giving it to me. I wasn't sure about that, but no one protested.

Ilya took his time reading it. I was too busy struggling to avoid a meltdown to try to read over his shoulder—or past his arm since I wasn't tall enough to see over his shoulder, let alone read anything.

He folded the eviction notice and handed it to me. When I started to open the paper, figuring I was supposed to read it now, he said in a voice as sharp as a slap, "Don't bother."

If Yorick started in on me, I would buckle. I knew it and Yorick knew it. His way of discussing anything had been to yell until I agreed with him.

"Mr. Dane, what makes you believe you are entitled to repossess this property?" Ilya asked, his voice still sharp but now also cold.

"This." Yorick produced another document with a flourish. He tried to hand it to me, but Ilya reached in front of me and snapped it out of Yorick's hand. "It's signed by both of us *and* it's notarized."

"It couldn't be," I protested.

"*Victoria.*"

Ilya using *that* tone of voice was his way of issuing a warning, so I clenched my teeth to avoid trying to stick up for myself. Of course, if Yorick and I went at it with all his friends taking his side, I'd probably end up in the hospital heavily sedated, so hoping that Ilya had a plan made more sense than having a breakdown.

"This document seems to be more obscurely written than most human agreements, but stripping it down to its essence, it says that since The Jumble had been in the possession of the Dane family for several generations, it came to you, Victoria, in the divorce settlement with the provision that you could prove it to be a viable living so that you wouldn't be a burden on the Dane family or a homeless embarrassment." Ilya paused. "Ah. You had six months to do this, and if you hadn't made sufficient effort to have income coming from the property, it would revert back to the Dane family—specifically back to Yorick Dane."

I couldn't stand it. I had to say *something*. "Even if I had seen that document, it isn't realistic to think this place could have been ready for paying guests in that amount of time. Not with all the work that had to be done."

"Vicki, Vicki." Yorick shook his head and tried to look sad. "You can see your signature right there. You knew the timetable, and you didn't meet it."

"I had people working on the main house and the first three cabins all winter, but some things couldn't be done until the spring! I wasn't ready for paying guests until mid-Maius."

"Conveniently two weeks past the deadline," Ilya murmured.

Just two weeks? I hadn't worked out the dates in my head. And something about being off by so little time struck me as odd.

"Two weeks, two days, two months, it doesn't matter," Yorick snapped at Ilya. "She didn't meet the terms of the agreement." He turned to me. "You're evicted, effective immediately. Hand over the keys and get out."

"No," Ilya said mildly. "That's not how this is going to work. Ms. DeVine will leave immediately. I'll arrange to have all her personal possessions packed and out of here by the end of the day. You, however, cannot take possession of the property until the utilities are informed that as of 12:01 a.m. tomorrow, you will be the responsible party for payment. Also, before you take possession of the property, I need to know how you are going to reimburse Ms. DeVine for the capital improvements she made on the property."

"Those are part of the property now," Vaughn said, narrowing his eyes.

"Not quite." Ilya smiled, showing a hint of fang. "The document says that if Ms. DeVine fails to develop the property in the agreed-upon amount of time, she will quit the property, leaving it in the same, or better, condition. My client chooses to return the property to Mr. Dane in the condition she found it after his family's decades of neglect." He opened his briefcase and pulled out a single sheet of paper, which he handed to Yorick. "Those are the capital improvements that were made to the main house and cabins. The total cost is listed at the end. You will agree to reimburse Ms. DeVine for all the money she put into this property to make it habitable again, or I can have crews here within the hour to remove the new septic system; dig up the new water pipes and remove all the new pipes that were put into the house and the lakeside cabins; and remove the new circuit breaker box and any other electric work that was done here."

"You can't do that." A vein in Yorick's temple began to throb as he turned to Grimshaw. "He can't do that."

"I wouldn't bet on it," Grimshaw replied.

"Fine," Vaughn said, looking like he would explode any second. "Yorick will reimburse Vicki for the capital improvements. You'll have a cashier's check first thing tomorrow morning. Now I want her out of here."

"The check will be drawn from a bank in the Northeast

that is still viable," Ilya said. "And, yes, Ms. DeVine will leave now. So will all of you. Until the check is deposited—and the bank it was drawn on is verified—Mr. Dane is within his rights to evict Ms. DeVine, but he has no legal rights to the buildings. We'll meet at the bank in Sproing at nine a.m. tomorrow. I'll hand over the keys at that time."

Ilya turned to me. "Please fetch your purse and *all* of your keys."

I thought he was helping me. Now I wasn't sure. When I looked at Grimshaw, he dipped his head in the tiniest nod, and I wondered if he knew something I didn't. Maybe Julian had said something?

As I walked across the hall, I dug the office key out of my pocket. I had gotten into the habit of bringing my purse downstairs and leaving it in the big bottom drawer in the desk, so at least I would have that much. But what about my clothes, my bits of jewelry? They didn't cost much, but I felt like I was being stripped of everything for the second time, even if Ilya *had* said I would retain my personal possessions.

I walked into the office and spotted Natasha Sanguinati, who raised a finger to her lips before I could say anything and alert everyone else to her presence.

She approached the desk, making sure she was still out of sight. "Don't worry," she whispered. "We'll take care of this."

I felt sick, and my hands shook as I took the purse out of the desk drawer.

Natasha held out her hand. "Ilya is giving you a ride. Give me your car keys. I'll make sure the vehicle gets to you."

The car keys were on their own ring, so I gave them to her and made sure I had my keys to the main house as well as the set of master keys for all the cabins. I left the office, closing but not locking the door. I gave Ilya all the keys, including the loose office key. He put the master set in his briefcase, along with the loose office key.

"It's time to go," Ilya said, staring at Vaughn.

"We'll stay a bit longer to look around," Vaughn said.

"You've already looked around while you posed as guests."

"You need help with the vermin?" Conan asked as he and Cougar came into the hall from the direction of the kitchen.

Cougar's lips peeled back in that disturbing smile. "Heh-heh-heh-heh."

I was pretty sure the boys weren't going to be invited to the main house to watch cop and crime night on TV.

"Let's go," Grimshaw said.

"Don't get comfortable with your promotion, *Chief*," Vaughn said as he walked out the front door.

Everyone who could be seen walked out of the house and watched Ilya lock the front door. Yorick took a step toward me, but Ilya got between us and hustled me to the black luxury sedan. We were the first to leave, but when I looked back, I saw Conan and Cougar standing guard at the front door and Grimshaw having words with Yorick and Darren. I also noticed an unfamiliar car parked next to the UV that belonged to Hershel and Heidi. Made sense. Eight people couldn't have come in one vehicle, but I wondered where they had rented a car.

"Could you drop me off at Ineke's?" I asked. I wasn't sure I would make it that far before I needed to throw up, but I really wanted to talk to a friend, and I wasn't sure Ilya qualified right now.

"*They* still have rooms there until checkout time," he replied, "and all of Ineke's rooms are booked for the week. More important, you would be more vulnerable to attack if you stayed at the boardinghouse."

"Yorick got what he wanted. There's no reason to attack me."

Ilya sighed. "You have so little faith in my skills as your attorney."

I guess Mount Victoria still had a little lava left. "Your *skills*? I didn't have a chance to see The Jumble before I had to accept the settlement or lose out on getting anything, but six months to clean up a place that hadn't been used for decades and bring in paying guests is ridiculous! I never signed that document. My signature was forged!"

"I know."

The calm acknowledgment stunned me. "You know?"

"Of course." He turned toward me. "Do you know how to kill a human, Victoria? *Could* you kill a human?"

Anybody could kill another person. You could throw a rock in anger and have the bad luck of hitting just the right place to kill someone. You could push someone and have that person fall and break his neck. But that wasn't what Ilya meant.

I shook my head. "No. I couldn't kill a human."

"I can," he said quietly. "I have."

Suddenly I was very aware that I was in a car with two Sanguinati who might have missed breakfast.

"Those men are predators," Ilya continued quietly, looking away as he opened his briefcase. "You are prey."

Like I needed the reminder. Yorick and his pals certainly saw me that way. But Ilya, who nature shows would call an apex predator, saw me as prey too. The difference was my attorney seemed to be struggling to look past that sharp reality and help me.

He removed a couple of sheets of paper from his briefcase. "When we get to the Mill Creek Cabins, which is where you'll be staying for the time being, I need you to sign these revised rental agreements that indicate you rented one of the lakeside cabins to Aggie, Eddie, and Jozi Crowe."

"I didn't rent to the three of them."

"This new document says you did. If Aggie stays there alone, she'll be too vulnerable, and the new caretakers can limit the amount of time any friends can stay with her. But three of them listed on an official document? One can always keep watch on the cabin."

"So we're going to forge a document?"

"Why not? They did." Ilya smiled. "Besides, our document won't be forged since you and Aggie will sign this one just like you signed the original. The agreement is merely revised. Something Mr. Dane doesn't need to know."

We turned off of Mill Creek Road—which was Main Street within the village limits—and drove down Mill Creek Lane. Like the access road to The Jumble, it was gravel, not paved. But it looked well tended.

"Why did you let them push me out?" I asked.

Ilya said nothing until the car pulled up at the second-to-last cabin and the driver got out and walked toward the water mill that generated the electricity for The Jumble as well as the cabins.

"Do you recall Julian Farrow's reaction when you all played Murder?" Ilya asked.

"Something upset him."

"His ability as an Intuit is to sense places. It's one of the things that had made him such an effective police officer and also the thing that had saved his life. In that, his ability makes him—and other Intuits like him—an effective barometer for the health of a place."

"But Julian is rubbish at playing the game," I protested.

"But that night, the game was altered to represent The Jumble, even to the point that some of the players were represented by teenies. It turns out that was enough of a difference for Julian to get a sense of place." Ilya looked me in the eyes. "He called me that night. When I met with him and Officer Grimshaw, Julian told me that once the businessman predator arrived, you would die if I didn't get you away from The Jumble."

I wanted to deny it, but Julian and Grimshaw *had* been acting weird since that night.

I shook my head. "Yorick would push me until he got what he wanted—he knows exactly how to push my buttons—but he wouldn't kill me." I couldn't have married a man who would do *that*, could I?

"Yorick isn't the dominant male. Vaughn is the leader of that pack, and he *is* a predator who could kill another human." Ilya patted my hand. "But Vaughn is also a small predator who believes he is powerful and does not yet appreciate how many other predators are now watching him. He will appreciate it very soon."

"And while you and Grimshaw and Julian get this straightened out for silly, incompetent me, I'll just sit in a corner somewhere and do nothing, because that's all I'm good at." I'd meant it to sound humorous—don't ask me how it could—but even to my ears it sounded bitter. Defeated.

"Can you kill a human, Victoria?" Ilya asked.

"No."

"Then let those who can deal with these predators."

"That's your plan? Kill Yorick and those other men?"

"Not if I can find a better way to solve the problem."

Oh, that did not sound good. I had a feeling that "better" meant a solution that was just as lethal but not as bloody.

"So while you're dealing with Yorick, what am I supposed to do?"

Ilya laughed softly. "First, you're going to sign this revised rental agreement. Then you're going to figure out how you want the furniture from your suite arranged in the cabin. And then you're going to decide which items you want stored in three of the other cabins that are available—we'll leave the one closest to the main road empty. The larger items that won't fit in the cabins will be stored in the outbuildings at Silence Lodge."

"My suite was basically an efficiency apartment within the main house. Everything I had there will fit in the one cabin."

He just smiled and escorted me into the cabin that would be my new home.

CHAPTER 52

Aggie

Sunday, Sumor 4

As soon as she heard the front door lock and the cars start up and pull away, Aggie flew down to the hall and landed near the office doorway. She shifted to human form, pushed the door open, and watched the female Sanguinati quickly filling a box with file folders Miss Vicki kept in the cabinets.

"Those belong to Miss Vicki," Aggie said.

"Yes, they do." Natasha looked at Aggie, then looked past her.

Aggie held out her arms like they were wings as she left the ground and landed several feet into the room when Cougar gave her what was meant to be a nudge.

"What are we going to do about this?" Conan asked, coming in behind Cougar.

"Call in all the *terra indigene* living in The Jumble who are willing to help," Natasha replied. "Fetch the packing boxes that are up in the attic. Fetch Miss Vicki's luggage as well. Trucks will begin arriving soon, but we'll need the donkey carts as well to take the items from two of the lakeside cabins down to the water. The supply barge will take those things to Silence Lodge."

"The Crowgard will pack up Miss Vicki's *personal* personal things," Aggie said. When Natasha gave her a questioning look, she added, "We'll be careful, and we won't take any little treasures." All the Crowgard would help Miss Vicki, who was not only their friend but the Reader. "And we'll pack up the books. Miss Vicki says they're a different kind of treasure, and she would want them in her new nest."

Natasha nodded. "All right. But we need to move fast. Everything has to be done, and we all have to be gone before the humans return tomorrow morning."

"How much are we taking?" Conan asked.

Natasha pointed to a thick file folder on the desk. "If Miss Vicki has a receipt for it, we're taking it."

CHAPTER 53

Grimshaw

Sunday, Sumor 4

Grimshaw watched Officer Osgood enter the police station with a delivery box from Come and Get It.

"I heard you didn't eat breakfast this morning," Osgood said as he opened the box and pulled out a thermos and a covered dish. "It's a bit early for lunch, but the meatloaf had just come out of the oven, so Helen made you a sandwich and coffee. There's also some sliced fruit in there."

Just the idea of having breakfast at the boardinghouse had burned a hole in his gut after Yorick Dane had waved that eviction notice in his face—not even having the decency to wait until he had gone to the police station and officially begun his workday. He'd walked out, saying they could meet him at the office. Since most of the residents in The Jumble woke up with the sun, he didn't think Vicki DeVine would sleep in, but he wasn't going to give Dane and his pals the satisfaction of rousing the woman out of her bed in order to kick her off her own property.

He'd toyed with the idea of calling Ilya Sanguinati and had come to the reluctant conclusion that that would be seen as taking sides and could get him called back to Bristol if Vaughn and his ilk complained to the right, or wrong, person. But he'd counted on there being enough of the Others up and about to see the cars crawl up the access road, forced to follow him at the speed he'd set. He'd counted on the couple of seconds of lights and sirens to draw attention to their arrival. And they had drawn attention, the best kind of attention. He'd breathed easier when Ilya had strolled in from the kitchen, as if he'd already been at The Jumble for an early-morning meeting.

He didn't know what was going to happen now. He just hoped he'd enjoy it more than he had carrying out the law this morning.

Grimshaw didn't touch the food. Not yet. One reason he had preferred to remain in the highway patrol division was that you didn't have to trust anyone but yourself. "Sit down, Officer."

Osgood sat in the visitors' chair in front of Grimshaw's desk. "Sir?"

"Something has been bothering me, and if we're going to continue working together, I need an answer to a question."

Osgood looked puzzled but not alarmed—and not *too* eager to be helpful. "What's the question?"

"Why do you think Swinn tapped you for this assignment?" He'd been trusting the baby cop because Osgood had survived the Elders' attack on the rest of the team. Now he needed to know if that trust was earned.

Osgood met his eyes and didn't flinch. "There were rumors at the academy about a special group, a club that could provide ways to enhance a career. When Detective Swinn said he'd heard good things about me, that I had a good record at the academy, I thought this might be an audition of sorts for the club. But the drive up to Sproing was long enough to convince me I didn't want to be beholden to someone like him, and I'd already decided I wouldn't join the club if I was invited." He hesitated. "So either I was tapped for the assignment to find out if I should be considered for membership . . ."

"Or?" Grimshaw prompted when Osgood hesitated again.

"Or Detective Swinn brought me along as the expendable member of his team."

"That meshes with my thinking." Grimshaw opened the thermos and poured a cup of coffee for himself, then gently wagged the thermos at Osgood in invitation—and felt the last whisper of suspicion quiet when Osgood fetched a coffee mug from his desk and held it out to be filled.

Grimshaw almost offered to share the meatloaf sandwich. Then he took the first bite. Nope. Not sharing. Best damn meatloaf he'd ever tasted.

He finished the sandwich, set the fruit aside, and sipped his coffee. Osgood sat across from him, waiting.

"Franklin Cartwright was working for Yorick Dane. When Cartwright is found dead, Swinn comes running up here to handle the investigation." Grimshaw weighed what he knew and balanced it against what he could see coming even before he went over to Lettuce Reed and talked to Julian. Then, to Osgood: "You sit there and just listen."

He called the Bristol Police Station and waited for Captain Hargreaves to come on the line. "Captain? It's Grimshaw. Could you call in another favor with the source who knows the ITF agent who has a direct line to the governor? I need a background check on some people and don't want to alert anyone in the Hubbney police force in case a member of a certain club hears that I'm digging. I especially need to know if any of the people I'm checking have had any combat training, even unofficially. We may have a lethal situation here."

CHAPTER 54

Them

Windsday, Sumor 5

Yorick opened the passenger door, tired of listening to Vaughn lay on the car horn and worried that the man might try to drive through the thick chain across the access road. Swinn and Reynolds were mad enough about being stuck in that camper site because there was nowhere else to stay in Sproing, and Swinn wasn't about to use up his personal fuel coupons to drive back and forth from Bristol or, gods help them, Crystalton, with all its freaks. If Vaughn wrecked Swinn's car trying to prove some point, it would be hard to find another ride. They had tried to lean on the bank's former manager for the loan of his car or the use of his house, but the man had run off with his family to parts unknown—something the rest of the Clippers weren't going to forget when the idiot came back looking for another cushy job.

"I'll move the damn chain," he said, getting out of the car.

The creep who had opened it the other morning had made it look easy, but the chain was heavier than he'd expected. He dragged it to one side of the gravel road and left it there. He didn't think Vaughn would leave him to make his own way up to the main house since he had the keys, but he didn't want any delays.

They'd done it. The whole thing had played out just like Vaughn said it would. Well, except for Franklin Cartwright ending up dead. But Yorick had a prime bit of real estate back in his possession, and once Vaughn and Hershel figured out how to get around the restrictions in the original agreement, they were all going to make a bundle of money, not just from creating a luxury resort for the discerning elite, but from the acres of timber waiting to be cut and sent to the sawmills as well.

He hadn't expected to be required to reimburse Vicki for the capital improvements she'd made on the property. He'd figured he could mess with her head the way he used to do and intimidate her into fleeing, stripped of every asset he'd conceded in the divorce settlement. But that damned attorney had been right there, looking at the paperwork, handling things, not giving him a chance to talk to her alone. She wasn't even at the bank this morning. Ilya Sanguinati had met them, verified the bank Yorick had used for the cashier's check, and deposited the check before handing over the keys.

So that money was gone unless he could talk to Vicki and convince her she didn't deserve to keep all of it. But that damn bloodsucking attorney wouldn't tell him where she was staying, wouldn't even give him her mobile phone number. There couldn't be that many places where she could stay, since he'd deliberately not given her any time to make plans. Maybe one of the cabins down on Mill Creek? Swinn had taken a look around there early in his investigation. Only one cabin was being used, but he hadn't been able to get close enough to find out who was living there. Or so he claimed. He never did explain why he couldn't drive to the end of the lane to poke around that last cabin. Vaughn thought Swinn and Reynolds were too spooked to be much good anymore, but for now they were better than nothing.

When they reached the main house, Yorick heard crows cawing but didn't see any of them around the house. Something else nearby yipped or howled. He shivered, anxious to get inside and put a stout door between himself and whatever was out there. Small shifters would be a nuisance, but something *big* had killed Franklin Cartwright and the detectives on Swinn's team.

He unlocked the door and they all walked into the large hall. Big enough space for cocktails and nibbles and other kinds of informal gatherings.

Would have to hire a cook. Maybe that girl who worked at the boardinghouse. He'd float that idea with Vaughn, Darren, and Hershel.

"Son of a bitch," Vaughn said, focusing Yorick's attention on the house.

"What happened to the curtains?" Trina said.

"Where is all the furniture?" Constance demanded.

Yorick hurried into the office. The desk and an old carpet were still there but nothing else. Not so much as a paper clip.

"Son of a bitch!" Vaughn shouted, his voice coming from the back of the house.

Yorick flipped on the light switch in the office, then looked up when nothing happened. What the . . . ?

CHAPTER 55

Vicki

Windsday, Sumor 5

"Tell me again," Ineke said when we took a milk-and-cookie break from unpacking my things and arranging them around the cabin.

"The *terra indigene* that Ilya assigned to clear out the main house and cabins took everything that hadn't been in The Jumble when I arrived. They even took the light bulbs."

Ineke's eyes gleamed behind her black-framed glasses; she looked like a child being told the Best Story Ever. "That is so amazing."

"I know! I couldn't believe it when they carted in the boxes of bulbs."

"No, not that." Ineke waved a hand dismissively. "Your attorney is literally a bloodsucker, so I expected him to wring everything he could out of your idiot ex. What's amazing is that you kept the receipts for light bulbs to prove you bought them."

I blinked. That wasn't quite the reaction I'd expected. "I thought I was supposed to keep the receipts for everything."

The attorney who represented me during the divorce made a passing remark about me keeping receipts since I would be running a business, and I'd been so afraid of not keeping something that would have a serious impact on my depleted savings when I had to send in my tax forms that I had saved everything, all neatly labeled in file folders.

Ineke leaned forward. "You kept receipts for *everything*? Even the paper products?"

"Well, you're the one who told me I should do that because I would need to buy in bulk. And things like paper towels and toilet paper aren't cheap anymore."

"The Others took those too? Even the partially used rolls of toilet paper?"

I looked at the box marked *paypurr* and wondered if all the rolls of TP had been riddled by Cougar's claws. "If I had a receipt for it, they took it."

Ineke laughed so hard she almost fell out of the chair. When she regained control of herself, she took off her glasses and wiped her eyes. "Want to bet on which woman is the first to sit down and make that discovery? Or how long it will take them to stop arguing about it so that someone makes an emergency run to Pops's general store or the grocery store in Bristol?"

"No bets." Personally I was hoping it would be the second Mrs. Dane who made that discovery.

"Spoilsport." Ineke took her milk glass and dish to the sink. "In that case, let's get the curtains on the rest of the windows and the dry goods into the kitchen cupboards. You want me to help you with the books?"

I shook my head and went outside, distracted by the sound of . . . bells? Ineke followed me out and we watched the goats for a minute. Well, we watched the goats that were grazing on the grass between Julian's cabin and mine, and the donkeys that were grazing between the cabins on the other side. There were even a couple of those chubby ponies grazing nearby.

"If the ponies aren't really ponies, what do you think the goats and donkeys are supposed to be?" I asked.

"Organic lawn mowers?" Ineke replied. "They cut the grass and fertilize it at the same time." She gave me a one-armed hug. "Let's tackle the rest of the 'need this done to-day' items. Then I have to get back to the boardinghouse, and you should sit outside with a book and catch your breath."

Catch my breath. Get my blood pressure out of the red zone. I liked that plan.

Besides, tomorrow was soon enough to start thinking about what I was supposed to do with my life. Again.

CHAPTER 56

Them

Windsday, Sumor 5

"You need to send someone out to unplug a toilet," Yorick said.

"Do you have a plunger? Have you tried to unblock the toilet yourself?"

"No, I don't have a flipping plunger." And he wasn't about to put his hands in a bowl full of floating turds.

Damn Pamella. She just plunked her ass down and pooped before realizing there wasn't a thing she could use to wipe her ass. So what did she do? She used the scarf she was wearing! Why was the woman wearing a long filmy scarf in this heat? But that's what she had, and somehow the scarf went down before the turds—along with enough water that the turds didn't end up floating on the bathroom floor. But now the only toilet downstairs was blocked, and none of the rest of the bathrooms in the main house had any flipping toilet paper either. So he needed the damn plumber to get off his ass and come out here to deal with it.

"Is that the only toilet in your house?"

"Doesn't matter if it is or not, I want you out here pronto!" Gods, what a place. Couldn't get service from anyone.

"We've got a full schedule for the next few days, but I'll send someone out as soon as I can. Where are you located?"

"The Jumble."

"Oh."

Yorick waited.

"You'll have to find someone else. Word around the village is someone stirred up the *terra indigene* in The Jumble, and I won't send my son out there until things calm down."

What the . . . ? He couldn't believe it. "Do you know who you're talking to?"

"A guy who plugged up his toilet."

"I'm Yorick Dane, the owner of The Jumble. You've heard of my family?"

"Yeah, I have. You people have a reputation around here. We're definitely not coming out."

Yorick stared at his mobile phone for a full minute after the plumber hung up. How dare a sewer jockey speak to him like that? Refuse to do the work?

And where was he supposed to find a new phone book that covered Crystalton and Bristol, the two closest human towns to this place? He'd been lucky to find a phone book for Sproing. The damn thing was years out of date, so he'd been lucky that the plumber hadn't changed the number. Had been lucky that the plumber was still in business.

That was the biggest problem. A new phone book hadn't been issued since last year, and with the number of people who vanished during those terrifying attacks last summer, there was no way of knowing if a business had gone under or the owners had died—or had run to some other place to escape.

Leaving the kitchen, Yorick went to the office, trying not to resent Vaughn's appropriating the desk to make some calls. Vaughn might have the vision of what they could do with this place, but Yorick *owned* this place, and if someone had to be shuffled off to use the kitchen counter, it should have been Vaughn.

Hearing the fury in Vaughn's voice, Yorick leaned against the wall near the open door and listened.

"I don't give a flying fuck if all your trucks are making deliveries today, and I don't want to hear any whining about having to drive all the way to fucking Sproing. If you want to remain a club member in good standing you will load the box springs, mattresses, and frames for four double beds, and you will get them to a place called The Jumble before the end of the workday." A pause. "If you move your ass, your men can get here, get the beds set up, and get back home before dark. If you drag your feet, they'll end up sleeping in the truck at a rest station."

Yorick shivered. There was no mercy in the wild country, no safety in the dark. The rest stations were supposed to be a neutral place where humans could spend a night without being attacked or killed. But "supposed to be" wasn't a guarantee.

The sun must have gone behind some clouds because the hall was suddenly darker than it had been a moment before. Gloomy. Forbidding. And Yorick had an uneasy thought: if The Jumble was considered wild country, were any of the people going to be safe here after the sun went down?

CHAPTER 57

Grimshaw

Windsday, Sumor 5

Sitting on Julian's porch, working on his second beer, Grimshaw looked at the nearest cabin. Curtains in the windows; a chair and small table on the porch; the large pots of flowers placed along the walls that bordered the front yard. Vicki's car was parked on the gravel rectangle that served as a driveway.

He'd eaten dinner at the boardinghouse, mainly to get a look at the new guests. A couple of salesmen who routinely stayed in Sproing to take orders from customers in the area. Two couples who wanted to get away for a few days and chose the village where they could see Sproingers and visit wineries. Nothing about any of those people made him think he needed to take a closer look, so he'd driven over to Julian's cabin in order to sit back and have a beer—and to check on Vicki DeVine.

"She need any help?" he asked when Julian joined him on the porch.

Julian shook his head. "Yesterday afternoon, Cougar and Conan provided the muscle for setting up the bed and placing the heavier pieces of furniture, and Ineke came over today to help Vicki set up the kitchen and put up curtains, things like that. When I went over after work to see if she needed any help, she sounded shaky, which isn't surprising, but she said she was okay."

"I didn't want to serve that eviction notice. It was bullshit." Grimshaw took a couple of long swallows of beer. "Got to hand it to the *terra indigene*, though. They picked up on my warning and got a message to Ilya Sanguinati fast enough for him to arrive at The Jumble by the time Vicki opened the door to that dickhead Yorick Dane and his slimy friends or business partners or whatever they are."

"You're letting your ire surface, Wayne." Julian sipped his beer. Then he sighed. "Truth is, I'm glad she's out of there."

"I had the impression that most of the people in the village were glad she had taken over The Jumble, including you."

"We were all glad to see her doing something with the place. Having The Jumble up and running would be a shot in the arm for all our businesses. I mean, gods, have you seen the public beach on the weekends when everyone is looking to cool off or row out on the lake to fish?"

"I've been a little too busy to even think about fishing," Grimshaw said.

Julian eyed him. "Do you fish?"

"Nope. But I've been too busy to even think about it."

"You should come by some morning. We can walk down to the creek and throw in a couple of lines."

"Why?"

"To look like we're doing something in order to do nothing."

"Ah. Best reason I've heard to go fishing." He spent—or had spent—his workday with his ass planted in the cruiser, so he preferred physical activity during his downtime. In his mind, fishing wasn't the same as lifting weights, or playing basketball during adults' night at the school gym.

Did they do that here? Not that he would be around much longer.

Julian snapped upright, tense and alert, a moment before a gust of cold air hit them.

"Crap," Grimshaw breathed. "I didn't hear anything in the weather report that said we'd get a blast of air coming out of the north."

"This isn't cold air coming from the north," Julian said quietly. "It's getting too cold too fast. This isn't natural. Something's changed."

Grimshaw touched the medal under his shirt. Most of the time, weather was just weather. But sometimes it was more— and it was devastating when it struck because there was something guiding it, shaping it. Creating it. "The Elementals?"

Julian nodded. Grimshaw's mobile phone rang.

"Osgood?" he said, wishing he'd tossed a jacket in the car. "You're on call tonight."

"One of the women was attacked." Osgood's voice shook. "At The Jumble. They said a hand came out of the bathroom sink and tried to choke her."

"Did anyone at The Jumble call the EMTs or Dr. Wallace?"

"Don't think so. One of the men called the station. I'm not sure which one. He was shouting and hung up before I could get any more information."

"You call Dr. Wallace and the EMTs, then stay at the station as a relay. I'll head to The Jumble."

"Yes, sir."

Julian drained his bottle and picked up the empties. "You're going to answer a call after having a couple of beers?"

"I'm not sending Osgood out there. Besides, it's getting dark. I should have been on my way back to the boarding-house before now."

"I could make some coffee."

"You could quit stalling." He wouldn't bring the baby cop with him, so why did he expect a man who quit the force years ago to back him up?

Because the man was Julian Farrow.

They stared at each other as the wind that swirled around them carried the sharp, cold bite of winter.

"I told you The Jumble wasn't a safe place," Julian said. "Well, it looks like you were right."

The EMT vehicle and Dr. Wallace's car were parked on the side of the road near the entrance to The Jumble, waiting for him. Their unwillingness to answer a call for medical help without police backup confirmed what Julian had said— The Jumble wasn't a safe place anymore.

The EMTs waited in their vehicle, ready to take someone to Dr. Wallace's office or to the hospital in Bristol. Dr. Wallace went into the main house, sandwiched between Grimshaw and Julian.

"What took you so long?" Yorick Dane demanded.

"Where is the woman who was injured?" Dr. Wallace asked.

When Dane didn't reply, Trina finally said, "She's in the kitchen. I'll show you."

Grimshaw did a mental roll call. Vaughn and his wife, Trina. Darren and Pamella. No sign of Hershel and Heidi, but there were two other men in the hall. "Detectives Swinn and Reynolds." He turned to Dane. "Since you have two members of a CIU team here, why did you bother to call the station? I'm sure the detectives could have sorted this out."

"We're not here in any official capacity," Swinn snapped. "We're on leave, visiting friends."

Vaughn didn't look pleased to be labeled a friend, but he didn't contradict Swinn either.

"Where are your other friends?"

"They're staying in their cabin," Darren replied. "Not enough rooms in the main house."

"But they called just before you arrived and said someone was outside their cabin, taunting them," Vaughn added. "They wanted to come to the house instead of being out there by themselves, but they don't want to walk over on their own. While you're waiting for the doctor to finish his examination, you should go to the cabin and escort them here."

"No," Julian said. "If they stay where they are, if they stay inside until morning, they should be all right." He looked at Grimshaw. "Going to the cabins in the dark would be a mistake."

When they were rookies, how many potentially lethal calls had he survived because he'd listened to Julian?

Grimshaw focused on Vaughn. "Tell your friends to stay put until morning."

"Coward," Swinn muttered.

"You're carrying, and you were here," Julian said. "But I don't see you going out there to help your friends. And doing *that* doesn't require that you act in any official capacity."

Swinn sneered at Grimshaw. "What's *he* doing here anyway? He washed up as a cop, so was he your date tonight?"

Snickers from Darren and Pamella.

"Officer Grimshaw?" Dr. Wallace walked toward him.

Grimshaw hurried to meet him, then cocked a thumb at the office. "Let's talk in here." He looked back at Julian, reluctant to leave his friend alone with that nest of vipers. But Julian wandered away from the rest of the people, putting a clear distance between them.

Getting out of the line of fire?

He closed the office door. "Doc? Are they trying to cover up a domestic dispute with a story about a hand coming out of the sink?"

Wallace studied him. "You worked highway patrol before coming here."

"I'm still officially part of the highway patrol."

"Then you've seen things. Know things about what lives in the wild country."

A chill went down Grimshaw's spine. "I've seen things. I know things."

"I wish I could tell you the bruises on Constance Dane's neck were consistent with a man's hand, but they're not. Too slender, for one thing. For another . . ." Wallace took a couple of deep breaths, as if to prove he could. "The man who served as the Northeast Region's governor before Hannigan."

"What about him?"

"There was a rumor going around the medical community that he died when water entered his lungs and then froze while he was taking a bath."

"What does that have to do with Constance Dane?"

"She was facing her assailant. And whatever grabbed her did so with a hand so cold it was like touching bare skin to a metal pipe when the temperature is below freezing. The hand not only grabbed her hard enough to bruise her neck; it pulled off a couple of layers of skin when it released her."

He and Wallace returned to the kitchen, where Trina and Pamella were hovering near Constance Dane but not getting too close, as if they were afraid to draw the attention of whatever had attacked their friend.

Grimshaw took a seat at a small table. Julian had mentioned that there was a couple who ran a used-goods business, everything from incomplete sets of dishes to furniture that was usable but not of sufficient quality to be considered antiques. Had someone made a run to that place to pick up the chairs and table, the dishes he saw piled on the counter in need of a wash before they could be used? He wondered which of the women would end up being the designated scullery maid.

"Can you tell me what happened?" he asked Constance.

Pretty simple, as long as you didn't think about it. She and Yorick had taken the manager's suite—meaning the efficiency apartment in the main house that had been Vicki DeVine's home until yesterday morning. Constance had been in the bathroom, washing her face at the sink, when she realized the water was draining so slow the sink was filling up. She started to tell Yorick that they needed to have the plumber look at the sink when they could get someone to show up. Then a hand made of water rose out of the sink and grabbed her throat, squeezing so hard she could barely breathe. And then it was so cold, so painfully cold. She tore free and managed to run out of the bathroom. By the time Yorick went in to investigate, the sink had drained and there was no sign of anything except some clumps of Constance's skin around the drain.

Grimshaw went through the motions of collecting evidence and taking statements. They might be despicable people, but they were still humans he had sworn to protect. Not that he had a chance of arresting Constance Dane's assailant. Or assailants. After all, Water couldn't have turned into a frozen hand without the help of an Elemental like Winter. And the thought that something had woken up Winter during the second month of summer scared him spitless.

It was full dark when he walked out of the house with Dr. Wallace and Julian. The EMTs were still there, in their vehicle, waiting for them.

The men looked terrified.

"The lash of cold has disappeared," Julian said as he opened the cruiser's passenger door. "It feels like the temperature is warming up, returning to normal for this time of year."

"Monkey man." A whisper in the dark.

Grimshaw paused, one foot in the cruiser.

"Mooooonkey maaaan." A different voice whispering the words. Mockery or threat?

"Wayne, let's get out of here. Please."

Was this the reason Hershel and Heidi had called their friends in a panic? Were these the voices they had heard?

"Wayne."

He heard the plea in Julian's voice.

No mercy in the wild country. No safety in the dark. As long as Dane and his friends stayed inside, they should be all right. But the doc and the EMTs were his responsibility, and a cruiser escorting another vehicle had the best chance of ensuring that everyone reached safety.

He drove back to Sproing, lights flashing to indicate he was on official business. The EMTs drove to the firehouse, where they would bed down until morning. He and Julian escorted Dr. Wallace to the man's home.

Julian had been unnervingly quiet throughout the drive, right up until they reached his cabin. Smoke rose from the chimney at Vicki's cabin. She must have figured out how to work the woodstove that heated the place. If Julian didn't start a fire in his own cabin, he would be in for a chilly night's sleep—if he slept at all.

"I wonder what those things are," Grimshaw said. "There were two of them."

"Five." Julian stared out the windshield. "There are five of them."

"How do you know?"

"I recognized the voices. Five of them come in once a week to buy books. They're the *terra indigene* who named the bookstore. I don't know what they are beyond that."

Grimshaw thought about that. "You don't feel threatened when they come into the store?"

"No."

"But you felt threatened tonight?"

Julian hesitated. "Not really. We didn't try to reach the cabins, so they had no reason to attack us. And those whispers? A warning, I think."

"Yeah. That's what I thought too." He just wished he knew where the line was that would tip a warning into an attack.

CHAPTER 58

Vicki

Thaisday, Sumor 6

It's funny how quickly a person can adjust to a routine. I started to put on my bathing suit before I remembered that I no longer had access to the lake, could no longer take a quick, refreshing dip before doing morning chores. Of course, the fire in the woodstove had gone out sometime during the night, so the cabin's temperature was better suited to jeans and a sweater.

Then I stepped outside. Chilly enough for jeans and sweater, but that would change by noon and we would be back to summer. Still, if I couldn't go for a swim, a walk would do just as well. If I kept the creek to my right going away from the cabins and to my left on the way back, I couldn't get too lost.

"Vicki? Wait up!"

And I had a better chance of not getting lost if I had company.

I smiled at Julian when he caught up to me. "I was going to take a walk before . . ." I looked at him. "I was going to say before work. Guess I'm just taking a walk."

"I'll go with you if you've no objection," Julian said. "It's a pretty walk, and even beyond the water mill, there is a footpath that follows the creek."

"Is there a wading pool?"

"A what?"

"Someplace where you can sit on a rock and dip your feet in the water? Seems like it would be a pleasant thing to do on a hot afternoon—bring a book and something to drink and dangle your feet in cool water."

He smiled. "I don't know. I haven't walked the path with that in mind. And this is my first summer here too. By the time I got the store up and running, it was a bit too cool to think of wading in the creek."

"Speaking of cool, thanks for sending your friend to help get the fire started in the woodstove. It would have been wicked cold last night without it."

"My friend?" Julian sounded odd.

"Aiden. Although, considering his choice of hair colors—red hair with blue and yellow tips—maybe he's Ineke's friend. Anyway, he showed up a few minutes after you and Officer Grimshaw drove off and said we had a mutual friend, so he wanted to check on me and make sure I knew how to work the stove because it was going to be a cold night. Not a freezing night, so I didn't have to worry about water pipes and farmers didn't need to fear for their crops, but it would be more comfortable with a fire."

"You let him in?"

Oh, definitely odd. "It would have been hard for him to show me how to work the stove if I hadn't. Anyway, he put in the wood and somehow got the fire started while I was still searching for some long matches. When I asked him how he'd done that, he laughed and said his name was a Brittannian word that meant . . ."

"Fire." Julian looked pale.

"Yes." I stopped walking. Not that I didn't trust Julian, but he was acting a bit weird.

"Vicki, when he said you had a mutual friend, he didn't mean anyone human."

Oooohhhhh. "He's *terra indigene*?"

Julian nodded. "One of the Elementals, I'd say."

"Fire." Oh golly. I had invited Fire into a cabin full of combustibles.

I bent at the waist and braced my hands on my knees, feeling anxiety wash through me.

"Vicki!"

I felt Julian's hand on my waist and wanted to pull away, wanted to shout at him not to touch me where he would feel the roll of fat—the roll that Yorick used to say made him want to vomit when he touched it while we were having sex.

Odd that it didn't seem to stop him from wanting to have sex even when he was exercising the Vigorous Appendage with someone else. It's not like he was worried that anyone else would come sniffing around. He'd told me often enough I didn't look good enough to screw.

But I couldn't say any of that. First, Julian would either agree with Yorick or would think I was nuts. Second, I heard a horse cantering toward us.

Julian's fingers tightened on my waist. So tense.

"Is she all right?" Aiden's voice.

Breathe, breathe, breathe. Don't give Aiden a reason to turn Julian into a large briquette.

I turned my head and squinched my face. "Hi, Aiden."

I couldn't see Aiden's face, but the horse . . . Black legs and a dark brown body. Pictures I'd seen of horses with that coloring usually had a black mane and tail. This one had a mane and tail that was the gray of storm clouds—and I was pretty sure I'd seen a pony with that coloring grazing around the cabin yesterday.

"What's your horse's name?" I asked.

"Twister."

Oh, I so didn't want to know that.

"Are you hurt?" Aiden sounded a bit testy.

"She's got a tight muscle in her back," Julian said. "That can happen when someone lifts a lot of boxes instead of accepting a friend's offer to help. Am I pressing the right place?"

It took me a moment to realize the question was directed

at me. "Closer to the spine." Not that I had any muscles that were . . . "Ow! Yeah. There." Guess I did have a few owie places.

"Is this typical in humans?" Aiden asked.

"It hadn't felt like I'd overworked the back muscles when I was moving things around yesterday," I said once I realized Julian wasn't going to jump in with an explanation. Probably just as well.

I stood up. Julian's hand lingered for a moment longer. It felt nice. More than nice.

I looked at Aiden. If I could forget the news reports I'd read last summer about fire tornados destroying entire human communities, I could see a handsome man on a pretty horse. But knowing who, and what, he was scared the crap out of me.

"Do you feel all right to help me shelve some books today?" Julian asked.

Shelve books? He hadn't mentioned me going to the store with him, and I had the impression Ilya Sanguinati wanted me out of sight. Then again, once Julian went to work, I'd be out here on my own with my new flaming friend and the goats.

"I'll be fine. I'll shelve and you can lift." I smiled at Aiden. "Thanks for lighting the fire last night. I was glad to have the warmth."

He studied me. Had he conversed with many humans, or was I a novelty?

"It should not get so cold again until Autumn is ready to sleep," he said.

"Why did it get so cold last night?" I had wondered about that.

Twister stamped a foot. I watched the dirt swirl around that leg and settle again.

"A female tried to claim your den," Aiden said. "We didn't like that, so Water asked her cousin for help in encouraging the female to leave."

"Which cousin?" I said it casually, as if I knew all of them.

"Winter, of course."

Oh golly. Breathe, breathe, breathe. Less than a month ago, I'd discovered that my lodger was one of the Crowgard, and I had a Panther and a Bear as employees. Now I was hobnobbing with the Lady of the Lake and Fire and acting all casual about other Elementals like Water and Winter taking an interest in The Jumble. Look at adaptable me.

I so wanted to sit down before I passed out.

"We should go if we're going to get some of the new stock shelved before the store opens," Julian said.

We waved and walked away. In my head, I could hear the voice of one of those nature show narrators. *A member of the team had direct contact with two humans in the wild. Though skittish, the humans remained long enough to exchange a few stilted sentences with the team member before making excuses to return to the safety of a human den.*

"I'm not sure Ilya wants me spending time in Sproing," I said.

"Do you want to stay at the cabin today?" Julian countered.

By myself? Well, by myself in the sense there would be no other humans around. I was pretty sure if I stayed at the cabin I would have plenty of company of a different sort. "Let's go shelve some books."

I missed Aggie, and I hoped she was all right. I doubted Yorick would let her stay in a prime location. Then again, I kept forgetting that even a small shifter could have large and scary friends. I wondered how long it would take before Yorick learned that too.

CHAPTER 59

Them

Thaisday, Sumor 6

Bicker, bicker, bicker, Yorick thought as he opened the front door and walked out of the main house. His business partners were bickering because no one had come to the cabin last night to hold Hershel's hand—the wimp—and the women were just being their usual bitchy selves. Except Heidi, who was in the kitchen washing dishes and proving she wasn't top-notch material. Then again, the only cleaning service in Sproing hung up on Trina when she told them she was looking for temporary help at The Jumble, and the fees quoted by the cleaning services in Bristol were outrageous. So they needed someone to do the washing up for the time being, and Heidi—good old fat Heidi—was the one to do it.

Vaughn shouldn't have invited a couple more Clippers to stay. They only had the one other cabin that was laughingly fit for human occupation, and the men said they were bringing a boat. They hadn't mentioned if they were bringing wives or mistresses.

Darren seemed to think that they could shuffle those freaking Crows to one of the primitive cabins if they couldn't kick them out altogether. Yorick wasn't so sure about that, especially since there were *three* of the creatures staying in that cabin. But they had to figure something out before their guests arrived that afternoon.

He watched the black luxury sedan drive up to the house. He recognized that car and was certain that nothing that came out of it would benefit him. And he was right.

When the driver opened the back door for Ilya Sanguinati, Yorick hoped Vaughn was still in a vile mood.

Ilya Sanguinati removed a document from his briefcase and handed it to Yorick. "I thought it prudent to review with all of you the original agreement between Honoria Dane and the *terra indigene* when she built the main house and the cabins on the land that became known as The Jumble."

"What's to review?" Vaughn snapped. "Yorick owns the land."

Ilya gave them all a cold smile. "Mr. Dane owns the buildings, not the land. By the original agreement, which you all should have reviewed before making plans to change The Jumble, you can tear down the existing structures, but you cannot put up any building that exceeds the square footage of the original structures. You cannot put up additional buildings without the landowners' consent, which they will not give—a message I was asked to convey. Also, before you raze any of the buildings, you may want to consider if you will be able to purchase sufficient material to build a new structure. I'm told it can take months, with all the repairs that are still being done throughout the continent and the constricted supply of raw materials."

"There is plenty of wood out there." Darren waved a hand toward the windows.

"Which Mr. Dane does not own and does not have permission to use beyond harvesting firewood sufficient to heat the main house and the cabins," Ilya replied. "Mr. Dane also has use of the cultivated land to grow crops to feed the residents of The Jumble, but the number of acres is quite specific and will not be enlarged."

Yorick didn't dare look at Darren or Hershel—and especially not Vaughn. But he *had* told them about the agreement, even if he'd glossed over the details. They couldn't say they didn't know. They'd just been sure they could rewrite what didn't suit them, so he hadn't seen the point of giving them a reason to be mad at him.

"You should also be aware that while the access road is wide enough for personal vehicles, it would not accommodate the kind of heavy machinery you would need if you were going to replace any of the buildings," Ilya continued.

"We can widen that road," Hershel said. "Going to have to pave it anyway."

Ilya smiled, showing a hint of fang. "Mr. Dane does not own the access road. Therefore, it cannot be altered without the permission of the landowners, and any attempt at alterations will forfeit the right-of-way and the road will be closed."

"You can't do that!" Yorick protested.

"The landowners can—and they will," Ilya replied mildly. "I repeat: Mr. Dane has claim to the five buildings Honoria Dane built within the boundaries of this *terra indigene* settlement and nothing more. Before you continue making plans for this place, I suggest you read the original document again since you will be bound by it."

Yorick followed Ilya Sanguinati to the front door. "This is ridiculous! We need to expand the buildings and improve the access road. Our guests will expect it."

"Then you should adjust your guests' expectations, Mr. Dane." Ilya turned toward the sound of a vehicle coming up the road.

Yorick swore under his breath as the pickup hauling a boat trailer pulled up near the house. Mark Hammorson and his friend had arrived early.

Ilya studied the boat on the trailer, then looked at Yorick. "Please advise your guests that motorized vehicles of any kind are forbidden on Lake Silence. Signs are clearly posted at the public beach at the southern end of the lake."

"But not here," Yorick said quickly.

"There has never been the need to post them here." Ilya waited for his driver to open the door. "But post a sign by all means, if you think your guests will not abide by that rule without one. Be assured, whether you put up a sign or not, the penalty will be the same if you break that rule."

CHAPTER 60

Ilya

Thaisday, Sumor 6

Ilya said nothing until Boris stopped at the end of the access road and turned to look at him. "Back to the lodge or to the office in the village?"

"The office," Ilya replied.

Aiden had appeared at the lodge just long enough to tell him that Victoria had gone into Sproing with Julian Farrow. At least, the description Aiden provided, along with talk of shelving books, sounded like she had gone to the village with Farrow. Confirming that she hadn't been lured into a dangerous situation by some other male wasn't meddling or interfering or undermining self-confidence or whatever a human female might choose to call it. Silence Lodge had a vested interest in Victoria DeVine, no different than their interest in a few other humans in the village. The *terra indigene* considered such humans nonedible prey because they were useful and could not be replaced easily. Protecting such a human was sensible, especially a human prone to those anxiety attacks, which left her vulnerable in ways that made it difficult to remember that she was *not* edible prey.

Well, once he verified that Victoria was working with Julian Farrow at the bookstore, he could focus on peeling back the layers of the Tie Clip Club to figure out if the humans who had arrived with Yorick Dane were secondary members, like Detective Swinn, who had been sent to drive Victoria away from The Jumble, or if they were the real enemy. Once he knew that, the Sanguinati would invite themselves to The Jumble for dinner.

"Those new humans brought a boat with a motor," Boris said.

"They did," Ilya agreed.

"You know what will happen when they put that boat in the lake."

"Of course." He met Boris's eyes in the rearview mirror and smiled. "I'm looking forward to seeing the Lady's response. Aren't you?"

CHAPTER 61

Aggie

Thaisday, Sumor 6

Aggie flew to the porch railing of the Crowgard cabin, then cawed in surprise when Jozi flew to the porch next to theirs, which was where the Hershel and Heidi humans were staying. The latticework on the sides of the porches provided some privacy, which Miss Vicki had said would be important when they had human guests, but right now it got in the way of Aggie seeing why Jozi had gone to the wrong cabin.

<That's not our place,> Aggie said.

Eddie came out of the Crowgard cabin holding one of the Wolf Team books that Miss Vicki had loaned to them when they had packed up her library. Well, she would have let them borrow the books if they could have asked her.

Aggie would fly over to Miss Vicki's new nest soon and tell her the Crowgard had borrowed the books.

<Something wrong?> Eddie asked, using the *terra indigene* form of communication despite being in human form.

Aggie fluttered to the ground, then walked to the front of the other cabin to see what had caught Jozi's interest.

<It's a shiny,> Jozi said, pushing at a small object on the porch floor.

Catching sight of the sparkly, Aggie moved closer. Earring. A shiny that human females pushed through holes in their ears, which sounded awful.

Did finding the shiny dropped on the porch floor mean the female no longer wanted it?

<Where are the humans?> Aggie asked.

<Up at the main house,> Eddie replied. <They're pecking at each other because they couldn't make us give up the cabin.>

When two more males showed up this morning, that Yorick human had tried to tell the Crows they had to leave, but Aggie told *him* that she and her kin had rented the cabin for the summer and they didn't have to leave. Then Yorick said they had to move to one of the other cabins because *they* didn't need the fully renovated place. But Ilya wanted them to stay here and keep watch over these cabins and the main house in case the humans started any trouble. Besides, the rest of the buildings already had *terra indigene* occupying one or two of the cabins in order to keep watch.

When Eddie said he would call Ilya Sanguinati and tell the attorney that Yorick Dane was reneging on the rental agreement, which would mean the *terra indigene* were also free to renege on *their* side of the agreement, Yorick had backed away, defeated.

Another bit of metal caught a beam of sunlight. The back of the earring.

After Yorick retreated, the human females had come down to the cabin to peck at Heidi, yelling that she hadn't done anything about clean towels and straightening the rooms at the main house. And Heidi pecked right back, saying she wasn't their maid and they could wash their own damn sheets and towels. Then they squabbled about who would go into the village to purchase the sheets and towels the new males needed, even though they didn't have a bed for the sheets.

Finally Heidi went into the cabin and fetched her purse. She locked up the cabin and stomped up the path to where the humans had to park the cars, saying she would buy the towels just to get away from the rest of the females.

The three remaining females had squawked at one another—or to one another; it was hard to decipher—before going down to the beach to lie on towels and overheat in the sun.

<Another shiny!> Jozi said when she spotted the metal backing.

<Leave that one,> Aggie said. <Take the sparkly instead.>

Jozi hesitated. <Why can't we take both?>

Jozi hadn't watched cop and crime shows with Miss Vicki, hadn't seen the story where a female had dropped an earring while struggling with a male who attacked her and then took her away from her nest. It turned out the dropped earring had been a clue for the cops who were searching for her. And Jozi hadn't had time to study humans closely enough to know that humans reacted differently to losing something and having something taken.

<If you take both, the female who dropped it will say we stole it and cause trouble,> Aggie replied. <But if she finds the metal piece, she won't know if she lost the other part around the cabin or if the sparkly fell out of her ear when she walked down to the beach.>

<Oh.>

<Hurry up,> Eddie said. <Someone is coming.>

Jozi grabbed the sparkly piece of the earring and flew off to hide it in her treasure tree. Aggie flew over to the Crowgard's porch and went inside their cabin to shift to her human form and put on clothes. There had been something about the way these new human males had looked at her and Jozi that made her wary of them seeing her without clothes.

By the time the males called Mark and Tony came in sight, she and Eddie were on their own porch, sipping cool water from the plastic glasses Miss Vicki had bought for the cabins.

The males walked by, predators assessing potential prey. She watched them too because something about the way they wore their shirts bothered her. Not that by itself, but combined with the look in their eyes . . .

<I think they have guns,> she said. <They are hiding guns under their clothes.>

Eddie cocked his head. <How do you know?>

<Miss Vicki and I watched stories about many kinds of bad humans. Some of them hid guns, or knives, under their clothes.>

<Are you going to tell the Sanguinati?>

Aggie nodded. First she would warn the rest of the Crowgard, who would warn the rest of the shifters living in The Jumble. Then she would tell the Sanguinati, and they would tell the Elders and the Elementals.

And all of them would make sure these two-legged predators never came close to Miss Vicki's new nest.

CHAPTER 62

Vicki

Thaisday, Sumor 6

I had ignored the increasingly sharp hunger pangs—brought on, in part, by skipping breakfast that morning—until Julian set a plate in front of me that had the sandwich special from Come and Get It, along with thick-cut fries. The sandwich—corned beef and sauerkraut with Helen's special sauce on toasted rye bread—was one of my favorites. So were the diner's thick-cut fries. Julian had just uncovered his own plate when he heard the store's screen door close with enough sound to be deliberate.

"Stay here," Julian said quietly. He left the office break room, moving swiftly. Within moments I heard him say, "Oh. Hi. I was just about to close for lunch, but you can browse."

Someone he knew.

I relaxed and took a big bite of my sandwich. All right, too big a bite. My cheeks resembled a chipmunk's when it was gathering food for its winter stockpile.

Of course, that was when my yummy attorney walked into the room. He stopped in the doorway, looking startled. Then he walked up to the table and studied the paperback near my elbow.

Ilya smiled. "Feeling Wolfish?"

"Mrph."

"Chew, don't choke."

I felt like a fool, burning up with embarrassment. Stuffing my face like that wasn't my usual way of eating, but hunger had overcome good sense and any nod to manners.

I chewed . . . and chewed . . . and chewed before I finally swallowed.

"Sorry," I said.

His smile was still there, but it had an edge now. "Don't you have food at the cabin?"

"Plenty." Did the Sanguinati ever binge eat because of stress? Probably a question I didn't want to ask. "I was going to have breakfast after taking a walk, and then I met Aiden and . . ."

"And?"

I put the sandwich down and wiped my fingers on the napkin to give myself time to figure out a safe way to explain. "I'm grateful for Aiden's help in getting a fire started in the stove last night. But this morning, when I realized who he was . . . I felt intimidated."

"Why?"

"Because he's *Fire*. An Elemental."

"The Lady of the Lake is also an Elemental. Does she intimidate you?"

"No."

"Why not?"

Huh. Good question.

"Is it because Aiden is male?" Ilya asked.

Ooooooooooh, trick question coming from my male attorney. And I hadn't been afraid of being around Aiden when I thought he was Julian's friend or Ineke's.

If Fire mates with Water, are the children called Steam? Focus, Vicki.

"It seems silly to be scared of someone who has minnows swimming around in her tummy. But Aiden . . . When he asked me if I was all right this morning, I was afraid of what he might do to Julian, who was with me. I was afraid of saying the wrong thing."

"You're often afraid of saying the wrong thing to men."

It wasn't quite a question, so I didn't feel obliged to answer.

"While both are Elementals, the Lady of the Lake's domain has boundaries," Ilya said as if there hadn't been an awkward beat of silence. "Fire does not. That makes him more dangerous. In that, you are correct. But he bears you no ill will. Please keep that in mind."

I nodded. "Was that what you came to tell me?"

Some subtle change of expression. "No. I came to tell you that Yorick Dane's new guests have come to The Jumble with guns and other weapons, and you need to stay away."

"Aggie."

"Don't worry about the Crowgard. The *terra indigene* who live around the northern end of the lake will help keep watch over The Jumble."

The sandwich didn't taste as good after Ilya left, but I ate it and the fries. I couldn't say if I was trying to store energy or was using food to pack down stress, but I ate everything in order to get ready for whatever was coming.

CHAPTER 63

Grimshaw

Thaisday, Sumor 6

Since Ilya Sanguinati had declined to sit in the visitors' chair, Grimshaw pushed to his feet to face the vampire. Julian had called to tell him that Vicki DeVine would be at Lettuce Reed today. Not an ideal situation, but they didn't have any reason to suspect she was in danger, except for Julian's reaction to the Murder game.

But Ilya's news added weight to the concern.

"Are you sure?" he asked.

"No," Ilya replied. "The Crowgard didn't see any weapons, and I suppose there are many reasons males don't tuck in a shirt."

"Did the Crowgard hear the men's names?"

"Not their full names, but other *terra indigene* saw papers that had their names—Mark Hammorson and Tony Amorella. Air says they run a security business."

Air. Gods above and below. There had always been stories about *terra indigene* called Elementals, just as there were rumors of forms known as Elders. Or there had been those kinds of stories where he had grown up. His grandfather had told him time and time again, "Mind what you do; there is always someone watching." When he was young, he thought it meant the adults in the family, who seemed to know when he made some mischief. But that wasn't the meaning of his grandfather's warning. There could be another form of *terra indigene* in the police station right now, listening, watching, judging, and he wouldn't know unless that being chose to appear—or attack.

And yet this was the world they lived in. Until the Humans First and Last movement started a war with the Others, most of the *terra indigene* had paid no attention to the humans who crowded together on the land they were allowed to use. Now *all* the *terra indigene* paid attention, even in an unremarkable place like Sproing.

Except Sproing wasn't unremarkable anymore because Vicki DeVine had unwittingly begun to restore a *terra indigene* settlement called The Jumble, and that one decision had attracted all kinds of potentially dangerous interest in this little village and the people who lived here.

Which circled back to the reason Ilya Sanguinati had come in to talk to him. Men with weapons had entered The Jumble. Yorick Dane might say the two men were there to protect the humans, but what could an armed man do against a sink full of water that suddenly took the shape of a hand and choked a woman? You couldn't shoot it. And taking potshots at any of the shifters . . . He'd seen the pictures of how the *terra indigene* responded when someone did *that*.

"I guess I should go out and take a look at those men."

The station door flew open and Osgood ran in. "Sir! A couple of flatbed trucks hauling construction equipment are heading for The Jumble!"

"You need to stop them before any of that equipment touches the access road," Ilya warned. "I told Dane yesterday that the access road wasn't part of his property and he couldn't do anything to it, or use it for anything but personal vehicles, without the *terra indigene*'s consent."

"Could someone have given consent? Maybe someone who wasn't actually authorized?" Didn't seem likely, but it was possible Dane had dangled the right bait in front of a shifter and gotten an agreement, figuring if he worked fast, the deed would be done before anyone could object—if you ignored the fact that Elementals like Air and Earth would be aware of the transgressors the moment those humans set foot in The Jumble.

If this underhanded way of doing business was typical of Dane and his pals, it made sense they would need security—and need men who also belonged to their special club.

Grimshaw checked his service weapon and made sure he had a couple of extra clips. Then he headed for the door. "Osgood, you keep an eye on things in the village. I'll be at The Jumble."

"I'll be in my office for a while if you should have need of counsel," Ilya said.

Grimshaw ran to the cruiser, tossed his mobile phone on the passenger seat, and drove away, lights flashing and siren wailing. Probably should have waited on the siren. He hadn't gotten past the village boundary when Julian called.

"Trouble?" Julian asked.

"Not if I can stop it." He ended the call and focused on driving. But his mind circled around the timing of all of this.

First Dane showed up in Sproing and his friends showed up at The Jumble for a long weekend. By Sunday, Vicki DeVine was evicted from the home and livelihood she had worked months to renovate. Two days later, two men in the security business arrived, swiftly followed by construction equipment, which must have been brought in from Hubbney since he doubted any construction company in Bristol or woo-woo Crystalton would have taken a job at The Jumble right now. Which meant Dane and his pals must have arranged for the arrival of men and equipment *before* they took possession of The Jumble.

He saw the flatbed trucks. They had to see him. But just as the first truck made the turn onto The Jumble's access road—where did the fool think he could go?—Grimshaw saw one of the trees next to the access road fall.

"No," he breathed. Dane had hired someone to cut down trees?

He reached for the cruiser's mic, intending to call dispatch in Bristol and request backup for a potentially lethal situation. He didn't know how many men were out there cutting trees. He didn't know how many men were in the flatbed cabs. And he didn't know if any of them were carrying.

He was almost on top of the second flatbed truck, so he pulled into the other lane to make sure the driver saw him. That's when he spotted the horse and rider. He didn't recognize the rider, but when he saw the red hair with the yellow and blue tips, he took his foot off the gas and tapped the brakes, wary of getting any closer.

One moment Grimshaw saw the horse and rider. Then, next moment, he saw the tight funnel of a fire tornado heading right for the flatbed trucks at a horrific speed. He put the cruiser in reverse and stomped on the gas, praying to Mikhos that he could get far enough away before the tornado hit.

The concussion of tornado hitting flatbed trucks and the heavy equipment they carried, followed by the explosion of the gas tanks a moment later, lifted the cruiser off the pavement. Grimshaw held on to the steering wheel, as if he had some control while airborne.

The cruiser's tires hit the pavement, and Grimshaw breathed a sigh of relief. It hadn't felt any worse than going over a speed bump too fast. Before he could think to apply the brakes, the cruiser rolled to a stop.

He stared out the window. The trucks were burning. The trees were burning. And the fire tornado had vanished as swiftly as it had appeared.

Grabbing the mic, he called Osgood. "Call out the volunteer fire department. I need firefighters, EMTs, doctors. We've got a mess here." He hesitated. "I need you too, Osgood. And Julian Farrow. And call the Bristol Police Station for backup. We need CIU, firefighters, cops—we need everything they can send. You escort Ms. DeVine to Ilya Sanguinati's office, then you hightail it out here."

"Yes, sir." A pale sound, but Osgood would be there.

He pulled the cruiser onto the shoulder of the road and ran toward the burning vehicles, but the fire burned too hot for him to get close enough to determine if anyone had survived. He hoped not.

"Anyone out there?" he shouted. The crews in the flatbed trucks were gone, but the men who had been felling trees might have seen the funnel in time to run.

Sirens. A lot of sirens. Too soon for any help from Bristol, but they would be coming. Captain Hargreaves would see to that.

The volunteer firefighters arrived first with the fire truck and a water tanker, followed by the EMTs and Dr. Wallace. Officer Osgood and Julian Farrow brought up the rear. Osgood stumbled out of the passenger side of Julian's car and stared at the fire, making Grimshaw wonder if a potentially good cop had seen too much too young.

Then Osgood shook his head as if to clear it and ran to where Grimshaw waited.

"Take the cruiser and go down the road," Grimshaw said. "Block it off. I'll have Julian block off the road at this end."

"Yes, sir." Osgood stared at the fire. "The Others are angry."

Grimshaw nodded. "But not with us. Get going."

As soon as Osgood headed for the cruiser, Grimshaw turned to Julian Farrow.

Julian said, "This morning Vicki and I met Fire, who calls himself Aiden. He was riding a horse named Twister."

"Gods," Grimshaw breathed. "How's Vicki?"

"How do you think? A fire was reported at The Jumble. No one could tell her if the buildings were burning or some other part of the property."

"I need you to man the barricade at this end of the road. I need to find one of those bridle paths or any kind of trail that will get me around to the other side of the fire. There were men out there cutting down trees. I don't know if they got away."

"And you have to check on Dane and the rest of them."

"Have to do my job."

"Caw."

Grimshaw turned toward the sound and spotted the Crow. He figured it had to be one of the Crowgard. All the ordinary birds would have fled from the fire.

"Aggie?"

"Caw."

"I need to find a trail to the main house."

The Crow flew off between a break in the trees. Grimshaw hurried to follow. If the fire cut him off from the road, he'd head for the lake.

"Keep reporting in," Julian called.

The game trail opened onto a bridle path. Grimshaw jogged to keep up with Aggie until she landed in a tree and didn't continue. Obviously she wasn't going to lead him any farther.

He pointed at the path in front of him. "The main house is that way?"

"Caw."

He took a step, then looked at the Crow. "If the wind doesn't change direction, more of The Jumble will burn. Miss Vicki would be sad about that."

No response, so he followed the path.

He didn't know if Aggie had delivered the message that fast or if something else had been listening, but when he reached the access road a minute later, the wind had shifted, blowing the fire back over already scorched earth.

The moment Grimshaw's foot crunched on the gravel, four armed men swung toward the sound.

"Hey!" he said, holding up his hands, palms out.

Swinn and Reynolds looked spooked enough that he felt lucky they hadn't fired out of reflex. The other two men? Yeah. Private security for sure.

Grimshaw turned to Yorick Dane, who was clumped with his business partners. "Is everyone all right? All the people staying with you?"

Dane stared at the charred husks of trees, then raised a shaking hand. "Is that . . . Is that a body?"

He moved in that direction for a closer look. *Gods, let those men be removed from all suffering.* He counted four bodies before he walked back to where Dane stood.

"What happened?" Vaughn demanded.

"Fire tornado," Grimshaw replied. "It hit the two flatbed trucks and the construction equipment you were bringing in, and then took out the crew felling trees." He tried to chain the anger swelling inside him. "You were warned."

Even Vaughn looked shocked. Most likely, they'd been getting away with underhanded deals since their university days, if not before. This should have been nothing different— except they weren't dealing with humans anymore.

"We'll have to leave," Darren said. "That truck is blocking the way and has to be moved."

He looked at the burned-out truck the loggers had driven and shook his head. "The firefighters are still bringing the fire around the flatbeds under control. You've got thousands of pounds—maybe a few tons—of burning, twisted metal blocking the access road." He pointed to the burned truck. "Nobody will be moving that one for a while."

The men stared at him.

"Then how are we getting out?" Dane asked.

"You're not," Grimshaw replied. "Well, you can pack a light carryall and walk out, following the bridle trails until you reach the road."

"Hammorson?" Vaughn said, turning to the beefy blond man.

"We can take my boat and go to the public beach and get help there," Hammorson said. "Or go across the lake to that big lodge I saw on the other side."

"Does that boat have a motor?" When Hammorson nodded, Grimshaw turned to Dane. "Didn't you tell your friends about the no-motor rule on this lake? Are you looking for ways to get these people killed?" He turned back to Hammorson. "Even if you take out a rowboat, you do not want to go across to Silence Lodge. Not today."

Hammorson narrowed his eyes. "Why? Who owns Silence Lodge?"

"The Sanguinati."

Uneasy now, all the men shifted their feet.

"Look," Grimshaw said. "The main house and the lake-side cabins are probably the safest place right now. Your cars aren't going anywhere until the road is cleared and that could take a couple of days." Or more. The flatbeds had been burning when he'd run to check on the people here, but his impression had been of metal twisted and melted into nightmarish shapes. Not the kind of thing you could roll out of the way.

"Vicki should have widened the access road and built a second entrance," Dane said. "We wouldn't be in this mess if she'd put enough money into this place."

Grimshaw stared at Yorick Dane. Was the man actually *pouting* because the ex-wife he was screwing on a business deal hadn't gone into debt to do more improvements?

He shook his head, disgusted with all of them. "Hear those sirens? That's the Bristol police and fire department coming in to help. You all do what you want. I'll inform the CIU team that you're all alive but there are burned bodies that need to be identified. I imagine someone will come in soon to talk to you. It would help if you could provide the names of the loggers you hired to illegally cut down those trees."

"Now, see here," Vaughn protested. "We did nothing illegal—"

Grimshaw held up a hand. "I'm not interested. That's for someone else to figure out. Just remember that the someone who is going to decide isn't a member of your damn club."

Ignoring their protests and vitriolic opinions about his parentage, Grimshaw followed the bridle path, then chose a game trail heading in the right direction. A few minutes later, he reached the road.

The firefighters had contained the blaze and were hosing down the surrounding grass and trees—and no doubt would continue until the water tank ran dry. They were being thorough because, like sweat and ash, fear was a taste in the air.

CHAPTER 64

Vicki

Thaisday, Sumor 6

As soon as the Bristol police arrived to assist Grimshaw, Julian drove back to Sproing and picked me up at Ilya Sanguinati's office. We stopped at Pops Davies's general store and bought some food that wouldn't spoil if we didn't eat it for a day or two. Then Julian drove us to the Mill Creek Cabins.

Beer wasn't my favorite drink, but I didn't say anything when Julian offered me a bottle before settling into the other chair on his porch. I could see the water mill from where I was sitting. It looked quaint, peaceful. I wondered if I would ever feel peaceful again.

"I feel bad about the men who died," I said. "Their boss might belong to that stupid club, but that doesn't mean those men did. They came here to do a job, just like any other job, and they died because Yorick and the rest of those . . . *men* . . . thought they could take whatever they wanted." Like Yorick had done with me. "And I keep thinking about all the men *I* had hired to renovate the main house and the cabins, the men who had brought in the bulldozer and backhoe and all the other equipment to replace the septic system. They could have been killed."

"I don't think so," Julian replied. "You were very careful about what you were doing. I remember you saying that you had reviewed the terms of the property agreement with all of your contractors to make sure you, and they, didn't violate the terms. And, Vicki? You hired firms from Crystalton, which meant you had hired Intuits. It stands to reason that at least one of the men on those crews would have known before the first shovelful of earth was dug up if they were doing something dangerous. The *terra indigene* wanted The Jumble restored, and you were doing that. And who was your first lodger? One of the Crowgard."

"A test."

"Probably."

"I thought she was a girl who had run away from home and needed a safe place to stay. Until the whole eyeball thing."

Julian sipped his beer. "I bet you didn't charge her anywhere close to what you could get for a week's stay in one of those renovated cabins."

I shrugged, unwilling to admit he was right. I'd wondered where she kept getting the money for the weekly rent, but she paid promptly and didn't cause trouble—and I didn't hear about any houses in the village being burgled, so I thought she'd tucked some money away before leaving home.

Come to think of it, I still didn't know where she got the money for the rent.

Thinking about the men who had done the renovations and the big improvements made me wonder about something else. "Why didn't the men Yorick hired look at using the farm track and the grassy lane that my contractors had used?"

Instead of taking another sip, Julian lowered the beer bottle. "What?"

"The farm track that forms the boundary between the Milfords' orchards and The Jumble—where Aggie found the dead man. The crews I hired came in that way. The foreman said it was the long way round but the grassy lane going into The Jumble was wide enough for them to reach the meadow where the septic tank was located." I frowned. "No, that wouldn't have worked. The lane ends at the septic tank."

"That grassy lane that connects to the farm track. Is the turnoff before or beyond where you found the body?"

I looked at Julian, who foolishly waited for an answer.

"You have no clue," he finally said.

"The only time I saw the lane was when the foreman drove me to the meadow to show me the new septic tank before they covered it up. Aggie and I followed a path in the woods to reach the body." I sounded defensive. I felt defensive. I tried, I really did, but the You Are Here map that everyone else seems to have in their head? I didn't get one.

"Vicki."

It was a soft warning. I followed the direction of Julian's gaze and saw Aiden walking along the road accompanied by a chubby brown pony with a storm-gray mane and tail.

I thought about the men who died today because the person who had hired them had knowingly broken the rules set down by beings who had no interest in the kinds of petty games humans played with one another. I thought about the men I had hired to do work in The Jumble. And most of all, I thought about the friends whose actions might be misunderstood.

I would never be able to rebuild my life again if a friend died because of me.

I set the beer bottle on the porch. "I'll be back in a minute."

"Don't," Julian said softly.

An expression of concern for me or a warning that he sensed something might happen? Either way, doing nothing was not something I could do and still believe I was a good person who deserved good people as friends.

I walked up to the gate in Julian's enclosed front yard, reaching it at the same time Aiden came abreast of the cabin. He stopped and looked at me. Maybe it was the light last night, or the lack of it. Maybe it was the shock of being evicted and scrambling to move into the cabin. Today, in daylight, I couldn't pretend Aiden was human.

"I wish I was stronger," I said. "I wish I was braver. But the truth is, even though you helped me yesterday, I'm afraid of you. I'm afraid of what you can do."

"You should be."

No attempt to tell me that what I felt was silly—because it wasn't silly.

"Your species has some things in common with the shifters in how you touch, and are touched by, the world," Aiden said. "My kind of *terra indigene*? We're connected to the world in a way you never will be. We may tolerate your kind, even feel friendly toward some of you. But we'll never be your friend, Vicki. Not like the Crows or even the Sanguinati." He took a few steps, then turned back, giving me a hint of a smile. "But if you need help lighting the woodstove, ask one of the Crows to contact me, and I'll come by to get the fire started."

He and Twister walked away, heading toward the mill and the creek. I returned to the porch and took a healthy swallow of beer. Julian and I sat quietly, not feeling a need to fill the silence with unnecessary words, giving me time to think about my recent encounters with the *terra indigene* in general and the Elementals in particular.

Friendly but not a friend. I understood the distinction. I just didn't know what that distinction would mean for the humans in Sproing in the future.

CHAPTER 65

Them

Thaisday, Sumor 6

Hershel stumbled out of the cabin and grabbed one of the posts that held up the porch roof. Feeling legless wasn't due to having too much to drink. It turned out fear had a way of keeping a man sufficiently sober. And fear could make a man feel weak.

Well, screw that. Screw all of it. Should have known a putz like Yorick Dane couldn't put together a solid deal, but Vaughn had said the property had potential. Even after they found out that Dane had given up the property, Vaughn didn't want to let go of a chance to have shares in a resort on one of the Finger Lakes since the human places around those lakes were so limited. And he had considered how Yorick's hanky ex-wife—the one who could be used until she was used up and then thrown away—could be worked to do the initial improvements before they came in to take over and build a *real* resort. But Dane had screwed up big-time, had glossed over the real reasons why his family hadn't done anything to develop what should be a prime piece of real estate.

They were surrounded by the Others here. *Really* surrounded by the Others. And not just the Crows and the furry guys. There was some seriously weird shit living in these woods. Like a tornado that targeted the two flatbed trucks and twisted them into an impenetrable tangle of burning metal that would take days to cut apart in order to reopen the access road. Like a fire that killed the loggers they had hired.

No, Dane hadn't been up front about a whole lot of things, including the fact that the land that was supposed to be his share of the investment didn't actually belong to him.

Hershel struck out for the beach. Nice beach, but that didn't mean anything if all you had to offer was unfurnished cabins, and most of them didn't have indoor plumbing! Sure, they could furnish the renovated cabins. He'd suggested buying the furniture off of Vicki DeVine—they could get it cheaper than buying new since *she* wouldn't have a use for it—but Constance refused to consider the idea, said Vicki's tastes were too pedestrian.

He wondered if Constance was starting to think that her choice of husband made her own taste a bit too pedestrian. After all, she and Vicki had married the same man.

Hershel paused at the beach, then continued walking until he reached the dock that stretched out into the water. Didn't seem to be much good for a boat. Did people fish off the end of it? Did kids jump off the end of it the way kids always wanted to do?

He walked to the end of the dock. A starry night sky and dark water. Not even a single light on in the lodge across the lake.

Piss on this place. As soon as that access road reopened, he was backing out of this loser deal and returning to Hubbney, where he had other deals in the works.

He grinned and put his hand in the opening in his boxers. Yeah. He'd piss on this place.

He huffed out a pleased laugh as his urine hit the lake.

"Monkey man."

No longer laughing, he finished up and tucked himself back into the boxers.

"Moooonkey maaaannnn."

"Spoiling our water."

"Soiling our water."

He started to turn, started to ask who was out there. But something—someone—hit him from behind, sent him flying off the end of the dock. He hit the water hard and went under—and felt something pinch the triceps of his right arm, the calf of his left leg. He surfaced immediately, focusing on the dock, but whoever had pushed him was already gone.

Something pinched his left forearm. He raised it above the water and stared at the wound. He'd been *bitten*.

Something yanked on his leg, followed by several pinches. Not pinches. Bites. *Something in the water was biting him.*

He took a breath, intending to yell for help. A hand rose out of the water, a hand with webbed fingers and curved, needlelike nails. The hand covered his face, the nails piercing his skin as he was shoved under the water.

Thrashing. Spinning as the things bit and bit and bit. He flailed, managed to break free a couple of times and reach the surface. But not long enough to call for help. Barely long enough to suck in air before being pulled under again.

Teeth sheared through one side of his neck. As he sank for the last time, he had the odd sensation of feeling his lower legs separate from the rest of him.

CHAPTER 66

Grimshaw

Firesday, Sumor 7

Grimshaw rinsed the shampoo from his hair, soaped up a cloth, and began washing himself. The Bristol CIU team had bunked at The Jumble, making do with sleeping bags rolled out in the social room. Ineke still had a full house, so Captain Hargreaves had been given Osgood's room, and the baby cop had slept on the sofa in the parlor. Today they would figure out whom to call in Bristol or Crystalton to disassemble the flatbed trucks and the construction equipment—and figure out where to haul it.

Thankfully, that was Hargreaves's headache, not his. With Bristol taking the lead on the latest trouble in The Jumble, he would stick to the village today, walk the streets, check in with the businesses. When he got tired of that, he would take the desk and let Osgood patrol and soak up the gossip.

He finished his shower and reached for a towel when he heard his bedroom door open.

Crap. He'd locked that door. Always did. His service weapon wasn't in plain sight but . . .

"Grimshaw? Wayne!"

"Captain?" He wrapped a towel around his waist and

walked out of the bathroom, beads of water running down his chest. Hargreaves stood in the middle of his room. Ineke stood in the doorway. She seemed to appreciate the view he provided but not the water he dripped on her hardwood floor.

He quickly stepped onto the area rug. Not that that was much better, but at least Ineke's presence—and the room key she held up for him to see—explained how Hargreaves had entered the room.

He took in his captain's appearance—hastily dressed and unshaven. Not showing pride in the uniform.

"Get dressed," Hargreaves said. "I'll wait for you in the car."

Ah, gods. "What happened?"

"The CIU team found part of a body at The Jumble. On the beach."

"A floater?"

Hargreaves shook his head. "They think it's one of Yorick Dane's business partners." He walked out of the room, closing the door behind him.

Grimshaw stared at the uniform he had hung on the hook attached to the back of the bedroom door. There were things he hadn't put in any report, things he wouldn't put on paper. But he should have told Hargreaves and the Bristol team about the creatures he and Julian had seen in the lake during the trail ride beach party. He couldn't have told them much, wasn't even sure what he'd seen. Except whatever lived in the lake probably weren't the same creatures that had been whispering in the dark the night Constance Dane had been choked by freezing water in her own bathroom.

Five minutes later, he was dressed and heading downstairs. Ineke met him at the front door and held out a large travel mug.

"Coffee," she said. "Sounds like you won't want to eat beforehand."

"Thanks." He took the coffee and walked out to Hargreaves's car.

* * *

Seeing what was left of Hershel, Grimshaw felt glad he hadn't had breakfast and wished he hadn't drunk the coffee.

"The bites aren't that much bigger than a human bite, but the teeth . . ." Samuel Kipp, Bristol's CIU team leader, shook his head. "Not an animal. Some kind of fish? Teeth could have been sharp enough that the victim didn't feel much more than a pinch or a tug when the creatures bit off chunks of him."

"Creatures?" Hargreaves asked. "More than one?"

Kipp nodded. "At least a handful of different bite marks. And the marks on the face? Claws maybe. I've got a man calling police stations located on the other Finger Lakes to see if they have any record of a similar attack." He looked at Grimshaw. "Anyone around here who would be the village historian?"

Grimshaw stared across the lake. "The residents of Silence Lodge probably could tell you exactly what did this, but I doubt the Sanguinati will be that forthcoming."

"Why not?" Hargreaves asked.

"Because they're close-lipped about the Elders who live on this land—and in the lake."

All the color leached out of Kipp's brown face. "Gods. We went swimming last night. Dane and his missus were bitching about us using that general shower area off the kitchen, so we all went down to the lake to rinse off and cool off. We could have—"

"Not likely," Grimshaw said. "I went swimming here too. Julian Farrow and I saw something out there—just a glimpse—but there was no indication we would be attacked." A sudden thought made his heart give one hard bump. "Except we were out here swimming when Vicki DeVine was still in charge of The Jumble."

He shook his head. Vicki was an important factor but not the only factor. "There hasn't been a lot of downtime since I got here, but I did take a quick look at the reports that were filed at the station. An attack like this would have been reported. If nothing else, there would be a missing persons

report or a copy of a DLU form. But people go fishing on the
lake all the time. They swim at the public beach. If this had
happened before, Ineke Xavier wouldn't have proposed
bringing her guests here for beach parties."

Activity behind him. Angry voices.

Marmaduke Swinn and Tony Amorella were squaring off
with some of Bristol's CIU team, while Vaughn, Darren, and
Yorick Dane were yelling and creating . . . a distraction.

Grimshaw looked around. "Where are Reynolds and
Hammorson?" They could be at the main house. The CIU
team could be taking statements. Or they could be . . .

A motor turned over, a sound coming from the other side
of the dock.

Crap!

Grimshaw ran for the dock. "Reynolds! You can't put a
motor in this lake!"

"The police aren't doing anything, so we'll handle this,"
Vaughn said, stepping in front of Grimshaw, getting in the way
of him stopping those fools before someone—*something*—
noticed them. "Going to make some chum."

Hammorson backed away from the dock, then headed for
the middle of the lake, motor roaring. Reynolds stood braced
against the windscreen, a shotgun aimed at the water, ready
to shoot anything that surfaced in response to the sound of
the motor.

The boat roared out of sight, heading toward the northern
end of the lake, then came roaring back before Hammorson
began driving in a big circle that could be seen from Silence
Lodge as well as The Jumble's beach.

Circling. Circling, circling, circling.

Even before Hammorson started shouting, started fighting to move the boat out of the circling water, Grimshaw
knew the circles made by the boat's motor had changed into
a whirlpool. Was it his imagination, or was he seeing the
shape of a steed emerging from the foaming water, racing
and carrying the water with it? Carrying the boat with it?

The boat was below the lip now. How soon before it
flipped? Could Reynolds and Hammorson survive long

enough to reach the surface, or would they be carried down to the bottom of the lake?

She rose without warning from the heart of the whirlpool, a giant female shape made of water. Her hands closed on the bottom of the boat and lifted it as her straight arms rose toward the sky. Her head. Her shoulders. Her torso. As her hips rose above the surface, she arched and dove back into the lake.

Reynolds and Hammorson screamed as they tumbled out of the boat and hit the water moments before she slammed the boat on top of them, her dive taking everything down with her.

The water circled, circled, circled, but it was residual motion. The whirlpool, like the female, had vanished.

The boat suddenly reappeared close to the dock, a projectile thrown by a giant hand. It struck the pickup truck still attached to the boat trailer, smashing through the cab and the windshield.

While Yorick Dane and his friends stood frozen in shock, Grimshaw ran to the end of the dock and searched the choppy water for any sign of the men.

"Do you see Reynolds?" Swinn shouted, pulling up at the land end of the dock. "Do you see him?"

The bottom of the lake had been churned up, turning the usually clear water cloudy. He couldn't see anything.

Then Grimshaw spotted something orange moving toward the dock, something under the surface, barely visible. A life vest? Reynolds had been wearing one.

The wooden ladder attached to the dock didn't look new, but he went down anyway, testing each step until his ankles were in the water.

"Check the boathouse for a gaff or fishing net," he called to Hargreaves and Kipp. Praying the ladder would hold his weight, he held on with one hand and squatted until his ass was almost touching the water. He stretched his other arm as far as he could, his heart pounding as his hand went under the water, as his fingers scrabbled to grab hold of what he could almost reach.

Hands with webbed fingers and needlelike nails closed over the sides of the vest and lifted it a little higher, a little closer. Close enough for his fingers to grab the strap.

"Thanks," he breathed.

The hands disappeared. Feet pounded on the dock and Kipp flopped on his belly before reaching to help pull up whatever Grimshaw had found.

Thanks, he'd said.

Nobody felt thankful when they hauled the life vest up to the dock and found Reynolds's severed arm and the shotgun secured to it.

Grimshaw shot up the ladder and kept going until he stood several feet from the dock and the water and whatever lived there. He bent over and braced his hands on his knees.

Hargreaves hurried to reach him. "Wayne, are you all right?"

He wasn't a coward. He'd seen plenty of grisly things during his years on the force. But remembering the bite marks on Hershel's body and what body parts he'd been dangling too close to the water a minute ago made him queasy. He hadn't seen the face or the mouth, but he'd seen the curved nails at the ends of those webbed fingers.

"That vest didn't float up by chance." He spoke quietly enough that only Hargreaves would hear him. "They're still out there, watching."

"Guess we're not putting divers in that water," Hargreaves said.

"Not today."

If Hargreaves was smart, today would turn into never.

Grimshaw straightened. "I have to close the public beach."

"Gods, yes." Hargreaves pulled his car keys out of his trousers pocket. "Take my car. I'll be here a while."

"I'll call Osgood to help me clear the beach and keep it closed."

He ran from the beach to the main house, then to the bridle path and game trail until he reached the road and the cars parked on the shoulder. A couple of the Crowgard followed him to the road. He didn't know if they were just curious or keeping tabs on him. At least he hadn't heard any of those unnerving whispers.

He still checked the front and back seats of the cruiser, then locked the doors as soon as he got in. He sagged in the seat for a minute. He gave himself that much time to wonder if the rest of the Finger Lakes held these kinds of secrets. Then he called Ineke Xavier and asked her to fetch his spare pair of shoes and give them to Osgood. Finally he called Osgood and gave the orders to meet him at Lake Silence's public beach.

Starting the cruiser, he touched the medal under his shirt and offered up a brief prayer to Mikhos before he put the vehicle in gear and drove to the beach.

CHAPTER 67

Vicki

Firesday, Sumor 7

I didn't hear about the beach being closed until I walked over to Come and Get It to pick up lunch. Julian had put up a CLOSED FOR INVENTORY sign on Lettuce Reed's door, which I thought was an odd thing to do on a weekday. I worried that he was turning away potential customers, and the needed income from book sales, in order to keep me out of sight. But when I offered to pick up lunch, he gave me his order without any fuss, so I guessed that meant he wasn't sensing any danger in the village.

The diner seemed more crowded than usual, and buzzing with people talking in low voices, as if they didn't want to be overheard but couldn't keep quiet.

I gave my order to Helen. I wanted to ask what was going on, but she seemed stressed and had a booth of snooty women—including the two who had tried to cause trouble for Julian—snapping their fingers in a demand for attention. As it turned out, everyone thought I was the one who had the answers.

"Miss Vicki." A middle-aged man wearing overalls and a T-shirt approached, twisting a cap in his hands. "Don't think we've met officially, but I've seen you around. I'm Fred, from the bait-and-tackle shop on the south end of the lake."

"Oh. Yes. Pleased to meet you." He was the one who approached me, but he didn't seem all that pleased about it.

"Do you know why the chief closed the beach?" Fred asked. "Does it have anything to do with all the police being at The Jumble?"

It took a moment to realize that "chief" meant Officer Grimshaw. It took another moment to realize that the buzz of voices had fallen to a few whispers from people in the booths farthest from the counter where I stood.

"Officer Grimshaw closed the public beach?" I asked.

Fred nodded. "Wouldn't say why, just ordered everyone out of the water and told them to go home. Then he put an officer at the entrance to the parking area to stop anyone else from going to the beach. There's talk that something happened to one of the people staying at The Jumble."

In school, I was not the kid who enjoyed presenting a report to the class. I wasn't the one who wanted to stand on the auditorium stage while people in the audience coughed politely or rustled their programs. But there I was, the center of attention, with my escape looking impossibly far away, not to mention the door being blocked by Gershwin Jones, who was wearing a caftan of somber earth tones instead of his usual bright colors.

A small village. I shopped here, had a passing acquaintance with most of the people who ran or worked in the businesses. I would have been one of the people who ran a business.

"I don't know what's happening at The Jumble," I said, looking at Fred. "My ex-husband repossessed the property and evicted me a few days ago. I don't have any information about what's going on there."

Fred pursed his lips and finally nodded. "Didn't know you'd been given the boot, but it makes sense that the trouble started when one of the Danes showed up."

Really? Did the police know people in the village saw a correlation? Should I tell Grimshaw? No, it sounded like he was already up to his eyeballs in dealing with this. Besides, he knew exactly when Yorick reclaimed The Jumble.

"I'm sure Officer Grimshaw will get it sorted out very soon." I wasn't sure of any such thing, but Fred looked relieved to hear me say it.

Suddenly color filled his cheeks and he wouldn't meet my eyes. "You got someplace to stay while you sort things out?" he asked.

I didn't know the details of Fred's life, just that he ran the bait-and-tackle shop with Larry. But I translated the blush as an offer of a place to stay, which was sweet—and a little confusing since this was my first conversation with the man.

"Thanks for asking. For now, I'm staying with a friend." Not exactly the truth, but Ilya Sanguinati was insistent that I not tell anyone exactly where I was staying and definitely not say that I was alone. It seemed silly; there were a limited number of places anyone could stay in Sproing, and if I wasn't staying at the boardinghouse, the Mill Creek Cabins would be the next logical choice.

"Staying with a friend. Is that what they call it these days?" That from one of the snooty women sitting in the booth.

Fred's hands tightened on his cap. Gershwin Jones, who struck me as a gentle if flamboyant man, took a step closer to the booth.

Helen thumped my lunch order on the counter, startling everyone. Then she leaned toward me and whispered, "Best if you go before someone gets riled. I put the lunches on your tab."

"Someone" meaning someone not human. Someone who might destroy the diner because a snooty customer took a verbal poke at me.

I thanked Helen, took the food, and hurried back to Lettuce Reed. When I entered the break room, Julian was on the phone.

"I'll talk to him if you think it will help, but I didn't see anything more than you did that day." Julian hesitated. "Stirred up, but that's been true for a couple of days. The current of fear is . . . more intense. Not dangerous, but you need to tell them something. Okay. Yeah." He spotted me. "Have to go."

I studied his pale face. "What happened at The Jumble? Why did Grimshaw close the public beach?"

"One of Dane's idiot friends took a motorboat out on the lake, and the lake's residents reacted as you might expect. Grimshaw closed the public beach as a precaution. Just until everyone calms down."

I set our lunches on the counter next to the sink, no longer hungry. "None of this would have happened if I hadn't tried to turn The Jumble into a viable business."

"By all the gods, Vicki, get over yourself," Julian snapped.

He couldn't have hurt me more if he'd slapped my face. I thought Julian Farrow was my friend. I should have known better.

"He trained you to do that, didn't he?" Julian said softly, staring at me. "He trained you to accept the blame whenever anything he did had consequences he didn't like. Vicki . . . Vicki, look at yourself. You're backed into a corner, trembling."

Meltdown approaching. Had to stay strong long enough to get out of there.

"Vicki." Julian held out a hand but didn't come any closer. "Vicki, let me help you. Come over here and sit down."

Couldn't. Meltdown approaching. Hysteria. Weeping. Guilt for being so inadequate, followed by agreeing with everything he said because that was the only way the yelling would stop.

I was in a chair, crying, and Julian was on the phone again. "I need you here, *now*."

Maybe Ineke would come. I could talk to Ineke. Maybe. Except she thought I was an interesting person capable of running a business, and I didn't want her to find out the truth. I didn't want her to know I'd been pretending, that I really wasn't capable of doing anything.

It wasn't Ineke who walked into the break room and

handed me a box of tissues to clean the snot off my face. It was Ilya Sanguinati.

"Who was your physician in Hubb NE?" Ilya asked quietly.

"I don't need medication." I'd always been afraid when he suggested that.

"When who suggested it?" Ilya asked, making me think I'd said the words out loud. "I didn't suggest it. Perhaps tea and whiskey? Isn't that a drink humans find calming?"

"I don't have the tea, but I have the whiskey," Julian said. He leaned against the doorway. Blocked the doorway.

"Victoria? Who is this *he* you speak of?" Ilya asked.

He knew. We all knew. I had reacted to one man's bit of temper as if he were someone else.

"I was interested in your X-rays."

I blinked. "Why?"

"They document broken bones." Ilya continued to look at me, quiet and benign.

Why did he think I would have broken bones?

Then I got it. "He never hit me. He threatened to sometimes when he was very angry, but Yorick never hit me." Words had been his fist of choice. So not something I was going to tell my attorney, who might be sitting quietly to avoid upsetting me but was far from benign.

How did I end up surrounded by scary men? Ilya, Aiden, Conan, Cougar, even Grimshaw. Even Julian.

"Would you take credit for someone else's achievement when you had nothing to do with that achievement?" Ilya asked.

"No."

"Then don't take credit for someone else's mistakes. Yorick Dane and his friends were told they couldn't bring heavy equipment into The Jumble. They were told motorboats were forbidden on the lake. They chose to ignore the rules. If you had been there, could you have stopped them? Would they have listened?"

"No," I said.

"Since they wouldn't have listened to you, I strongly suggest that you not accept guilt for actions you didn't commit and could not have stopped." Ilya stood up. "I still want the name of your former doctor. You can drop it off at my office on your way home."

Ilya and Julian left the break room. Julian returned a minute later and sat down.

"I'm sorry," I said.

Julian rubbed a hand over his mouth. Then he sighed. "During the months when you were restoring The Jumble and teaching yourself how to run a business—how to run a resort—I thought you were a little nervous sometimes, especially around men. I figured you were emotionally burned by your divorce, and definitely gun-shy about dating, but you were getting on with your life. I never imagined you experienced panic attacks this severe."

I felt sick with shame.

"It doesn't take much, does it? Just the wrong phrase or the wrong smell or seeing the wrong person and it all comes back. The pain, the fear." Julian tried to smile. "I can't watch the cop and crime shows you enjoy so much. I never know when the wrong combination of things will be in the story, and then I'm back in that alley trying to get away from men who want to kill me, not sure if I can get up and find help before I bleed out. I triggered this in you today, and I'm the one who's sorry. The last thing I want to do is sound like your ex."

"You don't. I'm not even sure what I heard."

"I understand that."

Sproing was such a marginal place there hadn't been any police officers working out of the station here until Grimshaw showed up, temporarily reassigned. Had Sproing's lack of crime been a relief to Julian, that the village could get along with calling the police in Bristol whenever there was trouble? What about now?

Had he closed his store today because *he* had needed to lock out all the trouble and turmoil?

"You've had some episodes recently, haven't you? With all

the police here investigating and the questions about the tie clippers . . . ?"

"I haven't had any bad episodes since I bought the bookstore, not even when I had some unusual customers. But since I've been helping the police with these inquiries, I've had a few bad moments."

"Does Grimshaw know?"

Julian shook his head. "And you're not going to tell him."

"You're his friend. Don't you think he should know what this is doing to you?"

"Vicki, if he knew, he wouldn't ask for my help. And I have a feeling, a very strong feeling, that some lives will depend on my helping him."

CHAPTER 68

Grimshaw

Firesday, Sumor 7

Grimshaw knocked on the back door of Lettuce Reed. When no one answered, he knocked again, louder. As he debated the wisdom of breaking down the door, he saw Vicki's face on the other side of the glass and heard locks turning.

"Officer Grimshaw."

He scanned her face. Puffy from a crying jag but no visible bruises.

Gods. He wasn't answering a domestic call. At least, he hoped not. Abusive relationships didn't always include sex. "I'd like to come in." He knew how easily he could use his size and the uniform to intimidate someone, so he made an effort not to lean forward. As Julian had said, he needed to be the good cop.

"Sure," Vicki said, stepping back to let him in. "I'm helping Julian inventory stock, and we're having a late lunch. Would you like something to eat? We have plenty."

"Thanks, I could use some food." Nerves. Awfully close to the behavior he'd seen when Detective Swinn had tried to bring her in for questioning in the death of Franklin Cartwright.

He followed Vicki into the break room. Julian's version of the Murder game wasn't in sight, which was good. Julian, however, looked pale and rough. And having seen that particular kind of shadow in the eyes of men who had served in the wild country for a little too long, he understood some things about Julian—and cursed his friend for hiding the difficulties so well.

He'd known better than to throw Osgood, who had seen *terra indigene* kill other members of Swinn's team, back into The Jumble. But he'd pulled Julian back into working with the police because he'd needed backup he could trust and he'd needed Julian's knowledge of the people living here as well as the man's investigative skills. He'd ignored Julian's half-hearted attempts to back away from this tangle of deaths; he'd thought the reluctance was because of the way Julian had left the force. He hadn't realized that by asking for help, he'd trapped his friend between feeling compelled to help and the need for self-preservation.

"Anything I should know?" he asked.

"Rough day," Julian replied, his tone warning Grimshaw to drop the subject.

Vicki found another plate and set out the food. The amount wasn't excessive, but Grimshaw figured neither she nor Julian had much of an appetite. He, on the other hand, was ravenous and felt grateful he didn't have to venture into a public place to find something to eat.

"I'm going to be making a public announcement later this afternoon," he said. "Have to explain about closing the beach and other things."

"You hate making public announcements," Julian said, almost smiling. "Can't Captain Hargreaves handle that? Isn't the Bristol station taking the lead?"

"He'll be there," Grimshaw replied sourly. "And Bristol is taking the lead. But I'm still stuck with the announcement. Anyway, we're going to close off this block of Main Street to vehicular traffic a half an hour before the announcement, which will be done outside the police station."

"You do recall that Main Street is the only way in or out of this village?"

"Yep." That was the reason he was closing it down. There was the odd chance of a stranger driving through, either on purpose or by accident, and hitting one of the villagers gathered in the street for an announcement he figured wouldn't take more than five minutes. "I might cause the first traffic jam in Sproing's history."

"How many vehicles constitutes a traffic jam?" Vicki asked.

"One percent of the population," he replied promptly.

She blinked. "But . . . that would be three vehicles."

"Yep."

Julian took a bite of a sandwich and chewed slowly. "I don't remember that rule of thumb."

"That's because I made it up."

A stupid conversation, but Grimshaw saw the change in Julian, saw the moment his friend stepped back from some personal abyss.

"Is this the first time you caused a traffic jam?" Vicki asked, as if his causing trouble this afternoon was a given.

He wasn't sure if that assumption was an insult, but she, too, was looking calmer so he'd run with it.

"No, I've done it a few times. The most memorable was a couple of years ago. I came across a young deer that had been hit by . . . well, probably a truck. It was across one lane of a two-lane road in the wild country, and the carcass was surrounded by crows." Maybe not the best story to tell while they were eating. Then again, Vicki didn't seem to notice. "Now, I couldn't tell if they were crows or Crowgard, but I figured the latter since several of them ran *toward* my cruiser with their wings raised, as if trying to intimidate me. I pulled the cruiser across both lanes, put on the lights, and got out."

"How many Crows?" Julian asked.

"A lot. They covered both lanes. I took some heavy gloves out of the trunk and approached the carcass, thinking to pull it over to the shoulder. Nothing doing. So I walked up ahead, getting my ankles pecked for my efforts, and I held up traffic for an hour before the Crows had eaten their fill and flown up into the nearby trees. Then I pulled the carcass over to the shoulder, got back in my cruiser, and I and the dozen cars who had waited drove away."

"I wonder if the Crowgard would do things differently now," Vicki said.

"How so?"

"Well, ever since Aggie moved into the cabin, she's been coming over to watch the cop and crime shows with me, so I think she would recognize police cars and understand police officers are there to help. So maybe now you could explain why it would be safer to move the carcass to the side of the road where the Crowgard could feed without being hurt by passing cars."

Grimshaw finished his share of the lunch. "Something to consider. At any rate, I wanted to give you a heads-up so you could get out before you're blocked in. Not that I expect the announcement to take up much time."

"Appreciate the heads-up," Julian said.

He pushed away from the table. "Thanks for the meal."

Julian walked him to the back door. "What time are you making the announcement?"

"Five o'clock." Grimshaw studied his friend. The shadows in Julian's eyes hadn't disappeared. Not completely. "You should have told me."

Julian didn't pretend not to know what he was talking about. "I had my own reasons for not telling you."

"Are they still valid?"

"Yes, Wayne, they are."

"It's part of the job," Captain Hargreaves said.

Standing in the police station, watching with his captain as a crowd gathered on the street, Grimshaw grunted. "I'm highway patrol. This isn't part of my job description."

"Now it is. Suck it up and do the job."

Hargreaves sounded testy. Grimshaw could understand that. If he'd been the one dealing with Yorick Dane and his pals today, he'd be testy too.

Checking the clock on the wall, he adjusted his belt and walked outside, glad of Hargreaves's support.

"Many of you already know there have been several fatal incidents at The Jumble. None of these incidents were human against human. The police are still investigating in order to understand what provoked the attacks."

"Ask the Dane family," a man in overalls shouted.

Grimshaw ignored him. "The latest incident involved two men who took a motorboat out on the lake, despite being told about the no-motor rule." Lots of headshaking and muttering in the crowd. "The response to the motorboat was of sufficient force that I decided to close the public beach for a day or two. While I don't believe anyone in Sproing is in danger of an unprovoked attack, I do believe allowing everyone to calm down is essential for public welfare. I'm in charge of this police station. Until that changes, I'm not taking chances with your lives."

Murmurs of approval.

"When are you chucking Dane and his hoity-toity friends out of The Jumble so Miss Vicki can go back home and get all this straightened out?" Helen from Come and Get It asked.

He heard a couple of sharp female voices protesting Helen's term for influential businessmen from Hubb NE, but mostly he heard rumblings of agreement. They wanted Yorick Dane out of The Jumble, out of Sproing, and far away from Lake Silence.

"That's not my jurisdiction." Before someone said the wrong thing and turned a crowd into a mob, Grimshaw held up a hand. "However, Ms. DeVine has an excellent attorney who is scrutinizing every document Mr. Dane presented."

"Sanguinati."

"Yeah, *he'll* sort things out."

He didn't recognize the voices, but he found the sentiment unsettling. When it came to choosing between businessmen like Yorick Dane and the Sanguinati, the majority of people in Sproing seemed to be voting for the vampires. Was that a change in allegiance, or had enough of the people here always been aware of who controlled their village from the shadows, and had they just pretended to be clueless?

"The beach will remain closed tomorrow," he said. "Barring any unforeseen circumstances, you should be able to resume water activities the day after."

Of course, Ames Funeral Home was currently filled to capacity with unforeseen circumstances.

The crowd dispersed. Grimshaw breathed a sigh of relief. But when the people scattered to return to their jobs or head home, he saw another crowd had formed in front of the bookstore.

Sproingers filled the sidewalk in front of Lettuce Reed, climbing on each other to see into the windows or cling to the screen door. Had Julian put out a treat this morning? Or were they focused on the store for some other reason?

"What's going on over there?" Hargreaves asked.

"Don't know." Before he could decide if it would be prudent to investigate, Gershwin Jones approached him. The big man studied the Sproingers, then looked at him.

"I have a feeling they're going to come for you soon, and when they do, you need to pay attention." Jones nodded to Hargreaves and walked away.

"What did he mean about them coming for you?" Hargreaves asked.

"I don't know. But Gershwin Jones is an Intuit, so if he has a feeling about this, I'm going to pay attention."

CHAPTER 69

Aggie

Firesday, Sumor 7

"Those police humans," Jozi said as she and Aggie followed the footpath to the main house, leaving Eddie to watch the cabin. "Why do they keep chasing after us? We haven't found any scraps, and it's not like *they* want the food."

Aggie slipped an arm around Jozi's waist. "The police are looking for clues."

They wouldn't find any—if the Elders left any scraps for the Crowgard and other small forms of *terra indigene*, they wouldn't leave them on the shoreline within The Jumble. But the police kept watching the Crows, and every time a Crow landed to inspect something near the water, one of the police ran over to see what the Crow had found. Very annoying. How could anyone look for a snack when another predator was waiting to snatch it?

Of course, she and Jozi and Eddie hadn't gone hunting for snacks because the police were paying special attention to them, with different men coming over to the cabin to ask if they had seen anything when the Hershel human ended up in the water. Didn't humans talk to each other? Was that why they all asked the same questions? Or were they trying to . . .

confirm . . . the information? Clearly humans weren't as good as Crows when it came to remembering things. And the police here worked sooooooo slowly compared to TV cops, but Miss Vicki had said stories on TV had to condense all the time it would take in the real world, glossing over the waiting and thinking time in order to keep the story interesting for the viewers. Having spent the day watching the police scour the beach for clues, Aggie approved of glossing over.

"What's she still doing here?" The raised voice sounded rough. Must be the bruised-throat female. "Things are bad enough now, but as long as she stays around, being here will only get worse. You have to do something! Force her out!"

Aggie retreated, tugging Jozi to come with her.

"That's so sad," Jozi said as they walked back to the cabin. "The Heidi human lost her mate, and now they want to force her to leave. Do you think the other females are afraid she'll try to steal one of their mates?"

"I don't think she wants one of the other males," Aggie said. But the Heidi human wasn't being included in the Dane flock anymore, had stayed alone in her cabin yesterday, not even venturing out to find food. And none of the humans who were supposed to be her friends had brought any to her.

As Jozi said, it was sad that the human females were so determined to drive the Heidi human away when they had been her friends the day before. But as the Crows spent the rest of the day watching the humans wander around on the beach, Aggie had the uneasy feeling that she had missed an important clue.

CHAPTER 70

Vicki

Watersday, Sumor 8

"Are you having trouble figuring out where to shelve these?" Julian asked, eyeing the books on the top shelf of the cart.

"No, no trouble."

"Then . . ." He reached for one of the books.

"If you didn't want me to look at the books, you shouldn't have asked me to dust the shelves." Helping Julian in the store for the past couple of days showed me why I could never work in the bookstore on a regular basis. I'd buy all the stock. "That's the first pass. I'll shelve the ones I'm putting back."

He considered the books. "Do you have a prejudice against authors whose names begin with . . ."

I raised my arm and stretched as far as I could without falling off the top step of the three-step stool, demonstrating that some books were not within the reach of a short person, which was why I hadn't selected titles written by authors whose names began with the first few letters of the alphabet.

Did Julian offer to find a taller stool or even a ladder? No, he did not. He just grinned.

"I'm going to the bank," he said. "It's a little early for

lunch, but I could pick up a pizza while I'm out and about. Does that have any appeal?"

"That sounds good. Thanks. Oh. Could you stop at the general store and pick up more carrots? I cut up the last ones for the Sproingers' treat this morning." I glanced at the books on the cart. "I'll put some of them back. Promise."

"No need. If I paid you for helping me these past couple of days, I think we'd end up even."

I wasn't sure about being even, but I didn't argue because I really didn't want to put any of them back. They were an escape from a shaky future. Maybe I should throw away all caution and look into going out west where you could apply to live in a town that was being repopulated. You had to be willing to work with the *terra indigene*, but I could do that. And leaving the Northeast should put enough distance between me and Yorick.

Of course, I had no idea how a human applied to live in one of those towns, but Ilya Sanguinati might know. I'd slipped my medical information under his office door, including the name of the physician in Hubbney. No reason I couldn't stuff the query about those towns under the door as well.

"I'll be back as soon as I can." Julian hesitated and rubbed the back of his neck. "Something doesn't feel right today."

"In the village?"

"On Main Street. I'm not sensing anything stronger than that. Don't always sense more than that until the trouble is almost at the door, so to speak." He looked at me, his gray eyes dark with worry. "I'll lock the back door when I leave. You have your mobile phone?"

"In my purse, which is in the break room."

"Get it. Keep it closer."

Now I was worried. "Should I warn Ineke to stay away from the shops today?"

Another hesitation. Then he offered a grim smile. "Better safe than sorry, right?"

Not really what I wanted to hear. "Right."

I followed Julian to the back of the store and listened as

he locked the back door. Then I dashed into the break room, fetched my mobile phone, and called Ineke. She couldn't insist that her guests stay away from the shops on Main Street, but she assured me that she and Paige and Dominique would stay at the boardinghouse. After promising to call with regular updates—we made a lame joke about calling it the Julian Report—I ended the call and immediately made another one. This time I got an answering machine.

"This is Silence Lodge. Please leave your name and . . ." Yada yada ya.

I left a message for Ilya, then went back to dusting the shelves, setting my mobile phone on the book cart so that it was in easy reach.

I wasn't sure how long Julian had been gone—I'd gotten a bit distracted reading the cover copy of a few books—when I heard someone fumbling with the lock on the back door. Figuring he had his hands full and that was the reason for the fumbling, I had just stepped off the stool, intending to help him, when I caught a movement out of the corner of my eye. "That was fast."

Except it wasn't Julian.

Before I could grab the mobile phone and even try to call for help, Detective Swinn shoved me against the bookcase, one forearm pinning me while his other hand rested on his service weapon.

"You're coming with me. You're not going to make a fuss or call any attention to us. Say it. *Say it.*"

I couldn't say anything at that moment.

"If you don't say it, if you don't promise not to make a fuss, we'll wait right here, and when Julian Farrow returns I will shoot him in the face. Not through the brain. I won't kill him. I'll shoot his face off. You got that, fireplug? He'll spend the rest of his life with no eyes, no nose, no mouth. He'll be fed through a tube, and *it will be your fault.*"

Swinn would do it. He *wanted* to shoot Julian, whether I cooperated or not. The only way to keep Julian from getting hurt was to go with Swinn and hope I would find a way to escape before he . . . hurt me.

Coward. I didn't even want to think the word "kill." He wasn't taking me somewhere to *hurt* me, and we weren't going somewhere for a chat. Yorick and his pals had decided I was a problem that needed to go away, and Swinn had been sent to fetch me.

Shoot-out in Sproing. It sounded like a frontier story, but I could picture the reality just fine. Shots fired on Main Street. Grimshaw running out of the police station, not seeing Swinn, a fellow cop, as a threat until it was too late.

Was Swinn's arrival the wrongness Julian had sensed, or was it something worse, something more like what I was imagining? Except I could prevent what I was imagining.

"Say it," Swinn growled.

"I won't make a fuss." At least not while we were in the village.

Swinn grabbed my arm and pulled me out the back door and over to the cruiser parked behind the bookstore.

"You stole a Bristol police car?"

"Borrowed. Get in."

He aimed his service weapon at me and kept it trained on me while he circled to the driver's side and got in. The windows were up; no one would hear if I tried to call for help. But the handful of Sproingers who visited the bookstore were at the edge of the parking area. Seeing me, they made the happy face. I made a sad face.

They hopped toward the cruiser.

Swinn drove off quickly enough to startle the Sproingers, then with more control as he turned onto Main Street and headed out of the village.

CHAPTER 71

Grimshaw

Watersday, Sumor 8

"*Wayne, something doesn't feel right.*"

Having cleaned his service weapon and backup, Grimshaw wondered if he should clean the shotgun next or walk down Main Street to remind people of his presence. Hargreaves had called a few minutes ago to say that he and the CIU team were heading back to Bristol, along with the officers he'd called in for backup. The access road to The Jumble was still blocked by the destroyed flatbed trucks and construction equipment, but all the bodies had been removed.

Grimshaw pushed back from the desk and rolled his shoulders. He could use some fresh air. Besides, Osgood was already out patrolling and, most likely, had answered the beach question a hundred times, so it was a good bet that no one would be asking *him* if the beach would reopen tomorrow.

And Julian Farrow had called to leave a warning while he'd been on the phone with Hargreaves. "Doesn't feel right" was a warning but not a cause for alarm. Not yet. Hopefully he could keep it that way.

He reached the door when the phone on his desk rang.

"Sproing Police Station, Grimshaw speaking."

"Officer Grimshaw? This is Agent Greg O'Sullivan with the Investigative Task Force."

Grimshaw's heart bumped hard. "You have something for me?"

"Probably not as much as you hoped for. I couldn't find anything of a criminal nature connected to the names on which you initially requested background information. That said, the men are known around the Hubb NE area as well-heeled entrepreneurs who have connections in a lot of businesses. Some of the deals they've put together look a little shady but nothing crossed the line into illegal, at least on paper, if you follow me."

"I do." Grimshaw swallowed his disappointment. He'd hoped the ITF agent would find some ammunition that proved Yorick Dane and his friends had used a forged document once before to take back property after enough money had been sunk into making capital improvements. "Thanks for your help."

"I'm not done. Like I said, I didn't find anything criminal connected to the names you initially asked the ITF to check, but the last two? Mark Hammorson runs a security business and has skated charges a couple of times for protecting a client's assets with a little too much enthusiasm. And while no evidence was found, Tony Amorella's name has been linked with a couple of suspicious deaths."

"Gun? Knife?"

"Garrote."

Grimshaw shivered. He pictured the Murder board as it had been the evening they'd spent at The Jumble, pictured Aggie setting a businessman on the square in front of teeny Vicki—the square with a garrote beside it.

Hearing an odd sound, he glanced toward the windows and froze. Sproingers scratching at the glass. Tumbling off their companions and climbing up again in an effort to look in the windows. *Scratch scratch scratch.*

"Grimshaw?"

"I have to go." He hung up on O'Sullivan and opened the

station's door. A dozen of the critters crowded the doorway, with more Sproingers heading toward him.

He scanned the street and spotted Osgood jogging toward him. He saw Julian walk out of the general store, stop at the sight of the Sproingers, and then look toward Lettuce Reed.

Closed store. A woman inside, alone. A predator with a garrote. Oh gods.

He ran across the street and down the narrow driveway that provided access to the parking area behind the store. Seeing the open back door, he drew his service weapon and approached cautiously. "Vicki? Vicki, are you there?"

Julian rounded the corner, skidding to a stop when he saw Grimshaw.

"I didn't leave that door unlocked. I didn't use the dead bolt, but I engaged the simple lock on the door."

"Could Vicki have let someone in?"

"Who?"

"Ineke Xavier?"

Julian hesitated, a silent acknowledgment of the possibility. He opened the screen door, allowing Grimshaw to slip in first.

"Vicki?" Grimshaw called.

"There's no one here," Julian said, pushing past him and rushing into the break room. "But Vicki's purse is still here."

Grimshaw moved forward. Bookshelves rising almost to the ceiling. Hiding places everywhere. "Julian, look at this."

Books on the floor, as if someone had dropped them—or they had been pushed off the shelves. A mobile phone on the book cart.

"She wouldn't leave without her purse," Julian said. "And she wouldn't leave without telling me, not after I'd told her that something didn't feel right."

Hearing the screen door open, Grimshaw stepped into the aisle that ran from the back of the store to the front. But it wasn't Vicki DeVine returning; it was Osgood.

"The Sproingers are fair upset about something," Osgood said. "They keep scratching at me."

"Vicki DeVine is missing," Julian said.

"Maybe there was an emergency? Did you ask Captain Hargreaves?"

Grimshaw frowned. "Why would I?"

"Just before the Sproingers started to mob the station, I saw a Bristol police car leave this parking area and head west out of town."

A car going to Bristol from that direction would turn onto the road heading south—the same direction someone would take to go to The Jumble.

"Osgood, go back to the station. Call Captain Hargreaves and make sure he didn't send a car for Vicki. I'm heading to The Jumble."

Osgood slipped out the door, tripping over Sproingers until he managed to get clear of them.

"I'm going with you," Julian said.

"I'm not asking you—"

"I knew something didn't feel right, but I left her alone here, thinking it would be a safe place. I left her alone because I was going to be gone a short while. Window of opportunity. Someone saw it and took it. So I'm going with you."

"Then let's go."

CHAPTER 72

Ilya

Watersday, Sumor 8

"*Ilya? It's Vicki. Julian says something doesn't feel right on Main Street. I thought you should know.*"

He looked at the rest of the Sanguinati who had come in to report a different kind of feeling. Something dangerous. Something lethal.

"Problem?" Natasha asked.

"Yes. Boris, please bring the car. We need to get to Sproing." Easier to travel in his smoke form, but the car would be necessary if he needed to quickly extract Victoria from the village.

The phone rang before he took a step away from the desk. "Yes?"

"It's Julian Farrow. Someone driving a Bristol police car abducted Vicki. The car was last seen heading west, so it could be heading toward one of the four-lane roads that provide access to bigger cities."

"But you think it's heading for The Jumble." Ilya wasn't asking a question.

"Yeah. We're on our way there."

Ilya hung up and hurried out to the lodge's multilevel deck, going down to the lowest level.

"Do you still need the car?" Boris asked.

On the other side of the lake, he saw the Crowgard flying up in alarm. "No. It's too late for that."

Where would they take Victoria? Farrow and Grimshaw—because he understood that was what Farrow had meant by "we"—would aim for the main house. But killing could be done anywhere.

Just before he changed to smoke to race across the lake and help with the hunt, Natasha grabbed his arm and said, "Look."

Shapes in the water.

<Stay where you are, bloodhunter. We will tell you if you are needed.>

He wanted to argue. After all, turning The Jumble back into a viable *terra indigene* settlement was the Sanguinati's responsibility—*his* responsibility—and that included keeping watch over the vulnerable human who was caretaker and Reader. But he knew better than to disobey a command when it came from one of *them*.

"Ilya?" Boris asked.

"We wait." The words tasted bitter.

"But our enemies are over there," Natasha protested.

He nodded. "So are the Elders."

CHAPTER 73

Vicki

Watersday, Sumor 8

I pictured opening the car door and flinging myself out of the vehicle while Detective Swinn had to concentrate on something in the road. I pictured him punching me in the face if I reached for the door handle. I was in the front seat with him—couldn't have me looking like a prisoner—but I didn't know if a passenger could unlock the door. So opening and flinging weren't good options.

I pictured myself grabbing the wheel like a plucky young woman in a TV show and sending the car out of control and off the road, rolling a couple of times. Of course, the villain would be trapped and Ms. Plucky would crawl out of the wreck with a couple of dramatic cuts but would still be able to show everyone why she had been a high school track star as she ran to warn the good guys that they were walking into a trap.

Since I wasn't plucky and, at thirty, I wasn't considered young, and my experience with track-and-field events did not make me any kind of star, I was more likely to end up looking like bug goo on the windshield while Swinn walked away from the wreck.

Cross off grabbing the steering wheel from my save-the-day list.

Then Swinn turned onto the farm track that ran between the Milfords' orchards and The Jumble.

"Where are we going?" I asked, feeling numb.

"Back to the beginning. You should have just rolled over like you were supposed to, fireplug. All this trouble happened because of you."

Actually, all of it happened because Yorick tried to renege on the divorce settlement, but I was pretty sure Swinn didn't want to hear that.

"What the . . . ?" Swinn said.

A chubby brown pony with a storm-gray mane and tail stood in the middle of the farm track, blocking our way. When he stomped one foot, dirt swirled around his legs.

"Oh no," I breathed, recognizing Twister.

Instead of stopping because, hey, there was a pony in the way, Swinn floored the gas pedal. Instead of running away from a speeding car, the pony charged—and disappeared in the center of a mini tornado.

Have you ever been on one of those stomach-churning spinny rides at a country fair? Well, spinning in a car is so much worse.

I screamed. Swinn screamed. And no matter what he might say later, it was *not* a manly yell.

The car stopped spinning—and flames erupted from under the hood.

Aiden?

I clawed at the door and tumbled out of the car, feeling Swinn's fingers slide over my butt as he tried to grab me. Since he had a gun and I didn't have so much as a nail file, I ran, figuring that having things like trees in the way would make it harder for him to shoot me.

"Come back here!" Swinn shouted.

Like that was going to happen.

Was this the trail I'd taken when I'd led Grimshaw to the first body? Didn't know and couldn't afford to care. I'd either end up at one set of cabins, or at the main house, or at the road. Hopefully I wouldn't end up back on the farm track and run into Swinn.

I didn't run into Swinn. But as I caught a glimpse through the trees of what I thought was the main house, I did run straight into a man wearing a business suit—and thin black gloves. I'd come around a blind curve in the trail and bounced off him, stumbling back a couple of steps. I didn't recognize *him*, but I saw the tie clip—one of those weird moments when time slows down and you fixate on one detail. So even though I didn't know him, I knew he wasn't a friend. Not to me.

I dodged him when he lunged at me. Don't ask me how. Adrenaline is an amazing thing. I was already puffing, so he wouldn't have to work hard to catch me. And I was sure that him catching me would be bad for my health.

Not having any sensible ideas of how to evade the man, I waved a hand over my head as if I was holding a ticket and wheezed, "I have the 'Elder Helps You' card!" Which shows you that, while adrenaline is an amazing thing, it can produce wonky thoughts in the brain, showing me a flashback of the Murder game we had all played that one evening.

Except . . .

I saw nothing, but I swear I felt fur brush the bare skin on my arm as something big rushed past me. As it passed, it gave me a negligible swat/shove/toss/take your pick that had me airborne. Reminded me of when I used to do the running long jump when we had the track-and-field segment in gym class. Not that my long jump was long. But this? I was *flying*. I had plenty of time to remember there was a safe way to fall and roll when I landed. I didn't remember *how*, just that there was a safe way and then there was the tumble the rest of us took.

At the moment my feet touched the ground, I heard a hideous scream—a terrified, mind-breaking sound. With my concentration shattered, I landed in a heap. Couldn't think about what had just happened. Couldn't, couldn't, couldn't.

As I pushed to my feet, I felt a sting in both knees, a sharp pain in my left wrist, and a queer feeling of sticky air along my right side. Couldn't think about that either.

I needed to be out in the open. The main house was probably stuffed with Yorick's friends, so I couldn't shelter there. But the beach? If I got to the beach and yelled for help, the Crowgard would hear me. Maybe even Conan and Cougar if they were hunting nearby. Someone would see me, would know what happened to me.

I ran and made rash promises to exercise more if I lived. Of course, if I died, exercising would be a moot point.

As I ran past the main house, following the path to the lakeside cabins and the beach beyond them, several things happened. A voice that sounded like Julian's yelled "Vicki!"; tittering female screams, not the I'm-being-eaten kind of screams, came from the screened porch; and Swinn, waving a gun, fought his way between a couple of bushes and came at me.

I was in sight of the lakeside cabins, sure that Swinn was going to shoot me at any moment, when fog suddenly started playing hide-and-seek with the ground, with objects, with people.

"Caw!"

"Caw!" "Caw!" "Caw!"

Aggie and her friends? I hoped so.

The fog thinned, revealing the sand.

"Bitch!" Swinn's voice, too close.

Sand would slow me down. So would the water unless I could get far enough out to be safe from bullets.

I changed course and ran for the dock. Was that sensible? Who knows? It's what I did. Behind me, I heard Swinn yell; I heard a big splash. A gun went off. And someone started screaming.

I was almost at the dock when Yorick ran toward me, waving something shiny and yelling, "Come back here, Vicki! It's all your fault! Come back here and fix this!"

I didn't know what he was holding. I just knew I couldn't let him get his hands on me.

Men with guns and other weapons behind me. Ahead of me? Something else.

The fog might have messed with my sense of distance, but it wasn't the reason I ran to the end of the dock and kept running until I hit the water.

CHAPTER 74

Grimshaw

Watersday, Sumor 8

Spotting the smoke, Grimshaw slowed the cruiser. "I need to call this in."

"I'll call it in," Julian said, plucking Grimshaw's mobile phone out of the console. "We need to reach The Jumble."

He glanced at Julian's pale face and stepped on the gas. They weren't more than a couple of minutes away, but a couple of minutes could make a difference in saving a victim or standing over a corpse.

"I don't know what's burning, but it's on the farm track between Milfords' orchards and The Jumble," Julian said to whoever was on the other end of the phone. "If the wind picks up, the whole area could be in trouble." He ended the call. "Volunteer fire department is on its way."

The mobile phone rang. Julian answered. "Officer Grimshaw's phone. Wait. I'll put you on speaker."

"Sir?" Osgood.

"We've already called the fire department to handle whatever is burning on the farm track, in case that's what you wanted to tell me."

A beat of silence. "No, sir. I called to tell you Captain Hargreaves is boiling mad. Seems two of the officers who came with him as backup let a fellow officer borrow their patrol car. The captain was mad enough about *that* since they didn't tell *him* about it, but when he threatened them with disciplinary action, they admitted they loaned the car to Detective Swinn. That's when he *really* got mad. He's on his way back with, and I quote, reliable officers."

"Tell Captain Hargreaves it's likely that those officers owe the Bristol station a car," Julian said.

"Why?" Osgood asked.

Grimshaw pulled to the shoulder near the game trail that they'd been using to reach the main house at The Jumble. "Because that's probably what's burning on the farm track."

"Do I have to tell him?"

"I'm heading up to the main house with Julian Farrow. You can tell him that."

Another beat of silence. "You should have backup. I'm on my way."

Grimshaw hesitated, then thought, *Either he has the stones for this work or he doesn't.* "The trail to reach the main house has been marked. If you don't see us, get up to the main house and hold anyone who's inside. You got that?"

"Yes, sir."

Julian ended the call and handed the mobile phone to Grimshaw, who tucked it in its spot on his belt as soon as he got out of the car.

"Damn," Julian said softly as they started up the trail.

Fog swirled around them as they hurried toward the main house. Not a thick enveloping fog, but almost . . . flirtatious, veiling and revealing. Just enough that Grimshaw couldn't see the ground, couldn't see something that might trip him up enough that he'd sprain an ankle or wrench a knee— injuries not normally life-threatening, but either would leave him useless and vulnerable.

Once they reached the access road, they ran toward the main house but stopped, frozen, when they heard a hideous scream.

Grimshaw took a step toward the sound. Julian grabbed his arm.

"No," Julian said. "We can't go there."

The look in Julian's eyes. He'd seen it at the academy—and he'd seen it on the streets before they'd been assigned to different stations. "Are you seeing the real place or The Jumble as it was represented in the Murder game?"

"They're the same now." Julian shuddered, then headed for the main house. "They're the same."

Not good.

"Vicki!" Julian shouted once they reached the main house.

Female screams coming from the back of the house.

"Wait," Grimshaw said as he pulled out his phone and called Osgood's mobile phone.

"Almost there, sir," Osgood said loudly. "I can see your car."

"Don't try to find me. Just get up to the main house and stay inside," Grimshaw said. He ended the call and almost dropped the phone when Julian bolted, no longer able to wait. "Julian . . . Julian!"

But Julian was running toward the far side of the house, following only Mikhos knew what. So Grimshaw went around the other side. He wasn't sure Swinn had brought Vicki DeVine to The Jumble. The man could have taken her farther down the farm track. Except . . . The damn fog. It was here and nowhere else.

He ran around the other side of the house. If Vicki was inside, he'd have to trust Osgood to deal with the situation as soon as the baby cop arrived. But he didn't need to be an Intuit to have a bad feeling that Vicki DeVine was out here. Somewhere.

The fog around him cleared abruptly. That was the only reason he didn't step on the body. Step *in* the body. Darren. Gutted. But not dead. Not yet.

He hesitated. Nothing he could do for the man, but it felt wrong to leave him alone in the fog where the predators waited. Then he heard a gunshot—and heard a man scream. That decided him. He ran to the back of the main house, heading for the dock.

Splashing, thrashing, screaming. He had a glimpse of Julian pulling something out of the water. Then the fog became a wall, cutting him off from everything except Vicki DeVine, running for the dock, and Yorick Dane holding something in his right hand and yelling, "Come back here, Vicki! It's all your fault! Come back here and fix this!"

Yorick reached the land end of the dock just as Vicki ran right off the other end and hit the water.

"Dane!" Grimshaw shouted. "Put the weapon down, *now.*"

Dane started to turn.

"Drop the weapon or I'll shoot."

Dane looked over his shoulder, his expression full of smirky disbelief. "You going to shoot me in the back? Won't look good on your record, *Chief.*"

"If I shoot you here, no one will ever find the body, so I can write up the report any way I please."

That wiped the smirk off Dane's face. "It's not a weapon. It's just a wrench."

"I don't give a damn what it is. Drop it and put your hands behind your head."

"Mooooonkeeey maaaaan."

Dane dropped the wrench and put his hands behind his head.

Yeah, Grimshaw thought. Given the current choices, being arrested was Dane's only chance of getting out of there alive.

"Vicki!" Julian, calling. "Vicki!"

Unfortunately, no one answered his call.

Grimshaw handcuffed Dane, then leaned in to speak quietly in the man's ear. "Just so you know. I don't care if you hire one of your tie clip pals to get you out of whatever charges come from all of this. I don't care what anyone else says about your guilt or innocence. If Vicki DeVine's body washes ashore, you and I are going to take a long ride deep into the wild country."

CHAPTER 75

Aggie

Watersday, Sumor 8

Air rode Fog around The Jumble, making it harder for the humans to find anything. That was good. The humans . . . Well, she wasn't sure what the humans had been doing before Air and Fog galloped into The Jumble, but it all felt sneaky.

<The Elders are hunting!> Eddie said.

Leaving the cabin's door open, Aggie went inside, removed her clothes, and shifted to her Crow form. Looking human would not be a good thing today.

Going back outside, she flew up to the porch roof—a good place to observe whatever she could see but close enough to the cabin door if she needed a place to hide.

Then Miss Vicki ran along the path, heading for the beach.

"Caw!" Aggie shouted. *"Caw!" Hide here! Hide here!*

But Miss Vicki kept running toward the beach, and moments later, that mean police human Swinn appeared and ran after her.

<Gun!> Aggie cawed. <He's going to shoot Miss Vicki!>

Miss Vicki swerved at the edge of the sand and kept running toward the dock, disappearing into a wall of fog.

Swinn stopped at the edge of the sand, turned toward Miss Vicki, and raised the gun. Before Aggie could call another warning, a big wave suddenly rose and flooded the whole beach, creating new shallows at the same moment Cougar raced out of his hiding place and pounced on Swinn.

The gun went *bang!* Swinn and Cougar landed in the water. Cougar leaped back to dry land—and Swinn began screaming as the Elders who lived in the lake, having ridden on the Lady's wave to reach their prey, grabbed the human and began to tear and slash while they thrashed in the receding water, feeding until the Lady made the next big wave to help them return to the lake.

The next wave arrived at the same time that Julian Farrow reached the sand. He ran into the water and grabbed Swinn, playing tug with the Elders who continued to bite and feed as they retreated to the natural shallows. Then Julian let go of what remained of Swinn and fell back, clear of the waterline. But he didn't leave, didn't move farther out of reach of the Elders. Instead, he stared at something stuck in the wet sand.

Had Julian found a shiny? She couldn't see what he had found, so she flew down to the beach. Coins sometimes fell out of torn pockets. Julian might share if there were several coins on the sand.

But it wasn't coins that held the human's interest. It was the gun. Did he need the gun? Why?

Another wave washed over the beach, higher than the usual waterline. Aggie saw the shape hidden in the water. Before Julian could lunge for the gun—and get in teeth-and-claw kind of trouble—Aggie flutter-hopped to the gun and closed one foot over the trigger guard.

"No!" Julian said, grabbing for the gun.

Water washed around her and Julian like they were rocks—and the Elder who had ridden in on that wave rose partway out of the water and took a swipe at Julian. He would have torn up Julian's arm, but Cougar smacked the human, knocking Julian out of the way.

<He's Miss Vicki's friend!> Aggie said, trying to tug the gun out of the sand and away from the water.

The Elder stared at her with those strange eyes before thrashing his tail and returning to the lake with the receding wave.

Cougar came up beside her and pawed at the gun.

"Wait." Julian's shaking hand closed over the gun.

Aggie pecked him. He was too close to the water. It wasn't safe to be human until the Elders stopped being angry.

"Have to put the safety on," Julian panted, his hand moving over the gun. "Can't have it go off by accident and hit someone."

Yes. That was smart. Since she didn't know how to do the safety thing, she stopped pecking him.

"Okay," he panted. "Okay." He let go of the gun and crawled up the beach until he touched the grassy edge. Then he looked at the lake. "Vicki! Vicki!"

No answer.

<Miss Vicki is in the water,> Eddie reported.

Nothing the Crowgard could do for her there.

Aggie shifted to human form, picked up the gun, and ran to where Julian lay on the wet sand. She set the gun beside him, remembering from stories to point it away from him, then shifted back to Crow and studied the human. Water leaked from his closed eyes. He was not paying attention. That wasn't smart with so many of the *terra indigene* feeling angry toward humans.

Did she care? Did it matter?

He was Miss Vicki's friend. And so was she.

Perched on Julian Farrow's raised knee, Aggie cleaned her feathers while she kept watch.

CHAPTER 76

Vicki

Watersday, Sumor 8

It didn't matter if I wanted to go back to The Jumble's beach or go on to Silence Lodge. I had reached the point of no return. I was done, exhausted—and hurt. My side felt strange, but I was too scared to touch it and find out why.

A wave caught me in the face, and I thought my side would rip as I coughed up the water I'd swallowed.

Then I saw the shapes coming toward me, saw a delicate dorsal fin, the flick of a tail. They surfaced all around me. If I hadn't been so brutally tired, I would have been terrified.

Imagine a creature whose ancestors had been a giant piranha that had mated with a lake-dwelling species of human. They had a humanlike torso that ended in that kind of tail shown in sketches of mermaids. The backs of their bodies were a blue-black that changed to a silvery-gray front. Big fish eyes. And triangular, interlocking teeth that could tear flesh from bone, easily stripping a carcass in minutes.

Elders. The long-standing, or long-swimming, residents of Lake Silence.

They raised their heads above the water, bobbing to keep the gills in their necks wet.

"I can't swim anymore," I said. I didn't know if I was asking for help or telling them that this prey didn't have the strength to fight them.

Two of them bobbed under the water on either side of me. When they surfaced, my arms were around their narrow shoulders, holding me up. I wasn't much help, but they maneuvered until we faced the shoreline near Silence Lodge.

An undulation of water lifted all of us, as if we were all riding on the back of something that had risen from deep in the lake to become a long, gentle swell. An arched back that rose and went back down. But the motion had brought all of us noticeably closer to the shore.

The third time that undulation occurred, I imagined I saw a giant head and shoulders right in front of me—a body that was never separate from the lake but still distinct.

We were in sight of the shore faster than I would have thought possible. Silence Lodge didn't have my nice beach. Dark pebbles, maybe shale. Shale had sharp edges. Landing on it would hurt. Not that I had a choice. I wasn't sure my companions understood human speech, and they weren't likely to spend their time pondering the preferences of shoreline material.

My vision blurred. The Elders who had been holding me up dropped away. And I rode that last undulation to the shore alone.

CHAPTER 77

Ilya

Watersday, Sumor 8

<Come to the shore, bloodhunter. We are bringing the Reader to you. She is wounded.>

"To the shore," Ilya told the rest of the Sanguinati. "Hurry."

He shifted to smoke and rushed to the shore, followed by Natasha and Boris. The other Sanguinati spread out to cover the rest of the shore in front of the lodge. As soon as he reached the water's edge, Ilya shifted back to human form and saw the swell—and the beings riding it.

Twice more a swell formed under the beings, carrying them closer to shore. Then the Elders swam away, leaving Victoria to ride the final swell alone. As the Lady of the Lake lifted Victoria DeVine above the stony shore, Ilya raised his arms to catch The Jumble's caretaker.

CHAPTER 78

Grimshaw

Watersday, Sumor 8

As Grimshaw marched Yorick Dane to the big screened porch at the back of the main house, he looked for Julian. Instead of spotting his friend, he saw Crows gathering near something on the beach. The land sloped, denying him a visual of the beach itself, but he could guess what would attract so many of the Crowgard.

Gods above and below.

Cougar appeared over the rise, moving away from the beach. The Panther saw him and stopped. As Grimshaw watched, Cougar looked back toward the beach. Then a front paw changed into a furry human hand that gave him a thumbs-up before the hand became a paw again and Cougar continued moving toward the cabins.

Somehow that human gesture to indicate something, or someone, was all right disturbed him more than the bodies he'd glimpsed in the past few minutes. But if he understood the message, Julian had survived.

"Osgood!" Grimshaw called as he and Dane approached the porch.

"Sir!" Osgood scanned the area, then unlocked the screen door and held it open while Grimshaw muscled Dane inside.

"According to Mrs. Dane, one of the women should be at the lakeside cabins."

"I'll check it out." He pushed Dane into one of the chairs. "Stay there."

"Where's Darren?"

"Where is Vaughn?"

Grimshaw eyed the women. There was fear under the bitchy attitude. "Darren is dead. I think Swinn is dead. I didn't see Vaughn." He hadn't gone looking.

"Why is Yorick in handcuffs?" Constance Dane said. "You can't arrest him."

"Yes, I can." He used the tone of voice that was so polite, so professional, no one had ever mistaken it for anything but a threat.

"Police!" Hargreaves, from the front of the house. Backup had arrived.

"Back here!" Grimshaw bellowed.

Hargreaves appeared in the kitchen doorway. He looked at the women, then at Yorick Dane. "Who is under arrest?"

"All of them," Grimshaw replied.

"What's the charge?" Constance Dane demanded, jumping to her feet.

"Fine." Grimshaw uncuffed Yorick Dane. "Either you're all under arrest or I chuck you all out the door, and you can take your chances."

Something near the porch laughed, a sound so full of terrible glee that it made Grimshaw's body clench, made Hargreaves's face tighten. Made beads of sweat pop up on the foreheads of the officers standing behind the captain.

"We'll take them to the police station in Sproing and sort out the charges there," Hargreaves said. "What are we starting with?"

"Abduction," Grimshaw replied as his mobile phone rang. "Possibly murder." He turned away from the people on the porch and covered one ear with a hand in order to hear the person on the phone. "Grimshaw."

"Bring a doctor and medical equipment to Silence Lodge," Ilya Sanguinati said.

Leaving the porch, he took several steps away from the house, ignoring Hargreaves's low protest. "You found Vicki? Do we need to take her to the hospital in Bristol?"

A slight hesitation. "I don't think she has time to reach Bristol."

Oh gods. "We'll be there." Grimshaw ended the call and shouted, "Julian! *Julian!* We need to get to Silence Lodge!"

He held his breath and almost gave up, almost turned back to the porch to tell Hargreaves where he was going. Then he saw Julian running up from the direction of the beach, Crowgard flying all around him.

"Grimshaw?" Hargreaves said as he left the porch's illusion of safety and joined him on the lawn.

He placed the call to the medical office while he waited for Julian to join them. Seeing the Crows land all around them, he resigned himself to a less-than-private report.

"Medical office," a female voice said.

"This is Officer Grimshaw. Tell Dr. Wallace that the Sanguinati found Vicki DeVine. It sounds like she's in bad shape, but she's still alive."

"I'll contact the EMTs. Their vehicle is equipped for emergencies."

"Do that." He ended the call.

"Hospital?" Julian asked.

Grimshaw shook his head. "Ilya says there isn't time." He looked at Hargreaves. "Can you take the lead on processing the scenes and handling the arrests?"

Hargreaves gave him an odd look, which didn't surprise him. The captain was still his boss, was still the one in charge, and yet he was treating the man like they were of equal rank.

"I can do that for you," Hargreaves said. "Would appreciate a call when you know Ms. DeVine's status."

Grimshaw nodded. Then he looked at the Crows. "Captain Hargreaves and his men have to collect the bodies and process the scenes, like the cops do in the TV shows. They're going to be walking around The Jumble, collecting evidence.

Can you let everyone else know that it's all right for them to be here?"

The Crows looked at one another. Then one looked up at him and said, *"Caw."*

Taking that as agreement, he and Julian ran down the trails to reach the cruiser and head for the lodge on the other side of the lake.

CHAPTER 79

Aggie

Being considered part of the team made watching all the poking and pecking done by the human police more interesting, but it was still frustrating.

<But why do they need *all* the shinies?> Jozi asked for the fifth time.

<The bad humans hurt Miss Vicki, so everything they had is evidence,> Aggie replied.

<But they're *dead*. Human police can't arrest them if they're dead. Can they?>

Aggie had never seen a TV cop arrest a dead man. Or parts of a dead man. Maybe Julian Farrow would know?

<They're going to let the eyeballs go to waste,> Eddie complained.

That was true, and it was sad. But the cops were just human and would never appreciate the edible qualities of fresh eyeballs, so there wasn't much the Crowgard could do.

The Crowgard living in The Jumble had gathered and then divided, several of them taking watch over each group of humans who were gathering evidence. Most of the Crows hadn't seen any of the cop and crime shows, hadn't talked about the stories with Miss Vicki, so they had many questions about what the human police were doing.

Was it usual for them to regurgitate food when they were collecting meat?

Aggie was pretty sure experienced cops didn't do that—not often anyway. She was also pretty sure most of the experienced cops who had come to help Officer Grimshaw had never seen what an angry Elder could do to a human body. But these cops seemed smart, even if they were human.

The one she was watching collect evidence held up a long piece of shiny string and said, "It's a garrote."

Garrote. She knew that word from the Murder game. Humans used it for killing other humans—and maybe smaller *terra indigene.*

Her cop looked up at the branch where she had perched to watch him. "Is this the reason he died like this? He was attacking the woman who was your friend?"

Was? That word made her sad, but she answered him anyway. *"Caw."*

A glint of something caught her eye, but the cop was moving away.

Aggie flew from the branch to the ground. Bit of black cloth. Small finger. And a gold ring clinging to the skin!

She looked at the cop still searching for evidence but moving away. She could pull off the ring, hide it under some leaves. She could . . .

Part of the team. You didn't hide things from the team.

"Caw." When he didn't answer, she tried again. *"Caw!"*

"Did you find something?" He returned and crouched near where she stood guard over the finger. "I guess you did."

When he reached for the finger, she pecked him. Couldn't help it. It was *her* shiny.

"Hey!"

Sorry. She moved out of pecking range to avoid pecking him again. After all, she was the one who had called him over to take the meat and treasure.

Once he collected the evidence, she flew back up to the branch in the nearest tree to have a better view of what the humans were doing. That's why she spotted the man walking toward them—a man with red hair tipped with blue and yellow.

"Sir," her cop said, "you can't be here. This is a crime scene."

Don't make him angry, Aggie thought. *Not him. Not in the woods.*

Recognizing that what approached him wasn't human, the cop took a step back.

Fire looked up. "I came to tell Aggie that the human doctor fixed Miss Vicki. She needs to be given medicine at specific times and needs to be watched for a day or two, so the Sanguinati are keeping her at Silence Lodge for the rest of today and tomorrow. They will tell you when you can visit."

"Caw!" Miss Vicki was alive!

Fire gave her cop a long look, as if memorizing his face. Then he walked away and disappeared.

Miss Vicki was alive. That news was even better than finding a shiny.

CHAPTER 80

Vicki

Watersday, Sumor 8

I woke from a dream where I was at The Jumble, serving raw fish sandwiches to my toothy guests and trying to explain the appeal of pickled herring.

"Easy," Ilya said. "Don't struggle." He restrained me with one hand while opening the blanket wrapped around me with the other. "We thought some fresh air would do you good but didn't want you to catch a chill. Not in your condition."

I had a condition? That didn't sound good.

"Do you want some water? Some juice? There is also chicken soup. I was told it is a good food for humans to eat when they have been ill."

"I've been ill?" I sounded like a frog, so that was possible.

"You were injured." Ilya took a seat near the lounge chair positioned in a shady spot on the lodge's top deck.

When he just sat there, looking like he did not want to be the bearer of bad news, I pushed the blanket open a little more in order to take stock. I was wearing a loose tank top and shorts. No bra. Or the bra had somehow missed my breasts and was hugging my ribs. A cast covered my left arm from knuckles to mid-forearm.

"You broke your wrist," Ilya said.

Right. I hadn't landed properly after the flying long jump.

"He didn't mean to hurt you," Ilya said.

"He certainly did!"

Ilya looked pained.

"The man in the business suit. I ran into him when I was running away from Swinn. He meant to hurt me."

"Not him. The Elder."

Oh. I remembered saying something about having an "Elder Helps You" card right before making the flying long jump.

I looked at Ilya. I think I squeaked. "That was an Elder? A real Elder?"

"Yes. He . . . Well, the male who threatened you was too close, so the Elder pushed you out of the way. A light swat, something one of their young would hardly notice. But humans are more fragile and . . ."

"Is that why my butt hurts? It's bruised from a helpful whack?"

"Yes."

I tried to change positions, then sucked in a breath when the attempt pulled at my side. "What else?"

"One of his claws sliced you along your back and ribs. It's not deep, but it is a long slice that flapped your skin. It required some stitches. A lot of stitches, actually."

You know what's worse than having one of the *terra indigene* look at you as if deciding which parts to have for lunch? Seeing one of the Sanguinati squirm like he was stuck on a nightmare blind date.

"You bled some, from the wound," he continued.

I liked him so much better when he was lethal and scary. "Some?"

"Enough that Dr. Wallace decided a transfusion was prudent."

Oh. *Oh.* Was *that* what he didn't want to tell me? "So I got some . . ." I touched my canine teeth to see if they were longer and sharper.

"Don't be ridiculous, Victoria. We're different species."

"Then . . . ?" By the time I dragged it out of him, I was going to need a nap.

"It turned out Officer Grimshaw had the correct blood type."

I blinked. Blinked again. "You gave me *Grimshaw blood*?"

Ilya sat back and studied me. "I realize I have a different view of human blood than you do, but I'm fairly certain that a transfusion of blood doesn't include a transfusion of personality."

"You never know. I could suddenly turn all stern and steely-eyed a percentage of days every month." I gave him my best narrow-eyed stare, an imitation of the mysterious heroes in some movies, who rode into frontier towns to take on the bad guys.

Ilya sprang out of his chair. "That's it. I'm calling the doctor. The medication he gave us for you is affecting your brain."

I stared at the empty chair, openmouthed, until Natasha walked out of the lodge and sat down.

"You shouldn't tease him," she said. "He's been concerned about you, and that's an unsettling feeling since your kind are . . ." She hesitated.

"Usually considered prey?" I suggested.

"Yes." She looked relieved that I understood.

The Sanguinati had their own reasons for helping me, for wanting me to run The Jumble. They might look sleek and sophisticated, they might have learned to mimic human behavior better than any other form of *terra indigene*, but they were, and always would be, predators. And humans would always be their prey, whether or not they chose to be friendly toward a few of us.

I tried to recall what happened when that last wave lifted me toward the shore and the lake Elders released me to wash up alone. I checked my arms, then looked at the skin I could see without lifting up the tank.

"Problem?" Natasha asked.

"I thought I would have some cuts from landing on the shale or the stones or whatever you have on your beach."

"The Elders told us they were bringing you to the lodge and you were wounded. We went down to the shore to help you." Natasha grinned, revealing her fangs. "When you washed ashore, you didn't land on shale; you landed on Ilya."

I had full-body contact with Mr. Yummy and wasn't conscious enough to appreciate it? How was that fair?

I did not say that out loud. At least, I hoped I didn't. Just like I hoped Natasha had another reason for laughing as she walked back into the lodge.

CHAPTER 81

Grimshaw

Watersday, Sumor 8

"Find anything?" Grimshaw asked Hargreaves.

Samuel Kipp and the Bristol CIU team, along with Captain Hargreaves and the officers he'd brought with him, had spent the day searching for Vaughn. It was possible the man had gotten away from The Jumble. Not likely, but possible. The possibility was the reason he had returned after giving blood to help Vicki DeVine survive her injuries. Serve and protect. That applied to fellow officers as well as the citizens of Sproing.

"Not sure," Hargreaves replied. "We brought in a couple of dogs, but something over there has them spooked. They won't go near the spot."

"I'll check it out."

"Wayne . . . Haven't you done enough today?"

He had done enough, and if he had any brains, he would go back to the boardinghouse and get some food and sleep. But . . . "Still my turf. I'll check it out."

He walked away before Hargreaves could object. In another hour, they would lose the light, and they were in a part of The Jumble that was a fair distance from any of the buildings. That meant Hargreaves would have to call off the search in the next few minutes and either pack up his men and head back to Bristol or make arrangements to bring in supplies for the night and have the men camp out in the main house. Staying in The Jumble tonight wasn't an assignment he'd want to give fellow officers.

The pile of branches that were stuffed with grass and leaves made him think of a land-based beaver lodge. It might be primitive, but it was a structure. A dwelling.

"Hello?" Grimshaw called quietly. "Anyone home?"

No answer.

An opening on the farthest side, big enough for a dog to enter. Big enough for a man to enter on hands and knees. Something had churned up the ground in front of the opening. Either something being dragged into the dwelling or someone fighting *not* to be dragged into the dark interior.

Swearing to himself—and at himself—Grimshaw turned on his flashlight and crouched in front of the opening, focusing the light on what lay in the center of the structure before sweeping the light all around to make sure there was nothing else inside.

From the look of the wounds, Vaughn had been bitten by something extremely venomous. Maybe an adult could survive one bite—if he received treatment in a hurry—but Vaughn's arms and lower legs were covered in bites.

Could the *terra indigene* who visited Julian's bookstore have a venomous form? Or was this something else that humans hadn't seen yet?

"Crap." Telling himself he was every kind of fool, Grimshaw crawled into the dwelling far enough to touch Vaughn's wrist and confirm there was no pulse. Then he held a hand close to Vaughn's nose and mouth. No feel of breath. Nothing more he could do.

As he started to back out of the dwelling, the light revealed three objects half hidden under the body. He stared, chilled by the implications.

He should not disturb a crime scene. He should not remove evidence. He weighed procedure against the promise to serve and protect. If people found out about this, it might cause a panic that would sweep through the village and that would stir up a shitstorm of trouble all around this lake. He would, of course, tell Hargreaves what he suspected . . . but later. He would tell Julian—and Ilya Sanguinati, on the odd chance that the vampire didn't already know. And he would tell Vicki DeVine.

Taking the three objects, Grimshaw backed out of the dwelling and breathed a sigh of relief when he was able to stand.

"Found him!" he shouted.

"Alive?" Hargreaves shouted back.

"No."

As he waited for Hargreaves, Samuel Kipp, and the CIU team to reach him, Grimshaw slipped the three chunks of carrot into his pocket.

CHAPTER 82

Grimshaw

Moonsday, Sumor 10

The courtroom was in the government building next to the police station. A village of fewer than three hundred people didn't need its own judge, so judges from Bristol and woo-woo Crystalton alternated holding court once a week in Sproing, and most of the time those men sat around chatting with government officials or reading a book.

Not today.

The only thing in the humans' favor was the Bristol judge wasn't wearing a particular tie clip, unlike the attorney who came in from Hubb NE to represent Dane and the widows of his business partners, and Yorick Dane didn't look happy when he noticed that little detail. But as Yorick and Constance, Trina, Pamella, and Heidi stood before the judge, Grimshaw looked at Captain Hargreaves and knew how it would go. That's why he didn't look at the other two men—males—in the room.

Had Ilya Sanguinati ever argued a case against a human attorney in a human court of law? In the case of *Dane & Company v. DeVine*, Yorick Dane's attorney had pulled out all the theatrical stops, playing to a nonexistent jury, and making Ilya Sanguinati's calm responses sound lackluster at best, as if he was simply going through the motions and didn't care about the outcome and the judge's decision.

But if the Sanguinati, if the rest of the *terra indigene*, didn't care about the outcome, why had the guy with the blue-and-yellow-tipped hair come to this hearing?

"To clarify," Ilya said mildly after Dane's attorney finished his dramatic summing up of all the trauma that had been done to his clients. "Despite the harm and injuries that Victoria DeVine suffered because of the actions of Yorick Dane and the other members of the organization known as the Tie Clip Club, there is nothing human law can, or will, do to punish the surviving adversaries?"

The judge was quiet and still for a full minute. Finally he spoke, slowly and deliberately. "Mr. Sanguinati, neither you nor the arresting officers can prove that Yorick Dane or the other people standing before the court today knew that Marmaduke Swinn would abduct Victoria DeVine. You can't prove these people knew that Tony Amorella would attempt to kill Ms. DeVine. Did Mr. Dane and his business partners disregard agreements that had been made with the *terra indigene* with regard to the property known as The Jumble? Yes, they did. But I think sufficient justice has been done in that regard. However, you did provide a convincing argument that the document Mr. Dane presented in order to repossess the property in question was, in fact, a forged document. Therefore, it is my ruling that the original settlement agreement between Yorick Dane and Victoria DeVine stands, and she is now and hereafter the lawful proprietor of the designated property."

Grimshaw held his breath, waiting for Ilya Sanguinati's response.

"The *terra indigene* will accept your ruling about the land known as The Jumble," Ilya said.

"Of course you'll accept it," Dane said in a voice close to a whine. "He ruled in your favor."

"But recent events have brought a group of humans to the attention of the Elders—and the Elementals," Ilya continued, "and *they* have made some decisions with regard to these adversaries."

Suddenly Grimshaw felt like he was standing next to a roaring fire. Hargreaves looked uncomfortable too. Ilya Sanguinati did not. As for the guy with the multicolored hair . . .

A chill went through Grimshaw as he considered why the room felt so hot.

"A few generations ago, a club was created in Hubb NE," Ilya said. "Its members were drawn from the private college, the university, the technical college, and the police academy. The purpose of the club was to form a pool of individuals whose various abilities would be made available to other members—a network, if you will. There is nothing wrong with networks—until they are used to manipulate other people in order for their members to take what doesn't belong to them. This particular club identifies its members with a distinctive tie clip—specifically, the one my learned colleague is wearing." Ilya looked pointedly at the other attorney.

Now Ilya focused his attention on the judge. "You have said that the humans standing before you cannot be punished according to your law, or have already been punished since Yorick Dane lost control of the land he coveted and three of the females have lost their mates. As the representative for the *terra indigene*, I am authorized to accept that judgment. In return, you must accept ours.

"Beginning this day and for the next hundred years, any human connected to the Tie Clip Club, as it is officially known, is banned from Lake Silence, the land around it, and the village of Sproing. The ban includes anyone connected to a member of said club by birth or marriage. Any member of the club who crosses into forbidden territory will be killed."

Ilya looked at Yorick Dane. "From this day forward, if any of you, or if anyone connected to you, tries to contact Victoria DeVine or distress her in any way or take any action that would damage the property known as The Jumble, a tight, intense tornado will form out of a cloudless sky and destroy your house and all that stands within it. It will destroy the building where you conduct your business. And it will also destroy the . . ." He turned to his companion. "What was it called?"

"Rut shack," the man with the multicolored hair replied.

"I think humans usually use a more genteel expression."

"Love nest?" Grimshaw suggested under his breath.

Ilya tipped his head. "Yes. Love nest."

Constance Dane turned on her husband. "You told me you hadn't renewed the lease on that place."

"I didn't!" Yorick said.

"He didn't," Ilya agreed. "He simply rented another one that you didn't know about. He successfully hid it from you. He can no longer successfully hide anything because now *we* have reason to watch everything he does—and everyone he does."

Grimshaw fought not to smile. If Ilya had been looking for a fitting kind of revenge against Yorick Dane, he'd found it.

"If any of you go near Victoria DeVine again, we will strip you, and anyone who helps you, of everything your greed has acquired," Ilya said. "And then we will strip you of your skin, your muscle, and your blood. But not all at once."

The other man picked up a rolled newspaper from the table behind him. He smiled as he held it up. "And what the tornado doesn't take . . ."

The paper turned into a torch that burned fierce and hot and quick. And the hand that held it was made of fire, not flesh.

"I think we all understand one another." Ilya Sanguinati walked out of the courtroom, followed by Fire, who dropped what was left of the newspaper.

No one spoke. Everyone watched the last pieces of burned, blackened paper float to the floor.

"Captain Hargreaves. Officer Grimshaw," the judge said. "You will escort these people to the nearest railroad station and see that they get on the earliest available train to Hubb NE. I will remain here until you return. In the meantime, I will call the governor and let him know about this latest . . . development . . . between humans and the *terra indigene*. This court is adjourned."

Hargreaves made the decision of who was riding with whom, giving Grimshaw the three widows and driving Yorick and Constance Dane himself. It was possible his captain wanted to give him a break and spare him from listening to the Danes snipe at each other. More likely, Hargreaves had made the decision to prevent Grimshaw from taking a very long detour into the wild country on the way to the train station.

Hargreaves knew him well.

CHAPTER 83

Vicki

Windsday, Sumor 12

"You're moving back to The Jumble tomorrow?" Julian asked as we settled in the chairs on his porch. He had a beer; I had orange juice over ice since I was still taking a nighttime pain pill in order to sleep.

"Yes, I'm going back, although I'm not sure for how long."

"Why?"

I hesitated. I went through so much to keep The Jumble; it was hard to admit defeat. "The Jumble is kind of notorious now." Kind of? Newspapers from Lakeside to Hubbney and all the Finger Lakes towns in between had written about the Tie Clip Club's schemes and scandals, and the *terra indigene*'s retaliation against said schemes and scandals. The one good thing that had come out of all of this was that the club had been exposed as a group of wheelers and dealers who were, quite often, underhanded in their business dealings with anyone but their own members.

"I don't think it's likely anyone is going to want to rent one of the cabins and take a chance of being eaten," I finished. Or bitten by critters whose happy faces hid a different, and very lethal, form of *terra indigene*.

"Do you want to know what I think?" Julian asked after a minute.

"Sure."

"Yes, The Jumble has some notoriety now, and with the ban on the Tie Clip Club members and their families, you're not likely to get the snooty crowd coming in for a weekend of summer fun." Julian leaned forward. "But ever since the story broke, I've been fielding calls from people who know people who were aware that I live in Sproing: professors from the Finger Lakes universities, and not just the Intuit university; writers and photographers who provide material for magazines like *Nature!*; even acquaintances from Crystalton who want to get away from home for a few days but don't want to go far. They all tried to call The Jumble directly but couldn't get through. I'm guessing your answering machine is full of messages. Since they couldn't reach you, they called me, and they're all asking the same thing: are you taking reservations?

"Vicki, this is a *terra indigene* settlement that not only allows human visitors to be on the land; it allows them to interact with the Others in a social setting. It's probably not the only place where that's possible, but I think it's among the few, and maybe the only one around the Finger Lakes. Think of it. You can swim in a lake ruled by an Elemental. You can talk to one of the Panthergard or a Bear. You can play a game of cards with a Crow. People who want to study the *terra indigene* in order to understand what we humans need to do in order to survive on this continent are leaving daily messages at Lettuce Reed because we need places like this. I think we always did, and that's why Yorick Dane's great-great aunt built this house and the cabins in the first place, so that the *terra indigene* could learn about humans and we could learn about them."

"There are *terra indigene* living in some of the cabins. I can't ask them to leave. It's more their home than anyone else's."

"You don't have to ask them to leave. In fact, you

shouldn't. Having a furry neighbor is part of the appeal. And I did mention that most of the cabins were basic accommodations with toilet and shower facilities in a nearby building. Apparently, when some of these people receive permission to spend a few weeks out in the wild country to do their research or take pictures, they're living rougher than that. They were excited and made it sound like having toilets and showers at all would be a luxury. And I'll give you one more reason for letting whoever is already living in the cabins stay on."

"What's that?"

Julian sat back and raised his beer bottle in a salute. "Somebody has to take care of the goats and donkeys."

CHAPTER 84

Grimshaw

Thaisday, Sumor 13

After suggesting that Officer Osgood go out for a foot patrol, Captain Hargreaves settled into the visitors' chair in front of Grimshaw's desk.

"So Vicki DeVine is moving back to The Jumble today?" Hargreaves said.

"She is. I'm taking a few hours' personal time to help out." Grimshaw cocked a thumb toward the windows. "Gershwin Jones is donating an upright piano in exchange for Vicki hosting a musical evening every couple of weeks. He figures it will bring people into his store for sheet music or smaller instruments. Might even encourage some of Sproing's residents to take music lessons from him. So I'm helping him muscle the piano into the truck and out again."

"Not so much of a loner these days?"

"Still like my space."

"You did a good job here, Wayne."

"Lost a fair number of people," he countered.

"No one could have stopped that except the people who provoked the attacks. Would have thought we'd all know better by now, but that wasn't the case." Hargreaves said nothing for a minute. "The governor wants this police station manned again. He's been apprised of why it's been difficult keeping it manned, but he believes it's vital to have a police presence here now. With more visitors coming in every day, the area around Lake Silence needs a faster response than people can get by calling the Bristol station if they need help."

"Can't argue with that."

"Of course, the Bristol station will continue to supply backup. So will the police force in Crystalton. But they need a chief of police here and one officer to work with him. Small place like this, two salaries are going to put a strain on the budget, but Silence Lodge has informed the village council that, if they approve of the people chosen to fill the positions, they will reduce the rent on the police station enough to help take the sting out of paying those salaries. The Sanguinati also said they would provide one of the Mill Creek Cabins as a residence for the new chief, all utilities except telephone included."

"That's generous."

Hargreaves studied him. "Wayne, you're a good officer, a good man. But you're too damn ornery and independent to rise up through the ranks in the usual way. It's a big jump, going from officer to chief, but I doubt an opportunity like this will come along again. That said, your temporary assignment is complete, and if you want, I'll put you back on the roster for highway patrol. You're being given the right of first refusal, so this is your decision."

"What about Osgood?"

Hargreaves hesitated. "The higher-ups have some concerns about him, about whether or not he'll wash out as a cop. He's already requested a transfer from the Putney Police Station, which is clear thinking on his part. He'd be shunned by a fair number of cops there, and that's not a good working environment."

Yeah. Julian Farrow would know about that. "Could Osgood stay here?"

"That would be the choice of the new chief of police."

He didn't doubt that he could do the job and do it well, but did he want the job? Small place where he'd know a lot more than he wanted to about the people he was sworn to protect. But there was also the wild country right outside his door. Dangerous? Gods, yes. And because it was dangerous, he could make a difference here.

"I need to talk to someone before I give you an answer."

"How much time do you need?"

"Fifteen minutes, maybe twenty." He wasn't going far, just up to the second floor.

"In that case, why don't I go over to the diner and pick up a couple of sandwiches?"

Grimshaw walked out with Hargreaves, then walked up the flight of stairs that led to two offices. He knocked on the door that had no stenciling on the glass that identified the business and walked in.

Ilya Sanguinati stepped out from behind the bookcases that formed the wall of his office. "Come in, Officer Grimshaw."

Ilya returned to the seat behind the desk. Grimshaw leaned against the bookcases.

"If I accept the position of chief of police here in Sproing, will you have a problem with that?" he asked.

"'You' meaning me, the Sanguinati, or all the *terra indigene* who live in and around Lake Silence?"

"All of the above."

"Then the answer to all of the above is no, we would not have a problem with that."

"You okay with Osgood staying?"

Ilya nodded. "You may choose whatever cabin would suit you for a residence, with the exception of the one already occupied by Julian Farrow. The rest are currently unfurnished . . ."

Grimshaw shrugged. "I have an efficiency apartment in Bristol. I can bring what I need."

"You should also be aware that Silence Lodge is considering offering three of the cabins for short-term leases—three months minimum."

"Good to know." It would certainly influence his decision of which cabin to claim for himself.

"Is there anything you'll regret leaving in Bristol?"

Wondering if that was Ilya's subtle way of asking about a lover, Grimshaw smiled. "I'll miss the pool hall."

Ilya sat back. "I beg your pardon?"

Now he grinned. "Pool is a game played on a felt-covered—"

"I know what it is." Ilya sounded grouchy. "I was just surprised by your answer."

Uh-huh. Couldn't be an easy transition going from the behind-the-scenes controlling power to having to deal with all the pesky humans directly. Considering his own job change, he felt some sympathy for the vampire, especially since that change happened by their own choices.

"There is a pool hall in Bristol, just seedy enough to have character. I would go there on my day off and shoot some pool, have a beer and a burger." It was as close to a social life as he'd had in a while. Not something he would share with one of the Sanguinati. "I won't miss the establishment all that much, but I did enjoy the game."

"None of the businesses in Sproing have a pool table?" Ilya asked.

Grimshaw hesitated, then decided there had to be honesty between them if nothing else. "There are a couple of bars in the village. Not sure if they're both open or if one has odd hours, but the one that does regular business has a pool table in the back. But I'd always be a cop there."

"Is that what you would call a deal breaker?"

He shook his head. "I just wanted to be sure we were good before I accepted the position."

"We're good . . . Chief Grimshaw."

And they would do some good, Grimshaw thought as he returned to the police station and gave Hargreaves his answer.

EPILOGUE

Vicki

Julian had been right. The Jumble's newfound notoriety might have scared off some people—and proved interesting to others, like the man who wanted to book a cabin in the hopes an Elder would eat his wife and save him the cost of a divorce. (I declined to take his reservation.) On moving day, my office was returned to working order first, and they—meaning all the big scary males I knew, plus Aggie—parked me behind the desk with the pad of paper containing all the names and phone numbers Aggie had carefully written down from the humans who wanted to rent a cabin. Between returning calls and answering new calls and making notes so that I could ask Fred and Larry at the bait-and-tackle shop which weeks would be ideal for fishing in the lake—and asking Conan when the trout returned to the creek, information I assumed he knew because he'd chosen to live in one of the creekside cabins specifically to get his paws on the fish— I had booked all the available cabins into late fall, when I stopped booking humans into the more primitive cabins, thinking of how I would feel if I had to put on boots and a winter coat in order to go out and pee. I had a waiting list for the two suites in the main house and the two renovated lakeside cabins. The three universities in the Finger Lakes area solved their inability to rent cabins in The Jumble or rent rooms at Ineke's boardinghouse by renting three of the Mill Creek Cabins from Silence Lodge on a year's lease, negotiating with Ilya Sanguinati to allow their people to explore The Jumble as part of the lease agreement.

I remained the Reader and, with Julian's assistance, continued to do a story hour three evenings a week. Gershwin Jones brought over a piano and a couple of drums, and we had a music night a couple of evenings a month. Hector and Horace acquired some ponies and ran a pony camp for visiting children—a couple of hours of learning how to ride combined with trail rides where the kids would see a Hawk or a Coyote up close. For people who didn't want to walk the trails in The Jumble for one reason or another, they could take a donkey-cart tour and attempt conversation with whichever *terra indigene* was driving the cart and who couldn't understand what the humans were saying half the time.

For reasons he wouldn't explain, Ilya Sanguinati purchased a pool table and installed it in one of the undesignated ground-floor rooms—and asked Julian Farrow to provide the information for proper decorations to make it look like a pool hall. A few women grumbled about their men disappearing into the pool room in the evenings instead of spending time with them, but I ignored the grumbles when I noticed that our new chief of police stopped by a couple of evenings a week to shoot pool. Sometimes he wanted solitude and played alone. Sometimes he played with Julian or even Ilya, who was learning the game. It felt strange to see Wayne—because when he was dressed in jeans and a T-shirt, he was Wayne, not Chief Grimshaw—looking relaxed, but it also felt good. And it felt good to spend time with Julian, to take walks and talk—and to go swimming once my stitches and cast were removed.

It was toward the end of summer when a young Intuit photographer came to The Jumble—a friend of a friend of Julian's. Because of that connection, and because this was his chance to build a portfolio of nature shots, I introduced the young man to Conan and Cougar, who permitted him to take photographs of them in both their forms—something they hadn't done for other people who had been busy snapping pictures. He took pictures of Aggie, Jozi, and Eddie as Crows and in the black-and-white outfits they had selected when I hired them to help me take care of all the guests. It worked out well. Smart guests gave them a shiny, inexpensive trinket. In return, you could count on those sharp Crow eyes finding a guest's missing earring whether it was under the bed, under a dresser, or in some other Crow's stash of shinies.

That day the young photographer wanted to photograph the lake, and he asked me to go into the water. I demurred. I protested. I whined. But he was a pleasant young man, and maybe, being an Intuit, he had a feeling I needed to be in the water that day.

I waded in, up to my waist. And she rose out of the water right in front of me.

I looked at the photographer, who was staring at her and not quite daring to raise his camera and take a shot.

"He would like to take your picture," I said. "Is that all right?"

"Our picture," she said.

"I don't like having my picture taken." You couldn't explain self-esteem and body image issues to an Elemental.

"Our picture. Then I will allow him to take one of me."

"Why with me?"

"So that you remember why it was possible for him to take the other."

He stood on the beach, with the water lapping at his feet, and took several shots of the two of us facing each other as if conversing. Then I moved away, and she turned to face him.

As a thank-you, he framed a copy of the photograph of me and the Lady of the Lake. He also gave me a framed copy of the photograph of her.

He won an award for that photograph. It appeared on the cover of *Nature!* and was part of a featured article full of photographs he took during his stay at The Jumble.

Those framed photographs hang on the wall in my bedroom. I look at both of them every day. I still wince when I look at the short, plump woman with unruly brown hair. Then I whisper, "You made the other one possible. Remember that."

The other one. In the photograph of the two of us, she is this wonder, with sunlight turning water droplets into diamonds falling all around her. But in the other one, the one where she looks directly at the camera . . .

She is power. She is lethal. She is the Lady of the Lake. If the Elders who live in the lake were the inspiration for stories of mermaids—as long as you didn't get a good look at them—then she is the siren song that lures sailors into dangerous water and takes them down to a dark, cold grave. Her eyes hint of temptation, but it's that little bit of something behind her smile that warns you of what can happen if you give in to that temptation, if you're not careful. She can be friendly, but she will never be your friend. And she is the little sister to the Elementals who live in the Great Lakes and in the seas and in the oceans. Challenge them at your peril.

I don't forget, but I do swim most days while the water is warm enough. Sometimes Julian joins me for an early swim before he drives to Sproing and opens the bookstore. Some days I swim alone.

Not really alone. She hasn't appeared to any of the guests since that photograph was taken, but when I'm on my own I can sense her nearby, sometimes see a face made from shadows in the water. And sometimes a dorsal fin will rise beside me, and the water's surface will be broken by the playful splash of an Elder's tail.

GEOGRAPHY
AND OTHER INFORMATION

NAMID—THE WORLD

CONTINENTS/LANDMASSES

Afrikah
Australis
Brittania/Wild Brittania
Cel-Romano/Cel-Romano Alliance of Nations
Felidae
Fingerbone Islands
Storm Islands
Thaisia
Tokhar-Chin
Zelande

LAKES IN THAISIA

Great Lakes—Superior, Tala, Honon, Etu, and Tahki
Feather Lakes/Finger Lakes (not all of them are named in
   this story)—Silence, Crystal, Prong, Senneca

CITIES AND VILLAGES MENTIONED IN THE STORY

Bristol—human town located on Crystal Lake
Crystalton—Intuit town located on Crystal Lake
Ferryman's Landing—Intuit village located on Great Island
Hubb NE (aka Hubbney)—human-controlled city; the
   government for the Northeast Region is located there
Lakeside—human-controlled city on the northeastern end of
   Lake Etu
Putney—human town located on Prong Lake

Ravendell—human/Intuit village located on Senneca Lake
Sproing—human village located near Lake Silence
Toland—human-controlled city on the East Coast

CALENDAR

DAYS OF THE WEEK

Earthday (a spiritual day and a day of rest)
Moonsday
Sunsday
Windsday
Thaisday
Firesday
Watersday

MONTHS OF THE YEAR
(not all the months have been named yet)

Janius
Febros
Viridus
Aprillis
Maius
Juin
Sumor
Messis

CAST OF CHARACTERS

HUMANS IN THE STORY

RESIDENTS OF SPROING

Horace and Hector Adams—owners of the stables
Sheridan Ames—owner of Ames Funeral Home, along with
    her brother, Samuel
Jane Argyle—postmistress
Pops Davies—owner of the general store
Victoria "Vicki" DeVine—owner/caretaker of The Jumble
Julian Farrow—owner of Lettuce Reed
Fred and Larry—owners of the bait-and-tackle shop
Helen Hearse—manager of Come and Get It, the village diner
Gershwin Jones—owner of Grace Notes
Silas and Ethel Milford—fruit growers
Dr. Steven Wallace—junior partner at the medical office
Dominique Xavier
Ineke Xavier—runs the boardinghouse with Paige and
    Dominique
Paige Xavier

POLICE

Officer Wayne Grimshaw—highway patrol, Bristol Police
    Station
Captain Walter Hargreaves—patrol captain, Bristol Police
    Station
Detective Samuel Kipp—leader of the Bristol Crime
    Investigation Unit (CIU)
Detective Marmaduke Swinn—senior investigator in the CIU,
    Putney Police Station

Swinn's team: Detective Baker, Detective Calhoun, Detective Chesnik, Officer David Osgood, and Detective Reynolds

THE REST OF THE HUMANS IN THE STORY

Franklin Cartwright—worked for Yorick Dane
Constance Dane (aka Constance Yates)
Honoria Dane—created The Jumble
Yorick Dane (aka David Yates)
Yorick Dane's business associates: Darren and Pamella, Hershel and Heidi, Trina and Vaughn, Mark Hammorson, and Tony Amorella
Steve Ferryman—mayor of Ferryman's Landing
Patrick Hannigan—governor of the Northeast Region of Thaisia
Greg O'Sullivan—agent in the Investigative Task Force

THE OTHERS (aka *terra indigene*)

Aiden—a Fire Elemental
Conan Beargard—Black Bear
Agatha Crowgard (aka Aggie Crowe)
Clara Crowgard
Eddie Crowgard
Jozi Crowgard
Elders—old, powerful forms; Namid's teeth and claws
The Lady of the Lake—a Water Elemental
Robert "Cougar" Panthera—Panthergard
The Ponies: Whirlpool and Twister
Boris Sanguinati—Ilya's driver
Ilya Sanguinati—attorney
Natasha Sanguinati—CPA
Vladimir Sanguinati—lives in the Lakeside Courtyard
Sproingers

Read on for the next
book in the World of the Others,

WILD COUNTRY

Coming March 2019 from Ace

A year from now, it would be called the Great Predation—those terrifying days when the Elementals and the Elders, the *terra indigene* who are Namid's teeth and claws, came out of the wild country and brutally thinned the human herds in Thaisia. In some cases, they wiped out the entire population of human towns in the Northwest and Midwest in retaliation for the slaughter of the Wolfgard and other forms of shifters who had kept watch over the human places.

Now, with death still fresh in everyone's minds, *terra indigene* and humans alike want to claim those empty places, especially the places of strategic importance.

Bennett is one of those places—and the Elders are staying nearby, waiting for the humans to make another mistake.

Waiting for them to make their last mistake.

CHAPTER 1

Windsday, Sumor 25

Jana Paniccia followed the gravel paths through the memorial park. There were no cemeteries on the continent of Thaisia, no individual gravestones, no family mausoleums unless you were very rich. Cities couldn't afford to waste land on the dead when the living needed every acre that they were grudgingly permitted to lease from the *terra indigene* who ruled the continent.

Who ruled the *world*. They had smashed and torn that harsh truth into humans across the globe, and only fools or the blindly optimistic thought there was any chance of things going back to the way they had been before the Humans First and Last movement had started the war against the *terra indigene* here in Thaisia and in Cel-Romano, on the other side of the Atlantik Ocean.

Instead of gaining anything from the war, humans had lost ground—literally. Cities had been destroyed or were no longer under human control. People were running to any place they thought could provide safety, thinking that large cities were less vulnerable to what the Others could do.

In that, too, humans were wrong. The destruction of so

much of Toland, a large human-controlled city on the East Coast, should have taught people that much.

But this wasn't a day to think about those things.

Jana found the large flower bed with the tall granite marker in the center.

There were no graveyards, no gravestones, in Thaisia, but there were memorial parks full of flower beds and small ponds, with benches positioned so the living could visit with the dead. She looked down the double column of names carved into the granite until she found the two she'd come to see: Martha Chase. Wilbur Chase. The foster parents who had taken her from the foundling home and raised her as their own. There hadn't been even a birth certificate left with her when the Universal Temple priests had found her on the temple doorstep. Just a printed note with her name and birth date.

All bodies were cremated and the ashes mixed with the soil in these flower beds, the names carved on the granite the only acknowledgment of who was there. Martha had loved growing flowers, and Pops had always tended a small vegetable garden in their backyard. Jana was the one who had no skill with the soil, no matter how hard she tried. She knew a rose from a daisy, understood the difference between annuals and perennials, and, most of the time, had dug up weeds instead of flowers when she tried to help Martha tidy the beds.

You have other talents, Pops used to say with a laugh.

Other talents. Gods, she hoped so.

They had died in a car accident just a week after Jana had been accepted into the police academy—one of only three women to be accepted. She'd spent the first few months struggling with her classwork and the hostility of her classmates while traveling from Hubb NE to a village near the Addirondak Mountains to meet with the Chases' attorney and take care of her foster parents' estate. There wasn't much. Martha and Pops had never been interested in things, but the sale of the house and furnishings was enough to pay off the school loans she'd taken out to attend a community college while she'd tried to get accepted into the police academy. It was enough to pay for the academy and living expenses. She'd been frugal, but if she didn't get a job soon . . .

"Hey, Martha," Jana said softly after looking around to make sure she was alone. "Hey, Pops." She sat on the bench, her hands folded in her lap. "I graduated from the academy. The only woman who stuck it out. Martha, you always said I was stubborn, and I guess you were right. I have a meeting with the academy administrator next week. Hopefully it will be about a job offer. The gods know, every human community needs cops right now, and everyone else in my class has already been hired by towns in the Northeast Region, which lost officers last month because of the war. But I know there are positions that haven't been filled yet because no one wants to take a job in a village stuck in the middle of the wild country. They say that's just delayed suicide. Maybe they're right, but I'd take that chance."

She looked at the flowers growing in the bed and wished she could remember the names of some of them. "I came to say good-bye. It's getting harder and harder to purchase a bus ticket, and I'm not sure I'll be able to get back here again. And if I'm hired—*when* I'm hired—I may be leaving in a hurry." She paused. "Thanks for everything. When I get to wherever I'm going, I'll light a candle in remembrance."

Jana hurried through the park, gauging that she had just enough time to reach the bus stop near the park gates and catch the bus back to Hubb NE. She hoped that by this time next week she'd be heading to another town to do the only job she'd ever wanted to do.

CHAPTER 2

Windsday, Sumor 25

"I quit."

Tolya Sanguinati studied Jesse Walker as they faced each other over the counter in Bennett's general store. The look in her eyes made him think of the lightning that sometimes filled the sky in this part of Thaisia. Despite being a dangerous predator—far more dangerous than the humans here appreciated—that look made him wary. "You can't quit."

"Oh, yes, I can."

He took a step back and considered. It was tempting to point out that, since she didn't actually work for him, she couldn't, technically, quit. But Jesse Walker was the unofficial leader of Prairie Gold, a small Intuit town located at the southern end of the Elder Hills. As such, she was his most important human ally. He couldn't afford to lose her knowledge or cooperation, so it probably wasn't a good idea to point out anything.

Erebus Sanguinati, the leader of all the Sanguinati on the continent of Thaisia, had told him to take over Bennett after all the humans had been slaughtered by Namid's teeth and claws. The town had a train station that serviced all the ranches in the area, as well as Prairie Gold. That made it an important place that the Elders would no longer allow humans to control because, when they had, the trains that traveled back and forth across the land had brought enemies to this part of Thaisia. Had brought death to the Wolfgard and other shifters.

Every place inhabited by humans was in turmoil right now because no one knew how many of those places had survived. With quick communication links between regions severed by the Elders, who had destroyed the telephone lines and tore down the mobile phone towers all along the regional boundaries, e-mail and phones of any kind were useful only to destinations within the same region. But even within a region, no one really knew whether a phone went unanswered because someone wasn't in the office at that moment or because there was no one left in that town to answer it.

But the rest of the Midwest Region wasn't his problem. Right now, his problem was the slim, middle-aged, grayhaired woman who had been helping him prioritize the tasks necessary to keep the train station open and to deal with urgent things such as food that was spoiling and pets that had been left in residences.

Until he traveled to Prairie Gold to be Grandfather Erebus's eyes and ears, Tolya had lived his whole life in Toland, one of the largest cities on the entire continent. He'd had the most extensive humancentric education available to the *terra indigene* and had been among the Sanguinati who monitored the television newscasts and the newspapers as a way of keeping an eye on what the duplicitous humans might be planning. And he'd been among the Sanguinati who had actual contact and dealings with government officials and businessmen. But those meetings had been formal, official, devoid of personal contact and feelings beyond the loathing each side felt for the other.

Nothing in his education or years of experience had prepared him to deal with messy daily interaction with humans who had no interest in being formal or official, or of limiting personal contact. Even his previous interactions with this

woman, when he had helped her and the other residents of
Prairie Gold prepare to hold out against humans trying to cut
them off from supplies, hadn't prepared him for dealing with
her now.

"Why?" he finally asked.

"Because you're not listening," Jesse Walker snapped.

"I listen to everything you say," Tolya countered.

Her right hand clamped around her left wrist.

Jesse Walker was an Intuit, a kind of human who had a
heightened sensitivity to the world, and her people had feelings about everything from animals to weather to sensing
whether someone was lying. Each Intuit didn't have feelings
about everything—their minds would break under that kind
of strain—but each developed a sensitivity that matched who
they were or the work they did. For Jesse Walker, it was
people, and an aching left wrist was her tell that something
about a situation made her uneasy—and the more severe the
ache, the more dire the situation.

"I have listened," Tolya reiterated. "But perhaps I'm not
understanding?"

He watched her anger fade. Her right hand still cuffed her
left wrist, but the hold was looser now. He wondered if
her wrist would be bruised.

"What are we doing here?" Jesse Walker asked. "Are we
just cleaning up what will become a ghost town, with a few
people manning the train station, or are we doing something
more?"

An important question. Looking at her, Tolya realized his
answer would do more than decide the fate of this town. It
would ripple throughout Thaisia in the same way that Simon
Wolfgard's decision to hire Meg Corbyn had started ripples
that were part of the reason he was here in this town trying
to figure out this woman.

If Simon were standing here right now, Tolya would
cheerfully snap the Wolf's neck. Then again, if Tolya was
fair, Simon hadn't known that taking in one stray human
female would end up with the *terra indigene* trying to help—
and even protect—packs of humans.

"Not a ghost town," he said carefully. "Bennett is no longer a human-controlled town, but that doesn't mean it has to decay."

"Or that its workers are transient?"

"They aren't meant to be transient. Some of the young humans who have come here don't feel this is the right place. They came for adventure . . . or something."

"They came for opportunities," Jesse Walker countered. "They came because their home communities in the Northeast Region are crowded and it's hard to find work, hard to learn a skill. And yes, many of them left home for the adventure. But they also left what they knew because, suddenly, there are a lot of empty human places in the Midwest and Northwest. I have the feeling that there won't be any new human places. Not for a long time. Not in Thaisia. Humans made too many mistakes over the past few months for the *terra indigene* to tolerate us anyplace we aren't already established. So if the empty places aren't reinhabited now, they'll fade away."

"I don't think the Elders will allow humans to move back into those empty places," Tolya said.

"Not alone, no. But there are *terra indigene* and Intuits working together here to take care of animals and make decisions about the food in the houses. And there's a lot more that needs to be done. Decisions have to be made about every single thing in every single residence."

"I can't do that," he protested.

"Neither can I. That's why you need more than strong young men who will happily eat all the ice cream and cookies they find in the empty residences but don't know what to do with the medicines. And regardless whether those Elders of yours were justified in killing everyone in Bennett, those people may still have family somewhere who would appreciate having the personal effects. Having young men with a lot of energy and strong backs is great, but you also need skilled labor and professionals if you want this to be a viable town. Why can't we create a place where *terra indigene* and Intuits and Simple Life folk and other kinds of humans can live and work together? Learn from each other. I got the impression that the Lakeside Courtyard and the Intuits in Ferryman's Landing were trying to do exactly that—build a new community that had room for everyone."

"Dangerous." Tolya looked out the big front window of Bennett's general store. "If the wrong kind of human comes here . . ."

"I know. No one can afford to make a mistake."

"Then how do you suggest we get these new citizens?"

They heard the clip-clop of a horse coming down the street. Barbara Ellen Debany, their pet caretaker and almost-vet, waved at them as she passed the store.

"Same way you got her," Jesse Walker said, smiling as she released her left wrist long enough to return the wave. "Have someone else screen the candidates before they get here, and then you make the final decision about who you want living in this town." She took a folded piece of paper out of the back pocket of her jeans and handed it to him. "Ideally, those are the professions and skills you should have in Bennett, for starters."

Tolya unfolded the paper. His eyebrows rose as he studied the list. Then he looked at Jesse Walker. "Anyone from Prairie Gold who might want to fill a position?"

"Kelley Burch. His skills are wasted in Prairie Gold, and there is a jewelry store here that needs someone to run it—and Kelley would have a better chance of selling some of his own designs, whether he sells them in Bennett or sends them on to someplace back east to sell on consignment. I'm going down to Prairie Gold tomorrow. I'll talk to him then."

"You want to spend time in your own store."

She nodded. "I need to be home for a couple of days."

"I'll get this list out as quickly as I can." The Elders weren't allowing the telephone and telegraph lines between the regions to be restored except under special circumstances. He could call or e-mail Jackson Wolfgard, who lived in Sweetwater, a settlement in the Northwest, but reaching Lakeside in the Northeast Region required extra time and effort.

As he left the store, he looked at the Intuit woman and wondered whether Jesse Walker would come back and continue to help him. Then he noticed that she was no longer holding her left wrist—and he breathed a sigh of relief.

Virgil Wolfgard stood next to a tree near the south end of the town square and watched the human female and the blue horse walk toward him. The wind was blowing in the wrong direction to carry his scent to the horse, which was meandering across the paved street toward the grass in the square, and the female seemed too preoccupied with something that wasn't right in front of her to control the horse or notice the predator who was watching her.

Not noticing was dangerous, something the female should have learned while she was still a puppy.

He stepped away from the tree, putting himself right in front of the horse.

The horse snorted and planted its feet, causing the female to grab the saddle horn for balance.

"Easy, Rowan, easy," she said. Then she gave Virgil a wary look. "Sheriff."

"Barbara Ellen." Virgil looked at her companion. "Horse."

His brother, Kane, who was in Wolf form, joined them, causing Rowan to snort again.

Barbara Ellen gave Kane a wobbly smile. "Deputy Wolfgard."

Virgil held up a small red collar. She took it and read the tag attached to the collar. "Fluffy," she said sadly. "She was a nice cat."

"We didn't eat it," Virgil said, anticipating the question she didn't dare ask. "Too much fur and not enough meat."

"Not much of an epitaph for poor Fluffy."

Maybe not, but that wasn't important. He and Kane hadn't killed the cat, but *something* had torn the animal apart. Not for food. For fun.

And that *something* wasn't any form of *terra indigene*.

"The horse was paying attention," Virgil said. All right,

the horse was more interested in reaching the grass, but it did notice him first. "You were not. Why?"

"I was thinking about some stuff," she replied.

He didn't ask what she was thinking about. He just stared.

"But I should pay attention when I'm riding," she added.

"Yes." Virgil stepped aside. So did Kane.

Barbara Ellen pressed her legs against Rowan's sides—and grabbed the saddle horn when the gelding bolted out of reach of the two Wolves.

Virgil shook his head as he watched her reestablish dominance and slow the horse to a walk. <Follow her,> he told Kane, using the *terra indigene* form of communication. <Make sure she doesn't fall off.>

The only good human was a dead human. He hadn't thought much of that species before the Humans First and Last movement had attacked the Wolfgard. He thought far less of them after those humans slaughtered his pack, leaving Kane and him as the only survivors, because they'd been ranging ahead of the pack, looking for game. They'd come running back when they'd heard the guns, but by the time they arrived, the pack members were dead or dying, and the humans were gone.

Virgil and Kane had followed the trail of the trucks until scent markers made by Namid's teeth and claws crossed the trail. Not willing to tangle with the Elders, he and Kane had returned to the small wooden den the pack had used to store items useful to those who could take human form. After packing the little they could carry in Wolf form, they had headed away from what had been their home territory, looking for humans to kill.

Instead, they ended up in Bennett, where the Elders had erased the enemy and yet were allowing those *creatures* to return.

He'd never seen one of the Sanguinati until he'd met Tolya, who had been given the task of making sure the wrong kind of humans didn't try to reclaim the place. But for that, Tolya needed humans as well as many forms of *terra indigene*. And he needed enforcers who were strong enough and feared enough that humans would follow rules and not become troublesome.

That was how Virgil ended up as the town's dominant enforcer, with Kane being the second enforcer. Virgil didn't know anything about human law, hadn't spent much time around actual humans until now. But if one of the two-legged threats caused trouble, he knew how to stop them dead in their tracks. And blood in the street would be a good reminder to the rest of them of why they should behave.

And then there were the two-legs like Barbara Ellen he felt reluctantly compelled to protect.

He walked along the edge of the town square, which served as a park surrounded by the town's original business district. A natural spring was the reason for the grass and trees—was the reason the town had been built there. The spring had been semicontained by human-made barriers, but the water still bubbled out of the ground, providing drinking water for everything with fur or feathers—and humans too.

When he came abreast of the general store, he stopped and waited for Tolya to cross the street and join him.

"Was there a problem with Barbara Ellen?" Tolya asked.

Virgil cocked his head. "Why do we call her that? The humans call her Barb."

"Barbara Ellen sounds dignified. I'm hoping she'll grow into the name, like a puppy grows into its big feet."

"Huh." That made sense, except . . . "She's young but she's an adult, not a pup. Do you really think she'll grow into a dignified name?"

"I am hopeful."

Tolya's dry tone made Virgil smile. Barbara Ellen Debany had ties to the Lakeside Courtyard because her brother was a police officer who worked directly with Simon Wolfgard. That made her special among the humans who were in Bennett. And her being special meant he had the task of trying to keep her out of trouble. Which made him think of the way she tended to want to befriend any and every critter.

"Are there any Snakegard here?" he asked.

"A couple of Rattlers arrived last week. Why?"

"Someone should explain to her about staying away from things that could kill her." Virgil thought for a moment, then added, "Things that aren't us."

"Speaking of things that are not us, Jesse Walker feels we need to bring in more humans to become permanent residents and take over the businesses."

"More." Virgil's lips pulled back in a snarl. "More of *them*?"

"And more of us. Enough *terra indigene* to maintain control of this place." Tolya met Virgil's eyes. "How would you feel about that? Being around them at all is difficult for you and Kane."

"I don't know human law," Virgil growled. "I know how to kill." Too often after a day around humans, he wanted to shed this terrible form and howl out his rage before he tore into throats and bellies and left bodies in pieces like . . . like . . .

"There is too much human bounty here for us to abandon this town," Tolya said quietly. "If we don't hold on to it, humans will flood in to claim what they can."

"Just because we hold on to it, you think the enemy *won't* find this place?"

"Find it? Yes. Even with the travel restrictions that limit humans' migrating between regions, they will find a way to reach this place. Control it?" Tolya shook his head. "The Elders won't allow that. If the Northwest, Southwest, and Midwest regions are purged of humans, they'll be held to the coasts and the towns available to them there."

"And we'll have back what was ours in the first place," Virgil snapped.

"Should a human like Jesse Walker die? She protected the young in the Prairie Gold pack. She's teaching a young Wolf human skills."

He liked Jesse Walker, as much as he could like any human. "There will be enough of us to stand against the humans if they turn rabid?"

Tolya nodded. "Enough of us who can work in the shops

alongside the humans and be ever watchful—and kill what cannot be allowed to remain among us."

"We need to find someone who knows human law."

"Another deputy. I'll add that request to the list of professionals I'll send to Lakeside. We'll see what help Simon and Vlad can provide in the way of humans while we send a message among our own for any who are willing to live near humans."

They walked up the street together, parting at the building that held the sheriff's office.

Going into the back, Virgil studied the three cells. Not a lot of space for wrongdoers, but it would have to be enough.

Humans. Couldn't live with them; couldn't eat them all.

CHAPTER 3

Thaisday, Sumor 26

"Did I do something wrong?" Rachel Wolfgard asked, an anxious whine beneath the words.

"No, honey. You did a great job," Jesse replied. "I just need time in my own place for a few days."

"Familiar smells are good." Rachel's hands gathered up the skirt of her summer dress and tightened into fists that would most likely crease the lightweight material. "I didn't mark territory in your store, even though it is my store too."

"Appreciate that. Urine smell in a store selling fresh food tends to put people off their feed."

"Why? One of the men came in yesterday and made a fart that smelled so bad Shelley Bookman left her shopping and went outside, and when she came back, she asked me to smell the food to make sure it still smelled fresh."

It took effort not to smile. "Smelled that bad, did it?"

Rachel nodded. "My eyes watered."

"Which man?" It hadn't escaped her notice that the juvenile Wolf had not named the bad-mannered lout. "It wasn't Tobias, was it?" If it *was* her son, she'd be having a few words with him.

"No," Rachel replied quickly. "Tobias wouldn't do anything that smelled that bad."

No longer able to hide her smile, Jesse turned toward the canned goods that filled the shelves along one wall. It sounded as if Rachel had a little crush on Tobias. She was too young for him, of course, just as he was too old for her—not to mention her being a *terra indigene* Wolf and his being a human.

Then her boy walked into the store.

"Howdy, Rachel," Tobias said. "That dress looks nice on you."

"Thank you, Tobias. I am wearing the underpants and undershirt too because that is what females should wear beneath the clothing that is seen." Rachel looked at Jesse. "And I have learned how to wash them. Ellen Garcia taught me while you were away."

"That's good," Jesse replied, studying the way Tobias blushed but gave no other sign that underclothes weren't something usually discussed with the other gender.

Not a crush on her son, Jesse decided as she watched the two of them. This was a very innocent younger sister revealing things to her older brother.

It made sense. With the exception of the nanny, all the adults in the Prairie Gold pack had been slaughtered by members of the Humans First and Last movement. Heeding Tolya Sanguinati's warning, she and the rest of the women in Prairie Gold had gathered up the children, human and Other, and headed into the Elder Hills to a spot where they would be safe from human killers.

Now the *terra indigene* settlement had a new leader, Morgan Wolfgard, and a new enforcer, Chase Wolfgard. Along with the Grizzly Wyatt Beargard they were the main contacts between the Intuits and the *terra indigene*—including the Elders who lived in, and protected, the hills.

Rachel continued to travel from the *terra indigene* settlement and work in Walker's General Store, under Jesse's supervision and on her own during the days when Jesse was in

Bennett helping to sort things out there. Morgan and Chase weren't happy about their lone juvenile female being surrounded by humans, but their allowing Rachel to be in town was the strongest indication that they were trying to get along with the humans who lived in their territory.

And Morgan and Chase didn't scare her half as much as Virgil Wolfgard, Bennett's new sheriff.

They needed workers in Bennett. They needed people to resettle the town. More than that, they needed someone Virgil would trust enough that he wouldn't look at every human as an enemy.

"Did you come in for supplies?" Rachel asked. "I could make up a box of supplies like cans of beans and coffee and—"

Jesse watched the back of Rachel's dress swish as the young Wolf lost control of her human form enough to regain her tail, which was wagging to indicate her eagerness to help. Fortunately, the girl was facing Tobias, so he didn't notice.

"Ellen is coming in for supplies tomorrow. I'm here to talk to my mother," Tobias replied.

"Okay."

When he didn't say anything, Jesse looked at Rachel. "Honey, why don't you finish stocking the shelves? Tobias, you come on to the back room with me."

A little whine, followed by a human-sounding sigh. Understandable that Rachel felt anxious anytime she was excluded, but the girl needed to learn that sometimes other people needed privacy and that not everything was shared by the whole pack—however "pack" was defined.

"You look tired, son." Jesse pressed her hand against one side of Tobias's face.

"We're all putting in longer hours." Tobias leaned against the wall. "Too few men for the amount of land we're trying to cover and the cattle we're trying to keep track of."

"There might be relief coming."

"If they can sit a horse, I'll hire them. Gods, even if they can't sit a horse, I'll hire them."

"Don't set your sights too low. I think I've convinced

Tolya Sanguinati that we need more people if he doesn't want Bennett to turn into a ghost town."

"You think he'll agree?"

"I think he will. But we'll need to be careful, watchful." Her right hand closed over her left wrist. "We need the people. We need to keep the town alive. But what is good for us won't be the only thing getting off the train."